SPECIAL MESSAGE TO READERS

Val McDermid comes from Kirkcaldy, Fife and was educated at St Hilda's College, Oxford, where she was the first student from a state school in Scotland. After graduation she became a journalist and worked briefly as a dramatist for BBC Radio, before embarking upon her career as a writer. In addition to her novels, she is a reviewer for several national newspapers, and broadcasts regularly on Radio Scotland. Val was inducted into the ITV3 Crime Thriller Awards Hall of Fame in 2009 and was the recipient of the CWA Cartier Diamond Dagger for 2010. In 2011 she received the Lambda Literary Foundation Pioneer Award. She divides her time between Cheshire and Edinburgh.

You can discover more about the author at www.valmcdermid.com

SPLINTER THE SILENCE

Psychological profiler Tony Hill is trained to see patterns, to decode the mysteries of human behaviour. When he comes across a series of suicides among women tormented by vicious online predators, he begins to wonder if there is more to these tragedies than meets the eye. Similar circumstances, different deaths. Could it be murder? But what kind of serial killer wants his crimes to stay hidden? Former DCI Carol Jordan has her own demons to confront. But with lives at stake, she and Tony begin the hunt for the most dangerous and terrifying kind of killer — someone who has nothing to fear and nothing to lose . . .

VAL McDERMID

SPLINTER THE SILENCE

Complete and Unabridged

2016

CHARNWOOD
Leicester

First published in Great Britain in 2015 by
Little, Brown
an imprint of
Little, Brown Book Group
London

First Charnwood Edition
published 2016
by arrangement with
Little, Brown Book Group
An Hachette UK Company
London

A catalogue record for this book is available
from the British Library.

ISBN 978–1–4448–2998–3

Published by
F. A. Thorpe (Publishing)
Anstey, Leicestershire

Set by Words & Graphics Ltd.
Anstey, Leicestershire
Printed and bound in Great Britain by
T. J. International Ltd., Padstow, Cornwall

This book is printed on acid-free paper

This one's for Leslie Hills for all the years of friendship — and because you, my dear, like so many of my female friends, refuse to be silenced.

1

Weekends were best. It was easy to avoid working then. So it was easier to watch the women he was interested in. Mostly they didn't go to work then either, so he had a chance to observe their routines and work out the best way to kill them.

He was good at watching. His teachers and later his employers had always commented on his attention to detail. How he would never attempt a project until he'd weighed up the risks and the possibilities. The first time he'd killed, he reckoned he'd still been in a state of shock, but even then he'd been able to make a plan and stick to it. Afterwards, he'd understood that act had opened a door to a mission. Now, his mission had assumed central importance in his life.

Like today. He hadn't quite made his mind up who was going to be next. He had a couple of names on his mental list and he knew how he wanted to kill the chosen one. It was mostly a matter of figuring out whether the logistics would work. When you were planning on hanging someone, you had to be sure there was something to hang them from. And he was in no hurry. The latest one remained fresh in his mind, a source of deep satisfaction. Perfectly executed.

This one, though . . . she ticked all the boxes. But he wasn't going to be rushed into making a final decision. Not like the first time he'd gone out into the wild, as he liked to think of it.

Sitting here now, watching a house where nothing was happening, it was thrilling to summon up the memory. Exciting but unnerving too. So many ways it could have gone wrong.

She'd been alone. It was so unexpected, he'd forgotten how to walk and tripped over his feet. He grazed his knuckles against the brick wall, a rash of blood spotting the skin. He couldn't quite believe it, but she really was alone. No minder, no driver, no PA, none of the chattering bitches she used to get her validation from. Just her, jogging down the five steps from her front door to the narrow sweep of gravel that divided her unfairly lovely home from the street where the likes of him were exiled. He half-expected the door to open again, one or more of her retinue to come blundering after her, running to catch up before she reached the gate.

But no. There was nobody. Only her.

He looked around wildly, his usual determination to blend in with the streetscape torn into confetti and scattered on the diesel breeze stirring the city air. But nobody was paying a blind bit of attention. Late afternoon in North London; nobody was paying any heed to anyone or anything outside their own tight little knot of concern, least of all to her. It wasn't as if she was recognisable beyond the Twitterati. To the average person in the street, she was simply another North London thirtysomething. Designer jeans and a fashion hoodie hugging her unexceptional frame rather than hiding it, that year's must-have leather satchel slung across one hip, multishaded blonde dye job caught back in a loose ponytail. Hardly worth a first glance, never mind a second one. Hard to believe anybody had ever taken any notice of anything she'd said or done.

Oblivious to his confusion, she opened the heavy iron gate with the gothic creak he'd grown familiar with lately. She closed it carefully behind herself and started walking.

He couldn't quite believe it was happening. For three weeks, he'd been keeping tabs on her whenever he could manage it. And she never ever ventured out alone. Running scared, he'd decided. Not scared enough to shut up, but scared enough to make sure there was always somebody around to watch her back.

After the things they'd said to her the night before, she should have been hiding under the duvet, cowed into submission. Not striding along the pavement acting like she was the one with the moral high ground instead of acknowledging the truth — that she was a destructive, disruptive, dangerous bitch who deserved everything that was coming to her.

He'd not planned on dealing with her today. He hadn't been expecting so golden an opportunity. But he wasn't going to let it slip away. Who knew when he'd get another chance like that? And it wasn't like he hadn't worked it all out in his head a hundred times, testing every element of the plan for weak points and figuring out how to overcome them.

'Get a grip,' he chided himself under his breath, falling into step behind her, a few metres and a couple of teenage girls between them. He knew it could be a long while till he got her alone again. 'Get a grip.'

Taking her off the street had been a lot easier than he'd expected. Women like her — middle class, secure in their status, used to the world running the way they wanted — had a false sense of safety. They trusted people until someone gave them good reason not to. She'd trusted him, because he made himself look and sound like all the other pathetic guys who let their women run the show — whipped into line and made into some bitch's gutless slave.

He'd done his research. He knew the names that would make his bullshit credible. She'd believed the tale he'd spun about her radio station needing her in the studio to cover for a sick colleague. She'd got in the car without a murmur. And then he'd shown her the photos on his phone.

He'd been proud of that. He knew how to plot, how to plan, how to prepare. Her daughter, doing a foundation course at film school, had been laughably easy. He'd pretended to be a photographer doing a project about hostages and protest. He'd got three of them involved, so he didn't look like a pervert singling out one girl in particular. Then he'd mocked up a series of shots of them apparently being held prisoner and tortured. And now he had a series of carefully edited shots on his phone that provided perfect leverage.

As soon as he showed her the first shot, she had frozen to stillness. A whimper from behind her closed lips. She'd pulled herself together and said, voice wobbling through an octave or more, 'What do you want?'

'It's more about what you want. You want your daughter to come out of this alive, don't you?'

'That's a stupid question,' she said, a flare of anger lighting up her face.

He wasn't having any of that. He took his left hand off the gearstick and backhanded her hard across the face. She cried out and shrank away from him. 'Don't make me call her babysitter. You won't like what happens to Madison if I have to do that.' He snorted. 'Madison. What kind of fucking name is that? We don't have any limits. We'll cut her, we'll rape her, we'll leave her so nobody will ever want to touch her again. Except out of pity. So do what the fuck you're told.'

Her eyes widened and her mouth formed an anguished O. He had to admit, there was real pleasure in seeing her pay the price for her bitching and whining and moaning. She'd called men like him misogynists. That was the opposite of what they were. Men like him, they loved women. They understood the kind of life that suited women best. They knew what women really wanted. Proper women didn't want to be out there in the world, having to shout the odds all the time. They wanted to build homes, take care of families, make their mark and exercise their power inside the home. Being women, not fake men.

After that, it had been easy. Back to hers after the staff had gone home. Into the garage. Wrist cuffed to the armrest to make it look like she was determined not to change her mind. Hose from the exhaust into the car. The book on the seat beside her, a reminder to himself of the roots of what he was doing. He could have changed his mind at any time, could have pardoned her. But what would have been the use of that? Even if she'd changed her ways, it wouldn't change anything. He took one last look and closed the garage door.

In the morning, they found her.

2

Carol Jordan swirled the last half-inch of port around her glass and thought almost wistfully of murder. To the casual observer, she hoped it looked as if she was fiddling with the stem of her glass. In fact, her grip was so tight she feared it might snap in her fingers. The man on her left, who didn't *look* like someone you'd want to punch, leaned forward to make his point more forcefully.

'It's absolutely not hard to find high net worth individuals if you target your efforts carefully,' he said.

And once again, like clockwork, she wanted to punch his narrow complacent face, to feel that sharp nose crunch against her fist, to see the look of utter shock widen his little piggy eyes.

Instead, she knocked back the last of her drink and pushed her empty glass towards her generous host, who casually poured another liberal slug of Dow's 2007. The man on her left had already pronounced it 'probably the best port Dow has ever produced', as he'd washed down another chunk of Stilton. She didn't know enough about port to argue but she'd desperately wanted to.

'I'm sure you're right,' Carol muttered again, trying not to sound ungraciously mutinous. She couldn't remember the last time she'd been at a dinner party of this formality but she hadn't forgotten the obligations imposed by accepting an invitation to break bread. They'd been drilled into her at her mother's table. Smile, nod, agree, stay away from politics and never ever start a row.

Fortunately for the rest of the company, years of serving as a senior police officer had reinforced her mother's injunctions against politics at the dinner table. When your budget and the very existence of your team was dependent on the largesse of politicians, you soon learned not to express an opinion that might come back to bite you in the neck with all the philanthropy of a vampire. Over the years, Carol had carefully cultivated the art of not holding controversial views lest she let something slip at the wrong moment. She left that to the junior members of her team, who more than made up for her reticence.

Not that there had been many occasions like this during her career as the boss of an elite murder squad. The demands of the job had consumed her, eating up far more than the forty hours a week she was contracted to provide. Carol hoarded the leftover time for things she wanted to do. Like sleep. Not spend endless hours at somebody else's table listening to obnoxious rich bastards holding forth about the iniquities of whoever they thought stood between them and their next million.

But now she had nothing but leftover time. The career she'd defined herself by was over. At moments like this, she had to remind herself that had been her own choice. She could have been

Detective Chief Inspector Jordan yet. But she had chosen to be plain Carol Jordan; just another incomer to a rural Yorkshire valley that had been remorselessly invaded by people who had no relationship to the landscape that surrounded them except that they liked it better than the suburbia they'd left behind.

Her host, George Nicholas, was an exception. His family had built the big Georgian manor at the head of the valley and lived in it continuously for a shade over two hundred years. His was the sort of background of comfortable privilege Carol was inclined to despise. On their first meeting, she'd taken one look at his scrubbed pink skin, his patrician profile and an outfit that could have come straight from a catalogue featuring country gentlemen's apparel and determined to distrust and dislike him. But she'd eventually been disarmed by the unflappable charm that met her hostility head on and chose to ignore it. That and the bloody dogs.

Later, she'd discovered the reason he believed he'd be the last of his line to inhabit the manor. He'd been widowed three years before when his wife had died in a road accident. He wore his grief lightly but for someone as well schooled in trauma as Carol, it was a clear and present pain.

Carol cleared her throat and pushed back from the table. 'I had better be going, George,' she said. Not a slur or a hesitation to betray the amount she'd had to drink.

The laughter lines round his eyes disappeared along with the smile the woman next to him had provoked with an ironic aside Carol had only half-heard. 'Must you?' He sounded disappointed. She couldn't blame him. He'd been trying for weeks to persuade her to come over for a meal. And here she was, bailing out at the first opportunity. 'We've not even had coffee yet.'

Carol aimed for rueful. 'Flash is still a bit young to be left on her own for too long.'

He mirrored her regret with a downward twist of his mouth. 'Hoist by my own petard.'

'Who's Flash?' The question came from an older man further down the table whose meaty red face and several chins made him look like one of the cheerier illustrations from Dickens.

'Carol kindly took on one of Jess's pups,' George said, the genial host again. 'One that's scared of sheep.'

'Scared of sheep?' The Pickwickian questioner looked as incredulous as he sounded.

'It happens from time to time,' George said mildly. 'All a ewe has to do is bleat and Flash puts her tail between her legs and runs. Carol saved the dog from redundancy.'

'And she's a great companion,' Carol said. 'But she's not much more than a pup. And like all collies, she doesn't like being on her own for great chunks of time. So I ought to get back.'

The man she wanted to punch snorted. 'Your dog sounds more tyrannical than our babysitter. And that's saying something.'

'Not at all, Charlie,' George said. 'Carol's quite right. You treat a pup reasonably and you end up with the best kind of dog.' He smiled, his dark eyes genial. 'I'll get Jackie to run you home. You can pick your car up when you're out with

10

Flash in the morning.'

Carol frowned. So he had been paying attention to how much she'd put away. The thought angered her. What she drank was her business. Nobody could be expected to endure what she had without some sort of support system. She knew she was in control of the drink, not the other way round, in spite of what anyone else might think. Or any one person in particular.

She pushed that thought away and forced a casual tone into her voice. 'No need. Jackie's got enough to do in the kitchen. I'm fine to drive.'

The man on her left made a faintly derisive noise. 'I'll get my driver to take you,' he said with a condescending pat to her hand.

Carol stood up, perfectly steady. 'That's very kind, but there's no need. It's only a couple of miles down the road. It's quiet as the grave at this time of night.' She spoke with the authority of a woman who has grown accustomed to being deferred to.

George hastily got to his feet, lips pursed. 'I'll see you to your car,' he said with his invariable politeness.

'Lovely to meet you all,' Carol lied, smiling her way round the table with its late-night chaos of crystal and silver, china and cheeseboard. Eight people she'd never have to see again, if she was lucky. Eight people probably breathing a sigh of relief that the square peg was leaving the round hole. George opened the dining room door and stood back to let her precede him into the stone-flagged hall. The subtle lighting made the elderly rugs glow; or perhaps that was the wine, Carol thought as she walked to the broad front door.

George paused in the porch, gauging the coats hanging from the guest pegs. He extended a hand towards a long black cashmere, then stopped, casting a smile over his shoulder towards her. 'The Barbour, yes?'

Carol felt a stab of embarrassment. She'd deliberately chosen her dog-walking jacket, stubbornly refusing to completely dress up for something she didn't want to do. And now it felt like a deliberate insult to a man who had only ever shown her kindness and a friendly face. 'It matches the Land Rover rather than the dress,' she said, gesturing at the black silk jersey sheath that fitted her better than it used to. She was a different shape from the woman who had bought it; hard physical work had broadened her shoulders and reconfigured her hips and thighs.

He handed her into the waxed coat. 'I rather like the contrast,' he said. She couldn't see his face but she could hear the smile in his voice. 'Thank you for coming, Carol. I hope it wasn't too much of an ordeal. Next time, I promise you a more relaxed evening. A quiet kitchen supper, perhaps?'

'I'm amazed at your persistence.' She turned to face him, her grey eyes meeting his. 'I'd have given up on me long before this.'

'Secret of my success, persistence. I was never the brightest or the best in my cohort but I learned that if I stuck with things, the outcome was generally acceptable. It's how I got Diana to marry me.' He opened the door and a shiver of chill air crept over them. 'And speaking of persistence — are you determined to drive? It's no problem at all to have Jackie drop you off.'

'I'm fine, George. Really.' She stepped on to the frosted gravel and crunched her way across, grateful for the closeness of his arm when her unfamiliar high heels unsteadied her a couple of yards from the vehicle. 'God, it's been so long since I wore these shoes,' she said with a forced laugh.

'One of the many reasons I'm grateful for being a bloke.' George took a step backwards as she opened the Land Rover door and swung herself up into the high seat. 'Do be careful. Maybe see you on the hill tomorrow?'

'Probably. Thanks again for a lovely dinner.' She slammed the heavy door closed and gunned the noisy diesel into life. There was a faint blur of frost on the windscreen but a couple of swipes of the wipers took care of it. With the fan on full to keep the windscreen clear, Carol eased the gearstick out of neutral and set off down the drive. George's mention of his late wife — killed in an accident involving a drunk driver — felt like a reproach for her decision to get behind the wheel after a few glasses of wine. But she felt absolutely fine, in complete control of her reactions and responses. Besides, it was less than three miles. And she was desperate to escape.

God, what a night. If they hadn't been such a bunch of tossers, she'd have been ashamed of being such a crap guest. As it was, she was dismayed at how poorly she'd repaid George's generosity. She'd lost the knack of being with people. Once upon a time, she'd been close enough to one man to tease him constantly about his lack of his social graces. Now she'd turned into him.

She swung out of the drive on to the narrow ribbon of road that stretched between George Nicholas's manor house and the stone barn she'd spent the past months stripping to its bare bones and rebuilding according to her own distinct vision. She'd peeled away everything that might provoke memories, but its history haunted her nevertheless.

The headlights bleached the hedgerows of colour and she felt relief as she recognised the markers that told her she was closing in on home. The crooked stump of the dead oak; the stile and the fingerpost for the footpath; the dirty yellow plastic grit bin, there to make up for the fact that the council were never going to grit a road so insignificant it didn't even have a white line up the middle.

Then, all at once, a different kind of marker. The kind that's never good news. In her rear-view mirror, a disco wash of blue lights.

3

Chief Constable James Blake was not a naturally patient man. Over the years, as he'd clawed his way to the top job, he'd forced himself to cultivate the appearance of patience. He'd imagined that once he was running the show, he could push the pace to match his desire. To his chagrin it hadn't worked out that way during his first command in the West Country. Trying to provoke a sense of urgency among his officers had been, as he often told his wife, like pushing clotted cream uphill. He'd put it down to the general sense that everything ran slower down there. So Blake determined to bite the bullet and take the first chance he had at a job somewhere they knew how to get out of second gear.

Bradfield Metropolitan Police, he reckoned, would have to be up to speed to cope with policing a modern urban environment. It would be absolutely his sort of place. An edgy Northern city with a decent slice of serious and organised crime, perfect for him to make a lasting impression. One that would guarantee a fistful of executive directorships when he came to hang up the uniform. He'd convinced the interview panel, persuaded his family they'd love big-city life, and sailed into Bradfield, certain that he'd have things running with speed and efficiency in no time at all.

It didn't help that he'd arrived simultaneously

with government funding cuts. In his eyes that was no excuse for the dogged stubbornness he encountered at every level as he battled to run the force more effectively and efficiently. It never occurred to him that the reason most of his officers had so little respect for him was his lack of experience at the sharp end of the kind of policing that Bradfield demanded. Instead Blake blamed it on their urban Northern prejudices — he must be a clueless bumpkin because he'd come from the West Country. He was disappointed and, he had to admit at times, discouraged. Which was why he had come to this meeting filled with anticipation. A working dinner with a junior Home Office minister, a pair of his civil servants and a special advisor. That wasn't something to be taken lightly, even if the special advisor was the retired chief constable who had preceded him at Bradfield. Blake didn't reckon much to John Brandon — if he'd done his job properly, Blake's task would have been a lot more straightforward.

Whatever they had in mind for him, nobody was in any hurry to get to the point. They'd been shut away in their private dining room for almost two hours, making their way through amuse-bouche, starter, sorbet, main course and dessert. The food had been abundant; luxurious, even. The wine, rather more sparing though no less good. The conversation had ranged widely around policing and politics, laced with entertaining anecdotes and a couple of mildly diverting indiscretions, but Blake remained no wiser as to why they were all there. His

16

impatience ate away at him, as aggravating as indigestion.

Finally, the waiters delivered a lavish cheese-board, fruit bowl and biscuit basket then retired, leaving the five men alone with no further interruption scheduled. It was, apparently, time to get down to business.

Christopher Carver, the junior minister, leaned forward and helped himself to an oozing wedge of Époisses. Judging by the beginnings of a paunch straining his shirt buttons, it wasn't the first time he'd indulged his appetite at the tax-payers' expense. He glanced up at Blake and gave a mischievous smile. 'You're probably wondering what all this is in aid of, James.'

As the evening had worn on, Blake had become convinced he was about to be catapulted into the professional stratosphere. A dinner on this scale, guests at this level; it wasn't simply a pat on the back because he'd worked wonders within his budget at BMP. 'It had crossed my mind, Minister.'

'You'll recall that we talked earlier about the principle of sharing the back office load among several forces,' Carver said. His face was flushed from over-indulgence, but his eyes were clear and focused on Blake.

Blake nodded. 'It makes sense. It's harder to manage with units as big as BMP, but we've had some success with merging crime scene management.'

'Some of us think there are more radical steps that we can take. Not only in terms of cost effectiveness, but also in terms of improving police response to major crime. John, would you like to explain our thinking to James here?'

Unlike Blake, John Brandon's career had all been at the sharp end. Nobody ever questioned his pronouncements when it came to operational strategies, which Blake thought was taking respect a little too far. Nobody was perfect, after all. But he smiled and gave Brandon a deferential nod as he sipped from his water glass then cleared his throat. The older he got, the more Brandon resembled a bloodhound, Blake thought. Long face, pendulous jowls, folds of flesh under his eyes.

'Murder,' Brandon said, his Northern accent dragging out the syllables. 'In spite of all those cop shows on the telly, we don't get that much of it outside the big cities. And what we do get is mostly domestic. Figuring them out wouldn't tax your average manicurist, never mind detectives. But every now and again, something comes along that isn't your run-of-the-mill homicide. You get a dismembered torso in the woods. Or an abducted child turns up strangled on a bit of waste ground. Or some lass doesn't make it home from a night's clubbing and a dog walker finds her mutilated corpse by the canal. Difficult, complex cases. Because they exist and because it's our job to solve them, every force identifies its best investigators and designates them a major incident team. Agreed?'

'Of course. You have to have specialist officers who are trained to deal with those difficult, complex cases. We have a duty to the public. But we also have to make maximum use of our personnel. We can't simply have them sitting around waiting for the next murder,' Blake said, trying not to sound defensive. 'Plus a reorganisation like Bradfield's means that, when we need it, we can pull together a very specific team to meet the needs of particular incidents.'

Brandon gave a weary smile. 'Nobody's criticising you for disbanding your MIT, James. We might not agree with the decision, but we understand the motivation.'

The minister pushed his floppy silver fringe back from his forehead and said, 'In fact, James, it was the boldness of your decision to scatter your specialists throughout the CID as a whole that made us reconsider our general policy in this area. If a force like BMP felt it was possible to manage without a standing MIT, what might make sense for other forces?' He waved a pudgy hand towards Brandon. 'So I asked John to think outside the box. Tell James what you came up with.'

Brandon began breaking an oatcake into crumbs with one hand. 'The drawback with pulling together an ad hoc team for major incidents is that it can damage the ongoing investigations those detectives were already knee-deep in. Not to mention the fact that you've got no idea what the personal dynamics of that rag, tag and bobtail bunch are going to be. Because that's what it is. Rag, tag and bobtail. It's not a team. Not like the cohesive unit you get when people work together over a period of time. When they've shed the dead weight or the awkward bastard or the sexist pig who pisses off the women on the squad. That's a team and that's policing at its most effective.'

'And its most expensive,' said the younger of the civil servants, his face screwed up in distaste.

'So I had to figure out how to square the circle,' Brandon continued, unperturbed. 'And I thought, if forces can share back room ops, why not share front of house as well? Why not create an MIT that operates like a flying squad? The ghost-busters of complex homicide, if you like. One team that stands outside any particular force and goes where it's needed, when it's needed.'

Blake realised his mouth had fallen open during the silence that followed Brandon's words. They were all staring at him, waiting for his response. His brain was racing to process the implications. They were going to ask him to mastermind this radical proposal. It sounded like madness. It sounded like the kind of thing you wouldn't want to touch with a bargepole. But on the other hand, if it worked . . . The sky would be the limit for the man who changed the face of British policing and made it happen. He clutched at something sensible to say. 'What if more than one complex homicide happens within a few days of each other?' It wasn't a stupid question, he told himself.

'They don't.' The younger civil servant pulled out his smartphone and fiddled with it, then turned the screen so Blake could see it in all its meaninglessness. 'We analysed the figures for the past five years. On only one occasion has there been sufficient proximity to give us grounds for concern.'

'And John has looked closely at that

conjunction of events,' the minister chipped in.

'That's right. And it seemed to me there were no insurmountable issues,' Brandon said. 'There are ways to extend resources in a digital world that didn't exist even a couple of years ago.'

'And so,' said Carver, 'we're going ahead with a pilot.' He attacked the cheeseboard again, this time slicing off a chunk of Ossau-Iraty and spearing two dates with the point of the cheese knife.

Blake felt the warmth of satisfaction rising through his body. One in the eye for everyone who'd ever said he lacked vision. 'That sounds like a tremendous challenge,' he said heartily.

Carver's smile was as sharp as the knife. 'Indeed. And that's why it's so important that we have the right person at the helm. That's why we asked you here tonight, to help us come to the right decision.'

Blake was so taken up with delight at the way he saw the evening going that he didn't quite absorb the nuances of what the minister had said. 'Absolutely,' he gushed. 'I'm ready to take on whatever you demand of me.'

Carver's eyebrows rose, to Blake's confusion. Why was he looking surprised? 'I'm glad to hear it. We're very clear about the person we have in mind for this role. But John was most insistent we shouldn't rely on his word alone when it came to appointing the new regional MIT chief. And so we turned to you as the last person to have worked directly with our first-choice officer.'

Blake heard a faint ringing in his ears, like a

brass bell struck a long way off. What the hell was Carver talking about? Who could he be thinking of? There was nobody in his Bradfield command who was up to a job like this, he'd have put money on it. 'I'm sorry? I'm not sure what you mean,' he stammered, his composure wobbling.

Brandon put his forearms on the table and leaned towards Blake, a smile bracketing his mouth with wrinkles. 'He means Carol Jordan. The minister wants to know what you think of Carol Jordan.'

4

Tony Hill opened his mouth in consternation. But the weird popping and crackling continued. The other three people round the table grinned, enjoying his discomfiture. The youngest, fourteen-year-old Torin McAndrew, started guffawing so hard tears formed in his eyes. Detective Sergeant Paula McIntyre poked him in the ribs with her fingers. 'Show our guest some respect,' she mock-scolded.

Her partner, Dr Elinor Blessing, took pity on Tony. 'It's popping candy,' she said. 'I sprinkled it on the chocolate topping before it set.'

Tony closed his mouth and frowned. 'And people *like* that . . . that weirdness in their mouths?'

'Most people do,' Elinor said.

'But Tony's not most people,' Torin said, still cackling.

'He's only known you a matter of months but he's already got you sussed, Tony,' Paula said.

Tony smiled. 'Apparently.' He shook his head. 'That is a deeply strange sensation.' Cautiously he took another spoonful of the chocolate tart Elinor had served for dessert. This time, he was expecting the popping candy, but he remained unconvinced that the sensation was pleasurable. However, he had to admit it was more interesting than anything he would have prepared for his own dinner. And interesting was always a plus point in his world.

'Elinor's been dying to try it out ever since she saw it on *Masterchef*,' Torin said.

'I can't deny it,' Elinor said. 'I don't often get the chance to cook a three-course dinner, so when I do I like to make the most of it.'

'I suppose A&E shifts get in the way of culinary experimentation,' Tony said. 'Which is a pity, given what a great meal we've just had. Weirdness and all.'

'Tell me about it,' Elinor sighed. 'Why do you think it's taken so long for us to have you round for a meal?'

Tony could think of plenty of reasons why most people would give the body swerve to the idea of inviting him to dinner. He'd always lacked the gift of building friendships. It was as if he'd missed out on the gene for social skills. In his professional life he was known and respected for his empathy with patients. Inside the walls of a secure mental hospital or a consulting room, he always knew the direction of travel. What to say, how to be. But on the outside, he was awkward, blunt, clumsy. Working with the police over the years, he'd been surrounded by the easy camaraderie that bound men together as mates. But somehow it never extended to him.

Paula, though. She was different. She'd become a friend, he thought. They'd started out as allies committed to the defence and protection of Carol Jordan. Paula, he suspected, was a little bit in love with her boss. Which probably made two of them. But their alliance had broadened and deepened, each answering some need in each other. And then she'd met

Elinor, which had released her from her pointless hankering for Carol. What had been left was a mutual affection between Tony and Paula that had only been enriched by the unexpected arrival of Torin in their midst.

The boy had been stranded by the murder of his mother, his only relatives miles away, strangers among strangers. He'd clung to Elinor, his mother's friend, like a drowning man to a spar. In spite of the scant time left from their demanding jobs, Elinor and Paula had made room in their lives for Torin. The boy's emotional damage had drawn Tony like a magnet; to his surprise, he'd found himself pulled into something approaching family life.

Paula interrupted his thoughts: 'You sure I can't tempt you to some pudding wine? It hardly counts as alcohol.'

Tony waved his hand at her, the thumb bandaged to twice its normal size. He tipped his head to Elinor. 'Your lot in A&E put the fear of death in me. Literally.' He assumed a grave expression and dropped his voice. ''Septicaemia's a very dangerous infection, Dr Hill. Take the full course of antibiotics and avoid alcohol.'' He grinned and reverted to normal. 'So for once I'm doing what I'm told.'

'Quite right too,' Elinor said.

Paula shook her head. 'I've never known anyone like you for unlikely injuries. Ripping the base of your thumb unscrewing a bottle of wine. Who knew a glass of Pinot Grigio could be so high risk?'

Tony looked down at the table. 'It wasn't Pinot Grigio.'

25

A moment's silence. They all knew who drank Pinot Grigio. Paula looked momentarily furious with herself. 'No. Sorry.'

'It was a cheeky little primitivo,' Tony said, surprised at himself for finding a way to lighten the moment.

'Very bloody cheeky,' Elinor said. 'How's it doing?'

'It throbs a bit when I've been using my hand.'

'It will do. Nasty business, infected cuts. So, who wants more tart?'

The diversion of dessert over, Torin reverted to teenage boy mode, pulling his mobile out of his pocket and succumbing to the seduction of its screen. While the adults rehashed the week's news, his thumbs danced over the phone, an occasional beep punctuating his silence. Then he stopped short, staring at the screen. 'Whoa,' he said. 'Never saw that coming.'

'What's that?' Elinor glanced across at him.

'Don't tell me some teen icon has cut his quiff off,' Paula said, flicking her fingers at Torin's carefully confected hairstyle.

'Ha! No, it's way worse than that,' he said. 'You remember that woman we were watching on *The Big Ask* a few weeks ago? Jasmine Burton?'

'The name doesn't ring a bell,' Elinor said.

Paula frowned. 'Yes, you remember. The one who was arguing that convicted rapists had no right to work in jobs where they came into contact with women or children after they'd served their sentences.'

'It's a point of view,' Tony said. 'I'd have to

26

say, given my experience of dealing with serial rapists, it has its attractions. Though it'd be pretty much impossible to accommodate without driving a coach and horses through the human rights legislation.'

'I remember now. She argued her case with real conviction. What about her?' Elinor asked.

'She's killed herself,' Torin said. 'She got totally trolled after *The Big Ask*. You know the kind of thing: 'You're too ugly to be raped', 'I hope you get cancer and die slowly and painfully', 'Lesbo feminist castrating bitch, what you need is a real man'. That sort of thing.' He gave an embarrassed apology of a smile. 'And worse.'

'But that's terrible,' Elinor said.

'Happens all the time,' Tony said. 'These days it's the first resort of men who don't perceive their privilege. They feel frustrated, they have a mostly unrealistic sense of powerlessness because they've not been taught how to value what they have and what they can aspire to. So they expend their energy creating victims wherever they get the chance. Online anonymity is their natural home.'

'Scumbags,' Paula said. 'But I've been following her on Twitter ever since *The Big Ask*. And she wasn't taking it lying down. People say you should ignore those arseholes. Don't feed the trolls. Report them, block them and move on. But she wasn't like that. She went at them head on.'

Torin nodded. 'That's right. She's been guest-blogging about it all over the place. It's like she moved on from what she was originally talking about and now she's been all over freedom of speech and Je Suis Charlie and standing up to the cyber-bullies. She was totally, 'Bring it on, I'm big enough and you are tiny little saddos'.'

'But now they've succeeded. They've driven her to kill herself,' Elinor said flatly, her disgust obvious.

Torin frowned. 'It makes no sense to me. I mean, that's a big journey, right? From having the nerve to take on whatever people throw at you to throwing yourself into the river.'

'I suppose it's similar to what we see in seriously ill patients.' Elinor pushed her long dark hair back from her face. Her eyes seemed to have lost their shine. 'They convince themselves there's hope. They talk in terms of a battle they can win. But that's not what's going on there. The disease is relentless. It doesn't let go. There's no respite. And one day the patient wakes up and believes a different narrative, one where fighting makes no odds because there is no light at the end of the tunnel. And very often, they die within hours or days of reaching that point of acceptance. Maybe that's how it felt for poor Jasmine Burton.'

'Or by sheer bad luck, somebody hit on the one thing she couldn't fight. Something that found a gap in her armour and pierced her to the heart,' Paula said. 'We've all got those secret places.'

'Have we?' Torin said. 'I don't think I have.'

Tony wasn't so sure about that. His mother's murder would always be the crack in Torin's psyche. Within hours of Bev McAndrew's death, Paula had taken responsibility for his protection, shutting down his social media accounts and making sure only a trusted handful of friends had initial access to him. By the time a wider circle found him, the focus of their unpleasantness had moved from his mother to the fact that he was living with lesbians. And that was something Torin felt pretty armour-plated against. 'Maybe not yet,' Tony said, trying to sound confident. 'But sooner or later you're going to do something you don't want anybody to find out about.'

Taking her cue from him, Paula chuckled. 'That's what being a teenager is for.'

'Do you see much online bullying among your schoolmates?' Elinor, always the concerned quasi-parent, hadn't noticed the others were trying to move the subject along.

The boy shifted awkwardly and looked to Tony as if for a cue. Tony lifted one shoulder in a half-shrug and gave him an encouraging smile. 'I don't think I know the kind of people who do that kind of thing,' Torin said.

'I don't imagine you do,' Elinor said. 'I only wondered whether any of your friends had been picked on like that.'

Torin grimaced. 'Nobody's ever said anything.' He gave a frustrated sigh. 'We don't really talk about stuff like that, Elinor. If one of my mates was upset about something, he might say. But, you know? He might not. Plus, we'd see it for ourselves on Instagram or Snapchat or Facebook or whatever.'

Elinor smiled. 'OK. You have to remember, your online world is a foreign country to us. When we were growing up, communication happened face to face almost all of the time.'

'Yeah, if I talked to one of my friends on the phone for more than five minutes, my dad would be standing in the hall, tapping his watch, muttering about the phone bill,' Paula said. 'If you wanted to bully somebody, you had to get up close and personal. None of this anonymous trolling.'

Tony fiddled with his knife. 'So we don't even know the right questions to ask half the time.' He looked up and met Torin's bland gaze. 'We have to rely on you to keep us straight.'

Torin rubbed the fingers of his right hand over the fine short hair above his ear. 'Right. Well, I don't know anything about what was going on inside Jasmine Burton's head. But you hear about people my age going over the edge because there's no more than a handful of people in their school giving them all kinds of grief. So I guess what she was getting was grief multiplied by loads. And she didn't know if they were people she'd never even seen in the street or people who sat next to her at work. That'd be the horrible bit, you'd think. The not knowing who hates you that much. At least with school bullying, you kind of know who's doing it, so you can maybe go, 'I know you're a numbskull, why should I care what you think about me?' But not knowing whether it's your so-called best mate or some total deranged stranger? That'd be a killer.'

5

The evening had turned into a steep learning curve. Among the things she knew now was that a police cell looked very different when you were locked in, as opposed to being the one doing the locking. Carol had always been satisfied with their inbuilt discomfort; the people she had banged up were there because they were criminals being kept in a holding pattern till she could nail them down unequivocally. They didn't deserve comfort.

Apparently, that was the judgement that applied to her now. A criminal who deserved nothing better than this. Cement-grey walls that seemed to sweat a faint sheen of condensation. A concrete platform with a plastic-covered mattress the thickness of a yoga mat. A thin blanket that would shame economy class on a long-haul flight. A stainless steel toilet with no seat, half a roll of paper on the floor next to it. The stink of stale sweat and piss. This was what she'd come to. This was what she deserved.

Now that she was on the inside, she was beginning to understand the insidious power of the cell. It was oppressive, no two ways about it. Nobody ended up here by accident. That was the message, and it was an environment designed to fuel the feeling of self-disgust that came with that realisation.

Carol had whirled through a series of

emotions when she realised the flashing blue lights were for her, not some urgent and distant emergency. This was not lightning striking someone else's house; this was the tornado ripping her up by the roots. First came indignation — what were the traffic cops doing on an empty back road when there were plenty of major roads in the county with dozens of potential offenders who posed a risk to others? Then came fear — she knew she was over the limit, knew if she was breathalysed that what lay ahead was not only shame but horrendous inconvenience. Next, a shot of defiance — until recently she'd thoroughly outranked these bobbies and she knew exactly how to put them in their place. But finally, as she sat with the Land Rover in neutral, waiting for them to arrive at her driver's door, she had to accept that she was comprehensively screwed.

There was no old pals' act to be pulled here. This wasn't Bradfield Metropolitan Police's patch. Here, she was on someone else's turf. Over the years, she'd had a few run-ins with West Yorkshire and nobody had walked away from those encounters feeling good about their opposite numbers. More than once, Carol had rubbed their noses in their own failures, and that was never going to make friends and influence outcomes.

So when the traffic cop tapped on the window and indicated that she should step out of the vehicle, she had nothing left but weary resignation. 'Can I ask why you stopped me?' she said as she got out, clinging to the faint hope that he might say something insufficient, something that might get her off the hook. She'd had a drink, for God's sake. She wasn't pissed. She knew where the slim chances lurked.

'We've been following you since you came out of the driveway back there,' he said with the offhand manner of a man who could sleepwalk through the next half-hour and still have everything perfectly in place. 'Your driving was erratic. You took the corner too wide and then over-corrected. You were weaving in a manner that suggested to me you might have been drinking.'

Carol straightened up, shivering at the night air, and cocked her head to get a better look at him. He must have struggled to make the height requirement but he'd compensated down at the gym. He filled his hi-vis jacket and his neck was a thick column of muscle. The hair that was visible under his cap was a dark bristle along the sides of his head. He didn't look like someone about to give an inch. 'I've had a couple of glasses of wine,' she said. 'I'm not drunk.'

He stretched his lips into a thin line, nodding. Heard it all before. 'We'll let the machine be the judge of that,' he said, raising his arm to show the breathalyser kit.

There was, she knew, no way to beat the machine. Her only hope was that when they came to retest her in two hours or so, she'd have metabolised enough alcohol to slip under the bar. How much had she had, after all? Not that much, not by cop standards, for God's sake. And so Carol steeled herself and submitted to the indignity of a roadside breath test.

He held the small yellow-and-black box up towards her face and she put her lips round the slim white plastic tube. She took a deep breath then exhaled. He'd tilted the machine so she could see the screen, watch with sinking heart as the figures climbed up past thirty-five, the magic number. *For fuck's sake, is it ever going to stop?* Forty-nine, fifty, fifty-one. And that was it. Fifty fucking one. Anything between a year and eighteen months off the road. She couldn't even begin to think how that was going to be possible.

Carol realised the cop was talking to her. His colleague was standing by the patrol car, the back door open. 'We're going to put you in the car and I'm going to move your Land Rover up the lane a ways to where I can get it safely off the road. There's a house about half a mile away, the road widens by their drive.'

'I know,' she said bitterly. 'It's my house. It's where I was going. A couple of minutes and I'd have been there. No harm done.'

'With all due respect, you don't know that when you get behind the wheel of a car after you've had a drink. You might well not have been the only person on this stretch of road. Now, you need to get in the car.'

'Are you arresting me?'

'We will be, as soon as we get your details. We'll be arresting you and taking you to the police station at Halifax where you'll be locked up pending a second breathalyser. You'll be entitled to a phone call when you get there.' As he spoke, he put a hand on her arm to steer her towards the car. She wanted to shake free and shout that this was ridiculous, she was Carol Jordan, scourge of murderers and rapists, queen of the crime scene. But she forced herself to stay calm.

It felt so strange to be the one directed into the back of a patrol car, the hand on her head to protect the officers from any accusation of carelessness or deliberate violence. While the arresting officer moved her Land Rover, his colleague ran her number plate through the national computer. 'Are you the registered keeper of the vehicle?'

'Yes.'

'So, you would be Carol Jordan?'

'Yes.'

And so it continued. Date of birth. Address. Yes, really. Just down the road. All the time biting her lip to keep a smart-arsed retort inside. All the checks done with, they set off in the Land Rover's wake. Less than three minutes and they were pulling into her own gateway. 'My dog,' she said, remembering her excuse for getting out of George Nicholas's dinner party. 'She's been indoors all evening. Can I let her out for a quick pee before you take me in?'

The driver turned in his seat and scrutinised her, trying to figure out if she was up to something. 'You're about to be arrested. You don't get luxuries like dog-walking.'

As he spoke, his colleague opened the door and looked in. 'Dog-walking? I heard barking coming from inside.'

'My dog. She needs to be let out. Only for a few minutes.'

'I've told her, you don't get off the leash when you're about to be arrested,' his colleague said, laughing at his own limp joke.

The first cop ignored him, leaning in to look directly at Carol. 'Is the dog all right with strangers? Friendly, like?'

'Yes. Very.'

'And has she got a lead?'

Carol nodded, seeing at once where this was going. He wasn't a bad guy after all, just someone doing his job. Unfortunately for her.

'Hanging up by the door. On the right-hand side. The door key's on the same ring as the Land Rover key, you've got it there in your hand. Would you let her out?'

'Andy,' his colleague protested.

'Dog's done nowt wrong, she shouldn't have to suffer.' Andy withdrew and headed for the converted barn where Flash would be dancing up and down behind the heavy wooden door. Watching the pair of them emerge and walk a hundred yards up the moorside had been the last moment of comfort she'd known.

They'd arrested her, processed her in the custody suite at Halifax's cheerless but chaotically busy police station and locked her up to await a second breathalyser. They'd offered her a phone call but she'd chosen to wait till after the second test. Carol continued to cling to the hope that she might not need to let anyone know the ignominious end to her evening.

She had taken one step to save herself. As she was being booked in by the custody sergeant, she had given him her best apologetic smile and said,

'I'd appreciate it if you could let John Franklin know I'm here. DCI Franklin?'

The sergeant had glared at her. 'Why? What's a drink-driving arrest got to do with CID?'

Carol kept the smile in place. 'Nothing, as such. But I'm sure he'd rather hear about it up front, from you, than on the grapevine.'

He'd given her a suspicious look but said nothing further. She had no idea if he'd called Franklin or whether there would be any response if he had. But it was the only roll of the dice she had left.

She kicked off her heels and paced back and forth in the tiny cell, hoping that physical activity would help her body process the alcohol faster. If it went badly for her, she'd have to call for help. She'd left the house with nothing more than phone and keys. No money for a cab, no card to hit a hole in the wall with. And no cab from Halifax would convey her to the middle of nowhere unless she flashed the cash first.

She could call Bronwen Scott, the best defence lawyer in Bradfield, a former adversary who'd recently turned into a sort of ally. But Bronwen was too hard-headed to schlepp all the way out here for a drink-driving case. Because there was no defence for what Carol had done. She hadn't been the victim of spiked drinks. She hadn't been fleeing in fear of her life or serious physical danger. She hadn't been in the throes of a medical emergency. None of the slender defences could be pasted on to her case. She was no more than another woman of a certain age who'd had too much to drink on a Saturday night. Nothing there professionally for Bronwen. And there wasn't enough between them personally to surmount that.

Paula would come, though. Carol was as sure of that as she could be of anything. Now she was no longer Paula's boss they were free to be friends. Paula herself had made that clear when she'd played the friendship card not so long ago. But if she called Paula, Elinor would have to know too. And the shame of facing that cool, understanding gaze the next time they met would be too much. Sometimes kindness was the hardest thing to bear.

She could call George Nicholas, who was too much of a gentleman to refuse her. But he'd been drinking too. He'd have to delegate the job to Jackie. Or worse, one of the guests' drivers. It would be mortifying. But even worse than that, it would be the hot gossip of the valley. Everyone would know she'd disgraced herself, getting sloshed on George's generosity. There would be tutting about women who couldn't hold their drink, who didn't know how to behave, who were a real disappointment after the previous owners of the barn.

Carol pushed that thought away. The bloody history of the barn was something she only allowed herself to think about when she was at her strongest. Her brother and his wife, slaughtered in their own home, and all because Carol had failed them. She'd stripped the barn back to its bare bones and covered them with new flesh, but still the past leaked through into the present. Tonight, that memory linked directly to the one other person she could count on in a crisis. The one other person she truly didn't want to call.

Before she had time to reject the very idea, the metal hatch in the middle of her cell door slammed open. A pair of eyes appeared, then disappeared as the hatch closed again with a hollow echo. She stopped pacing and stood facing the door, bare feet apart, hands open at her sides, shoulders back. Poised for fight or flight.

The man who walked in and pushed the door to behind him was no stranger even though he'd changed since she'd last seen him. The thick dark hair swept back from his jutting brow was threaded heavily with grey and he'd grown a ridiculous goatee in the shadow of his prow of a nose. He was even more gaunt than the last time they'd been in each other's company, but he'd bought new clothes to accommodate the shrinkage. His shirt no longer ballooned at the waist under a jacket that resembled a superhero's cape. Now, he was wearing a fitted shirt under a lightweight leather jacket that looked surprisingly stylish. John Franklin had found something approximating a mojo, Carol thought, almost smiling at the notion. 'Carol,' he said, acknowledging her with a nod.

'DCI Franklin. Thanks for coming out.'

He leaned against the door. 'I was in the office anyway. You've fucked up royally this time, haven't you?'

'Looks that way.'

'I can't do owt for you, you know that? Even if you were still a DCI, I wouldn't be able to make this go away. Even if I wanted to. Face it, there was never any love lost between your team and my lot.'

Her heart sank even though she'd had no real expectation of anything different. 'I always thought there was respect. You can't blame me for trying.'

'Oh, I think I can. You should know better than to try and pull strings. It makes me look bad, getting calls from the custody sergeant about people he's got banged up.'

Carol's chin came up. 'I'd have thought it would take a lot more than that to make a copper with your stellar reputation look dodgy.'

'You should know better than anybody what it's like these days. It's a perpetual night of the long knives.' He pushed off from the door. 'I'm sorry, there's nowt to be done. It won't be easy for you, living out there in the middle of nowhere with no wheels. I suppose you can always get a quad bike and go up across the moor.' He gave a sardonic smile and opened the door. 'The lads who brought you in will be coming back in a minute to do the second test. The custody sergeant will bail you and let you make a phone call.' He cleared his throat. 'But you know all that. Good luck, Carol.'

And he was gone, leaving her to stare at the blank door for what felt like moments before it opened again to reveal the custody sergeant. 'Let's be having you,' he said. 'Time to blow in the bag again.'

6

Brandon couldn't help enjoying the sight of James Blake struggling with his composure. The cocky fool had thought he was being touched up for a job that was so far beyond his reach as to be laughable. Blake had never run a murder inquiry, never mind an MIT. People's capacity for self-delusion never ceased to amuse Brandon.

'Interesting,' Blake managed after a long moment. He lifted his glass of port and took a slow sip. 'But of course, she's not actually a police officer any longer.'

Carver flapped a hand idly, as if that were an insignificant detail. 'Easy enough to have her apply for the job. People come back on board all the time, I'm told. Different force, different rank, even. I'm not interested in fiddle-faddle. What I want to know is whether this Carol Jordan is the woman for the job.'

'Maybe it would be easier if we went through the specifics,' Brandon said quickly, seeing a glint in Blake's eye that he didn't like. 'What's your opinion of her as a detective?'

A flush darkened Blake's cherub-pink cheeks. 'She's good.' It wasn't quite a grudging response but it wasn't enthusiastic either.

'Clever?' Brandon asked.

'Oh yes, she's very intelligent.'

'Quick on the uptake, would you say?'

'You don't have to explain things to her twice.'

41

Blake stared at the table, avoiding everyone's eyes.

'And resourceful? I always thought she made a little go a very long way on that MIT squad.'

Blake breathed heavily through his nose. 'She's not the budget option, but she doesn't waste what she's got at her disposal. She fights hard for what she wants in terms of the wherewithal to get the job done.'

'What about teamwork? Is she a team player?'

'She built a very tight team round her in Bradfield. So in terms of her junior officers, yes, she's very much first among equals. They're not afraid to bring things to her, but she also instils the confidence in them to strike out on their own if they've got a theory to pursue.'

It was like pulling teeth, but Brandon reckoned his presence made it hard for Blake to be dishonest or to appear too partial. He must know Brandon would jump all over any attempt to paint Carol in a bad light unless he could justify it with chapter and verse. But before he could ask his next question, Blake was off on a flanking move.

'Having said that, ex-DCI Jordan's team support didn't travel in the other direction. She always put the interests of her team, her cases, above everybody else. She didn't see the bigger picture of the force's best interests.' He thrust his chin up, making contact with his natural belligerence. 'I did offer her the chance to return to the fold recently, but she made it clear she wasn't about to revisit her decision to go.'

Brandon gave him a sharp look. This was the first he'd heard of an olive branch. Before he could follow up, the minister butted in. 'A bit of a maverick, then?' Carver didn't sound as if he thought that was a bad thing. The public did enjoy that in a politician, even if party leaders hated it. Brandon wondered about Carver's relationship with the whips' office. 'Can you give me an example of what you're talking about?'

Blake darted a glance at Brandon, who read its malevolence. 'I can. The MIT had developed a very close relationship with a psychological profiler. I believe DCI Jordan was actually his tenant at one point.'

'You mean she was living with him?' Carver leaned forward like a wolf picking up a scent. *They do love their gossip, our lords and masters.* 'Something more than a financial arrangement?'

'I couldn't say,' Blake said loftily. 'At the very least, he was her landlord.'

'If you're talking about Dr Hill,' Brandon interrupted, 'there was nothing more to it than that. When she first came back to Bradfield she wasn't sure whether she'd stay. She didn't want to sell up in London and burn her bridges so she rented. Her flat was completely self-contained. Tony and Carol have never been more than friends. I know them both and neither of them would presume to work together if their relationship had ever stepped across the line.'

Carver looked startled at his adamantine certainty, then smiled. 'I'll happily take your word for it, John.'

'That wasn't my point,' Blake said firmly. 'The point is that Dr Hill worked extremely closely with the MIT. He was never away from their ops room when they were running a case. And his word was law. DCI Jordan would listen to him ahead of senior colleagues. He was one of the most significant expenses of the unit and, frankly, I thought most of what he came up with amounted to little more than the application of common sense.'

'I'd have to disagree with you there,' Brandon grunted.

'With all due respect, John, of course you would since it was you who brought Dr Hill to BMP in the first place.' Blake's voice was tart, his mouth prim. 'So when we were looking to make significant savings across the piece, I told Carol Jordan to stop using Dr Hill. And what happened on their next major case? There was Hill, back in the driving seat. And let's bear in mind that this is a man who ended up under arrest as a suspect in the first major murder inquiry following DCI Jordan's departure from BMP.'

'A murder for which somebody else is currently awaiting sentence,' Brandon said, eyes dead as flint. 'I'm amazed you think it's a good idea to use another officer's incompetence to try to blacken Tony Hill. After all he's contributed to BMP and other UK police forces over the years. Of course Carol wasn't going to give him up. Taking Tony off the payroll would be like having the sniffer dogs put down because they don't work every day.'

'Gentlemen,' Carver said smoothly. 'Whatever the merits or otherwise of Dr Hill, I think the point James here was making is that Carol Jordan can be something of a law unto herself?

Would that be fair?'

'Exactly,' Blake said.

Brandon harrumphed, then nodded. 'I suppose that's one way of putting it.'

'Splendid,' Carver said. 'I like someone who thinks outside the box.'

Brandon was disconcerted, but less visibly so than Blake. 'She's not easy to work with,' he said. 'I can imagine her putting people's backs up if she was parachuted in as the visiting firefighter.'

'They'll soon shut up if she starts getting results,' Brandon said. 'Which she will do. James, do you think she's resilient enough to operate a team outside the usual management structures?'

Blake's eyebrows rose slowly. He looked as if he couldn't quite believe what he was being handed on a plate. 'Resilient? I don't know, John. Twice in her career she's had a major crisis. And twice she's walked away. I offered her the chance to come back inside the tent, but she threw it in my face. And even if we put that on one side, we both know, I think, that she is liable to take comfort in the bottle.'

His words hung in the air between them like a gauntlet thrown down in a challenge. Brandon rubbed his long chin, then shook his head regretfully. 'You've got a point, James. But here's what I think. I think very, very few of us have ever been tested to the limit as Carol Jordan has. I don't know that I would have survived what she's been through. What I find admirable is that she hasn't let either of these terrible events destroy her. She's still standing, James. In spite of everything, Carol Jordan's still standing.'

7

By the end of dinner, Tony had felt mellow and relaxed. Good conversation, good food and the sensation of being among friends continued to be a novelty, one that he was slowly learning to trust. But walking home across town had woken him up, then he'd discovered he'd forgotten to adjust the heating timer before he went out. Now it was too chilly on the narrowboat where he lived to strip off and get into bed. Muttering under his breath, he boosted the thermostat. Half an hour of blasting heat and he'd start to get warm and sleepy again.

To pass the time, he opened his laptop and pulled up a news site. What caught his eye was the story of Jasmine Burton's suicide, and he clicked on it.

Charity organiser Jasmine Burton was driven to suicide by internet trolls, friends said last night.

Jasmine, 36, came under fire from a string of vicious bullies after her recent appearance on the TV current affairs debate show *The Big Ask*. Controversially, she demanded that convicted rapists should never be allowed to take up jobs after their release that would put them in direct contact with women and children.

Jasmine, chief executive of SafeHouse, a charity that supports women and children trafficked into the UK sex trade, was criticised by organisations supporting offenders who have served their sentences. One said, 'There's an important principle at stake here, that we should help people reintegrate into society after they have paid their debts. We must not treat people like pariahs when they show they want to be rehabilitated.'

A colleague from SafeHouse told us, 'Jasmine had no problem with people who disagreed with her and wanted to enter into a proper debate around the issues.

'The problem was the trolls who piled abuse on her personally via social media. The things they said to her were beyond vile. Some of it made me feel physically sick.

'At first, she stood up to them. She took them on directly, she complained to the social media sites, she made it clear that she wasn't going to shut up. But it got worse and worse. SafeHouse actually complained to the police, who were investigating the most atrocious and threatening messages.

'We all thought she was handling it. She would come into work and mock the trolls, poking fun at their appalling spelling and grammar. She was determined to carry on as usual. But obviously, beneath the surface, it was a different story. We're all in shock. We can't believe we've lost such a champion for people who are victims of exactly the kind of men Jasmine spoke out against.'

Tony stared unseeing at the screen while he thought through what he'd read. Suicide had never been a central part of his practice, but inevitably he'd ended up dealing with patients

47

who'd attempted it. Most of them had also cut themselves, often over a long period of time. He'd come to think of self-harm as the junior partner of suicide. People spoke of suicide as a cry for help, but he'd always thought it was more like, 'See how bad it really was?' By the time people killed themselves, they'd gone past the point of believing help was a possibility. But when they were still at the stage of cutting themselves, he knew it was possible to intervene and bring the patient back to something like safety.

Of course people killed themselves without necessarily going through a literal blood-letting as a way of releasing their anguish. But there were generally other signs. It never came from nowhere. When nobody noticed, it was mostly because there wasn't anyone close enough. But it didn't sound to him as if Jasmine Burton lacked support. Which made him wonder.

Frowning, he started trawling his social network sites to see what the world had to say about Jasmine Burton's end. Most of the trolls had been shocked into silent retreat, but a few were poking their heads out of the cave even now to crow over what they were already claiming as a success for rapists' rights. Rapists, in their world, being the victims as often as the women they were convicted of attacking. Tony was fascinated and repelled in equal measure.

'How did we get to here?' he muttered. He knew better than most that poison pooled below the surface in the dark psyches of men who raped and mutilated and killed. He'd spent his professional life dealing with the results. But the level of venom that the apparent anonymity of the internet had provoked was significantly higher than he would have predicted ten years before.

What troubled him most was how much of the vitriol was deployed against women. Yes, men in the public eye were insulted, derided and belittled. But the treatment dealt out to women for offences as trivial as suggesting Jane Austen should appear on a banknote was infinitely worse. They were threatened with sexual violence, demeaned and intimidated. If his patients had spoken of women in those terms, he'd have recommended they stay inside the walls of a secure mental hospital.

'OK, so you attracted the haters,' he said. 'But what else is going on here?' Beyond the vilification, there was love. Dozens of people — not all of them women — had posted comments regretting Jasmine's death, praising the work she'd done in life, even suggesting a memorial fund. There was anger here too, that she'd been pushed so far that ending her life had seemed the only answer.

There was also more detail about the circumstances of her death. Apparently, Jasmine had been spending a few days at a friend's holiday cottage in Devon. She'd had dinner with a former colleague and his wife in Exeter then left to drive back. At some point in the early hours, she'd walked into the River Exe estuary, her pockets full of stones, and drowned.

'Why drowning?' Tony said. 'It's not an easy way to go, walking into the sea. Or the river. It's not like jumping off a bridge, where there's no going back once you've gone over the parapet. But walking in? There's got to be a moment when the survival instinct kicks in, when you have second thoughts. Walking in, you've got the chance to change your mind. Take the stones out of your pockets. Stumble back to the shore. Give yourself a good talking to. But keeping going? That takes a lot of nerve.'

Maybe it hadn't been a matter of choice. Maybe she'd been overwhelmed with the urge to end it all in a place where other options hadn't been available to her. Most people didn't carry the means of an overdose in their overnight bag. She was off her own turf, so she might not have been able to access a tall building or a motorway bridge to jump off. And holiday cottages were notorious for their lack of sharp knives.

But still. She'd have had to be pretty bloody determined. Tony felt a heaviness in his heart for her, that she had felt so isolated and vulnerable in spite of a clearly devoted circle of friends and workmates. That someone so respected and so cherished should end up walking into the chill waters of a dark river in the middle of the night was hard to understand for him, a man who spent his life empathising with the damaged, the deranged and the despairing. For those who knew and loved her, it had to be so much worse.

Tony got up and made himself a hot chocolate, topping it up from a can of spray cream from the tiny galley fridge. It was one of his few indulgences. He took his first sip, not paying any attention to the treat. There was something niggling him about Jasmine Burton's death, but he couldn't pin it down.

Before he could chase the idea any further, his phone began to vibrate, doing a little dance on top of the saloon table. His heart sank. This time of night, it was almost certainly Bradfield Moor Secure Hospital. A crisis with one of his patients. Or a new admission that they were struggling with.

He lunged for the phone, a splat of hot chocolate barely missing it. 'Number withheld,' the screen said. Definitely Bradfield Moor. He fumbled the slider but managed to catch the call before it disappeared. 'Dr Hill,' he said, hoping the person on the other end caught the note of resignation.

'Tony? It's Carol.' Not that she needed to identify herself. His name in her voice was enough.

'Hi, Carol. I thought you were work. How are you doing?' He didn't know what else to say. They'd both tried building bridges lately. A few exchanges of texts. A tentative arrangement to meet for dinner that fell through because he had to go to Nottingham to testify in a court case. But the gulf between them yawned wider than their efforts to span it. Though if she was calling him late at night, that was something, surely? Even if the chances were that she was only calling because she'd been drinking. Dutch courage was better than no courage at all.

A pause. Then, 'I'm truly sorry about this, but I need a favour.' Her voice was tight, angry almost.

A small leap of delight that he was who she'd turned to. Unless of course it was one of those favours that only he could provide. Except he couldn't think what that would be now she wasn't a cop any more. 'No problem. What can I do for you?'

'I'm at the police station in Halifax. I've no way of getting home. I came out without any money. And they won't give me my car keys back. I know it's late and — '

'Of course I'll come,' he said, cutting her off. He had no desire to make her beg. 'The car's outside. I'll come straight away.'

There was no sigh of relief, no gushing thanks. Three simple words, but there was warmth in her voice now. 'I appreciate it.'

'Are you all right? Why are you at the police station?'

'I'm fine. I'll explain when you get here.'

'I'll see you soon.' The line went dead. Automatically, Tony slipped the phone into his pocket and made for the companionway and the hatch leading outside. He grabbed his coat from its peg and his keys from their hook as he passed. Everything in the right place. That was how he lived now, a change of habit forced by his environment. A literal battening down of the hatches to match the emotional equivalent; adjusting to life without Carol at its heart.

He stepped out into the damp chill of the Minster Canal Basin. Even on the cusp of midnight, it was still lively, the last stragglers leaving pubs and restaurants, standing around in chattering knots taking their leave of each other. The ebb and flow of conversation and music drifted across the water from some of the other houseboats. A tram drew a line of light against the darkness as it crossed the Victorian viaduct, its arches a bold silhouette against the glow of the city beyond. Normally, he'd have paused for a moment to drink it in, to remind himself of the unlikely haven he'd found here. But not tonight. Not with Carol waiting in Halifax police station.

Tony slipped behind the wheel of his car and headed for the motorway link that would take him to the M62 and onwards across the Pennines to Halifax. He was trying not to speculate about the story that lay behind Carol's call. He suspected that, whatever it was, it involved drink. And that, whatever it was, it would involve trouble.

Trouble, after all, had always occupied the heart of their relationship.

8

Tony wasn't the only person in the city confounded by the puzzle of his relationship with Carol Jordan. Elinor raised her voice to compete with Paula's electric toothbrush and said, 'I think Tony's getting the hang of coming out to play.'

Paula grunted through toothpaste.

Elinor stretched out in bed and yawned. 'I mean, he actually had conversations. He talked to Torin about console games. And we all discussed that poor woman who killed herself. Jasmine what's-her-name.'

Paula spat. 'Burton. Jasmine Burton. Yes, he did well. We're fighting an entire lifetime of not actually managing to achieve social interaction, but we're definitely making progress.' She came through from the shower room and slipped under the duvet, snuggling into Elinor's side and giving her a minty kiss.

'Do you have any sense of what's happening between him and Carol?' Elinor shifted on to her side and fitted her body into her partner's in a familiar configuration.

'He doesn't really talk about her. I think they're in touch. I'm amazed he's hanging in there. He nailed Blake to the wall for her. Forced the Wurzel to offer her a job at her old rank. And what did she do? Told him to stuff his job up his jacksie. Tony used all that leverage for her and she pissed all over it. In his shoes, I'd have cut her loose.'

Elinor chuckled, one hand rumpling Paula's short blonde hair. 'No you wouldn't. You're scarily like him. The pair of you would walk into machine-gun fire for Carol Jordan.'

Paula made a wordless sound of protest.

'Well, maybe not machine guns. But close. You miss her, don't you?'

Paula burrowed closer, pulling Elinor tight. 'She's the best cop I ever worked with. I look at the bosses I have to deal with now and I wonder how the fuck they got where they are. And truly, Elinor, I wonder whether I should be looking to transfer my skills somewhere they'll be appreciated.'

Elinor shifted, leaning back so she could see Paula's face. She knew her partner was frustrated with the narrow scope her job had assumed, but this was the first time she'd talked about walking away from it. 'Like where?'

'There's opportunities. Carol always said I was the best interviewer she'd ever seen. Counter-terrorism's big business, private sector as well as governmental stuff. Or maybe I could go totally over to the dark side and get some corporate head-hunter job.'

'Well, I wasn't expecting that,' Elinor said. 'I thought you were settled.'

'I was, until Blake broke up the band and sent us off to play with people who have no sense of rhythm.'

Elinor smiled. 'Ooh, extended metaphors.'

'It'll be zeugma next.'

'I love it when you talk dirty to me.' Elinor kissed the skin next to Paula's mouth, the closest she could get to her lips. 'Promise me you won't do anything rash and impetuous.'

Paula laughed softy. 'Now why would I promise you that when the last rash and impetuous thing I did was snog you in a lift?'

'Because you have me now. But if you're serious about making changes, I think you need to talk it over with the people whose opinions you respect.'

'That would be you.'

Elinor gave Paula's nose a gentle tap. 'That would be me, but also Tony and Carol. We should kill two birds with one stone and have them both round for dinner. That way they're forced to deal with each other, and you can use them as sounding boards for your thoughts.'

Paula gave a mock-shudder. 'Mmm, you know how to turn a girl on.' Then she sighed. 'OK, let's do it. Either they'll talk to each other, or they won't. I can hardly wait.'

9

The London night was raw and damp, a sharp contrast to the warm comfort of their private dining room. James Blake and John Brandon had been billeted in the same hotel so they were condemned to walk back together from the restaurant. Even a balmy summer evening wouldn't have thawed the chill that had become obvious between them the minute they said their farewells to the minister and his officials.

After Brandon had made his defence of Carol Jordan as a staunch and tenacious officer, Blake had tried a last throw of the dice against her. 'There's one key issue you're not taking into consideration, John,' he'd said, his voice dripping condescension. 'Whoever we choose for this job is going to be the focus of a huge amount of media attention. And Carol Jordan simply won't stand up to that level of scrutiny.'

'She has a remarkable record,' Carver said. 'The roster of her successful cases includes some of the most high profile killers of the last decade or more. The Jacko Vance cases alone guarantee she comes out covered in glory. I'd be hard pressed to come up with another officer we can parade in front of the media as more of a star.'

'Look, this isn't personal. I think she's an excellent detective. I'm the one who offered her a job at her old rank, after all. What I'm considering is what's best for the police service.

Because dealing with Carol Jordan isn't straightforward, is it? There's a lot of bodies in her wake. Not least her own brother and his wife. In the wrong hands, she could come over as a sort of angel of death.'

There had been a sticky silence before Brandon jumped back into the fray. 'Are you seriously suggesting that the fact her brother and sister-in-law were murdered is somehow a skeleton in Carol's cupboard? I don't think I've ever heard anything more offensive.'

Carver placed his forearms on the table and leaned forward. 'I don't think you've quite grasped the nature of the British press, James. Can't you picture how well that story will play in the *Daily Mail*? Carol Jordan as the heartbroken crusader for justice. My God, they'll be putting her forward for the fourth plinth in Trafalgar Square.'

'That doesn't mean there won't be plenty of others looking to dig the dirt,' Blake said obstinately.

'Let them try.' Brandon's expression was as grim as his voice.

'She has a drink problem.' Blake, apparently, could be as dogged as the woman he was determined to discredit.

'It's not a problem,' Brandon insisted. 'Nobody has ever suggested she's been drunk on duty. Or that drink has impaired her professional judgement.'

Blake snorted. 'She could be as hammered as a Geordie hen party and that team of hers would cover her back. Listen, John. If I know she's got a drink problem, how many others know it? And how many of them has she pissed off over the years? It only takes one with a grudge to hold her below the waterline.'

Brandon shook his head in disgust 'It's not public knowledge. It's not even canteen gossip. I know exactly where you got your information from. And he's one of that loyal team you've been going on about. Except he's only loyal to himself. You forget, Bradfield was my patch before it was yours and I know who can and can't be trusted. And so does she. Your boy will keep his mouth shut because he's too ambitious not to. Carol Jordan's secrets are safe, believe you me.'

'The point is,' Carver said, 'the media will be looking for a hero, not a villain. We'll be pitching this as a remarkable new initiative that could change the style of British policing. Unless and until they screw up, they'll have a following wind of approval. I think we can manage the media, James. I think we can make them love her.'

And that had been the end of it. Blake finally understood that he'd been a crucial part of Brandon's long game to win the new post for Carol. Brandon knew perfectly well that Blake would try to trash her. And he also knew that if there were any buried bodies, Blake didn't know where they were. In the end, Blake had been a straw man, there because Brandon knew he could push him over with a flick of his wrist. It was humiliating. He lengthened his stride, determined to get away from Brandon as soon as possible.

Long-legged Brandon easily matched the increase in pace. 'So, how are you enjoying Bradfield?' he asked genially.

'It's never dull.' Blake's words were clipped and tight.

'That's what I liked about it. It kept me on my toes.'

'Retirement must be pretty tedious by comparison.'

Brandon didn't rise to the spite. 'I'm never short of things to keep me occupied. The Home Secretary is full of interesting notions that need to be analysed and evaluated.' He smiled. 'It's good to feel useful.'

Before he could reply, Blake's mobile produced the ring tone of an old-fashioned landline. He pulled it from his pocket and frowned at the screen. 'Bloody number withheld. Though at this time of night, I'd better . . . ' Another time, he'd have given an apologetic look, but he chose instead to go for the triumphant smile of a man who is too important to ignore his phone. 'Blake here,' he announced briskly. Then, 'Yes, I do remember . . . ' He stopped dead. A spasm of some unidentifiable emotion flashed across his face, then nothing. He listened, then said, 'And where is this?' More silence, but this time, his shoulders relaxed. 'Of course. No, you're quite right. Nothing. But thanks for letting me know.'

Blake ended the call and carefully replaced the mobile in his pocket. He took a couple of steps to bring himself level with Brandon. 'Well,' he sighed, his voice and his expression indicating deep satisfaction. 'That was a very interesting conversation. Tell me, John, did you ever come across a DCI Franklin in West Yorkshire?'

Brandon gave him a wary look. 'John Franklin? Oh yes. Not personally, but he did cross swords with one or two of my detectives over the years. Is he working for you now?'

Blake shook his head. 'He's still with West Yorkshire. But he had some information he thought I'd be interested in. Given what we've been talking about this evening, I'd have thought you'd be interested too.'

Now Brandon was on full alert. When a man like Blake allowed his smugness to creep past his better instincts, there was trouble in store for someone. He thrust his hands deep into his overcoat pockets, letting them form fists. 'Come on then. Spill it. I can see you're dying to.' He swivelled on the balls of his feet to face Blake's profile. He couldn't help noticing the younger man's jawline was starting to blur, his cheekbones to disappear under a slather of flesh. He'd lost the habit of fitness, if he'd ever possessed it. A mark of a man who was, at heart, lazy, Brandon thought, wishing Blake would get past this gloating silence and get on with it.

'DCI Franklin wanted to pass on some information about an arrest on his patch.' Blake paused, but Brandon wasn't about to beg. At last, he said, 'The Home Office might have to rethink their plans for the new MIT. Carol Jordan's been arrested for drink-driving.' He turned to face Brandon. 'So that's that, then. I hope you've got a first reserve.'

10

Carol had never felt more chastened. The humiliation of having to consent to police bail was bad enough, but sitting in the custody area waiting for someone to turn up and take responsibility for getting her home was mortifying. She'd only ever seen snapshots of the Saturday-night parade of misery and hell when she'd been dropping off her own prisoners. She'd never actually endured the constant procession of people off their heads on drink and drugs, people bruised and bleeding from injuries too minor to warrant a trip to hospital, people with no inhibitions and no desire to discover them any time soon. The cocktail of smells was vile — sweat, drink, smoke, vomit, urine, and the occasional hit of something unspeakable and thankfully unidentifiable.

And she was right in the thick of it. There was no hiding place. A bare wooden bench bolted to the floor ran along the wall opposite the counter that protected the custody sergeant from the onslaught. Whoever was waiting for the next stage of their custodial experience was dumped on the bench and there they slumped. One or two looked her over, as if she was an unexpected possibility in the wreckage of their evening, but mostly they were too drunk, stoned, ill or terrified to pay her any attention. Her flesh crawled at the occasional contact.

As if all of this wasn't bad enough, she had to contend with the shame of needing to be rescued. It all might have been bearable if she'd still been mistress of her own destiny. But no. That had been stripped away along with her dignity. She'd had to call Tony to come out in the night and save her from herself. What did it say about her that he was the only person she could turn to with absolute certainty that he'd drop whatever he was doing to help her? A man married to a job ministering to people so fucked up they couldn't be allowed out to play with the rest of humanity. A man who had all the social skills of a dormouse. A man who persisted in sticking around even after she'd blamed him for every disaster in her own life.

Carol sighed so deeply the junkie next to her jerked upright, as if he'd lost sight of the fact there were other people in the room. 'Wha'?' he shouted, looking around wildly.

She inched away and told herself to skip the self-pity. *It could be worse, you could be one of these lost souls.* Instead, she reminded herself of all the reasons she should see Tony Hill as a blessing. She knew no one who was a better reader of human beings and their behaviour. He was clever and surprising; once he admitted you into his world, it was impossible to be bored. He was loyal and kind in his own distinctive way and he made her laugh. Though not generally when he intended to. He refused to abandon her in spite of everything, and if she would only let him, he was more likely to help her climb out of the hole of her misery than anyone else.

Her brother Michael had once accused her of being in love with him. She didn't think love was the right word. She didn't think there actually was a word for the complicated matrix of feelings that bound her to Tony and him to her. With anyone else, so much intimacy would inevitably have led them to bed. But in spite of the chemistry between them, in spite of the sparks and the intensity, it was as if there was an electric fence between them. And that was on the good days.

Lately, there had been no good days.

Tonight was simply another spit to add to the trench that separated them now. Another unreasonable demand that he would meet with an equanimity that would be worse than anger. Maybe it was time for her to acknowledge that she missed him more than she blamed him.

The custody sergeant put the phone down and glanced across at her. 'Carol Jordan? There's someone in reception to pick you up.' He looked around. 'PC Sharman, take her through to reception, there's a good lad. You'll get confirmation of your court date in a day or two. Don't forget to turn up. Come round sober tomorrow and you can have your car keys back.'

She followed the young officer through a door, down a corridor and through another door into an identikit reception area. It could have been any police station in any town. There he was, sitting on a plastic chair under a poster about home security, intent on some stupid game on his phone. He didn't even look up when she walked into the room.

64

The PC left her to it and she crossed to where he sat, thumbs busy on the screen. 'Thanks for coming,' she said.

Startled, he jumped up, almost dropping his phone. 'Carol,' he said, a smile lighting up his tired face. 'How are you?'

'I feel stone-cold sober, though the breathalyser doesn't agree with me. Can we get out of here?'

He gestured towards the street doors and followed her in silence out into the bitter cold of the night. 'I'm parked round the corner,' he said, taking the lead when she stopped and gave him a questioning look.

Carol sat hunched in the passenger seat while Tony scraped ice from the windscreen with the edge of a credit card. She wasn't looking forward to the conversation that lay ahead but there was no way out of it. It was the price of rescue and it couldn't be worse than spending the night in a cell.

Eventually they set off, locked in silence. As they reached the outskirts of the town, Tony said, 'You'll have to direct me. I don't know the way to yours from this side.'

'Stay on this road through Hebden Bridge, then I'll tell you where to turn.' It was a novelty, being driven by Tony. By unspoken agreement, she'd always driven them, whether they'd been on police business or not. He was, in her eyes, the very definition of a bad driver. Easily distracted by other road users, not to mention whatever was going on in his own head, then twitchy on the brakes, vague on priorities at junctions and always four miles an hour under the speed limit except when he forgot about it altogether. Fortunately, Tony's clapped-out Volvo was almost the only vehicle on the road, so she'd be spared any indecisive attempts at overtaking on the minor roads they'd be driving down.

'Did they say when you'll be up in court?'

'Wednesday. They don't hang about.'

He was silent for a moment, then he said, 'That's fine. There's nothing I can't rearrange.'

'You don't have to be there. I just needed a lift home, that's all.' She knew she seemed ungrateful but she was struggling so hard not to give way to tears that she didn't dare invite sympathy or kindness.

'Of course I have to be there. Somebody's got to get you there and home again. Plus, you shouldn't drive between now and the hearing.' The streetlights ran out and he leaned forward, peering into the darkness.

'It's perfectly legal for me to drive between now and then,' she said, not caring that she sounded peevish.

'The magistrates would like you better if you stayed off the road.'

Carol snorted in derision. 'It makes no odds whether they like me or not. It's a twelve-month driving ban and a fine and my insurance fucked up and a criminal record, and no amount of grovelling will make any difference.'

'It might make the difference between twelve months and fifteen months,' he said.

'What? Suddenly you're the expert on drink-driving sentencing?'

He said nothing.

Carol threw her hands in the air, exasperated with herself. 'I'm sorry, I don't mean to be a bitch. I appreciate you doing this.'

His lips tightened but he said nothing.

'I can't quite believe it, you know,' she said, needing to fill the silence. 'It's less than three miles from the end of George Nicholas's drive to my front door. Three miles of road that goes from nowhere to nowhere. Talk about bad luck. What are the chances of that?'

'You ran out of chances tonight, Carol,' Tony said. 'That's because you've been taking chances for a while now. Going by the law of averages, you're long overdue tonight.'

'Bullshit, Tony. Really, bullshit. I know my limits, I know when I'm not safe behind the wheel. I never drive when I've had too much.'

'You might think you're safe, but you'd have been over the limit. Be honest. We both know you've spent most of the last few years over the limit. And I'm not talking about a one-off Saturday night out. Carol, this is your wake-up call.'

'Oh, for fuck's sake,' she exploded. 'Just because I'm a captive audience doesn't mean you get to preach a sermon.'

'It's not a sermon, it's an intervention. Tonight's made me realise I've been biting my tongue for too long. I can't stand by any more and watch you destroying yourself, Carol.'

'What? I've hardly seen you in months. You've not exactly been watching me do anything. And I'm not destroying myself, I'm trying to put myself back together. Which you'd know if you'd actually been acting like a friend.' Streetlights again. Shop windows and traffic lights. Carol squirmed round in the seat so she could stare out of the side window. She didn't want him to see her face. She didn't want him reading what he wanted to believe.

'I know,' he said. 'I've not been acting like a friend. I've been running scared. For too long I've been telling myself that if I told you the truth I might lose you for good. And I didn't want to risk that.'

She could feel a lump in her throat, tears threatening to break through her armour. 'Next right, past the chippie,' she said.

Tony swung the car off the main road and drove between tall ranks of terraced stone houses, looming dark apart from the occasional dim glow from a stair light or an opaque bathroom window. And then they were back in open country. 'You've got to stop drinking, Carol. It's a wall between you and the rest of us. The people who care about you. The people who might care about you if you gave them half a chance. Look at you. You're a brilliant woman. You're tough, you're tenacious, you're beautiful and you're bright as hell. And what are you doing with your life? You've cut yourself off. You're using Michael and Lucy's death as an excuse to focus on your love affair with Pinot Grigio and vodka. And where has it brought you? A Saturday-night police cell, along with the other drunks and the junkies and the terminally fucked-up.'

'I'm not a drunk,' she shouted. 'Liking a drink doesn't make me a drunk. You are completely out of order.'

'I'm not. I'm back in line for the first time in a very long time. And this time I'm not walking away.' He stopped at a T-junction. 'Left or right?'

'Left. Then a mile down the road, you take a right. Actually, no. Drop me at the corner. It's only a mile from there. I'd rather walk.'

Tony gave a sardonic laugh. 'In those shoes? My company must be worse than I thought. I'm driving you home, Carol. And then I'm staying over.'

'What? What do you mean, staying over? There's nowhere for you to sleep.'

'There's a whole barn. I brought my sleeping bag in case you don't have a spare bed.'

'No.'

'Can we talk about this when we get there? Only, I need to concentrate.'

'There's nothing to talk about.'

'You can pretend all you like, but I know you're not happy like this. And I can't ignore that any longer. Whether you like it or not, Carol, it's time you took your life back from the bottle.'

11

Watching again. Waiting again. Wondering again whether this was the one. Ideally, he'd like to see inside her home before he made a final decision. He needed the kind of stairs that had a balustrade with spindles. You couldn't hang someone when the bannister had a solid wall beneath it.

He didn't mind waiting. He had plenty to occupy his mind. Killing time like this reminded him of where the debt he was owed had begun. It was a Sunday evening. His dad had promised him his mum was coming home that night. He'd been excited at the news, though he knew better than to show it. Lately, his life had changed in ways that enraged his father and baffled him.

It all started when his mum had announced she was going on a day trip to somewhere down south called Greenham Common. He'd never heard the name before. He'd only been eight years old; his world consisted of Bradfield, where all his family lived, and Torremolinos, where they went every summer on a charter flight from Bradfield airport for a week of sunburn and Spanish tummy. He'd heard of London and Manchester and Leeds but he'd never been to any of them and had only the haziest notion of how far away they were. Greenham Common, apparently, meant getting up at six because it was at least three hours on a coach. And it was women only.

He'd asked her what was at Greenham

Common. Was it like a hotel? Or a beach? His mum had laughed and said no, it was American nuclear missiles and a women's peace camp that was protesting about them. He didn't understand why people were protesting about missiles. Missiles were good things, they meant you could fight back when people attacked you.

'Nobody's going to attack us,' his mum had said.

'You know that, do you? You've got the Russians' personal guarantee of that, have you?' his dad had demanded with a tired belligerence.

'Nobody's going to use nuclear weapons, Pete, don't be stupid. They all know now about nuclear winter. It'd be the end of life as we know it. We'd be back in the Dark Ages, only worse, with mutations and all sorts.'

'So if nobody's going to use them, what's the problem? They might as well be here as anywhere else.'

'Apart from anything else, they're a symbol of how this island's nothing more than a giant floating aircraft carrier for America.'

He'd tuned out somewhere around there. He hadn't properly understood much except that his mum and her pals were going to make a human fence round the place where the missiles were. Which seemed a weird thing to do. Like giving them a great big hug.

Him and his dad had watched the news that night and they'd seen a story about Greenham Common with pictures of women shouting at policemen then being carried away by them. There had been soldiers too, staring straight in

71

front of them as if the women and the police were in another dimension. He'd been in bed by the time his mum got home, but at breakfast the next morning she'd been as excited as he'd been the day before his birthday party. His dad had just grunted.

It turned out that there was a whole camp at Greenham Common. Not like the cub camp he'd gone to the summer before, where they'd slept inside wooden huts and done lots of activities on the site and in the woods around it. There weren't even proper tents, according to his dad. Only plastic sheets stretched over tree branches bent over and pegged to the ground. That's why they were called benders, his mum said. His dad said something he didn't understand and his mum flared up at him and said a word he didn't know. When he asked her later what a lesbian was, she said he was too young to understand but it was a way of people showing they loved each other.

Anyway, his mum had got a taste for going camping at Greenham, even though it wasn't summer. At first, it was just for a couple of nights at a time. Then she started going every other week for the whole week. He didn't like it when she was gone. They had boring tea every night. Beans on toast or bacon and eggs with the yolks all hard and the edges of the whites all crispy. And his dad was always in a bad mood.

But his mum kept on about saving the planet for the future and the importance of sisterhood and how women united were strong. 'I thought that was the miners,' his dad had muttered.

'Them too. Solidarity, that's what it's about. We're fighting a war here.'

Which had confused him because he thought the whole point of Greenham was that it was a peace camp. His dad swore about it a lot when there were pictures on the news. He said the boy's mum had been led astray by gobby bitches who wanted to convert normal women to their unnatural ways. That she'd been happy enough with her life before they'd started pumping their nonsense into her head, brainwashing her with their feminist ideas. She took to reading as well, in a big way. Later, he came across some of the books at school. Sylvia Plath. Virginia Woolf. Going to Greenham had made his mum somebody else's puppet, his dad complained.

That Sunday night, they were waiting for her to come home. His dad had tried shouting and arguing to make his mum stay at home, but this week, he said he was going to try something different. 'Soft soap,' he said. And that made sense because there were no bathrooms at Greenham and his mum always came home gagging for a bath and clean clothes. His dad had prepared a special tea too. He'd gone to Marks & Spencer and bought two tins of chunky chicken in a special white sauce, and they were going to have it with oven chips and frozen peas. Then his mum would know how pleased they were to have her home.

She was due back about four o'clock. By the time it got to five, his dad was totally fed up. He'd opened a can of beer and he was smoking one cigarette after another till the living room was like a gas chamber. He'd left his dad to it and gone upstairs to his bedroom where he could look down the street and watch out for the battered old Volkswagen camper van that his mum's pal Muriel gave her a lift in. He sat cross-legged on his bed, willing the orange-and-white van to appear, as if desire could make it happen.

That's how he knew the police were coming before his dad did. The blue-and-white panda car stopped outside their front door and two cops got out, a man and a woman. He hurtled downstairs and yanked the front door open before they'd even reached it.

'Is your dad in, son?' the man asked.

Before he could say anything, a waft of acrid smoke answered for him. All at once, his dad was there, a protective hand on his shoulder. 'Oh, bloody hell,' he said in tones of disgust. 'Has she gone and got herself arrested?'

'If we could come inside?' the woman said, a sympathetic smile on her face.

When he looked back, that had been the last moment in his childhood that had held any promise of happiness. Right then, in his head, his mum was still alive. Still there for him. Still somewhere between Greenham Common and his bedroom.

They'd been less than an hour from home when it happened. A fuel tanker in a crash. A diesel spill. A camper van sliding through 360 degrees and ending up wrapped round the central reservation of the M6. Three women dead. But only one he cared about.

His dad had taken refuge in rage. It was as if he wanted the boy's mum back so he could shout at her and tell her how stupid she'd been to listen to those bloody women. It did make sense, the way he told it. Even if the boy had wanted to argue the toss, he couldn't have faulted the logic. Until the women at the peace camp turned his mum's head, she was perfectly happy, and so was he.

Some of the women turned up at the funeral. He expected his dad to kill them. But instead, he stayed deadly calm, like a ninja. He went right up to the undertaker and told him to tell them they weren't welcome. Then he led the boy into the crematorium, dignified and head high. Only a bit of colour in his cheeks to betray how angry he was.

But once the funeral was over, there was no need to keep his fury in check. It seeped out, it seethed through everyday life, it seized every possibility of happiness and shook it by the scruff of the neck till it was dead. Those women had poisoned his whole life.

And now bitches like that were everywhere he turned, interfering in other people's lives, making misery for other kids like him. He couldn't escape them. He'd reached the point where he couldn't keep taking their crap. He needed to put a stop to it.

But he had to be clever about it. Just killing them would make martyrs of them. He had to strip them of anything that might make them admirable. Make them worthless. Make it look as if their own behaviour had driven them to their deaths. That their guilt and shame had finally kicked in.

Now he'd started, he felt so much better. After Kate Rawlins, there was a kernel of peace in his heart that hadn't been there before. It grew stronger with Daisy Morton and Jasmine Burton. Now the bodies were starting to pile up, these bitches would have to take notice. It might take a while, but eventually they'd begin shutting up.

Or he'd keep on doing it for them.

12

In the end, Carol had made Tony sleep in her bed. 'I have to get up early and walk the dog,' she'd insisted. 'That way I won't disturb you.' And so she'd finally found a use for the air mattress Michael and Lucy had kept for the children of visiting friends. 'It's intended to discourage them,' he'd once said. Now she'd discovered he hadn't been joking. Luckily Tony's sleeping bag was thick with down and she hadn't had to add cold to discomfort. She'd bedded down in a corner of the long stone barn she'd been systematically destroying then restoring over the past few months. Flash, accustomed to having the open-plan area to herself at night, was ecstatic to share her territory with her adored mistress and immediately curled up against her legs. Feeling the additional warmth, Carol couldn't help wondering why she'd barred the dog from her bed until now.

Tony meanwhile was in the self-contained end section of the barn, where Carol had been living. He was gratified that she trusted him enough to give him free access to her most private domain. He hoped she'd eventually grasp that what he was about to do wasn't a breach of that trust.

Carol had stamped her own personality on the space now. Michael, a successful games software designer, wouldn't have recognised the place. It had been designed as an office that could double as a guest suite. A desktop ran along one wall, power points arrayed along its length like a strange design statement. Where there had once been an assortment of computer monitors and peripherals, there was now a single laptop and a neatly folded pile of T-shirts. Another wall was shelved and held Carol's books and CDs. There was a king-size bed and a walk-in wardrobe, a shower room, and beyond that, down a short hallway, a decent-sized kitchen with a breakfast bar and a couple of stools. It was sound-proofed and air conditioned; to Tony, it resembled a bunker more than anything.

Sleep had been elusive, but that wasn't unusual. Tony had struggled with sleep for years, seldom managing more than four or five hours without waking and staring at the ceiling, listening to the wheels going round inside his head. The atmosphere between Carol and him before they'd parted hadn't helped. He'd hoped she'd see the sense in what he was saying. He knew she wouldn't be able to capitulate directly, that she'd make him drag her to the point of agreement, but he believed that she was ready for change. Ready to admit that it was time to reclaim her life.

That hadn't been how it had gone. He'd barely made it to the barn door in time to stop Carol slamming it shut in his face. Her eyes had blazed with anger as he'd barged in behind her. 'I've told you. This is none of your business,' she'd said, storming through the barn to her living area. By the time he caught up with her in her kitchen, she was pouring a large glass of white wine.

'Straight to the bottle,' he said. 'You've been busy telling me you don't have a problem, but what's your first response to any kind of criticism? Have a big drink. Classic, Carol. Classic alcoholic behaviour.'

She took a defiant swig from the glass. 'I'm not an alcoholic. I like a drink. And frankly, after the night I've had, I think I deserve a little pleasure.'

'I don't think there's any pleasure in that glass. I think there's relief. I think there's release. And I think there's dependency. You needed that drink, whether you wanted it or not.'

'You think I can't do without it? You couldn't be more wrong. I'm perfectly happy to do without drink.'

'Really? So why did you always have a quarter-bottle of vodka in your desk drawer? Why do you always carry a hip flask in your handbag?'

She'd made a little 'tcha' of disgust. 'What? You're spying on me now?'

Tony shook his head, sadness in his eyes. 'Not me. Your team. People who care about you, who came to me because they didn't dare go to you.'

That hit home. He wasn't ashamed of landing such a low blow. He wanted it to sting, wanted her to feel the shame of what she was doing to herself. She couldn't meet his eyes. 'You've never seen me falling-down drunk. Throwing up over myself. Out of control. I've always been able to do my job. Always able to function.'

Tony shrugged. 'So you're a functioning drunk. You don't have to be falling down in the street or pissing yourself or sleeping with unsuitable men or losing whole days at a time to be a drunk. All it takes is for you to be dependent. And you are. We both know it.'

Carol looked at Tony as if she hated him. 'I don't need to drink. I could stop any time I wanted to.'

He'd given her a long level stare then. 'You think? Prove it. Let me stay here with you till Wednesday. It's only four days. You go on the wagon and I'll be here to support you. Believe me, Carol, I'd love to be proved wrong.'

She glowered at him, her expression a shifting mosaic of petulance and dismay. He wasn't sure if she was more pissed off at the thought of going on the wagon or having to put up with him in her face all the time. 'Fine,' she said, clipped and tight-lipped. 'If that's the only way to get you off my case, fine.' She tipped the last inch of wine down the sink in a defiant gesture. 'You sleep in here, I'll take the sleeping bag. I have to get up early and walk the dog. That way I won't disturb you.' And she'd stalked off. He suspected she thought she'd got the better of the exchange.

She was wrong. After she'd gone, he took advantage of the soundproofing to search the annexe for alcohol. Three bottles of malt whisky, two bottles of pepper vodka from the freezer, a bottle of gin, five bottles of Pinot Grigio, two bottles of cava, a bottle of brandy and five bottles of craft beer. He swallowed his qualms about her privacy and went through every handbag in the wardrobe, discovering three miniatures of vodka and one of whisky. Then, one by one, he opened the bottles and poured the contents down the sink. The fumes rose up, making his nose tingle. She'd be furious in the morning when she saw what he'd done. But eventually, she'd be grateful.

★ ★ ★

Twenty miles away, on the outskirts of Bradfield, Ursula Foreman read through what she hoped would be the final draft of her monthly column for *TellIt!*, the popular online news site she'd helped to set up two years before. She ran both hands through her ginger curls in a bid to wake herself up and sharpen her concentration. As she read, she chewed one corner of her lower lip absently, her eyes narrowing as she weighed her words.

Four months ago, she'd written what she considered a thoughtful and measured piece about the effect on young women of unthinking, everyday sexism in TV soaps.

She'd been taken aback by the flood of vilification it had unleashed. A torrent of hate and anger had saturated her social media feeds. At first, she'd laughed about it, complaining about the lack of imagination displayed by the trolls. In response, they'd upped their game. Until then, Ursula had stuck to the accepted axiom — don't feed the trolls. But she found it hard to stay silent in the face of such grim abuse. Her next column had probed the reasons why men — for it was, she was convinced, almost exclusively men — harboured such powerful negative feelings towards women they'd never met and whose words were unlikely to have any direct effect on their lives.

The second shitstorm was even worse than the first. Ursula wasn't daunted by her attackers, though she was a little shaken when her partners in *TellIt!* told her to keep it up; her foul-mouthed critics were actually drawing more people to the site than ever before, which was good for business.

The following month, she wrote about the underlying fear that infused the abuse she'd experienced, and its wider impact on women's lives. A lesser person might have buckled under the loathsome bile that was by now a daily feature of her online life. But Ursula stood firm. Her only concession to the depravity was to ask *TellIt!*'s IT guy to ID the worst culprits, in the hope they could hand the police enough evidence to prosecute the cowardly bastards.

The door of her study swung open to reveal a burly man in a T-shirt and checked fleece lounging trousers. He was waving a pair of steaming mugs in the air. 'Fancied hot chocolate and thought you might too,' Bill Foreman said, moving into the room, surprisingly light on his feet for so stocky a man. 'Put a splash of rum in as well. Reckoned you deserved a bit of a livener.'

Ursula sighed happily. 'You are my hero. I was about to send this off then call it a night.'

Bill handed her one of the mugs and she cradled it in her hands, savouring the warmth and the rich aroma of the chocolate and the rum. He lowered himself into a battered chintz armchair and Ursula swivelled her office chair round to face him. 'So what did you go with in the end?' A journalist himself, he understood how often the finished piece ended up in a different place from the initial plan.

'A tangent. I'm writing about female genital mutilation. How we've become much more aware of it in the past couple of years here in the UK and how we need to make a safe space for women to be able to speak without fear of reprisals.'

Bill grinned. 'Nothing controversial, then. It's not hard to imagine how they'll come back at you on that one. You've found a way to upset the fundamentalist Muslims and the right-wing arseholes in the same article.'

Ursula sighed. 'Depressing, isn't it? It was a lot easier to be optimistic about equality when you didn't have to confront the Neanderthals on a daily basis. When you could imagine that people were actually changing their minds because they'd stopped groping secretaries at the photocopier.'

Bill's mouth turned down at the corners. 'And all the time, it was burrowing underground, hibernating and growing stronger. Baffles me. I'm a bloke. I like football and beer and playing *GTA* with my mates. But that doesn't mean I have to despise women. It's not a binary. I genuinely don't understand the thought processes that go into the kind of abuse you've been getting.'

'That's because it's not got much to do with thought processes.' Ursula leaned forward, her face animated. 'It's emotional. I think it's got a

83

lot to do with the fact that the kind of work men do has changed dramatically. Their fathers and grandfathers did hard manual labour. Yes, it was brutal and exploitative, but society constructed an identity round that. That kind of work made you a man. That was how you could prove yourself.'

Bill swigged his cocoa and nodded. 'A kind of indoctrination, and the memory lingers on. There's a lot of men out there with a feeling that they don't measure up. Buried so deep they don't even know it's there, never mind how to fix it. And shouting at women makes them feel better.'

'Literally or figuratively. I used to feel sorry for them till I found myself on the receiving end.'

Bill stared at the carpet between his feet. 'Speaking of that, have you been looking at the news feeds at all tonight?'

'No, I only pulled up what was relevant to what I was writing about. Why? Is there something I should know about?'

Bill sighed and shifted in the chair. 'That woman we liked on *The Big Ask* — Jasmine Burton. The one you emailed about writing something for *TellIt!* She's . . . ' He scanned the room, corner to corner, as if he'd find the right words there.

Alarm made Ursula sit up straight, eyes wide. 'She's what? Has someone attacked her?'

Bill shook his head. 'No, it's . . . it's worse than that. Ursula, she's killed herself.'

The words vibrated in Ursula's head like a plucked string. She couldn't make sense of them.

She smiled and shook her head. 'You must have got it wrong, Bill. You've misread it.'

'No mistake, my love. I double-checked it on half a dozen sites. Her body was washed up by the mouth of the River Exe. Looks like she walked into the river with a pocketful of stones to weigh her down.'

'The River Exe? Isn't that in Devon, some-where like that?' She gave a false laugh. 'There's obviously been a mistake. Jasmine Burton lives in Birmingham.'

Bill shook his head. 'She'd been staying down there in a friend's cottage. Apparently she wanted to get away from it all. The trolling, it was start-ing to get her down, one of her workmates said. Out there on her own, it must have got to her.'

Ursula turned away, putting her mug down with a clatter. 'I don't believe it. I can't believe it. We were only emailing last week.' Her fingers started clattering over the keys as she summoned up the news sites she visited most often. The BBC, the *Guardian*, the *Huffington Post*, the *Indepen-dent*, the *Daily Mail* — they all told the same story as Bill. He sat in silence as she browsed the screen. 'Poor woman,' Ursula said at last, her strong voice made small. 'She seemed so tough. Like she'd never lie down and give in. If she reached the end of her rope . . . Well, it's a scary thought.'

Bill hauled himself out of the chair and put his hand on her shoulder. 'Thing is, my love, she was on her own. According to what I read, anyway. She wasn't living with anyone. No kids. And no matter how supportive your colleagues and your mates are, when you shut that front door behind you at night and it's you all alone with the nutter-sphere, it's hard not to feel the walls closing in. It's not like that for you. You've got me, our family, our friends. Plenty of validation when you start to wonder about the crap that's being sent your way. Jasmine didn't have that safety net.'

Ursula reached up and grasped his hand. 'I know. But all the same . . . It feels like the bastards have won.'

'Totally get that. And I'm sorry for what Jasmine went through. But you're not Jasmine and they're not going to wear you down like that.'

His stout confidence should have made her feel better. But as she sat there staring at the screen, all Ursula could think about was the cold creeping up Jasmine's body as she walked into the estuary, the mud sucking at her feet, the steady rise of the water covering mouth then nose then eyes, the instinctive gasp for air, the choke and struggle as the river claimed her for itself, the terrifying moment when she knew it was too late to change her mind.

And then the peace.

13

The light of morning disturbed Carol's sleep. No curtains hung at the windows in the main body of the barn. No point when she was doing work that constantly kicked up grit and sawdust. No reason when she welcomed no overnight visitors. Half-awake, she grumbled as she turned over. That was all the encouragement that Flash needed. The dog was on top of her, long pink tongue washing the sleep from her face. 'Oh, for fuck's sake,' she complained, crawling out of the sleeping bag and shivering in the unheated air.

She'd had the foresight to grab her dog-walking clothes the night before and she quickly dressed in the warm weather-proof gear that blended in with the landscape and the locals. There was a dull ache at the base of her skull and her body craved coffee. But she wasn't ready to confront her overnight guest yet. Fresh air and a brisk walk up the moor at the back of the house would give her the upper hand.

She deliberately chose a route that took her in the opposite direction from George Nicholas's house. The last thing she wanted was to have to explain how her evening had ended. He'd have to know, of course. But she couldn't face him yet.

Half an hour later, she came down the hill at a good pace, moving swiftly over the bent yellow grass from tussock to tussock, the dog ranging round her in wide loops. The cold air had brought colour to her cheeks and seen off the pain in her head. So many mornings like this, a prelude to a day of hard work and mindlessness.

The light in her kitchen window gave her a jolt. She'd never seen that before, coming off the hill. The barn was always in darkness. It was an unwelcome reminder that today wasn't going to be like all the others. Today she was going to have to deal with Tony and his determination to interfere in her life. She was inclined to tell him to piss off as soon as he'd had a cup of coffee, but she knew him well enough to realise that would be a waste of breath. For a man so well endowed with empathy, he could be remarkably deaf when it suited him.

At the front door Carol paused, getting her breathing under control, composing herself. Then she squared her shoulders and marched inside. Two dozen steps brought her to the door of the separate section where she lived. Without knocking, she walked in. It was, after all, her home. Not his.

The room was empty. Tony's jacket was slung over her office chair; the annexe was warm and cosy, thanks to the ground source heat pumps that Michael had installed when the barn had been renovated the first time. Carol carried on past the bathroom and into the kitchen, where Tony stood frowning at her coffee machine. Hearing her approach, he turned round and smiled apologetically. 'I was going to have some coffee ready for you, but I'm not smart enough to figure out how to work this beast.'

'It's not that hard,' she said, unzipping her waxed jacket and tossing it over a chair. 'Move over, I'll sort it.'

That was when she saw the array of empty bottles on the draining board. For a moment, she couldn't quite believe her eyes. Then she rounded on him. 'What the fuck?'

'It's a lot easier not to drink if there's no drink in the house.'

'How dare you? Who the fuck do you think you are?'

'I'm the friend who's here to save you from any more humiliations like last night.' He spread his hands in a placatory gesture.

Carol was not placated. 'This is your fantasy, not mine. I never said I was going to stop drinking forever. OK, I gave in to your stupid challenge. I agreed to stay off the sauce till I go to court. But that's all. Where do you get off, pouring my booze down the sink? Apart from anything else, that's a couple of hundred quid's worth down the drain. You may not have noticed, but unlike the drunks you're comparing me to, I drink premium brands. I drink for the taste, not just to get pissed.' She shook her head, her mouth a bitter line. 'You bastard.'

'I'll reimburse you,' he said, mild as milk.

'It's not the money, it's the principle,' she shouted. 'You have no right.'

He half-turned away from her. 'If I don't, nobody does.'

'And that's how I like it.'

He stood up. 'I'll leave you to it, then. Next time you're in the shit, find someone else to call.'

He swung round to face her again, eyes hard as flint, chin up ready to take the hit. 'If you can find someone who can be bothered.'

It was below the belt, but that didn't make it any less true. He'd never spoken to her like this before. Her pride wanted to tell him to fuck off. But her fear wouldn't let her. 'Sit the fuck down and stop grandstanding,' she growled. 'I'll make the coffee.' She turned her back on him and went through the ritual of grinding and tamping and expressing coffee. Surely he wouldn't walk? And when she turned round, he was still there, hands clutching the chair back so tightly his knuckles were white. Wordlessly, she put the espresso cup on the table near him before processing a second cup for herself.

She took a deep breath. 'I usually have beans on toast with scrambled eggs. I'll make some for you too if you want.' It was the nearest she could come to an apology.

'That's fine. You've branched out a bit from an orange juice and a granola bar.'

She gave a grim little smile. 'I learned the hard way. You can't do a day's physical work on that.'

Tony sat down and sipped his coffee while she assembled the breakfast with the efficient economy of movement she'd developed since she'd started working on the barn. Everything to hand, a system clearly worked out. No fuss, no mess, no hesitation. In the kitchen as it was in the barn. She'd learned that the hard way too.

She plonked the plates down and sat opposite him, her face stiff with anger. Annoyingly, Tony seemed unmoved by her reaction. He thanked her then said, 'What's the plan for today?'

'I don't know about you, but now I've finished the first fix for the electrics, I'm going to start plasterboarding the end wall.' The fresh air had sorted Carol out; she attacked her breakfast as if George Nicholas's lavish dinner party had been a week ago rather than the night before.

'Good eggs.' He swallowed another forkful. 'I've got a couple of pre-sentence reports to write up, and I've got my laptop with me, so that's me sorted. And if I finish them . . . well, I've made a start on writing a book.'

'A book?' Carol was startled. A book was a major project. And she'd known nothing about it. That was a measure of the distance they'd allowed to grow between them. 'What kind of book?'

'What kind of book would you expect me to write?'

She smiled, in spite of herself. 'I suppose you could do a mash-up of your interests and do a cartoon guide to profiling for beginners.'

He made a self-deprecating face. 'With a caped crusader showing up to save the day.'

'You'd look silly in tights. So what's this book, then?'

'It is about profiling. My supervisor — you know, the psychologist I go and talk to so I stay on the relatively straight and narrow — he thinks that if the police are going to try to save money by doing their own profiling instead of paying people like me, we shouldn't be dogs in the manger and wash our hands of them. He thinks I should write a book that gets away from technical language and theory and lays out in the most practical way possible what it is that I do. Jam-packed with examples of profiling in action from my casebook.'

Carol frowned. 'Isn't that like collaborating with your executioners?'

Tony shrugged. 'One of two things will happen. Either they'll get it and they'll learn how to do it properly, which is a good thing because, even when they were paying me, I could only be in one place at a time. Or they won't get it and they'll realise there's actually some expertise involved and they'll come back to us professionals with a renewed respect.'

She spluttered with laughter. 'You can't renew something that was never there in the first place, Tony. You've never had the respect your work deserves.'

'Some people have valued what I do. John Brandon. You. A couple of mandarins at the Home Office.'

'Just not enough to make ignorant arseholes like James Blake do the right thing.' She shovelled the last of her breakfast into her mouth and stood up, wiping the back of her hand across her mouth. She caught him watching her and felt the blood rising in a blush. Working like a labourer, she'd somehow acquired the same habits. The old Carol Jordan would have used a napkin or even a sheet of kitchen towel. The new Carol Jordan didn't care.

★　★　★

Left to his own devices, Tony set himself up with laptop and notebook. He could focus on his own work without having to keep watch over her. Unless she had a secret stash in the main part of the barn. But there was no reason for that. Besides, he reckoned she would be fired up with determination to prove him wrong. That righteous resolve would be enough to keep her going for a while. The problems would come on Monday or Tuesday, faced with the impending disaster of the court case and the loss of face and driving licence. That would be when he had to watch over her like a mother hen.

What she needed was something proper to focus on. Manual labour was all very well, and it had clearly fulfilled a need in her. But it was repetitious; for great tracts of time, it made no intellectual demands. And Carol was a woman who needed to occupy her mind. He had to figure out something that would engage her intelligence. If she couldn't be a cop any more, there had to be something else she could do that would stretch her and challenge her in the same way. But maybe with slightly lower stakes. Stakes that didn't push her back towards the bottle.

With a sigh, he turned to his notes and started to compose the pre-sentence report on a serial rapist who had tried to convince the court that he was driven to attack women by the voices in his head. Tony thought not. He reckoned he was dealing with a high-functioning psychopath who was aiming for a secure mental hospital as a preferable alternative to the sex offenders' wing of a prison.

By the time he'd finished, it was past noon. He stood up and stretched, then went through to the barn where Carol was nailing battens to the rough stone walls with six-inch nails. 'Do you want me to throw something together for lunch?' he asked.

She stopped hammering and turned round, pushing her damp hair back from her forehead with her bent wrist. Her plaid shirt clung to the contours of her body and her jeans were tight, revealing sculpted muscle. She was grimy and sweaty, and he knew it was a cliché, but he couldn't help but feel his blood stirring at the sight. 'There's bread and cheese and pâté and tomatoes,' she said. 'I usually have that with some fruit.'

He nodded. 'I'll make some sandwiches.'

'OK.' She turned back to the work. 'I won't be long, but I want to finish this section before I break for lunch.'

Back in the kitchen, he assembled clumsy sandwiches with cheap supermarket cheddar and tomatoes that would taste of cotton wool and water. Carol might drink for the taste, but he suspected she was only eating for the fuel. There was a bowl of apples and pears on the side and he moved them to the table beside the plate of sandwiches. It wasn't exactly a feast, but it would do. He poured two glasses of water and set two places opposite each other. There was nothing more he could do to make it look appealing so he went back to his laptop to pass the time till she joined him.

Tony didn't want to start work on the second

report only to have to pause. Instead, he navigated to a news site and checked out Jasmine Burton to see if there was any more information on her death. He sifted through several reports but nothing fresh seemed to have emerged. 'Stones in your coat,' he muttered under his breath. The detail bothered him but he couldn't pin down the echo that was resonating in the back of his mind.

'What did you say?'

He'd been so absorbed in what he was reading that he hadn't heard her come in.

'Nothing important. Just something that's niggling in the corner of my brain.'

She leaned over him to check out what he was looking at. He could smell clean sweat. It would have been erotic, he thought, if not for the slightly rancid edge to her breath. The drink working its way out of her system, he guessed. Even if they'd been at a point in their relationship where they might have kissed — and there had been moments of that intensity — her breath would have given him pause.

'Why are you so interested in a suicide in Devon?' Carol asked.

'I'm not sure. I was round at Paula and Elinor's last night and Torin brought it up. We got talking about cyber-bullying and trolls and how it looks like that's what drove Jasmine Burton to kill herself. But there was something about it . . . ' His voice tailed off.

Carol scanned the story in the top window. 'The media does love a good stick to beat the internet with,' she sighed. 'I know why this has caught your attention and got you puzzling.'

'You do? That's a relief.' He looked up at her expectantly. There was a familiar teasing half-smile on her lips. 'So are you going to tell me?'

'You can't help yourself, can you? Your subconscious is always building patterns.'

'So what's the pattern? What are you seeing that I'm not?'

The smile broadened. 'She's not the first one, Tony. At some level, your brain has clocked that she's not the first one.'

14

Detective Constable Sam Evans stretched luxuriously, loving that he was in a bed so big his limbs didn't make it to the outer limits. He admired the contrast of his latte-coloured skin against the white sheets, enjoying the sculpted contours of his muscles. The light fabric blinds on the high skylights cast a flattering light, and Sam smiled, knowing Stacey would gasp with grateful delight at the sight of him when she returned with his coffee.

At the far end of the loft, Stacey Chen poured beans in the hopper of her coffee grinder with one hand, while she tapped on the screen of a mini tablet with the other. She couldn't help herself. Even with the overwhelming and very tangible distraction of the man she'd never believed she'd tempt to her bed, the intangible world of cyberspace exerted its fascination.

Stacey knew she was a geek. Probably an uber-geek, if she was honest. Her immigrant parents had wanted the traditional route for her — the law, medicine, accountancy. But the first time she'd sat in front of a computer screen, she knew she'd found her natural home. She wanted to know how it worked so she could make it do her bidding and she'd plunged into the silicon world as if she was the bastard love child of Steve Jobs and Bill Gates.

While she was an undergraduate, she'd written

a piece of game code that she'd sold to a major developer for an eye-watering sum. It was earning her royalties all these years later. Her fellow students had expected her to join a games company or a software giant. Nobody expected her to join the police. Now she was the leading digital forensics expert with Bradfield Metropolitan Police. And every other force that managed to snag some of her wizardry. In her spare time, she still wrote code; in the past year, she'd developed two mobile apps that had each earned more than her annual salary.

Very few people knew the extent of her success. Stacey didn't want too much speculation about her reasons for staying with the police when she could have a much more lucrative life elsewhere. When pressed, she would talk about giving something back to the society that had welcomed her parents. The truth was too shaming to admit.

Stacey loved sticking her nose into other people's data. And being a police officer gave her access and licence. Nobody knew enough about her world to have the faintest idea how extensively she crawled and trawled her way through people's secrets. She'd wormed her way into almost every significant official data collection in the country and she had the back-door keys to all sorts of places whose users thought they were secret. It was helpful professionally. But nothing fired her up more than breaking through some high-level firewall into other people's privacy. Not even Sam.

Stacey dumped the ground coffee into a

cafetiere and poured the boiled water over it. As she waited for it to brew, she allowed herself a dreamy moment. They'd had a brilliant night. They'd ordered dinner from a local gourmet restaurant that delivered three-course meals, they'd opened a bottle of champagne, they'd streamed a movie that Sam had been eager to see, then they'd ended up in bed for twelve hours, alternating sex and sleep in a deeply satisfying combination. This was the first time Stacey had been in a serious relationship and she loved Sam so hard it made her stomach clench. After a night like this, the conclusion was irresistible. He loved her too.

It had been a few months now since she'd screwed up her courage and made her feelings known. He'd been a little wary at first. But they'd gone out to dinner and when she invited him back for a nightcap to her loft, he'd finally relaxed. They'd stood by the big windows, looking across the scatter of light that was Bradfield by night, and his arm had crept round her shoulders.

It had been a moment of pure magic. Stacey shivered at the memory, then plunged the coffee, glancing back at the screen of her tablet. As she read the alert she'd set up when she'd first joined the Major Incident Team, her mouth opened in a silent O.

Sam would be gobsmacked.

★ ★ ★

When Carol went back to work, Tony tried to be dutiful and prepare his second pre-sentencing report. But what she had said intrigued him too much. Carol hadn't been able to remember much detail but she was convinced she'd read recently about a case where a woman had killed herself after being trolled for speaking out about something vaguely feminist. Carol couldn't remember that either. 'I'm getting old,' she'd said with bleak humour. 'Things don't stick like they used to.'

That was quite an admission from a woman who was known for her eidetic memory for speech. Carol could repeat any conversation or interview verbatim, from memory. It was an occasionally inconvenient gift. Thoughtlessly, he'd said, 'Old age and alcohol. They both kill off brain cells at an alarming rate.' And that had been the end of any chance of Carol trying to be helpful. They'd eaten lunch in glum silence and she'd escaped back to work as soon as she could.

He tried various combinations of keywords in a series of fruitless searches. He wished he was still working with Carol's old team. Stacey Chen would have tracked the answer down in a matter of minutes. His years of gaming had left him adept at hunting down zombies but they hadn't trained him to scour the internet as successfully.

He was about to give up when he tried 'suicide trolling rape' and finally got what looked like the answer. Kate Rawlins had been a commercial radio presenter, responsible for an upbeat, anodyne drive-time show in London. She'd spoken up in support of the anonymity of rape victims after a controversial case involving a soap star who wanted his old job back after serving a sentence for rape. His fans had named his victim and persecuted her in spite of the guilty verdict and Kate had started a campaign to have the violators of the victim's privacy prosecuted.

She'd been buried under an avalanche of abuse. Her social media accounts had been deluged with a disgusting torrent of insults, threats and rage. They'd even tracked down her teenage daughter, an art student, and demanded she disown her mother for her shameful hostility to men.

Kate, a woman who'd always relied on warmth and charm to woo her audience, had discovered depths of defiance and determination. She'd stood up to the bullies, using her access to the airwaves to call them out. All that did was to provoke more baying for her blood. On the face of it, she'd taken it all on the chin, winning a broad swathe of support from broadcasters, journalists and her followers on social media.

And then one morning, her PA had turned up at her North London house and found her in the garage with the engine running. In case of second thoughts, Kate had handcuffed herself to the passenger armrest so she couldn't reach the ignition button.

There was a storm of shock and outrage. Fingers pointed at the soap star, who threw his hands up and denied that he'd ever encouraged the beasts who'd tormented her. The story commanded inside-page headlines for a few days and then it died.

Similar circumstances, very different deaths. It

was interesting, but finding out about Kate Rawlins hadn't stilled the niggle in his head. Something was bothering him about Jasmine Burton's death.

But worrying at it was getting him nowhere. Experience had taught him that the best way to access what was swimming under the surface was to focus on something else. So he forced himself back to work.

When he emerged from the other end of the tunnel of concentration, it was late afternoon. He strained to listen but he couldn't hear the distant muffled banging that had kept him company just below the level of consciousness earlier in the day. He wondered whether Carol had taken the dog out. He hoped not; he'd been planning to suggest accompanying them on their next walk. He needed the fresh air and walking was always where he got his best ideas, whether for his book or about Jasmine Burton.

He opened the door and Flash was at his side in an instant, weaving round his legs. Not dog-walking, then.

She wasn't working either. At the far end of the barn, Carol was sitting on a sawhorse, her arms wrapped around her body, her shoulders hunched. Even from that distance, he could see that she was shivering even though a couple of big space heaters made the barn a tolerable temperature. Tony took his time walking towards her, trying not to show the level of his concern. The last thing she needed right now was the emotional complication of his feelings for her spilling out all over the place.

As he drew nearer, he could see a sheen of greasy sweat on her face. She tried visibly to get hold of herself and stop shaking. But her body betrayed her, trembling like a beaten dog. He sat down beside her and put his arm around her. They'd avoided any physical contact for a long time, both nervous of where it might take them. The intimacy that had once been second nature to them had been shattered by Michael and Lucy's death and since then they'd been like a country riven by a civil war whose opposing sides don't know how to rebuild diplomatic relations. Feeling her warmth against him after all this time filled him with a nostalgic sadness. He wished the embrace came from wanting, not needing that physical contact.

'I'm sorry,' she said, her voice barely above a whisper.

'This'll pass,' he said. He could feel the tremors passing from her body through his, smell the sharp acidity of her sweat. 'Do you feel like going for a walk? The fresh air might help.'

Carol leaned her head against his shoulder. 'It can't be any worse than this. Give me a minute.' She closed her eyes and shuddered. Then she pulled a grimy rag from her pocket and wiped her face. She managed a weak smile. 'My mother would have a fit if she could see what I've become.'

Tony gave a strangled laugh. 'That's nothing to what my mother would say.'

Carol squeezed out a weak chuckle. 'She never liked me.' She forced herself to her feet, slightly unsteady. 'Come on, then, if you're coming. I warn you, though, that moor isn't for the faint-hearted.'

He gave her a lopsided smile. 'After this morning, you think I'm faint-hearted?'

15

Stacey bustled back into the bedroom with the coffee, so excited that she was virtually unmoved by Sam's naked display. 'You're never going to believe this,' she said, putting both coffees down, slipping out of her silk wrap and sliding back into bed alongside him.

'Are you going off me?' he teased, reaching over and pulling her into his arms. She could feel him stiffening against her thigh but right then, that wasn't the only thing on her mind.

'Don't be silly. But this is totally shocking.' She kissed him lightly on the nose. 'Pay attention for a minute, Sam. Really. You won't regret it. I'll still be here.' She squirmed away from him and reached for the tablet she kept by the bed. Her fingers danced over the screen till she found the alert that had stopped her in her tracks in the kitchen. 'Look at this.'

Sighing, Sam propped himself up on one elbow. 'I can't believe there's anything more exciting than what my cock has planned for you. OK, let me see it.' He held out his hand like a banqueting Roman expecting the sweetmeats.

Stacey flicked his shoulder with her fingertips. There was a primness to her that would never enjoy his occasional vulgarity. There was no need, in her world, for crudeness of behaviour or speech. 'You don't deserve me.' He poked his tongue out at her and she passed the tablet to him.

For a moment, he wasn't quite sure what he was looking at. It was a computerised custody record from West Yorkshire Police, that much was obvious. Halifax cop shop. Drink-driving. Why was Stacey so excited about a drink-driving arrest?

Then he saw the name and whistled softly. 'Carol fucking Jordan.' He checked the date and time. 'This only happened last night. How the fuck do you get this stuff?'

Stacey shrugged, trying to look modest but failing. And why should she try? She was proud of her skills. She was, however, dimly aware that not everyone appreciated her sticky fingers all over their personal stuff. 'It's easy. I set up an alert on my system to trawl all my database access for any mentions of people or things I'm interested in.'

'And Carol Jordan is one of those?' Sam shuffled up the bed and reached past Stacey for coffee.

'I put an alert on her when I first started working for the MIT. It seemed . . . sensible?'

'To spy on your boss?' He giggled. 'That's brilliant. No wonder you're always one step ahead of the game. Can you do the same for my boss? I know next to nothing about the bastard. And knowledge is power.'

Stacey pretended to frown. 'And would you use your power for good or evil, Sam?'

He laughed and kissed her. 'I'd use it for us, sweetheart.' He looked back at the tablet. 'That is fucking amazing. I knew she was drinking. I told Blake about it but he could never nail her.'

Stacey was shocked. 'You told Blake the boss was drinking? Why would you do that?'

He gave her an innocent look. 'Because I care about the job, of course. I didn't want us to lose cases because she'd had one too many vodkas. She was my boss, not my friend, Stacey.'

Stacey was taken aback. 'But she was a good boss, Sam. The best I've ever had. The work was interesting, she treated us fairly and she always fought our corner with Blake. Why would you go behind her back to the very person who was trying to destroy her?' She desperately wanted him to come up with a valid reason; this early in their relationship, she couldn't bear the thought that he might be less than she believed him to be.

He handed her back the tablet. 'You make it sound much more melodramatic than it was. Like I said, justice came first. Plus I wanted to make sure Blake knew which side I was on when the chips were down.' He reached an arm round Stacey and tried to pull her down on to him.

Stacey was struggling to make sense of her feelings. Carol Jordan had been the perfect boss as far as she was concerned. She hadn't cared what Stacey did or where she sneaked in, as long as she delivered what the team needed when people's lives were at stake. Carol had plucked her out of a pretty dull job and offered her the chance to make a difference, and she'd appreciated Stacey's talent in a way that no other senior officer had before or since. Stacey suspected it was because Carol's brother had been a geek too, that that had given her an insight into the world

Stacey inhabited for most of her waking hours.

But Sam was the man she loved, the man she'd lusted after and longed for since the first day he'd walked into the MIT squad room and looked around with those assessing brown eyes that seemed to see inside her head and her heart. It had taken her a long time to admit even to herself what she felt, and it had been Paula who had finally pushed her into making her feelings known. Stacey still couldn't quite believe he'd chosen her, and she wasn't secure enough in his love to challenge him. Part of her despised herself for not sticking up for Carol the way Carol had always stuck up for her officers. 'But she was always on our side,' was all she said.

Sam nuzzled her shoulder, his mouth moving down towards her breast. 'Never mind Carol Jordan,' he said. 'We've got better things to occupy us now.'

And so Stacey let herself succumb to his seduction, entirely unaware that with part of his mind, her lover was calculating whether there was any way he could use this new information to his advantage. When she'd said he didn't deserve her, Stacey had been more right than she knew.

16

Metal ground against metal as Tony crashed the gears of the Land Rover. 'I am going to want to drive this again one day,' Carol grumbled.

'It's been a while since I drove anything so primitive.'

She snorted. 'You're not exactly Jeremy Clarkson when it comes to wheels.'

Tony winced. 'For which we should both be grateful. My Volvo might be close to clapped-out but at least it was built after synchromesh was invented.' The easy banter as they drove up the moor edge towards the Bradfield road was a welcome relief to Tony after the fraught and sometimes tetchy evening they'd spent after their walk up the hill behind the barn. He'd feared she was going to lose her temper, but he'd held back before he pushed her that far.

And this morning, Carol seemed calmer. They'd sat at the kitchen table, Flash at her feet, and managed to talk without scoring too many points or scratching too many scabs. He'd broken the silence with a question he hoped she wouldn't take as a challenge. 'What do you normally do in the evenings?'

She'd raised her head and pushed back the thick curtain of silvering blonde hair from her forehead. 'When I'm too tired to work any longer, I watch TV. Anything except crime dramas, which means I sometimes end up watching very bizarre documentaries on Channel 4.' This last with a wry smile.

'Maybe it's time you started gaming?'

She gave a shout of derision. 'What? Pretend I'm Lara Croft, like you do? Run about the landscape with improbable tits, killing people?'

'You know better than to give a cheap answer like that. The kind of games I play involve strategic thinking, quick reactions, forward planning. They're heuristic. You learn from your mistakes and develop alternative approaches to problems.'

Carol hooted with laughter. 'And that's your justification for hours in front of a screen acting like one of the crazies you spend the rest of your waking life treating?'

Tony shook his head. 'It's the truth. It takes my conscious mind off the crazies. And it frees up my subconscious mind to solve the problems the crazies set me.'

'And you think that would help me how?' Her grey-blue eyes sparkled, blazing a dare at him. She took a defiant swig of the coffee that was the sum total of her breakfast that morning.

Deep breath. Hard talk. 'I think it might give you space to work out what you want to do with the rest of your life. Sooner or later you're going to run out of barn to renovate and then you're going to have to make some choices. I know you, Carol. You're not going to settle for burying yourself away here in the middle of nowhere, walking the dog and joining the WI and watching bad TV.'

She looked away from his direct gaze. 'And you think *Grand Theft Auto* will fill the gap?'

'It'll take your mind off the gap till you know what's going to fill it. I need to go into Bradfield today. I've used up the clean pants in my emergency overnight bag and I need to go in to Bradfield Moor to make arrangements for other therapists to pick up the slack for me for the rest of the week. I thought I'd grab my — '

'The rest of the week?' Carol cut across him, a mixture of outrage and surprise on her face. 'Who the fuck asked you to move in?'

This was where he would normally have stepped sideways to avoid a direct confrontation. He'd spent years avoiding head-on collisions with her. Partly because professionally he didn't believe in warfare as a means to lasting peace. But mostly because he hated the hollow feeling in the pit of his stomach that came hand in hand with fighting Carol. Today, though, he knew there was no escape. 'You need me, Carol.'

'Fuck you, Tony. I don't need you. I don't need anyone.' She scraped her chair noisily on the floor as she pushed it back. The dog jumped to her feet, ears pricked, sensing trouble. Carol waved an arm expansively around her. 'Take a look around you. I'm managing fine by myself.'

'No, you're not. You keep telling yourself that, but it doesn't make it true. You're hurting and you need healing. You need help, Carol. You need help from somebody who believes you deserve to be helped. And I'm not going anywhere. I'll be here for as long as it takes.'

He saw the sparkle of tears in her eyes as she turned away. 'Christ. Am I to have no peace ever again?'

'If you genuinely want me to leave, I will. But I won't come back again.'

'And then who would you bug the hell out of? Face it, Tony. If I'm Billy No Mates, like you said yesterday, then so are you. You need me so you can feel needed. Well, I've been getting along without you very well lately. I can do that again.'

Then, uncharacteristically, he'd raised his voice. 'Will you stop this? I'm tired of fighting with you. All these years, every time we get close, we let something come between us and one of us lashes out or walks away. I'm sick and tired of it, Carol. I want us to be at peace with each other. You're right. Neither of us has anyone else who even comes close to the way we understand each other. You can't manage without me and I can't manage without you.' He punched one fist into the other palm. 'Just. Please. Stop it.'

Carol reached out blindly to Flash, who laid her head on her mistress's lap. She fondled the dog's soft ears, buying herself time. When she could trust her voice, she said at last, 'If we're going to Bradfield, we'd better go via the builder's yard and the bed shop, then. I've got a spare set of keys for the Landie and we can swing by Halifax nick and pick up the other set if we've got time.'

And that was that. As settled as anything could be between them.

As they crested the moor, he took his second gamble of the morning. 'By the way, I've arranged for us to meet Paula for a coffee,' he said.

'Oh, for fuck's sake,' Carol muttered. 'More humiliation.'

'You don't have to tell her if you don't want to,' he said. 'But she might already know.'

'She'll know. The thin blue grapevine will have been working overtime.'

'Whether she knows or not, she's not going to judge you. Not Paula. But that's not why I want to see her.'

Carol swivelled in her seat, her curiosity piqued. 'Why, then? What are you up to?'

'There's something bugging me about Jasmine Burton's suicide. And because of that, I want to know more about Kate Rawlins too.'

Carol's mouth lifted at one corner in a crooked smile. 'You're still suborning Paula to do your heavy lifting, then?'

'I'd do it myself if I could, but she's the one with her hands on the levers. And she keeps in touch with Stacey, who isn't averse to doing foreigners for an old friend either.'

'One of these days you're going to land her right in the shit. And she won't have me to pull her out of it next time.'

Tony gave a wry laugh. 'That's not fair. Paula and I have been a good team in the past. If it hadn't been for her going the extra mile and dragging you out from under your stone, I might be languishing in prison right now.'

Carol's look was sour. 'You say that like it's a good thing.'

'It is from where I'm standing. Anyway, I thought it might be interesting to see what she can find out. It might keep us amused, you and me.'

'What? A fake investigation? You think that's

what I need at this point in my life?'

He'd shrugged. 'It might not be fake. Depending on what Paula turns up. Come on, Carol. I know you've developed lots of new skills lately but you've got a bunch of existing ones that need a bit of exercise too.'

She'd groaned. 'Enough. So before we even spoke this morning, you were expecting me to come into Bradfield with you? What? You don't trust me alone? You think as soon as you were out the door I'd be calling George Nicholas to fetch me a bottle of vodka?'

Tony tried to look hurt. 'It never crossed my mind,' he lied. 'I merely thought you might appreciate a change of scenery. And somebody else's company apart from mine.'

Carol muttered something under her breath but let it lie. He was, he thought, making some progress, even if he felt as if his skin was being flayed from his body with every step forward. He kept reminding himself of what he knew in his heart. Nobody was worth it more than Carol Jordan.

17

Paula brushed her teeth in the locker room, trying to rid her mouth of the taste of the office brew. If she was going to a proper coffee shop, she wanted to taste what she was drinking. Back in the days of the MIT, they'd had proper coffee, beans freshly ground, sometimes brought back from artisan roasters by whoever had been out on the prowl. Her new team was led by a DCI who was clinging to her job by her French-manicured fingernails and who drank Yorkshire tea so strong it would have defeated builders. DCI Fielding and Paula had got off on the wrong foot when Fielding had arrested Tony on suspicion of murder, only to be proved spectacularly wrong by Paula, with more than a little help from Carol. In spite of the humiliation, Fielding had kept her job. But she'd made sure ever since that Paula's life was as uncomfortable as it could be. Yet another reason to mourn the passing of the best squad she'd ever worked with.

When Tony had texted her the night before, Paula had startled Elinor by squealing with delight at the prospect of seeing him and Carol at the same table, actually talking to each other. There were few things more painful than watching two people who clearly loved each other tearing that connection apart. For anyone who cared anything for Tony or Carol, the past year had been purgatorial. She couldn't help wondering what had brought them back to this point.

The question had been answered as soon as she'd walked into the CID office that morning. She hadn't even got her coat off when DCI Fielding had appeared in her office doorway. 'Did you hear about Carol Jordan?' she said, unable to hide the feline smile twitching the corners of her mouth.

'What about her?' Paula had turned away under cover of hanging up her jacket. She wasn't about to give Fielding the satisfaction of seeing her reaction to whatever piece of bad news she was clearly on the point of dishing out.

'She's been done for drink-driving. West Yorkshire picked her up on Saturday night. Nothing marginal about it either. Well over the limit, I hear.' Fielding couldn't keep the satisfaction out of her voice. She might not be half the detective Carol Jordan had been, but she was damn sure she was never going to be caught out doing something that stupid; that was what Paula read in her tone.

Paula hid her dismay and turned to face her boss. 'That must be a relief to a lot of people,' she said blandly.

Fielding frowned. 'Meaning what, Sergeant?'

'With a criminal conviction like that, there's no prospect of her being wooed back on to the force.' She turned her mouth down at the corners in a sardonic expression. 'So she's not going to be challenging anybody else's job.' Then she'd walked away, not waiting for Fielding's reaction. She armed herself with a cup of execrable instant and headed for an interview room without a backward glance.

When she sat down to interrogate an arrogant rape suspect, she put Fielding's words out of her head. There would be time for that later. Right then, she had to focus on stripping a young man of his swagger and introducing him to the world of uncertainty and fear. This was what she lived for, in a professional sense. Her natural environment was the ritual dance of the interview, where she could use all her wiles to wheedle and worm information out of men and women who had come into the room armoured with certainty that they weren't going to reveal themselves. Nobody was better than Paula at shredding that certainty and leaving them exposed to their own venality and criminality. It was, she knew, the reason Carol Jordan had recruited her in the first place.

By the time she'd done with the rapist, it was time to slip out and meet the two people whose brilliance had helped shape her into the cop she was now. She told nobody where she was going, only that she had someone to see about a case. Fielding wouldn't like it, but the way Paula was feeling these days, that was a bonus.

When she walked into the hipster coffee bar on the fringes of the university campus where Tony had told her to meet, she wondered momentarily if he'd misjudged the rendezvous. But of course it made perfect sense. None of the patrons here would have the faintest idea who any of the trio was; they'd just be three old saddos who had walked in by mistake.

117

Paula spotted Carol and Tony right away, sitting hunched over a corner table at the back of the room. Even from this distance, Tony looked tired, dark smudges under weary eyes, his cheeks hollow.

Paula picked up an Americano at the counter and joined them. Carol was pale, her skin blotchy and dry. Her hair needed a good cut from a proper stylist, not whatever local snipper she'd entrusted herself to. In the weeks since Paula had seen her last, she appeared to have withdrawn even further into herself. But Paula was determined not to show her worry for her former boss. 'Good to see you,' she said cheerily as she settled into the third chair, wondering what the etiquette was when it came to mentioning drink-driving charges.

'You too,' Tony said.

'Thanks for sneaking out to meet us,' Carol said.

Paula grinned. 'How did you know there was sneaking involved?'

Carol shrugged. 'I don't imagine DCI Fielding would have let you out of the building if she'd known where you were going. Especially in the light of the latest gossip.'

Paula stared at her coffee, as if there was some fascinating message there. 'I heard,' she said. Then she felt ashamed of herself for her lack of support. She raised her eyes and put some spirit in her voice. 'That sucks.'

Carol fiddled with her coffee spoon. 'I was over the limit.'

'Even so. Is there no way of sorting it? I could

talk to DCI Franklin, I always got on with him better than you did . . . '

Carol held up a hand. 'No point. John Franklin is no friend of mine, but even if he were, I think he'd struggle to make it go away. It was a fair cop, Paula.' She shook her head, resigned. 'I was on a back road, a mile from home, in control of my vehicle and myself, which makes it sound unlucky and unfair, but in all honesty, I've got no grounds for complaint.'

Paula couldn't help admiring Carol's honesty. In her shoes, she doubted she'd be quite so accepting of her fate. 'Makes it sound like a conspiracy,' she grumbled. 'But I hear you. If there's anything I can do to help. I mean, practically. When you . . . '

'Lose my licence? Thanks, I might take you up on that. It's not exactly straightforward, living where I do.'

'You could move back into town for the duration,' Tony said. 'There's always houseboats for rent down at the Minster Basin. We could be neighbours again.'

Paula had the feeling this was news to Carol. He'd probably waited till there was someone else around so she couldn't explode at the suggestion.

'Yeah, right,' Carol said. 'The dog would love that. Cramped and confined and constrained by the inner city. No thanks. I'd rather put up with the inconvenience. Besides, I'm not doing all this work on the barn so somebody else can have the benefit of it.'

'Well, if you ever need a bed for the night

when you're in the city, we can always squeeze you in, there's a sofa bed in the living room.'

Carol gave an involuntary shudder. A less understanding woman than Paula would have been offended. 'That's kind of you, Paula, but I wouldn't want to intrude. I think I remind Torin too much of what happened to his mother.'

'Speaking of death?' Tony said with his usual flair for derailing the small talk.

'Which we weren't,' Carol said.

'We sort of were.' Paula made an apologetic gesture with her hands. 'Let's face it, that's what generally draws us together. I should have known there would be something more than a decent cup of coffee on the agenda. Fire away.' She raised her coffee cup in a toast.

Carol and Tony exchanged a look. 'You do it,' he said. 'You're better at briefing detectives than me.'

Carol shook her head. 'Oh no, you don't get out of it that easily. This is your bloody mad idea.'

Tony shifted in his plain wooden chair, hooking one arm over the back of it. 'It's probably a chimera. Remember we were talking about Jasmine Burton on Saturday night?'

Paula nodded. 'Yes, Torin was outraged about the trolling. He was talking about it again yesterday.'

'There's something about it that's niggling at the back of my mind and I can't put my finger on it. I don't have any idea what it relates to, but there's something there that's bothering me. We were talking about it, me and Carol — ' He

120

gestured for her to take over.

'And I remembered Kate Rawlins. Does that ring a bell?'

Paula shook her head. 'Sorry. Should it?'

'The radio presenter who stuck up for the anonymity of rape victims after that twat from *Northerners* kicked off about being an innocent man found guilty because of a lying accuser. You remember?'

Light dawned on Paula, bringing a blast of self-disgust with it. 'Yes, of course, sorry. I'd forgotten her name. How crap is that? A woman gets driven to suicide because of a bunch of bullying bastards, and I can't even remember her name.' She flushed, feeling a wash of shame. 'But what's that got to do with Jasmine Burton? They didn't even choose the same method. Didn't Kate Rawlins do the car exhaust thing?'

'That's right,' Tony said. 'And I know this is incredibly tenuous, and my cause is not helped by me not being able to summon up what it is that's bothering me, but it's my job to see patterns where other people see white noise. And in my head, there's a pattern here. Two women. Strong, competent, professionally respected women who stuck their heads over the parapet all the time, except that one time it was picked up on by the internet trolls.'

'I prefer to think of them as inadequate wankers,' Carol said. 'The trolls in Terry Pratchett's books are quite lovable. Not even their mothers could find anything remotely lovable about these twats.'

Tony scrunched his face up, as if her words

pained him. 'Well, strictly speaking, most of the people who do this have been revealed as quite pathetic and even vulnerable young men whose mothers probably do love them.' He held his hands up to ward off the protest Carol started to voice. 'But some of them are much more dangerous and insidious than that, you're right.'

'All of this is very interesting, but . . . ?' Paula gently interjected.

'The pattern. Yes. Strong women with a mind of their own who didn't back down. They stood up to the trolls — sorry, bastards. They didn't run away and hide, they didn't backtrack, they stuck to their guns. They acted as though they felt brave. They behaved with conviction. And then out of the blue they killed themselves. Pattern.'

'Are you suggesting they were murdered?' Paula had heard some wild theories from Tony over the years, but seldom anything that had strained her credulity quite this far.

'Not as such,' he said hesitantly. 'Not in the conventional sense of someone killing them directly. But something happened. Something intervened between their determination to see off the bastards and their deaths. Once would be an oddity. Twice makes me wonder.'

'And he thinks I need something to keep my detective skills from atrophying,' Carol said drily. 'Though what I'm going to use them for in future is anybody's guess. So we're all going to play at running a case.'

There was a long silence while everyone suddenly became very interested in the contents of their cups and the beardie weirdie indie track playing in the background. It was Paula who spoke first. 'So what exactly is it you want me to do?'

'You might want to get Stacey on board,' Carol said. 'We want everything you can get your hands on. Investigating officer reports, interview product, pathology, the works.'

'We're looking for something we don't know exists and we won't know what it is till we find it,' Tony said. 'But if it does exist, you know you can rely on us to spot it.' He flashed her his sweetest smile, the one that made men and women alike eager to do whatever it took to provoke it again.

'And meanwhile I'll be backtracking through the news sites online to see whether I can find any more that fit the pattern,' Carol said cheerfully.

'Great,' Paula said.

Tony twinkled at her. 'Go on, admit it. You've missed us, haven't you?'

18

The books were talismans that linked him to his past. They were the physical representation of the journey his mother had made away from him and into the embrace of the peace camp that had taken her life. Those were the texts she'd relied on to justify her absence. Any time his resolve wavered, he could go back to those books and remind himself of the lesson they carried. They were written by women who preached about feminism and women's rights and demanded change to the way things had always been. Even to this day, stupid feminists held them up as texts that showed the way, that illuminated a path other women should follow.

But what their followers never talked about was the fact that it was a path to the grave. Those women his mother had read and admired — Sylvia Plath, Virginia Woolf — and those others he'd discovered since, they realised that what they'd been shouting about wasn't a blueprint for life, it was a set of directions to hell. They'd invented a life of misery for themselves. They'd created a recipe for disaster. Their feminist revolution had led them straight down a one-way street to self-destruction.

And so they'd done the logical thing and killed themselves. And since the message he wanted to send was that these loud-mouthed women were setting themselves and their so-called sisters on the road to perdition, the books would serve to hammer home the message. They would act as a kind of suicide note, there to reinforce the act itself, to still any doubts on the part of the authorities. They would be an easily solved code that indicated these women had brought about their own deaths.

This was the message he wanted to go viral: failing to fulfil yourself as a wife and mother would make you want to kill yourself. He wanted there to be no misapprehension in the eyes of the audience. He didn't want to cloud the issue with the notion that there might be something else going on. He didn't want them martyred as murder victims so he had to strengthen that image of suicide. Trying to forge suicide notes would have been asking for trouble; the books served the same purpose and couldn't be exposed as forgeries.

And besides, after the first two or three went public and people began to sit up and take notice, they'd become a fashion statement in themselves. Silly women driven to death and despair would pick their own texts to say goodbye with, so they'd become part of the movement he was creating. The ones who got it would join his very own sisterhood of their own free will.

The books had been a late addition to his plans. But a brilliant one. He had to scrabble to get them all together in time. But the more he thought about it, the larger their significance loomed. The little stack on the shelf in his garage had turned into one of the most powerful elements of his campaign. Women who had killed themselves raising their voices in support of women who were killing themselves. It had an almost poetic symmetry.

And of course, they led him directly to the next death.

19

They had started with a post-apocalyptic world recovering from a deadly fungal infection. To Carol, who hadn't looked properly at a video game since the blocky polyhedrons of the nineties, *The Last of Us* looked as slick as an animated movie. 'It's a quest, like all the best books and films,' Tony said. 'I guarantee, you'll care as much about Joel and Ellie as you did about Scout and Atticus Finch. Well, maybe not quite that much. But they will get under your skin and into your emotions.'

At first there had been a lot of swearing and walking into walls. Carol's aim was appalling, her co-ordination little better. But Tony was encouraging, occasionally taking over the controls to show her how to negotiate a particular difficulty. And gradually, she got the hang of it. Watching her immerse herself in the world of pixels, Tony cursed that he hadn't managed to persuade her to do this years ago. With the game as their focus, they slipped back into an easy intimacy that he thought they'd lost forever. They teased each other, made jokes, groaned at her failures and cheered her victories. They jostled each other's shoulders like a pair of teenage gamers, both lost in what she was trying to achieve.

When he'd suggested they pause for a cup of tea, Carol had been astounded to realise they'd been playing for more than three hours. 'I'd no idea. I thought it was about ten o'clock. Not midnight. I have to be up in the morning,' she said in tones of wonder.

'Take the dog out now, she'll cut you some slack in the morning, won't she?' He yawned and reached for his tablet.

Carol gave him a derisive look. 'It's clear you've never had a dog. I'll be lucky if I get an hour's grace with this one.'

'At least you've got a proper bed to sleep in tonight.'

They'd spent an hour earlier in the evening assembling a king-size bed at the far end of the barn. Carol had insisted on the widest option in the shop. 'If I've got to share my bed with a bloody dog, I need as much space as possible,' she'd pointed out.

'It doesn't matter what size bed you buy, she'll snuggle up to you anyway. You're the leader of her pack, she wants to be close to you.'

Carol had grunted but opted for the big bed regardless. And now she'd surfaced from the game, she intended to crawl into it as soon as possible. But by the time she came back from a short jog along the shoulder of the hill, Tony was deep into 80 Days. 'That looks a bit dull,' she said, looking over his shoulder.

'Try it.' He offered her the tablet and sat back. 'It's got narrative, which might appeal to you. And it looks good.'

An hour later, she surfaced, dazed. 'Christ, this is addictive,' she groaned.

'But you haven't craved a drink all night, have you?'

She glared at him. 'So that's how it goes, is it? Replace one addiction with another?'

'Whatever works. And it's not like you've had a shit time, is it? If you stick with it, it won't take over your life. At least, I don't think it will. I love gaming. It helps me work things out. And yes, there have been times when a new game has kept me up pretty much all night. But mostly, I just play for an hour or two, when there's nothing urgent needs dealing with. And then I put it to one side. It's a less demanding mistress than drink or drugs, I promise you.'

She looked mutinous for a moment, then she yawned. 'I'll take your word for it. But right now, I need to sleep. If you're going to be around for a while, I need to install a second bathroom.'

'I don't mind sharing.' He sounded almost wistful.

'Maybe not, but I do. I've lived alone for a long time, and I don't like my ablutions dictated by someone else's timetable. Besides, it was the next job on my list after plaster-boarding the end wall. You can help me with the plumbing.' She stood up and patted him on the shoulder. 'Thank you.' And then she was gone. It wasn't much, but it was more than enough for him.

★   ★   ★

For once, Stacey was almost relieved to have her penthouse to herself. Sam and his team were out celebrating a double arrest in a violent armed robbery, and they'd both agreed that him staggering in pissed in the small hours would be a satisfying experience for no one. So he was spending the night in his own flat, a modern box in Kenton Vale overlooking the scabby park that the developers had claimed was about to be given a makeover. They hadn't made it clear that the makeover would be in a downward direction. Sam didn't care. 'Do I look like a man who takes a walk in the park?' he'd said. What he liked best about his building was the basement gym where he could hone his muscles in relative peace and quiet. Stacey would have killed herself before she'd be seen in a gym. She liked having an apartment that was big enough to accommodate a pilates ball and a yoga mat so she could follow her own, private fitness regime. But if the price of Sam moving in was one of those big multi-function gym machines in her space, she'd learn to live with it.

Not that living together was on the agenda. Well, not yet anyway. And although Stacey often fantasised about how wonderful it would be to share their lives even more completely, she had to admit there would be a downside. When would she find the time to invade other people's systems, never mind write her own code? How would she keep secret from Sam the extent to which she was privy to all sorts of data that was supposed to be held safe behind firewalls and real walls? It wasn't that she didn't trust him. She did, of course. But his desire to do the right thing — like telling Blake about Carol's drink habit — could be dangerous, given some of the information Stacey came by in the course of her compulsion to creep around other people's confidentiality.

Take tonight. How would she explain that to Sam? He liked concrete lines of investigation, not this vague trawling around in the dark on a whim. He'd think she was wasting her time. Worse, he'd think she was pandering to her old boss, unable to let go and move forward as he had done.

He wasn't a big fan of Paula's either. He thought she'd been Carol Jordan's teacher's pet, that she got preferential treatment when assignments were being handed out. Stacey wondered if he was a little bit jealous of Paula's success rate. She was, after all, the queen of the interview room and that was so often where the case was wrapped up. They'd all contributed to take the case to the point where the crucial interrogation could happen, but because it was always Paula asking the questions and making the final nail-down, she looked like the star baker every time.

Stacey didn't mind that. In fact, she quite liked being lost in the background, pixelated out till she was 'the Chinese one' in the minds of outsiders to the team. That meant they didn't look too closely at what she was actually doing so she could keep on getting away with it. That was one of the reasons she'd liked working for Carol Jordan. The boss cared about her results, not the minutiae of how she got them, provided that nothing Stacey did was going to come back and bite them in the arse at a later stage. Sometimes they had to find alternative explanations of how they'd made what looked like an extraordinary leap in the dark. But that was part of the fun.

Tonight, though, was different. There was no

MIT invisibility cloak to protect her if things went wrong. She was on her own. And being a white-hatted version of the darkside hacker wouldn't help her if she was caught with her hand in the biscuit tin of another police force. For Stacey, that was like a gauntlet thrown down in front of her skills. Paula had offered her a chance to do the kind of thing she did best, and these days, such opportunities were hard to come by. The work that was officially being thrown her way could have been completed by an A-level student. She'd have taken that as an insult were it not for the fact that she realised the officers handing out the orders knew so little themselves that they had no clue how far beneath her capabilities their requests were.

Normally she'd have said no to a drink after work on a Monday evening. She was always eager to get back to her own devices after the first brain-numbing day of the week. But Paula had sweetened the invitation with the teaser that Carol and Tony were looking at something they wanted her help with. Stacey didn't care that Carol was outside the official tent. What tempted her was the promise of something different and probably difficult. So she'd said yes.

They'd met in a dingy bar on the edge of Temple Fields, where the gay village blurred into the domain of the sex trade. So early in the evening, it was more or less deserted, apart from a pair of wan young men leaning despondently on the bar. 'You know all the best places,' Stacey said, sipping her vodka tonic with an air of deep suspicion.

'I know how to hide in plain sight.' Paula took a swig of overpriced Eurolager. They worked their way through the catch-up but Stacey's heart wasn't in it. She thought of Paula as a friend — probably her closest female friend — but she didn't think that meant she had to be interested in her girlfriend or their weird domestic set-up with a murder victim's teenage kid. But that was the way the world worked. You had to pretend you cared.

'I presume you heard Carol got nicked for drink-driving?'

Stacey nodded. 'It showed up on my radar.'

'If you were paranoid, you might think Franklin had set his lads up for it. She was a mile from home, not driving like a maniac, the usual Carol Jordan buzz on. And where she lives, it's a back road that goes from Bumfuck, West Yorkshire, to Bumfuck, Lancashire. You'd have to sit around all night waiting for a car to collide with.' Paula sounded angry. Stacey recognised the signs. She'd been brooding all day and now she was ready for a little rant.

But Stacey was going to lance the boil. 'I thought of that too. So I took a look. There's no trail of breadcrumbs in the system that says anything other than this was righteous. Franklin actually emailed the arresting officer yesterday, wanting to know what they were doing on that road. The yellow jacket said they use it regularly as a cut-through from Todmorden. Which it sort of is, if you're trying to avoid making too many inconvenient Saturday-night traffic stops.'

Paula sighed. 'I know. I'm just raging against

the machine. Anyway, the bottom line is Tony's trying to get her off the sauce — '

'What? Dry her out?' Stacey couldn't help showing her scepticism.

'Well, there's nobody else with a snowball's chance of getting her to even try. He seems to think if he keeps her occupied every waking moment she'll get through the worst of it and out the other side.'

'Good luck with that,' Stacey said. 'But I thought she was gutting her brother's place?'

'She's at the rebuilding stage now, Tony says. But because it's hard physical labour, there's only so much she can do in a day. And then she's got all evening to sit around and get tanked up. So he thought he'd find some other things to take her mind off the next drink.' Paula gave Stacey an up-and-under look over the rim of her glass. 'He's going to get her gaming.'

Generally Stacey aimed to conform to the stereotype of the inscrutable Chinese. Give people what they expect and they won't look twice. But now her eyes widened and her hand flew to her mouth. 'Carol Jordan? Gaming? But she despises gaming.'

Paula nodded. 'But he's managed to get her to agree to give it a go.'

'It's the invasion of the body snatchers. Are you sure this is Carol Jordan we're talking about?'

'Looked like her this morning. And I think I have some evidence to back it up. The other thing he's come up with to keep her occupied is a classic Tony and Carol ploy. They think they've

134

found a case to investigate. A case that's so far below the radar it doesn't even exist yet.'

Stacey straightened her face. 'Now that I can believe. And since it's supposed to be keeping Carol occupied, of course he's gone down the far end of the obscure spectrum. And that'll be where I come in, I take it?'

Paula grinned. 'You know you want to.'

'You only want me for my baud rate.'

'I don't even know what that means, Stace. Anyway, here's what it is. Two women, each with a bit of a profile, express separate opinions online that set the trolls off. There's bile, there's vile, there's threats and there's all sorts of unpleasantness. But neither of them backs down. They're taking it on the chin and fighting back. And then they kill themselves. When you say it like that, it sounds like one of Tony's famous patterns. But there's a lot speaks against that. There's about three months between the two suicides. One did the car exhaust thing, the other drowned herself. We don't know if they'd ever even met, never mind knew each other.'

Stacey automatically took out her tablet and started typing. 'Names? Addresses?' She went through her list of basics and Paula answered where she could. 'Any question marks over their suicides?'

'Nothing more than the usual disbelief from friends and family. Tony thinks there may have been some kind of intervention. Something that tipped them over the edge. But that's total speculation at this stage.'

'I presume they want everything?'

'Yesterday. I'm going to have a look at our caseload tomorrow, see what we've got in terms of troll complaints so I can use that as a springboard for an official request for a background briefing. But you know what'll happen. I'll get some overworked DC reading from someone else's notes because it's not in any sense a priority. So we need you to get all of the stuff that counts.'

'You'll be wanting their digital data, I suppose? Phones, hard drives, tablets?'

Paula shrugged one shoulder, affecting nonchalance. 'Only if you can manage it.'

That was the challenge. And now it was time to roll her sleeves up. Literally. Stacey folded back the cuffs of her perfectly tailored Egyptian cotton shirt and set her fingers flying over the keyboard. Only if you can manage it? Who did Paula think she was talking to?

Before Carol Jordan walked into court on Wednesday, there would be some answers.

20

The past few months had taught Carol that there was a good reason why builders always had the radio blaring. The work was repetitive and boring; without distraction, her thoughts ran like a dog biting its tail. Having the radio as a constant companion forced her out of the rut she'd worn in her brain and allowed her to move tentatively to other thoughts. She'd tried speech stations, but they intruded too much. She had to keep stopping what she was doing to shout at the ignorant and the bigoted and the mad. Classical music was useless because there were too many quiet bits. And too many ladies singing, fat or otherwise. She'd worked her way through various commercial stations but the ads drove her to distraction. And then she discovered music streaming. Now she paid what seemed to her to be a ridiculously small amount to have an apparently infinite amount of music at her fingertips. She'd compiled playlists, rotating them and adding to them regularly. And it had worked.

But the morning after Tony had set about distracting her with gaming and investigating, nothing was as it had been. For once, she needed to concentrate on what she was doing. Plumbing in a bathroom was not a dull, repetitive task. It required focus and attention, otherwise she'd be condemned to a lifetime of cold showers and recalcitrant flushes. With or without music, she seemed incapable of fixing her mind to the task in hand for any length of time. Her thoughts kept drifting off, exploring possible reasons why a strong-minded woman might suddenly kill herself. And if she managed to drag herself away from that, strategies for getting round the world inside eighty days crept in like something glimpsed out of the corner of her mind.

When Tony emerged from what Carol still thought of as Michael's office towards the end of the morning, waving a shopping list and announcing that he was going down the valley to the supermarket, she took that as a signal to take off her tool belt and reclaim her desk. It never occurred to her to sneak off in her Land Rover to do some shopping of her own. If Tony was expecting her to fail, he was in for a surprise. Although her body was reminding her of withdrawal with aches and pains, trembling and unsteadiness, in her head she'd already made a choice.

Whether she'd manage to keep to that decision was the big question she wasn't even going to ask herself.

As she waited for her laptop to boot up, Carol found herself paying attention to her hands in a way she hadn't for a long time. Her skin was dry and rough, her nails chipped and uneven where they'd broken and she'd bitten them straight rather than file them as she once would have. She turned them over and felt a mixture of pride and surprise to see calluses and scars, all of whose origins she could point to in the barn. She wasn't who she used to be, not in any sense. But could she access those old skills again? That was the pressing question.

Stacey was unquestionably the queen of the data search. But Carol had picked up a few tricks over the years. There was an understanding that went beyond algorithms and when it came to mining the internet for the trace elements that made the kind of connections detectives loved, she reckoned she did pretty well.

She started with the basic subject of internet trolling examples. An unnerving half-million search results showed up in a matter of seconds. That so much had been written, that so many had been moved to put finger to keyboard to protest was as worrying as it was depressing. Carol browsed a series of newspaper articles, blogs and academic research, her anger growing as she went. The majority of the victims were women and teenage girls. Although there were vulnerable boys and young men in the mix, overwhelmingly this looked like a misogynistic phenomenon.

Intriguingly often, when a culprit was identified, their response seemed to be consternation followed by a desperate claim not to have meant anything by it. They called it 'banter'. They blamed drink or drugs or depression. Their mothers, their sisters, their girlfriends (when they had them) sprang to their defence, saying they weren't really like that, that their victims shouldn't be so thin-skinned, that it was just a laugh. 'Is this for real?' Carol said out loud.

'Telling someone you hope their baby gets raped by a black man is a laugh?'

And when women spoke out against what was happening, they simply attracted more insults, threats and contempt. In such a morass of unpleasantness, it was hard to see what might have distinguished Kate Rawlins and Jasmine Burton from the crowd. Carol ploughed on, feeling tainted simply by reading the stuff that was out there.

After a while, she realised she was attacking it from the wrong end. She was looking at the cause when she should be looking at the effect. What made Kate and Jasmine stand out was not that they had been trolled but that they had ended up dead.

So she refined her search and came at it from another angle. Whose experience of being bullied online had ended on the mortuary slab? Even here, there were more instances than anyone should be comfortable with. But most of the cases Carol uncovered didn't come anywhere near the template of the two women who had piqued Tony's curiosity. Teenage suicides of girls who had been beaten down by abuse were tragic but not characterised by vocal defiance of their attackers. Nor were the deaths of women who had been plagued by mental health problems before they were picked on by faceless bullies.

After what felt like a long journey, Carol finally found something that sounded like it might squeeze under the wire into their territory of interest. Daisy Morton had been a part-time teacher and a city councillor in Bradfield. 'Right on our doorstep,' Carol muttered. She'd delivered a blistering attack on dead-beat dads who didn't contribute to raising their children.

'I'm not only talking about the disappearing divorced dads who do everything in their power to avoid their responsibilities,' Daisy had said. 'I'm talking about the nice middle-class men who are never the ones who leave work early so they can spend time with their children. Who cheerfully spend forty grand on a new car but won't spend forty minutes with their kids. Who think it's a woman's job to do the parenting so they're free to go to the pub. Those are the dead-beat dads who are responsible for the dead-beat teenage lads who have no respect for women because they've never seen a woman being respected.'

Carol could see that Daisy Morton had gone out of her way to cause a shitstorm. And that was exactly what she'd got. It had started with online abuse but it had escalated to more direct attacks when Daisy had refused to apologise or retract what she'd said. A brick had been thrown through her living room window; dog shit had been smeared on the windows of the office where she held her constituency surgeries; and the tyres on her car had been slashed. And still Daisy berated the men she believed were letting their children down.

And then, dramatically, Daisy Morton had died. She'd been in the kitchen of her house when it had exploded and caught fire. The intensity of the blaze had made it impossible for firefighters to rescue her. The inquest report revealed a few anomalies; Daisy had been found with her head inside the oven, which was electric rather than gas. And the pathologist said that death was due not to smoke inhalation but asphyxiation from natural gas. The explosion had been laid at the door of the burners on the stove. However, there was nothing to suggest foul play and the coroner had recorded an open verdict. That did nothing to prevent speculation by a handful of bloggers and a couple of newspaper columnists that Daisy had been driven to kill herself by the pressure of the bullying she'd experienced.

It was far from satisfactory, but Carol knew from experience that when pieces didn't fit the jigsaw, there was no point in hitting them with a hammer till they appeared to slot in. The coroner had taken the easy way out. The one that would spare the family the grief of a suicide verdict on top of the loss of a wife and mother. The one that let everyone off the hook.

She printed out a few of the relevant pages and left them sitting on Tony's laptop. Then she picked up her phone and called Paula.

★   ★   ★

The CID room at Skenfrith Street police station was empty save for a couple of officers hammering light-touch keyboards with heavy fingers. Neither looked up when Paula walked in. 'Where is everybody?' she asked, taking off her jacket and draping it over her chair.

'A shout came in while you were at court,' one

said without looking up from his screen. 'Armed robbery at the coffee stall on Station Approach.'

'Armed robbery at a coffee stall? You're kidding.'

He looked up and shrugged. 'Cash business, mostly. A few hundred punters on their way to work, call it a fiver a time, soon adds up. Two lads with a shotgun and a motorbike. Sounds like the same pair that knocked over the hot dog van on Campion Boulevard at the weekend. Fielding grabbed every available body and took off.'

The other officer stood up and stretched. 'She said if you got back from court, you were catching any calls that came in.'

'And has anything come in?'

He shook his head. 'Nothing that needs immediate action.'

Exactly what she'd hoped. As usual, Paula had a hefty caseload, but there was nothing so urgent that Fielding would notice she'd parked it on the back burner. She turned on her computer and called up the list of pending cases. This was her division's home for lost causes: hard-to-solve minor incidents whose victims were so resigned to not seeing justice done that they never picked up the phone to complain; complicated stories that nobody had been able to make sense of or even decide whether a crime had been committed; and the occasional internet scam that seemed impossible to get a handle on. Somewhere among the orphans of the storm she thought she'd find what she needed — a complaint about online stalking or bullying that would give her a legitimate reason to gain access to the official record on the two cases Tony and Carol were interested in.

It was a wearisome and depressing trawl. So many stories with no ending, so much pain and anger with no consolation, so many problems with no obvious solution. Paula soon lost count of the incidents that might have been resolved if only the person concerned had simply had someone to confide in, someone to turn to who could have taken the sting out of a problem before it escalated to the point where the police seemed to be the only available answer.

About halfway through the case listings, she found what she was looking for. A young Asian fashion designer called Shakila Bain had been interviewed on the local TV news, saying that although she didn't support Islamic fundamentalism or terrorist violence, it was obvious that the demonising of young Muslim men in the UK was creating a battalion of willing young jihadists eager to fight for a cause. For a couple of weeks, Shakila had been showered with hate messages and assorted threats of violence. She'd reported the harassment to the police but before an investigation could grind into gear, the trolls had lost interest and moved on to someone else. So the case had been filed under 'let's forget about this' because nobody ever wanted to get into something with so much potential for aggravation.

Paula called up the case files and began to read. Shakila had been interviewed twice — once when she'd made her initial complaint then, a few days later, there had been a follow-up conducted by Terry Browning, one of the detective constables on DCI Fielding's firm. He was a couple of years off retirement; his laziness was a legend in the CID room. Any case Fielding assigned to him was, by definition, one that the DCI didn't care about. Chasing it up would piss off the boss but, on the other hand, anything worked by DC Browning would inevitably have loose ends she could tease into something worth pursuing. And it would give her an excuse to talk to the officers responsible for Kate Rawlins and Jasmine Burton. Result all round.

Paula picked up the phone and keyed in Shakila's mobile number. Unsurprisingly, it went straight to voicemail. If Paula had experienced the hatred Shakila had been subjected to, she'd be screening her calls too. At the beep, she spoke, 'Hello, Shakila. This is Detective Sergeant Paula McIntyre from Bradfield Metropolitan Police. I'm conducting a review of your complaint of harassment and I'd like to meet you to talk through your experience. Can you call me back or text me on my mobile?' She recited her number, repeated it and hung up.

It didn't take much research to identify the officers who had dealt with the suicides of Kate Rawlins and Jasmine Burton. Her first call was to a detective sergeant in the Met. Lee Collins sounded young and brash, his voice the glottal whine of Estuary English. But his attitude didn't match his accent. As soon as Paula explained her interest, his tone softened. 'Bloody awful thing,' he said. 'It's hard to imagine how much pressure she must have been feeling, to do that.'

'Exactly. And I'm keen to make sure we don't get a repetition up here. I was wondering if you'd mind sending me a copy of your reports so I can check whether there were any signs we should be looking out for.' Even as she spoke, Paula knew it sounded thin. But it wasn't unusual for cops to make requests of colleagues that didn't make a lot of sense. There was an assumption that you didn't want to waste another officer's time with lengthy explanations.

'Sure, no problem. You thinking it might be some of the same arseholes doing the trolling on your patch?'

'Could be. How did you get on with tracking them down?'

His sigh was heavy enough to be clearly audible. 'It's still with the hi-tech crime unit. You know how long it takes them to come up with IDs from digital footprints.'

'Tell me about it. But I'd like to see what you've got anyway.'

'Sure, but I don't think you'll find anything. There was nothing to show she was feeling that bad. She was obviously bottling it all up. But she clearly meant it. It was no cry for help that went wrong. It was almost clinical in its precision.'

Paula picked up the regret in his voice; something she could use for her benefit. 'Clinical? How do you mean?'

'She'd left nothing to chance. She was in the passenger seat and she'd handcuffed herself to the armrest on the door so she couldn't reach far enough to turn off the engine.'

'I've never come across that before.'

He sighed. 'I've not come across that, specifically. But I've seen cases where the suicide has gone into the back seat. Some people are determined not to give second thoughts a chance.'

'If you say so. I'm on uncharted territory here.'

'It was all of a piece, you could say. Her handbag with her phone in it was locked in the boot. She had definitely set her mind on doing it. The only thing she had with her was a book of poems.'

'Poems?' Of all the things Paula would choose to comfort her if she ever got that low, it wouldn't be poetry. 'What kind of poems?'

'Hang on a minute . . . ' There was the sound of clattering keys, then DC Collins was back. *The Death Notebooks.* By Anne Sexton. She was an American poet who killed herself the same way. Locked herself in the garage and turned on the car engine.'

'Was Kate a big fan of this Anne Sexton, then?'

'The daughter, Madison, says she never saw the book before. Apparently her mum wasn't much of a one for poetry generally. I think she was telling the truth. I had a quick look at the bookshelves in the house and there wasn't any poetry there.'

'That's a bit odd, isn't it?' There was nothing Paula loved more than odd. Years of working alongside Tony had instilled in her an understanding that odd was often where the answers started.

'I don't know. I think when you're at the point where killing yourself feels like the answer, you're not thinking straight. Nothing you do counts as odd, because the whole thing is off the scale of odd.'

'I suppose so. So, is it OK for you to send me a copy of your files?'

'I don't know what help it'll be to you, but be my guest. It's not like there's any doubt about what happened. She got bullied to death. And the bastards who pushed her into it will probably walk away scot-free. That's the bottom line.'

It might be now, Paula thought as she ended the call. But that might change with Carol Jordan on the case. As the thought crossed her mind, Paula's phone rang, the screen revealing the caller was her former boss. 'Hi, chief,' Paula answered automatically.

'I think I've found another one,' Carol said. 'And this time it's right in your backyard.'

21

Carol placed a steaming platter of penne puttanesca on the table next to the salad Tony had already tossed with a sharp French dressing he'd concocted. The air filled with the aroma of olives and garlic. 'I don't want to talk about tomorrow,' she said as she sat down.

Tony knew that adamantine tone of voice. Might as well try to argue with El Capitan. And if he was honest, he wasn't sorry to avoid discussing Carol's court appearance, a subject that would only lead to tension and awkwardness between them. The morning would be soon enough to deal with that. 'Sparkling water?' he asked, waving the green plastic bottle with a placatory smile.

Carol turned her head, looking down at the table. 'Why not?' It came out as a snarl.

They helped themselves to pasta and salad in silence. Three forks' worth in, Tony said, 'So, did Paula know about the Daisy Morton business already?'

Carol shook her head, chewing a mouthful of salad. She swallowed, washed it down with a swig of water and said, 'It never crossed Paula's professional radar — Daisy lived outside the city centre, in Northern Division territory. But fortunately for us, Paula has a good contact up there. A DS called Franny Riley. He looks like the missing link between Neanderthal Man and rugby league, but he's actually a pretty shrewd operator. She's going to talk to him and see what he's got to say beyond the official reports.'

'Does she agree with you, that this might be another one that fits the pattern?'

'She's not completely convinced. Kate and Jasmine, they were clear-cut suicides. No doubt about it. But Daisy's death looks less well-defined.'

Tony paused with his fork halfway to his mouth. 'That's not necessarily an issue. Real life isn't neat and unambiguous. Stuff often happens outside the control zone of the criminal, stuff that plays havoc with their careful plans.'

Carol nodded. 'I know. And if I've learned one thing from you, it's that serial offenders aren't static. They develop. They change what they do, how they do it, because they come up with better ways to get to where they're aiming for in their twisted, fucked-up imagination. So in a way, it would be more surprising if there was an identical pattern time and time again.'

'So what is it about Daisy's death that makes you uneasy?'

Carol drank more water, reaching for the bottle to top up her glass. Giving up alcohol had made her thirst constantly. She felt as if she'd drunk gallons of tea, coffee and water in the past couple of days. And none of it satisfied her desire. But right now, the act of refilling her water gave her a moment's pause to get her thoughts in order. 'According to the inquest, the pathologist said she'd died from asphyxiation from the inhalation of gas. You have to work extremely hard to kill yourself using natural gas. There has to be a pretty intense level of concentration. I looked it up, and to be sure of it killing you, you need seventy-five per cent gas to air.'

'That's not impossible, surely? I mean, wouldn't she basically have to turn on the gas and wait for the room to fill up?'

'It's not quite that straightforward. Natural gas is heavier than air so it forms a layer close to the ground. It seeps away under doors and through gaps in the floor.'

'But she was close to the ground, right? You said something about her having her head in the oven?'

Carol nodded pensively. 'But it was an electric oven.'

'So why . . . ?' Tony's voice trailed away and he stared over her shoulder. Carol knew the look of old. The wheels were going round, taking Tony in a direction that most other people wouldn't even consider. 'It's not a very reliable way of killing yourself, is it?'

'Depends what you're planning,' Carol said. 'You're right, it's a bit chancy in terms of asphyxiation, but on the other hand, if you've filled the house with gas, all it takes is someone turning on a light switch or a mobile phone ringing to blow the place sky high. So if you're not already dead from the gas, the chances are the explosion will kill you.'

He frowned and studied his plate as if he'd never seen food before. He prodded a piece of black olive with his fork and slowly said, 'I'd like

151

to know whether she was lying with her head on the edge of the oven or if she was jammed in.'

'Does it make a difference? Surely what we're concerned with is whatever pushed her over the edge?'

'It makes a difference. If she knew the gas was heavier than air then it makes sense for her to get as close under the burners as she could.' He loaded up his fork and resumed eating. 'What else is bothering you about Daisy?'

'According to the inquest report, she didn't leave a note.' Carol held a hand up to forestall the objection she could see coming. 'Yes, I know she might have left something that was destroyed in the explosion, but I think she'd have thought of that. There are lots of ways to leave a message. She could have sent an email, she could have put something in the post. She could have left a note in her council office.'

'Did Kate or Jasmine leave a note?'

'I don't know yet. I need more information.'

'I'd have expected some sort of communication if there was something that tipped them over the edge,' Tony mused. 'These were women who knew all about getting the word out there. Even if they'd been pushed beyond bearing themselves, wouldn't they have wanted to save other women from the same fate?'

'Unless what pushed them carried a wider threat,' Carol said. 'To their children or their partners?'

'That would make sense.'

There was nothing more to say, but they carried on worrying at the few facts they possessed long after they'd finished eating. He loved seeing her animated by what she'd always done best — analysing, rearranging and making sense of disparate pieces of information. Watching the shifting expressions cross her face, the pain of missing her hit him afresh. He couldn't bear it if he let her slip from his grasp again.

Carol produced Paula's email and they picked their way through that, finding nothing more substantial to add to the little they already had. That, Tony thought, was the trouble with trying to build something out of thin air. This had started with the most slender of notions and now they were behaving as if it had genuine substance. He'd been intrigued by a detail and he'd wanted to give Carol a bone to chew to take her mind off drinking and what it had brought her to. And now they had real police officers carrying out clandestine trawls for information. He'd got them all chasing a chimera. He'd created an expectation he wasn't certain he could fulfil. The let-down could end up causing more grief than the original problem. And all because he'd been so desperate to find a way back into Carol's good graces.

He was on the point of trying a gentle warning when the dog leapt to her feet and made for the door in a blur of black-and-white and a cacophony of barking. Tony glanced at his watch as Carol got up. 'It's a bit late for visitors.'

'I don't get visitors,' she said, heading out into the barn, snapping on a work lamp as she went. Tony followed because, if it wasn't visitors, she shouldn't have to face whoever it was alone. He was at her shoulder when she pulled the door open to reveal a man in a tweed flat cap and a waxed jacket with a plaid scarf knotted carelessly at the throat. His beard reminded Tony of the portrait on King Edward cigar packets. He suspected it of being camouflage for thin lips at odds with a slightly bulbous nose. The skin round his eyes fell into deep wrinkles when he smiled. The dog had stopped barking and dropped to her haunches.

'Sorry to call so late, Carol, but I was passing.'

Carol cast a quick look over her shoulder, checking where Tony was. She stepped back and the man came inside. He was bigger than Tony in every way — taller, broader, more obviously confident of his place in the world. 'Tony, this is my neighbour, George Nicholas. George, this is Tony Hill. Tony's a former colleague of mine.'

George offered his hand and Tony accepted it. The grip was exactly as firm and dry as he expected. George gave him an appraising look. 'You're a police officer?' He sounded almost amused.

'No, I'm a clinical psychologist. I offer advice in a variety of areas.' Tony met George's eyes with a measured stare. He was standing alongside Carol, the pair of them effectively blocking any further advance by the visitor.

'All a bit beyond me, I'm afraid,' George said. He crouched to pet the dog, scratching her head and rubbing her ears. Then he stood and turned his attention to Carol. 'I haven't seen you out on the hill for the last few days. Not since you came to supper on Saturday. I just wanted to check everything was all right?'

Tony imagined Carol's dismay but he knew it wouldn't show in her face. Time to come to the rescue. 'That's my fault. I've been staying for a few days and I've knocked Carol's routine for six.' Tony grinned cheerfully.

'And I completely forgot my manners, George. I meant to drop you a thank you note. I'm sorry,' Carol said, picking up his cue.

'Oh no, no need. I was simply a little . . . concerned, that's all.' He gave Tony a wry smile, as if conceding defeat. 'I've grown accustomed to seeing Carol and Flash out on the hill in the morning.'

'It's nice to know there's somebody looking out for you when I'm not around,' Tony said, well aware that he sounded condescending to both of them.

George tipped his cap and backed out of the door. 'I'll be on my way. Good to see you, Carol. And to meet you, Tony.' He turned and walked away without a backward glance. Carol closed the door and leaned against it, shaking her head, her expression a mixture of amusement and incredulity.

'What?' he said, knowing perfectly well what.

'You. Pretending to be all territorial.' Then her face grew serious. 'Thank you for saving me from having to tell him.'

Tony shrugged. 'He'll find out soon enough. You've got plenty of humiliations to come without seeking them out.' He turned away and started walking back to the kitchen. After a few steps, he turned on his heel and walked backwards. 'You don't fancy him, do you?'

Carol stopped dead. 'George? No, what made you think that?'

'I didn't. But I wanted to be sure.'

'It's kind of none of your business.'

'I know that.' Tony stopped too. In the stark light and shade cast by the work lamp he couldn't see her eyes. He didn't know if there was humour or anger lurking in their shadows. 'But I think he fancies you.'

'You think so?' There was definitely humour in her voice.

'It's obvious. Well, it's obvious to me, but then I am a clinical psychologist. So I wanted to clear things up because I don't know if you noticed us doing the guy thing just now, where I more or less told him to back off? Only, if you do fancy him, you'll have to go and apologise for your friend Tony who has no social skills.'

She laughed. 'Well, that much is true.' Her voice softened. 'But there's no need to apologise. I've got no romantic interest in George.'

He wanted to sigh with relief. Instead, one side of his mouth twisted up in a half-smile and he swung round and walked back to the kitchen. Sometimes there was no need to have the last word.

★ ★ ★

Stacey Chen was beginning to feel as if she was drowning. It hadn't taken her long to hack her way into the official accounts of Kate Rawlins' suicide, the ongoing investigation into Jasmine

Burton's presumed suicide and the later addition to the roster — the gas explosion that had killed Daisy Morton. As well as the formal documents, she'd accessed the emails of individual officers, filling in some of the blanks of what they'd pursued and why they'd pursued it. Text messages would take longer and even Stacey had to acknowledge she might not manage to get them. She'd punted everything straight on to Paula so she could pull a report together for Carol Jordan that cut out all the repetition and white noise.

Now came the hard stuff. Which was also the interesting stuff. She'd started with Kate Rawlins, chronologically the first of the three. Gaining access to her social media accounts hadn't been hard. The password was Madison, her daughter's name, and the year of her birth. Stacey couldn't understand why people chose passwords that wouldn't fool a drunken teenager. When she voiced this opinion, her colleagues always complained that it was too hard to remember random strings of letters and numbers. 'So use your car registration as the basis for your password,' she would tell them, not bothering to hide her exasperation. 'You should be able to remember that. Add something to it like the number of the house where you lived when you were ten, and Robert is your father's brother.'

What was staggering was the volume of abusive messages that had filled her timelines and home pages. Tracking down everyone who had posted was a huge task, even with the automatic programs Stacey had at her disposal to find individual IP addresses and the associated service providers. Getting through the service providers' security systems to the names of individuals was generally a lot more difficult, even with the accumulated data she'd acquired over the years. She debated whether to go through the posts and focus only on the worst of them, but dismissed the idea. There was no way she could do that objectively and if it wasn't objective, it wasn't worth doing. One person's traumatic was another person's trivial, and vice versa.

Once she'd set those searches in motion, she turned to email. Kate's email address wasn't one that could readily be guessed so Stacey didn't expect to find messages from her harasser there, but if Kate had had any unsettling encounters there was a chance she'd have told a friend or a colleague. Once she'd penetrated her email account, she shipped the whole lot on to her own server, setting it to one side to work through later.

She'd repeated the process for the other two women, then finally settled down to fillet the emails for anything that might be relevant. She'd barely started the tedious trawl when Sam's face swam into view on the security camera screen. 'Hi, babe,' his voice squawked from the speaker. 'I come bearing salted caramel truffles.' His face was replaced by a cellophane bag of chocolates.

'I wasn't expecting you,' Stacey said as she buzzed him in. She was torn; she still felt her heart contract when he walked into a room, but she was gripped by the challenge of the hunt and she didn't want to stop now.

She met him at the door and her misgivings

swam away on the tide of rising hormones that swept through her when he pulled her close and kissed her, one hand running across the back of her neck, making her tingle. 'I missed you,' he said. His voice was thickened with alcohol; she tasted stale wine on his breath. She knew him well enough now to see he'd had a drink, but was a long way from drunk.

'It's Tuesday. You usually go to the pub quiz and stay at your place,' Stacey said, snuggling close as she pulled him inside the flat.

'Pete and Rick are both out of town,' he said, pulling the door closed behind him and freeing himself so he could shrug out of the navy cashmere overcoat she'd bought him after she'd heard him admiring it in the window of Harvey Nick's. 'There didn't seem much point with just me and Mitch. So I thought I'd give you the pleasure of my company.'

'And it's lovely to see you. But you're going to have to amuse yourself for a while because I have something I need to work on.'

Sam pouted, giving her his best kicked-puppy look. 'And here was me thinking you'd be pleased to see me.'

'I am. Very pleased.' She ran a hand up the inside of his thigh and he shivered. 'But you have to let me work for a while.'

He gave a theatrical sigh and crossed to the giant plasma screen TV that dominated the end wall of the living space, tossing his jacket over a chair as he went. 'I'll watch the football, then.'

Perfect, Stacey thought. She poured him a glass of wine and retreated to her workspace, putting on her noise-cancelling headphones to cut out the frantic wittering of the football commentary. She began winnowing Kate Rawlins' email, efficiently getting rid of everything that wasn't a personal exchange. Once she'd done that, she sidelined everything written or received before Kate had made her pronouncement about rapists then started the tedious business of reading them. She was so engrossed that she didn't realise Sam was looking over her shoulder till he touched her arm. She pulled off the headphones and frowned up at him. 'Do you need something?'

'I need you,' he said, leaning down to kiss her ear. 'The football's finished and I am more interesting than some stranger's email. What are you doing, anyway? Don't you have grunts in the office for this kind of thing? And why are you doing it at home?'

Stacey sighed. With anyone else, she'd tell them to piss off and mind their own business. With Sam, she wouldn't have risked that, even if she'd wanted to. 'Because it's a foreigner. I'm doing a favour for Paula,' she said. She understood enough not to risk Sam's irritation by invoking Carol. 'If it was official, of course I'd be able to hand it off to a junior officer to free me up for the things that needed my skillset. But there's nobody to dump on here so I have to do it.'

'Why can't Paula do her own grunt work?' he grumbled.

'Because she's got other fish to fry.' Stacey tried to focus on her screen but it was hard when

Sam was playing with her hair.

'So have you.'

Stacey sighed. She knew when she was beaten. And besides, what Sam was offering was a lot more appealing than a dead woman's gossip. It wasn't as if there was anything urgent there.

And there was definitely something urgent here.

22

Halifax Magistrates' Court looked like an unfortunate collision between a Victorian town hall and an Italian military academy, complete with a tall, square campanile towering above the entrance. The pale sandstone seemed to glow from within in the morning sun as Carol and Tony arrived far too early that Wednesday morning. In spite of Tony's insistence that she should have a solicitor to plead in mitigation, she had refused. 'There's no point. It'd be a complete waste of money. I'm screwed, Tony, and no matter how aggrieved I feel, there is no defence.' That had been her last word on the subject.

Tony found a car park a couple of streets away and they sat in silence for a moment, both staring out of the windscreen. 'We've got time to find somewhere for a coffee,' he said. It was the first thing out of either of their mouths other than directions since they'd left the barn.

'I think I'd throw up.' She clamped her mouth shut, the muscles along her jaw bunching tight beneath her skin. She'd worked wonders with make-up. It made him wonder how much she'd been covering up during all the years of drinking when he'd seldom seen her look as haggard as she deserved. She'd dressed carefully too. A loose-fitting navy gabardine jacket over a high-collared shirt, smartly pressed grey tweed trousers, low heels. She looked like someone who should be taken seriously but not high enough up the wealth ladder to be punished for it.

'Do you want to go for a walk?' Tony asked.

Carol looked around. Drab and dirty Victorian buildings housed pound shops, charity shops and cheap takeaways. Occasional grim concrete frontages broke up the vista like old amalgam fillings in a mouth of discoloured and decaying teeth. 'Maybe not,' she said. 'It's not exactly going to lift my spirits, is it? Even on a sunny day it looks like it's been shot in black and white.'

And so they waited. There was nothing he could say that would make things better. *Some therapist*, he thought. The man who was paid to fix the broken people, exposed for the fraud he probably was. All his working life, he'd been held up as the expert in empathy, the one who knew how to stand inside other people's skin and report back on what they felt and why they felt it. And every time, Carol Jordan proved how wrong the world was.

The minutes crawled like parasitic worms under his skin until eventually it was a respectable time to show up at court. Carol pressed her fingertips against her forehead and screwed her eyes shut. Then she straightened up. 'Let's go,' she said.

They walked the short distance side by side, steps rhyming like a Leonard Cohen song. Tony tried not to think about what lay ahead, focusing instead on the other lives on the street: youths in hoodies and trainers with the crotches of their jeans halfway down their thighs; elderly women with shampoo-and-sets and tartan shopping trolleys; men with big bellies and cheap jeans smoking outside the betting shop; women pushing prams, their youth buckling under the weight of their make-up; and everywhere, people yammering or stabbing at their mobiles, more interested in someone else, somewhere else. Nobody like him. He'd never fitted in and the passage of time was making no difference to that. For years, Carol had been the only person who had made him feel he belonged. And then she had walked away from him. Now, Paula had made him part of her family and that mattered. But not as much as the prospect of fixing things with Carol.

Inside the court building, neither of them knew where to go, what to do. The time they'd both spent in courtrooms had been on the other side of the fence. There had always been someone available to shepherd them through unfamiliar places. Tony spotted a woman shielded by a high curved desk and a computer screen. He approached, Carol at his shoulder. 'Excuse me. My friend is appearing before the magistrates this morning. Where should she go?'

The woman barely glanced at them. She looked like a victim of gravity; everything about her tended downwards, from the angled fold of skin above her eyes, through the sagging cheeks to the defeated shoulders. 'Name?'

'Carol Jordan.'

She tapped at a keyboard. At once, her attitude changed. Her eyebrows jerked upwards and her eyes opened wide. She looked at Carol, then back at the screen. 'It says here you have to

164

go up to the first floor. To conference room two. I don't understand that. That's not a court. But that's what it says here. 'Carol Jordan. Please direct to conference room two.' Well. I've never seen that before.'

Tony exchanged a worried look with Carol. She simply shrugged and set off towards the stairs. He followed in her wake, even more uneasy than he had been earlier.

Conference room two was near the head of the staircase. They paused outside. Carol shrugged again and muttered, 'Nothing ventured.' She knocked briskly, and a muffled voice told them to come in. She gave him one last anxious look then turned the handle.

The only person in the wood-panelled room rose to his feet as they entered. He inclined his head to Carol, then to Tony. 'Nice to see you both,' John Brandon said. As he settled back down, all Tony could think was that the modern plastic chairs and pale Scandinavian wood table were both at odds with their setting. Shock would do that, he thought, recovering himself. He should have worked it out on the way upstairs. If he'd thought about it, John Brandon would have been in the top three guesses as to who might be in the room. He glanced at Carol. Her face had closed down, unreadable.

'I wasn't expecting to see you today,' she said, her voice neutral.

'No, I don't suppose you were,' Brandon said, his lugubrious face breaking into a smile.

'Not that I'm not pleased to see you. But why are you here?' Carol pulled out a chair opposite

Brandon and sat down. Tony hovered for a moment, then chose a seat between the two of them, on the third side of the table. In case an umpire became necessary.

Brandon leaned back in his chair. 'Think of me as your fairy godmother. If you want to take a chance on what I'm offering, all of this unpleasantness will go away.'

'What do you mean, 'go away'? It was a righteous arrest. I've gone through the system. Been processed and spat out at the other end. How can that go away? It's all on the record.'

Brandon fiddled with his watch strap. He wasn't as comfortable with this as he wanted them to think, Tony decided. 'Carol has a point,' he said. 'It's not like nobody knows what happened to her. The police are gossip central, you know that.'

Brandon nodded graciously. 'Of course I do. That's why the news that Carol was tested with a faulty breathalyser machine will also spread like wildfire. Carol and three other people who were also victims of the wrongly calibrated breathalyser will all have their arrests quashed. No further action.' He paused, then said, 'If you agree to what we want from you.'

Tony imagined Carol felt as stunned as he did but she showed nothing. 'Whatever it is, you must want it very badly to be willing to pervert the course of justice, John. I always had you down as an honest copper.'

Brandon winced. 'That's how I like to think of myself, Carol. But what we have in mind for you is more important than making a criminal of you over this.'

'I was driving under the influence of alcohol. I could have killed someone.' There was no defiance in her voice, merely a bald statement of fact.

'You drove for less than three miles on an empty country road. I've seen you drinking, and I suspect that at that level of blood alcohol, you were driving perfectly adequately.' Brandon shrugged and spread his hands. 'It's right down the bottom of the scale.'

'It's still a criminal offence.'

Brandon sighed. 'Do you want to martyr yourself, Carol? Or do you want to play your one and only get-out-of-jail-free card?'

'You say there are three other people caught up in this?'

Brandon nodded. 'Arrested by the same officers in the course of their shift.'

'So they'll all have had second breathalysers and possibly blood tests that back up what happened out there at the roadside,' she said.

Brandon looked as if he wasn't quite sure where she was headed with that. 'Yes.'

'And you think they're not going to think it's a bit strange for the charges to be dropped because the first breathalyser was faulty? Fruit of the poisoned tree isn't a legal principle in this country, unless they've changed the law since I was working the streets.'

Brandon shrugged. 'You know it's the CPS policy not to pursue cases unless there's a fifty per cent chance of success. And the faulty first breath test opens up the gates for the hip-flask defence.'

'Can we back up a minute?' Tony butted in. 'What's the fruit of the poisoned tree? And what's this hip-flask defence?'

Carol waved a hand at Brandon to indicate he had the floor. 'Fruit of the poisoned tree is an American legal principle that mostly applies to searches. If the search isn't legal, nothing you get from it can be produced as evidence. And anything that stems from it, you have to be able to prove you came at it from a different route. What Carol's saying is that even if the first breath test wasn't accurate, she thinks the subsequent one at the police station will stand.'

'And won't it?'

Carol shook her head. 'The hip-flask defence is where I say, 'Oh, your worship, I was so shocked and stunned at the breath test that I had to take a swig from the hip-flask in my handbag while I was in the back of the police car on the way to the station. And that's why the second test was over the limit.''

'Do people actually get away with that?'

Brandon nodded. 'There's precedent. So the CPS can legitimately say the wheels could come off these cases very expensively so let's not bother. And if anybody asks, we can provide that as a legitimate excuse.'

Tony held his breath for what felt like an impossible length of time before Carol spoke. 'So what's the big deal to make all this worth fixing?'

'You come back into harness.'

'I won't work for James Blake again.' It was obviously a red line, not a bargaining chip.

Brandon smiled, his mouth a wry curve. 'You

won't have to. This is something quite different.'

Before he could say more, she cut across him. 'The last time you dragged me back into the ranks, it didn't go well. I lost one officer and came close to losing another.'

Brandon sighed. 'Nobody's more aware of that than I am. But between the two of you, you've saved a lot of lives too. And that's why you're held in such high regard. Why you're the one and only person in the frame for this job. What I'm offering you is the chance to run a free-standing Major Incident Team. You'd hand-pick your officers. You'd be on standby to pick up murders, serious sexual assaults and the like over six distinct forces here in the North.' He leaned down and picked up a computer bag. From it he drew a file. He flicked it open and spread a map out on the table. It showed the force areas of Bradfield Metropolitan Police and five others across the North of England, from East Yorkshire to Cumbria. 'The Home Office has chosen these forces as a test-bed for this because they already share scenes of crime teams and forensic services. You'd be in charge of high-level investigations with a core team who would call on local CID and uniform for back room support.'

'The grunt work,' Carol said. 'That'd make a team like this popular with the locals.'

Brandon shrugged. 'Something you've never had to finesse before.' The sarcasm was only thinly veiled.

Carol finally cracked a smile. 'How to keep your friends close and your enemies even closer. My motto.'

'Where's the catch?' Tony said.

'I don't think there is one,' Brandon said. 'We get a first-class detective back doing what she does best, we have the chance to try out a new style of policing, and Carol avoids her life crashing and burning. Do you think there's a downside in there, Tony?'

'Where would we be based?' Carol asked.

Brandon laughed. 'My God, Carol, you haven't lost your knack. Straight to the only unattractive part of the whole equation. You'll be working out of an office in Bradfield. That's not negotiable. It's logistically the best choice and they have space. However, you won't be at force HQ.'

'Where will we be?'

'Skenfrith Street. The third floor's been empty ever since they took the station out of mothballs. It's all cabled up and ready to roll, but it's never been used.' Brandon's smile was encouraging.

'Skenfrith Street,' Carol said flatly. 'Home of DCI Alex Fielding, who hates me even more than Blake. Fabulous. The last time I was in Skenfrith Street — ' she gestured with her thumb at Tony — 'he was under arrest for murder. She's going to love having us under the same roof, reminding us of her finest hour.'

Startled, Tony yelped, 'Us?'

'Well, duh.' Carol rolled her eyes. 'I wouldn't even consider this if I wasn't allowed a proper team.'

Brandon gave a satisfied nod. 'I take it that's a yes, then?'

'I'd like some time to think about it.'

Brandon shook his head. 'That's not going to

be possible. The court is gearing up downstairs. If we're going to get you off the hook, it has to be now.'

'I don't believe you,' Tony said. 'If you've got enough weight behind you to make a drink-driving charge go up in smoke, you've got more than enough juice to get the CPS to ask for an adjournment. Long enough to give Carol a chance to consider this properly.'

'As I said earlier, there are three other people who are also being let off the hook to make Carol's case dismissal look kosher. So it's all got to happen this morning. There's no leeway.' Brandon's voice was steely, his face implacable. It was a stern reminder to them both that, behind his geniality, Brandon was capable of unyielding obduracy. They'd seen it employed on their behalf in the past; it was uncomfortable to be on the receiving end now.

Carol knew when she was beaten. 'One more question,' she said, defeat conceded. 'And it might be the deal-breaker. Obviously there's a chain of command. Who am I answerable to?'

'The Home Office in the final analysis. For now, while we're putting the pieces together and seeing how things pan out in practice, I have oversight on their behalf. The chief constables of the various forces will have to come through me.'

This time, everyone smiled. The relief was palpable. Carol took a deep breath and squared her shoulders. 'Given the alternative . . . when do I start?'

He stood up and extended a hand across the table. 'Tomorrow morning suit you?'

Carol accepted the handshake. 'What time?'

'I'll see you there at nine,' Brandon said. 'Don't let me down, Carol. There's a lot riding on this.'

A flush coloured her cheeks. 'I'm done with letting people down, John.' She tipped her head to Tony. 'He's always on about redemption and rehabilitation. I'll try and prove both of you right.'

23

After Kate Rawlins, he'd felt an odd mixture of triumph and jitteriness. He hugged his knowledge to himself, pleased he'd taken the first step on this evangelical undertaking. But when he closed his eyes at night, anxiety kicked in. He'd exercised power over life and death. His had been the last face Kate Rawlins had seen. And yet, a current of apprehension ran through him like the tremor you got in your arms from using a hammer drill. Would he, could he get away with it? But as the days had passed and it became clear that everybody was convinced she'd killed herself, he began to relax.

What helped to soothe him was the preparation for the next one. He'd shortlisted another three women and started watching each of them whenever he could. This time, Sylvia Plath would be his template. He knew from the start it would be a challenge. Plath had gassed herself, but that was back before the days of natural gas. Then, stoves and household fires were fuelled by poisonous coal gas. People put their heads in the oven and turned on the gas and they died. Painlessly, by all accounts. But it was the gas that killed them.

That wasn't going to work so well for him. But he'd been thinking about this for a long time and after testing out a raft of different ideas and rejecting them, he finally had a plan. Daisy

Morton had a public profile. And so he'd pretended to be a journalist from a women's magazine. 'At home with Daisy Morton' was the pitch. Appealing to their vanity always worked.

And then it had been laughably easy. He'd turned up at the agreed time, and of course she'd offered tea. He'd slipped the GHB into her tea. While he waited for it to take effect, he'd had to listen to the rubbish she spouted. If he'd had any doubts about what he was doing, that would have crushed them. Once she'd started slurring her stupid words, he'd given her a couple of valium to make sure she stayed calm and controllable; if they did a post-mortem toxicology screen and it showed up, they'd assume she'd taken it to calm herself down and make sure she went through with her plan.

Once the drugs kicked in, it was easy. Plastic bag over the head, gas from the hob via a piece of vacuum cleaner hose, and patience. She'd barely twitched as the gas filled her lungs, displacing the air and slowly suffocating her. He'd watched the plastic membrane move in and out with her breathing until it finally stopped. There was a thrill in knowing, as with Kate, that he could stop it any time he wanted. It was almost sexual. But he was stronger than that. He had a goal and he wasn't going to be deflected by pity or shame.

He checked her pulse, then checked it again a few minutes later. When he was satisfied she was really gone, he removed the bag and the hose and turned on all the burners on the hob. He fetched towels from the bathroom, wet them and stuffed them along the bottom of the back door. He put more behind the kitchen door as he closed it on the way out. They wouldn't stop the gas escaping but if there was the sort of explosion he was hoping for, the remnants of them would be in the right area. And if there was no detonation, the assumption would be that they'd been pushed back when the kitchen door was opened.

He found Daisy's mobile in the pocket of her jeans and rigged it up to the old-fashioned answering machine he'd brought with him, setting them both down close to the stove.

His last act before he left the house was to pull the pages loose from the Sylvia Plath book and leave them in the hallway. He was no expert, but he thought an explosion would blow them out into the garden. Some of them would survive.

Then he settled in for the long wait. If things went according to the routine he'd observed four times now, nobody would return to the house before four in the afternoon. By then the house would be filled with gas. When her kids came home, as soon as they approached the front door, he would call Daisy's mobile phone. That in turn would set off the answering machine, creating a sustained electrical arc that would be enough to ignite the room full of gas.

That day, waiting had been almost unbearable. He could have left it at Daisy lying with her head in the oven but he wanted something more spectacular, something that couldn't be ignored. These deaths needed to make a mark. They needed to make women sit up and take notice.

To understand that being like Daisy and Kate wasn't going to end well.

24

Working in Carol Jordan's MIT had placed Paula firmly at the leading edge of modern policing. But when it came to teasing information out of other cops, she was perfectly capable of stepping back in time. And so she had arranged to meet Detective Sergeant Franny Riley in a gloomy pub a couple of streets away from Bradfield Police's Northern Division HQ. The pub consisted of a series of small rooms furnished with dark wooden tables and heavy chairs. Although it had been years since smoking had been banned in pubs, Paula could have sworn the penetrating stink of stale smoke hung in the air. It wasn't coming from her either — it had been six weeks since she'd replaced her heavy-duty habit with an e-cigarette, much to Elinor's relief and delight.

She bought herself a pint and settled down to wait at a corner table, her back to the wall. Five minutes drifted by, then a man shouldered his way into the room, looking more like the stereotype of a villain than a cop. Bull-necked, his nose badly repaired after an old break, his ears misshapen and unmatching, he walked on the balls of his feet as if expecting fight or flight to hit the agenda at any moment. His dark eyes glittered as they swept the room, then, seeing Paula, crinkled and twinkled in a smile that turned his piratical face benevolent. 'Mine's a

Guinness,' he said, parking himself opposite her.

'Good to see you too, Franny,' she said, getting to her feet and heading for the bar. By the time she returned, he was surreptitiously sucking on a discreet e-cigarette of his own. 'Is that strictly legal?' she asked, setting his drink down.

'Landlord doesn't give a shit. Draws the line at full-on fagging it, but vaping's OK with him. Half his customers and most of his profits come from us anyway, he's not going to make a fuss.' He took a long pull of his pint then wiped the foam from his upper lip with the tip of his tongue. 'Good pint. So. You'll be wanting me to do your job for you, as usual?'

Franny Riley was defiantly old school. But she knew that he knew she was a good cop in spite of her gender, as he would have put it. She'd proven herself when their paths had crossed before, and in spite of his abrasive approach, Paula trusted his acumen and his information. 'More like satisfying my curiosity, Franny,' she said, raising her glass in a silent toast.

'Daisy Morton, you said on the phone?'

'That's right.'

'What's your interest? You're Skenfrith Street now, right? No more mighty MIT? What's Skenfrith Street got to do with Daisy Morton? Are you doing some kind of a foreigner?'

He was, she remembered, a lot shrewder than you might expect. 'You remember Tony Hill?'

Franny's lip curled in a sardonic grimace. 'Funny little bugger with a blue plastic bag and a conversational style that goes all round the houses? That Tony Hill?'

'That Tony Hill. Not just a funny bugger, Franny, a clever bugger too. Anyway, he's got a bee in his bonnet about a couple of cases of suicide. I said I'd have a look around as a favour to a friend.'

Franny took another deep swallow. Half the pint had gone in two gulps. 'He got nicked a while back, didn't he? Ended up making DCI Fielding look like a right arse?'

Paula gave a wry smile. 'And that didn't exactly help my career. The DCI is not my friend these days.'

'Not like DCI Jordan, eh?'

'Oh, Franny, if you only knew the ways ... Anyway, I'm interested because Tony's interested in Daisy Morton's death.'

'Suicide. Whatever the coroner said, we were satisfied there was nothing going on beyond that. I can see why he gave an open verdict to spare the family, because it was an odd one. But I don't think there's any room for doubt. She was getting seven shades of shit from every corner of the internet, and it all got too much for her.'

'Fair enough. But you have to admit it wasn't a bog-standard, straight-down-the-middle-of-the-fairway suicide.'

He gave her a speculative look. 'Is there any such thing?'

'You know there is. Overdose, chucking yourself in front of a train, hanging yourself from the bannisters. Sticking your head in the gas oven used to be all the rage, but not since we changed to natural gas forty years ago. It's really hard to do yourself in with natural gas because it's not toxic. It only works when you manage to displace the oxygen with carbon monoxide. Or am I teaching you to suck eggs?'

The word 'suck' reminded Franny of his e-cig and he took a deep drag. 'It worked, though. She was obviously determined to go for it. The post-mortem says carbon monoxide poisoning. No smoke in the lungs. So she was dead before the explosion and the fire.' He raised one shoulder in a half-shrug. 'You're right, though, it's not the obvious route. But who knows what goes through a woman's head when she's had enough? Come to that, who knows what goes through a woman's head at any time?'

'Did you check out the harassment she got online?'

Franny nodded. 'Bloody awful. Those twats need a good kicking. Relentless, it was. But there was dozens of them. It wasn't like it was only one person giving her the needle. So if your Tony's looking for a single arsehole driving her to it, he's barking up the wrong tree.'

Smarter than the average bear, as she'd always known. 'I don't know what he's thinking, to be honest. Was there anything else about it that was out of the ordinary?'

Franny drained his pint. 'Hard to say.'

'Meaning what?'

'There was one thing. But we both know fire and explosion do funny things.'

'Like blowing people's clothes off?'

'That kind of thing. So this might be something Daisy did herself or it might have been caused by the explosion.'

Paula waited while Franny exhaled a cloud of vapour and considered.

'All over the front garden there were pages from a book of poetry. Scattered everywhere.'

'A book of poetry?'

He nodded. 'Something called *Ariel*. By that lass Sylvia Plath who's buried up by Heptonstall. Married to Ted Hughes. Him that was Poet Laureate.'

Paula hoped she was hiding her astonishment at the extent of Franny's literary knowledge. 'She gassed herself,' she said. 'Sylvia Plath.'

Franny nodded. 'That she did. So maybe that was Daisy's last message to the rest of us. Like Sylvia Plath, she couldn't take any more.'

'She didn't leave a note, then?'

Pointedly, he sucked the last drops of stout from his glass. 'Not a word. Now, are you for another pint or are you off like a scalded cat now you've sucked me dry?'

Paula laughed. 'Just a half. Because I'm not really supposed to be here at all.'

Franny guffawed. 'You and me both, pet. You and me both.'

★   ★   ★

When they'd been kids, Carol and her brother Michael had had their own cure for hiccups — thumbs in the ears, index fingers jamming the nostrils closed, eyes shut to avoid distraction, the deepest breath you could squeeze into your lungs, then hold it for as long as possible. Till you could feel the hot tide of blood in your cheeks and you thought your eyeballs might explode. Then, an eruption of breath like an explosion. The hiccups would be gone, but the sufferer would stagger around for a few moments, light-headed and disorientated. That was how she felt all the way back to the barn. She'd screwed herself up so tight to face the consequences of her stupidity and then suddenly, all that tension had been released.

She said next to nothing on the journey home. Tony kept starting sentences without finishing them, fading to a halt a few words in. She was accustomed to him talking to himself when he was working out a problem. What she wasn't used to was being the problem.

It wasn't even lunchtime when they walked into the barn. Carol closed the door behind them and crouched down to accept the adoring welcome from Flash. As the dog licked her hands, she buried her face in the black-and-white fur of her ruff and tried to calm herself. Tony stood a few feet away, watching them with an expression of curiosity. She looked up. 'What? You've never seen a dog welcome its owner before?'

'It's an aspect of you I'm not entirely familiar with yet. Obviously it's some sort of displacement, but I'm not sure for what.'

Carol glared at him but her heart wasn't in it. Just because he managed to come out with so many unsettling lines didn't mean he wasn't trying to help. She stood up and leaned against the wall. Christ, she needed a drink. She was determined not to have one, but the desire burned through her like electricity in the vein. A vodka and tonic, so cold the glass would sweat condensation over her fingers. Or the smooth glide of a Pinot Grigio slipping down her throat, taking all the tension with it. A few of those and she would feel no fear.

Because fear was exactly what she was feeling right now. Coursing through her, making her heart race and her hands damp. She could feel a drop of cold sweat trickling into the small of her back. What in the name of God had she agreed to? Her eyelids fluttered and she drew in a ragged breath. 'You can go home now,' she said, pushing off from the wall and heading for what had been her private domain until Tony had decided to move in. 'I don't need a chauffeur any more.'

She could hear his footsteps on the concrete floor as he slowly followed her. 'I want to help,' he said.

'And you have.' Carol kept her back to him, walking through to the kitchen and filling the kettle, shielding it with her body to hide the tremor in her hands. 'And now it's time for me to stand on my own two feet. I'm not drinking and I'm not going to.'

'I thought it might be useful for you to use me as a sounding board. This is a huge challenge you're taking on. And Brandon clearly expects you to hit the ground running even though you've spent the last six months being a builder, not a copper.' He sat down at the table, reaching for a satsuma and starting to peel it. The bitter-sweet tang of the orange peel filled the air between them.

'You can't follow me round holding my hand.' She blocked any response by activating the coffee grinder. When it stopped, she spooned grounds into the cafetiere and poured on the water.

'I know you don't need me to hold your hand,' he said, the gentleness in his voice almost as infuriating as if he'd offered to do the opposite of what he'd said. 'And I have my own work to get back to. But you told Brandon back there that you wanted me on your team. If I'm going to risk my reputation on this mad enterprise, the least you owe me is the chance to help you shape it. Don't you think?'

He was, she had to admit, a clever bastard. By making it about him and not her, he'd left her nowhere to go. She poured two cups of coffee and sat down facing him. 'OK. What's your T and Cs?'

That familiar frown of bewilderment that she had learned was not always to be taken at face value. 'T and Cs?'

'Terms and conditions.'

Enlightenment spread across his face. 'Well, I do already have a job and I'm supposed to be writing a book.'

'Your job at Bradfield Moor is only part-time, though. You've always managed to squeeze in police work before.'

He pulled a face. 'I am the man with no life.'

Carol rolled her eyes. 'Poor, poor pitiful me.'

'I didn't know you were a Warren Zevon fan.'

She groaned. 'Linda Ronstadt. All I'm saying is that I know we can't have you full-time, and

184

that's fine. We've always made it work before and we'll make it work again. It's better for the budget, anyway.'

Tony recoiled in mock-horror. 'Oh my God! You're channelling James Blake.'

'Ha. As if.'

'So who else do you have in mind for this crack team?'

He'd been right, as usual. The very act of talking about it, figuring out the practicalities, was releasing some of the tension that had been creeping up her neck and into her scalp. 'Paula, obviously. And Stacey, because she's wasted anywhere outside an MIT. Then there's Kevin.'

'He's just retired, hasn't he? Didn't I get invited to his retirement do?'

'He's got his thirty in and yes, he's off. But I think I might persuade him back. I've got a little something up my sleeve to run past Brandon in the morning.'

'Very intriguing.'

'You'll find out soon enough. Do you think Alvin Ambrose would be interested in moving up here?'

Ambrose, a tenacious and talented detective sergeant from West Mercia, had worked with Carol's team a couple of times before when their paths had crossed. He'd impressed her with his reliability and his resourcefulness. And Tony, she thought, had almost made a friend.

'He was pretty pleased when he thought you might be heading for West Mercia,' Tony admitted. 'He'd be a good man to have on the team. And he gets on well with Paula.'

'I'm going to ask for him anyway. I think he might be up for something a bit more demanding than a couple of murders a year. And that's pretty much as far as I've got right now. I'll need one or two DCs, but they can wait. Paula mentioned a lad she's got under her at Skenfrith Street, Hussain?'

Tony shook his head. 'No idea. Don't know whether I've met him. What about Sam Evans? He's still a DC, isn't he?'

Carol shook her head, her mouth a thin line. 'I'm not having Sam.'

'He's a good digger.'

'Yeah, but he's too fond of digging in places where he's got no business. I don't trust him, Tony. A small, tight team like this? There'll be enough people on the outside ready to stab us in the back without having someone on the inside with a stiletto up his sleeve.'

'I'm not sure you're right.' He held up a hand to make her pause. 'I know he's not trustworthy. But the thing about Sam is that he's all about Sam. And a place on a team like this, the first standalone MIT, that's his ticket to the stars. He wouldn't put that at risk.'

'He'd do it in a heartbeat if it meant he came out of it smelling of roses. He'd be the man who shot Liberty Valance. Except of course, I'd be John Wayne, shooting myself in the foot for taking him on in the first place.'

Tony frowned, working his way through her tortured metaphor. 'If you say so. But it's going to be hard on Stacey.'

Carol glowered defiance at him. 'Stacey's a big

girl. She loves what she does. She won't pass up a chance like this just because her boyfriend's sulking.' Tony looked sceptical. 'I'm telling you, Tony. Stacey loves data more than she could ever love a human being.'

He shrugged, his face keeping his thoughts to himself. 'It's your team. And it sounds to me like you've got the makings of a good one.'

'So can I take it you're in?'

'Did I not make that clear? Of course I'm in. I love my clinical work, don't get me wrong. There's nothing more satisfying than helping somebody mend the bits that are broken inside. But profiling is something else. It stretches me. It makes demands of me. It forces me to look at everything I know from a different angle. It meets a need in me I didn't even know was there until I started doing it.' He cleared his throat, as if overtaken by embarrassment. She had never heard him speak so eloquently about the work he did for law enforcement. Generally he spoke only of the mechanics of what he did, not what it meant to him. Hearing him talk like this made sense of the way he worked. She'd met other profilers, men whose egos swamped the investigation they were supposed to be helping. And others whose profiles were so hedged about with qualification that they were worse than useless. But Tony brought a humility to the process that meant he was always open to possibilities that others might never consider. It wasn't that he lacked certainty or conviction. More that he was flexible.

'Good,' she said.

'So how do we get started?'

'I think a little practice run would be good for us. So we might as well carry on with these internet trolling cases.'

He shook his head, bemused. 'That was . . . I don't know, something for us to play around with. There's no real evidence of anything suspicious.'

'Except that we are trained to have suspicious minds, and something rang a bell for you. Look, we need time and experience to bed down together. And I don't think we should be doing that on a live case with the eyes of the media on us. This is perfect practice.' She ran her fingers through her hair, tugging at strands, pulling it one way then another. 'And Christ knows when I'm going to have time to get a proper haircut. He'll want to blow the trumpet about this, Brandon will. And I can't hold a press conference looking like this.'

'You look fine to me,' Tony said. From another man it would have been gallantry. From Tony, she suspected it was surprise that she looked anything out of the ordinary.

Carol rolled her eyes again. 'Would you even notice if I dyed it pink? This is one area where I rate your observational skills at zero, Tony. Trust me, I need a haircut.' She pulled her phone out. 'I wonder if Wendy still remembers how I used to like it? Maybe she could fit me in on Saturday . . . And I'll need to take a pile of stuff to the dry-cleaner's.' She looked at him brightly, as if something had occurred to her as she spoke. 'You could do that for me on your way home. There's that dry-cleaner on the way into Bradfield, the one that used to be a petrol station. You know where I mean? Right after the Morden roundabout?'

'You're determined to get rid of me.'

She couldn't deny it. 'You were here for me when I needed it,' she said. 'I've not had a drink since Saturday night. I'm over the worst and now I need to be able to trust myself. I need to prepare for tomorrow. It's been a long time and now I need to get my copper's head back on.' Carol did her best to sound apologetic. She didn't want to hurt his feelings. But she knew she had a rough night ahead; the desire for a drink would grow as her fears loomed larger in the small hours. She didn't want him to see her like that. She didn't want pity from him. She cupped a hand round his. 'I want to sleep in my own bed, Tony. I need to reclaim my own space.'

That did the trick. She could see in his eyes that it made sense to him. He dipped his head. 'OK.' His smile was pained but it was a smile. He stood up, almost tripping over the dog. 'For what it's worth, I'm glad you said yes to Brandon. You're not a builder, Carol. You're a detective. It's time to go back to what you do best.'

25

After Tony left with the dry-cleaning, time slowed to a dull trickle. Carol laid out a suit for the morning — dark navy wool mix that didn't crease and didn't create showers of static sparks. She'd realised in preparing herself for court that quite a few of her more tailored jackets weren't going to fit her new shape, with its broader shoulders and more muscular arms. There would have to be shopping on a serious scale. She stifled a sigh and made a note to arrange a raid on the outlet mall with Elinor. Paula's partner had a better sense of style than any of them; with her dramatic fall of black hair, her pale skin and her wiry slenderness, she carried off clothes better than most, but she was always happy to share her discriminating eye. Carol added a rich fuchsia shirt to the pile then swapped it for kingfisher blue, then a vibrant scarlet. Then back to the first one. She recognised an unfamiliar indecision and scolded herself under her breath.

But once she'd settled the matter of her wardrobe, she found herself at a loss. How exactly did you prepare for a return to work? Being a cop wasn't a job like any other. It wasn't like working for an advertising agency, where you could check out what the opposition were doing; or the oil industry, where you could familiarise yourself with new processes; or teaching, where there was always some new aspect to the organisation of the curriculum. Yes, there might be some advances in forensic techniques, but she wasn't going to find those out till she was in the thick of an investigation that needed them. Other than that, it was business as usual. Dig out information, make connections, develop a theory of suspicion, arrange the available evidence to support or destroy the theory, make an arrest and interview the suspects till one of them turned into a perpetrator.

There was, of course, the case of the questionable suicides to think about. But that was making bricks without straw. She needed more information before any of them could take the matter any further. Probably it was nothing, and she'd have plenty of real cases soon enough. The best she could do right now was to clear her head.

'Come on, Flash,' she said, stuffing her feet into her walking boots and pulling on her waxed jacket. Some sunshine brightened the moor, though it was struggling now with a thin layer of cloud drifting in from the west. A light breeze coursed up the valley, enough to freshen without chilling. Perfect weather to be out on the hill. Woman and dog climbed the moorland on a long diagonal that eventually brought them to the top of the ridge, the dog coursing back and forth, covering four times the ground Carol had.

Halfway along the ridge, she caught sight of movement below. It soon resolved itself into George Nicholas and Jess, Flash's mother. So much had happened since he'd turned up at the barn the day before; it felt like far more time had passed. Today, she had nothing to hide. It was probably time to build some bridges after Tony's odd intervention. So she gave a civilised wave in his direction.

George returned the gesture and altered the line of his approach so he would cross her path. He was breathing a little heavily when he reached her, but there was nothing strained about his smile. 'Your friend Tony didn't fancy a walk, then?'

'He's gone back to Bradfield. Actually, he does do quite a lot of walking, but mostly in the city. He says it helps him think. That and video games.' She shook her head with an indulgent smile, recalling her own reluctant entry into that world and the shock of its attraction.

George fell into step with her and together they began a meandering descent towards the barn. 'I hear you had a bit of a brush with the law,' he said with an air of nonchalance.

'News travels fast.'

Most people would have been put off by her repressive tone, but George had been to boarding school; he was tougher than he looked. 'There's so little genuine news in the valley that we have to fall on what we have like vultures. Did you think people wouldn't get to hear about it?'

Carol exhaled sharply. 'There's nothing to hear. I was stopped driving home, the breathalyser was faulty, case dismissed. Hard to think of anything more dull.'

'Except that you had been drinking.'

She smiled, but in a way that would have

made her junior officers find something urgent elsewhere that needed their attention. 'Within the limits of the law.'

George's eyebrows jerked upwards. 'I'd have thought rather more than that.'

'What? You count your guests' drinks? How very bourgeois, George. I wouldn't have expected that of you.' Her tone was light but her eyes were dark with suppressed anger.

'No, of course not. One notices, that's all. Especially if they're going to be driving. One wouldn't want anything on one's conscience. If anything were to happen.'

A frosty look. 'Well, George, your conscience is clear. In the eyes of the law, no offence has been committed. More than that, I'm about to go back into harness.'

'You're going back to the police? But I thought you'd resigned?'

Carol picked up a stick and threw it as far as she could. The two dogs flashed over the yellow moorland grasses in pursuit. 'I did. But they've come to me with an offer I can't refuse, so I'm going back.'

'To your old job?'

The dogs were performing a tug of war with the stick, pulling each other in circles, their play-growls filling the silence. 'Not quite,' Carol said. 'The same sort of thing but with a much wider remit. And a different line of command.'

'What about the dog? How will you manage Flash? She won't like being left alone all day.'

Carol hadn't given it much thought. But she'd always been good at making things up on the

193

hoof. 'I'll take her with me. She can come into the office. That's the advantage of being your own boss.'

George looked a little bleak at her response. 'I see. Well, if you ever need any dog-sitting, you can always bring her round to mine. As you can probably tell, Jess is always happy to see her.'

'Thanks. I may have to take you up on that.'

'You'd be very welcome.' They'd reached the path that ran along the side of the hill close to the bottom. The natural order of things would be for George to turn right towards his house, and for Carol to go left to the barn. He looked hopefully towards the barn, the nearer of the two. But Carol wasn't playing.

'I'd better get home,' she said. 'Lots of preparations to make for tomorrow.'

'You're starting work already?'

She shrugged. 'I've made the decision. No point in hanging about. I'll see you around, George. The barn's close to being finished, I'll probably have some people round for drinks to celebrate. So I'll see you then, if not before.'

He looked shocked. She understood why. In one brief exchange, she'd robbed him. No more morning hikes up the hill with the dogs, no more casual chats about the weather and their history and the neighbours. Carol wondered whether she'd allowed him to harbour false hopes about where their friendship might go and felt a moment of guilt. But not enough to change her mind or her plans. She sketched a little wave then turned away. A hundred yards on, she could still feel his eyes on her and she glanced back.

George was where she'd left him, crouched beside his dog, hand in its ruff, his gaze fixed on her. Carol kept going, heading for home, not doubting her choice, but wondering whether she could ever steer herself into a position where she could have what she actually wanted.

The answer, as it always was when she asked herself such questions, was Tony. In all its fucked-up combative glory, that was the place where she felt most herself.

Carol let herself into the barn, taking her mind off men by returning to thoughts of her wardrobe. She should try on that blouse, make sure it still fitted. Five minutes later, she had discovered that none of the three did her any favours. Swearing loudly, she pulled on her sweater again. At least it was Wednesday. Late-night shopping at the Bradfield outlet mall. She had time enough to find something that made her look like a copper, not a bra advert.

She went through to the kitchen and reached for the Land Rover keys. The hook was empty. She tutted. Bloody Tony had walked off with the keys in a typical moment of inattention. Thankfully, there was a spare set in the cutlery drawer.

Except that there wasn't. She searched through every compartment and came up empty. Then it dawned on her. He'd been afraid she would crack and go out to buy drink. So he'd made it impossible. 'You bastard,' she yelled pointlessly.

If Tony Hill was the answer, she had to be asking the wrong question.

＊ ＊ ＊

Carol wasn't the only one who had been reconstructing their world recently. Thanks to circumstances beyond anyone's control, Tony was living on a fifty-foot narrowboat in the Minster Canal Basin in the heart of Bradfield, a vessel he'd inherited from the father he'd never known. He'd surprised himself at how easy it had been to adapt to such confined living. He'd always been one of life's clutterers, every surface piled with books and papers and game boxes and journals, with the occasional dirty coffee cup hemmed inaccessibly in the middle of the stacks. But when every inch of space had to earn its keep, that kind of messiness made life impossible. It had taken him a long time to get there, but finally he understood that chaos did indeed expand to fill the room available.

And so his world aboard had become neat and ordered. Things were put away after use; nothing was admitted to *Steeler* unless its presence could be justified. He wasn't entirely a reformed character — his office in Bradfield Moor secure mental hospital was as untidy as it had ever been, presenting a bipolar contrast between the area where he worked and the section of the room where he talked to patients, a corner containing a pair of comfortable armchairs separated from the anarchy by a pretty Japanese screen.

But one problem remained. Half of the walls in his former home had been lined with bookshelves, crammed from end to end with a catholic mix of psychology, philosophy, fiction, history and true crime. There was no room in either his office or his new floating home for his library, and Tony missed his books with the kind of ache normally reserved for an absent lover. That they were still there, albeit boxed up in a storage unit, did nothing to assuage his grief.

It was one of his colleagues who unwittingly solved his problem. She was considering investing in a new form of student housing — the conversion of cargo containers into self-contained studios, stacked in blocks on undeveloped city sites. Tony recalled that the storage company who were currently looking after his books also had shipping containers for hire. He'd gone down with a pad and pencil and measuring tape and worked out that he could construct a neat little maze of shelving with a comfortable chair at the heart of it only five minutes' walk from the boat. His own personal library.

Over the past few weeks, he'd erected flatpack industrial shelving in the arrangement he'd settled on and now he was unpacking and stacking the books. He seemed to have packed them randomly, so he was making an attempt to sort them as he went, a process that involved a lot of rearranging and swearing. Not to mention being sucked into books he hadn't opened in years and reminding himself of why they'd grabbed his interest in the first place. It was the perfect task to distract him from fretting over things he couldn't alter.

Tony had gone straight there after he'd

dropped off Carol Jordan's dry-cleaning, knowing he'd be incapable of anything more constructive. He knew the need for a drink would be gnawing at her and he didn't have her confidence that she could resist that. So he'd taken the high-handed step of helping himself to her car keys. He wondered how long it would take her to make the discovery. He hoped the first she would realise what he'd done was when he turned up at the barn in the morning acting stupid and repentant. It wasn't as if that was so unlikely a scenario.

So he was disappointed when his phone rang a couple of hours after he'd left and the screen showed it was Carol calling. As soon as he picked up, she was off. 'How dare you?' she began. 'Who died and made you God? What the *fuck* do you think you're doing, walking out of here with my car keys?'

'I just thought — '

'No, you didn't think. You made a decision about me with no authority. You decided I couldn't be trusted to keep my word. You decided I needed to be kept prisoner in my own home. You're supposed to be the one who's full of empathy, so where was your fucking empathy this afternoon? You didn't think for a nanosecond how I would feel, to be treated like someone who can't be trusted.'

'I thought about how you'd feel if you failed.'

She snorted. 'You think that's a defence? To tell me you have so little faith in me? That you thought I was more likely to fall off the wagon than hold my nerve? Have you any idea how hard this is for me? My body and my brain are screaming for a drink and I am absolutely not listening and it's tearing me apart but I. Am. Not. Giving in. Fuck you, Tony.'

'I was trying to help.'

'Brilliant. So here I am, stuck in the middle of nowhere with no transport and a new job to start in the morning.'

'I know that, I was planning to bring the keys back first thing so you could get to work.'

Now her voice went deadly calm and cold. 'And that would be perfect if I had some clothes to wear. I can drive into work but all I'll be wearing under my jacket is a bra. And a pretty functional bra at that. Tony, my shirts don't fit me properly any more. I was going to go late-night shopping at the outlet mall for tops. Not down to the supermarket for cut-price booze.'

His stomach felt like he'd descended thirty swift floors in a lift. He'd thought he was being so clever; that although she'd be angry at first, in the long run she'd thank him. He was supposed to be good at making choices like that to help patients understand how to make positive choices for themselves in future. And he'd blown it comprehensively with the person who meant most to him. 'I'm sorry,' he said, angry at the inadequacy of the words. 'I could come out right away with the keys?'

'I don't think there's time for that. I'm going to get a cab to the mall. You can meet me there with my Land Rover keys then drive me back after I've finished shopping.' She didn't sound in the least mollified, but at least she was still talking to him. There had been times in the recent past where not a word had passed between them for weeks on end and it had been the hardest emotional loss he'd ever endured.

'I'll text you when I get there,' he said. But he was talking to dead air. How the hell was he going to redeem himself this time?

26

The top floor of Skenfrith Street police station had an unrivalled view of the multi-storey car park opposite. That was probably its finest feature. Right now, it was an empty rectangular space with grey industrial carpeting and pale grey painted walls. The dropped ceiling had banks of fluorescent lighting that stripped everything of its humanity, including the humans. John Brandon sucked his teeth and frowned a question at the man from Building Services.

An eager-looking hipster with a waxed moustache, skinny jeans and a canvas jacket, he tapped his tablet and held it out to reveal a bare floor plan. 'We've got a team standing by to knock it into whatever configuration you want with a view to being ready to roll on Monday,' he said, fingering his quiff with his free hand.

Carol looked around, considering. 'I want a corner office over there,' she said. 'With a window. Six metres by six.'

The hipster drew a box with his finger on the floor plan. Black lines appeared. 'That sort of size?'

Carol nodded. 'A desk, two four-drawer filing cabinets, a proper ergonomic chair and two visitor chairs. And a coat stand.'

More tapping and suddenly, there it all was from a bird's-eye view. 'You'll want a waste paper bin,' he said.

And so it continued. A separate office for Stacey with enough power points for a small factory, enclosed so prying eyes couldn't see what illegalities she might be perpetrating. Open plan for everyone else, with a couple of small meeting rooms where private conversations could be conducted when necessary. Whiteboards for displaying case progress. A flip chart. A long run of desks in the middle of the room and a few scattered on the periphery. Computers, obviously. And the coffee area.

'We need a proper coffee machine. From bean to cup. We're very particular about our brew in this MIT. I don't care what you call it on the official requisitions, but it's a necessity.' Carol's chin came up in a challenge but she was tilting at the wrong windmill.

The young man grinned and nodded. 'That is an excellent call. It's yours, provided I can stop by when I'm in the building.' He started to say something then stopped.

'Go on?' Carol said.

'There's a new roaster opened on Bellwether Square, Coffee Temple? Everywhere else is third wave but they're proper old school, you know? Mellow and chocolatey.' He shrugged. 'If that's the way you roll, it's as good as it gets. You might want to pick up your beans from there.'

Carol smiled and thanked him. 'What do you say, John? Will we try the new coffee shop and let the guys get on with their work?'

'Sounds like a plan,' he said, leading the way to the lifts. As the doors closed, Brandon said, 'I suppose you understood every word of that?

About the coffee?' he grumbled.

'Pretty much. When it comes to my team, I think I can safely say that as far as coffee is concerned, we're old school. Trust me, John, you don't want to go down the acidic and fruity route.'

'I remember when coffee was just coffee. Sometimes frothy,' he muttered as he followed her out of the building. The sky was low and louring, the air damp and sour as they walked briskly through half-empty back streets to Bellwether Square. Five minutes later, they were huddled over their drinks at a corner table in Coffee Temple, where the aroma of roasted coffee mingled with fresh scones. Carol thought it was going to be hard to resist escaping there whenever she could sneak out.

'So,' Brandon said. 'No second thoughts?'

Carol shook her head. 'No. For the first time in ages I'm excited about the idea of working cases.' She twisted her mouth in a wry expression. 'Working with Blake knocked a lot of the satisfaction out of the job, to be honest. I'm looking forward to having a bit more control over how we manage our budget.'

'It will be your responsibility,' he said. 'You've got pretty tight constraints, but at least you get to decide your priorities. So, who have you set your heart on?'

'DS Paula McIntyre, DC Stacey Chen and a young DC, Karim Hussain from BMP. I'd like DS Alvin Ambrose from West Mercia. And I'd like to bring Kevin Matthews back out of retirement.'

Brandon frowned. 'I don't see any problem with the serving officers. But why would Kevin want to come back?'

'I've given that some thought. You remember years ago he got bumped down from inspector to sergeant?'

A grim look settled on Brandon's face. 'I remember. He leaked details to the press. He was having an affair with that hack Penny Burgess, wasn't he?'

'That's right. But it was a long time ago.'

'That was the first case where we used Tony, wasn't it?'

Carol's eyes clouded at the memory. 'Anyway, Kevin paid the price. He dropped a rank and he stayed there. He could have tried to get back to inspector, but he wanted to stay on the MIT and I didn't have the budget for a DI. So I'm proposing we not only bring him back into the fold but we bring him back as an inspector. Ideally, every MIT should carry an officer at that rank anyway. And Paula's not ready.'

'You're going with a very small team,' Brandon said.

'You promised us local back-up for all the routine tasks, so I'd rather keep the team small and tight so we can use our budget where it matters. On the forensic experts. Tony, for one.'

Brandon stared into his coffee, considering. It was a bold set-up, but bold was what they'd asked for. If it all went horribly wrong, all he had to lose was some lucrative Home Office work. They wouldn't starve, him and Maggie, if they had to fall back on a chief constable's pension.

The only one taking a risk here was Carol, and that would be a hell of a spur to make things work well. He looked up and gave a curt nod. 'I think we can live with that arrangement,' he said. 'The beardie weirdie said you'd have the office up and running by Monday. I'll do my best to make sure the paperwork's in place for you to have your team then. It'll be tight, but I haven't forgotten how to wave a big stick.'

'How about tomorrow? If I can get them on board?'

Brandon was surprised and it showed. 'Why do you want them tomorrow? There's no case for you yet. You'll have a few days to bed down before anything gets punted your way.'

'The sooner the better,' she said. 'I think they might need an exercise to get back up to speed, given they've none of them been working exclusively on major cases.'

'An exercise?' Brandon looked nonplussed. 'What sort of exercise?'

'A little something Tony and I are putting together that will get them working as a team and set their brains ticking over,' she said with a nonchalance that could only have fooled someone who didn't know her.

Brandon sighed. He knew he couldn't complain. He was the one who had unleashed the juggernaut. 'Why don't you have an unofficial word with them, see what they have to say? I'll see what I can do to make those transfers immediately effective.'

Carol's face lit up in a way he hadn't seen for a very long time. 'Thank you, John. And thank you for having the confidence in me to give me this chance. I needed something to kickstart my life after what happened to Michael. I just didn't know what it was.'

★ ★ ★

Shakila Bain had an air of apparently effortless glamour that Paula knew a lifetime of practice would never grant her. Her glossy hair hung in blunt lines without a split end in sight, her make-up was striking without being grotesque, her nails were perfectly shaped and without a single chip. She looked both younger and more mature than the twenty-eight years her website credited her with. She was wearing a silky plaid tunic over skinny-leg trousers made from some shimmering black fabric. Paula, who had made the effort of clean black jeans and lightweight layered T-shirts under her Puffa jacket, came under a critical gaze and felt wanting.

She'd invited Paula to meet her at her studio in Manchester's Northern Quarter. The area was clearly trying to brand itself as edgy and stylish but it had quite a way to go, Paula thought. Tired wholesalers with windows full of cheap clothes and second-hand jewellery shops rubbed shoulders with juice bars and craft workers' outlets. Shakila's studio occupied the entire second floor of a shabby brick building in a scruffy back street. It was surprisingly bright, which was probably a good thing for the eyesight of the dozen women hunched over industrial sewing machines amidst a riot of colourful fabrics.

Large sketches of tunics and shirts were loosely pinned to the walls, adding to the blitz of colour.

Shakila led her into a small white cube of a meeting room where she was the only splash of colour. When she closed the door the clatter of machinery subsided to a low mutter that was quieter than the buzz of the CID office Paula had left. 'Thanks for making the time to see me. You're obviously busy,' Paula said, settling on a white leather ottoman.

Shakila shrugged. 'I'm kind of surprised to see you, to be honest. Because I didn't get a whole lot of interest from your colleagues when the shitstorm hit. I don't know whether it was because I'm a Muslim or because I'm a woman, but I so didn't feel the love.'

'I'm sorry about that. All I can say is that this is a relatively new crime and some of my colleagues don't quite grasp how serious it can be for people like you on the receiving end. It's no excuse, I know. But that's why I'm here now. I've been doing case reviews and I thought you deserved better from BMP than we delivered.' Paula meant what she said. The hardest part was knowing that the only reason she was there was because another investigation interested her more than what had happened to Shakila. Without Kate and Jasmine and Daisy, nobody would ever have come near the designer again.

Shakila shrugged. 'I appreciate what you're saying but it doesn't change the facts. I was threatened and frightened and I came to the police for help and you guys didn't help. If they hadn't lost interest in me because something more tasty came along, if they'd acted on those threats, it wouldn't be any consolation to me that you're here now.'

Shakila was, Paula thought, a lot less confrontational than she'd have been in her shoes. 'I've read the file, and I do sympathise. Would you mind talking me through what happened?'

'One of the reporters on the local news channel went to the same school as me. He said he was looking for somebody who confounded expectations of what a Muslim woman looks like to talk about the alienation of young men and why they go off to become jihadis.' She sighed. 'I didn't think it was that controversial. I mean, you only have to think about it for five minutes. Teenagers, they're always looking for a cause. If your average white boy had the equivalent of jihad to nail his idealism to, they'd be signing up round the block. It's the kind of stupid thing that appeals to boys when they're at their most stupid age, it's not a Muslim thing. It's the reason half of them join the army.'

'And then the sky fell in?'

Shakila's expression took on a wry twist. 'You could say that. For the first couple of days, it was just a local thing. But then what I like to think of as anti-social media got hold of it. Before I knew it, I was getting abuse by the bucketload.'

'What were they saying?'

'Nothing very original. I needed to have some sense raped into me, I was a dirty Muslim terrorist-lover, I should go back to where I came from. Not bloody likely, I said, I'm not going back to Bingley.' A forced smile. 'It was pretty horrible. When it got to 'We know where you live and we're coming for you', my brother persuaded me to go to you lot.'

'Then what happened?'

She spread her hands. 'Nothing much. I made a report, somebody took some notes and I went home. And then that woman MP went on *Question Time* and said more or less the same thing I'd said and they all lost interest in me.' She shrugged. 'I'm prettier than her but she gets more attention in the media, so there's more traction in trying to terrorise her.'

'And nobody turned up at your house?'

Shakila shook her head. 'That doesn't mean they wouldn't have, if some other bright shiny thing hadn't caught their eye. These people are scum, you know?'

Paula knew. 'I expect you were very upset.'

'Upset doesn't begin to touch it. I was frightened for my life. And for the women who work for me. What if one of those bastards had set fire to this place? What if a bunch of them had taken it into their heads to attack me on my way home? I couldn't sleep, I couldn't eat. I had a couple of weeks of absolute hell. I'm a tough woman, Sergeant. You have to be tough to make it in the rag trade. But I was buckling under the stress of it all. Thank God I have a strong family around me.' For a moment, her composure slipped and Paula caught a glimpse of the unravelling that had threatened her.

'This might sound like a strange question, but I'm asking because we're looking at other women who've had similar experiences to you.

Was there anyone suggesting you should kill yourself?'

Shakila gave a shaky laugh. 'There was all sorts. To tell you the truth, I stopped reading them after a couple of days. I decided I didn't need that shit in my head. I didn't delete them, in case anything happened and your lot finally decided to do something. But I didn't go through them. If you want to take a look, send somebody over, they can go through what's on my laptop. They'll have to do it here, though. My life, my business, they're all on that machine, I'm not letting it out of my hands.'

Paula smiled. 'That's OK. I have a colleague who can make a shadow copy of your hard drive in next to no time. Then she can take it away and analyse all that crap. But you don't remember anyone specifically encouraging you to kill yourself?'

'Plenty telling me the world would be a better place if I was dead, quite a few saying if I loved jihad so much why didn't I become a suicide bomber. You can see for yourselves.'

'I'll arrange for DC Chen to come over and copy your hard drive,' Paula said. 'And we'll see whether we can track down any of the men who have been harassing you.'

'I'm happy to press charges,' Shakila said. 'Even if it means I get more of the same. All I did was express an opinion. Somebody has to show these people they don't get to shut the rest of us up because they don't like what we have to say.'

27

Everybody seemed to like Skype except him, Tony thought, closing his office door then settling in front of his screen. His dislike was both personal and professional. Everybody looked weird on Skype. Everyone, frankly, looked like a potential patient. There was something very unsettling about that fish-eyed stare. Even people he liked looked deranged. From a professional perspective, the trouble was you could never see enough of the person you were in conversation with to gauge their body language. They might be giving off all sorts of signals you'd be aware of in what his boss had taken to calling 'F2F encounters', but the Skype interface could hide a multitude of clues.

But sometimes it was impossible to avoid. Like this morning. Paula was in Manchester, interviewing Shakila Bain, the British Asian fashion designer who'd been a recent victim of harassment. Stacey was in the digital forensics unit of BMP grinding her way through routine analyses of the hard drives of suspected fraudsters. And he was seeing patients at Bradfield Cross. They'd settled on a time; all he had to do now was get his Skype up and running.

He was only four minutes late joining the other two, who were deep in discussion of Paula's interview with Shakila. Paula broke off to greet him, adding, 'Shakila was incredibly helpful. She's given us access to her hard drive and her social media accounts so Stacey can check out the bastards who were harassing her, see if we can come up with any crossover.'

'Great,' he said. 'So, have we got anything at all to suggest linkage between the three victims?'

'Before we get on to that, what happened yesterday? Was it adjourned, or what? Neither of us could find anything online about it,' Paula said.

'Which is very strange, in my experience,' Stacey added. 'What with the courts being open to the public.'

Tony rubbed the back of his head, screwing his face up. 'I should have called you. Sorry. It all got a bit complicated. The case was dismissed.'

There was a moment of shocked silence. 'Dismissed? How can that be?' Stacey looked almost affronted. Almost as if she'd known how rock solid the case had been.

'I thought they had her bang to rights?' This from Paula. 'She sounded like she was resigned to losing her licence. The works.'

For once, Tony was glad Skype robbed them of the ability to see his body language. 'The breathalyser was faulty. So Carol and three other people had their cases dismissed.'

Paula grinned like a birthday child. 'So she's off the hook? No record, still driving?'

'Still out there, able to do it again, you mean,' Stacey said gloomily. 'Not that I wish anything bad for Carol, but she shouldn't do it.'

'She's not drinking,' Tony said. 'It was a wake-up call, Stacey.' He cleared his throat.

'Anyway, I know she'll be in touch herself later.'

Paula gave him a quick sideways look. 'What are you not telling us?'

That, he thought, was the downside of building friendships. People could see more than you necessarily wanted to show. 'Nothing you won't find out in due course from the appropriate source,' he said stiffly. 'Please, Paula, don't put me on the spot.'

'So Carol's got something to tell us and it must be a big deal or you'd have spilled the beans by now.'

'Stop teasing him,' Stacey said with mock-severity. 'There's no point. He won't tell us and we'll only make him even more uncomfortable.'

Tony couldn't remember Stacey ever having so much to say that wasn't directly related to the digital universe. Apparently her relationship with Sam had mellowed her to the point where she noticed other people existed. He liked that people still had the power to surprise him in a good way. 'So, now we've established I'm not going to tell you what's not mine to tell, can we move on to the purpose of this conference call?' he said.

Paula rolled her eyes. 'Stacey, you go first.'

'OK. I won't bore you with all the numbers of troll posts, which are surprisingly high across all social media. I knew this was an issue, guys, but I hadn't quite grasped that it was the same scale of epidemic as images of child sex abuse. I know I'm a geek, but even I regret some of what the internet has made possible.'

'Bloody hell, is that the sound of the sky

falling?' Paula demanded.

'Not funny. The key figures for our victims are these — only seven people trolled all three women. Of those seven, only five did so repeatedly. So if you're looking for a starting point, I'd say that's one possibility.'

'And do we actually know who those five individuals are? In flesh-and-blood terms, I mean?' Tony was cautiously interested.

'I have ID on three of them. The other two are being a bit more elusive but I should be able to crack them.'

'That's amazing work, Stacey. It's good to see you've not lost your touch, even though they've got you doing the equivalent of shovelling coal,' Tony said. 'That definitely gives us a place to start pushing.'

'There's something else that's a bit odd,' Paula said. 'Kate Rawlins had a book of poetry on the driver's seat next to her. According to her family, she never read poetry and they don't recognise the book as belonging to Kate. It was by some American called Anne Sexton who killed herself. She apparently had a lot of mental health issues. But what makes it even more intriguing is that the pages of a book of poetry by Sylvia Plath were scattered all over Daisy Morton's garden after the explosion. Plath was also an American. Also with mental health problems. Also killed herself. As if that's not enough of a coincidence, Kate and Daisy killed themselves in roughly the same way as the dead poets did. Sexton locked herself in the garage with the engine running and Plath stuck her head in the gas oven. Though there wasn't an explosion.'

Abruptly, Tony slapped his forehead. 'Of course,' he shouted. 'I am so stupid sometimes.' He spread his hands and grinned. 'It's been bothering me for days — Jasmine's death. Walking into the river with her pockets full of stones. I knew there was something nagging at the back of my mind.' He looked triumphant.

'What?' Paula said. 'You're going to have to give us more of a clue.'

'Virginia Woolf. Not an American, admittedly, but another woman writer who killed herself. She committed suicide by walking into a river with her pockets full of stones. Honestly, some days I think I'm losing it altogether. Did anyone say anything about finding a Virginia Woolf book?'

Paula shook her head. 'No. But they're not very clear where exactly she went into the river. I imagine they didn't think it was important to know the precise point. Apparently there's a cycle-way and footpath that runs along the estuary. She'd parked her car near the path but they're not sure how far she walked along the bank before she walked in.'

'Do we know anybody down there who might take a look for us?' Tony asked.

The two women looked at each other, blank. 'I got nothing,' Paula said.

'Me neither. At least, not that I know of. I don't know the geographical whereabouts of all my network.'

Tony said no more. If Carol decided to pursue this, she could organise liaison with the local force. If she wasn't plunged directly into a live case. Which was always a possibility. Before he could say more, Paula started. 'My phone,' she said, turning away. She glanced back at them. 'Gotta go, it's Carol.' She disappeared from the screen, leaving Tony and Stacey staring uncertainly at each other.

'Send me what you have on those three you've identified,' he said. 'I'll see if anything jumps out at me.'

'Didn't she write *A Room of One's Own*? Virginia Woolf?'

'Yes. She said women needed a room and five hundred pounds a year if they were going to be writers. I suppose that was a kind of middle-class feminism,' he said.

'The feminism of privilege,' Stacey said. He could hear her fingers whispering over the keys. 'That's more than twenty-seven grand a year in today's money. She wouldn't have done very well on the Jobseeker's Allowance.'

'All of our victims were making their own living, though. They weren't expecting a man or the state to keep them. They were modern feminists.' Tony sighed. 'I wonder, are we making this up as we go along?'

Stacey smiled. He wasn't familiar with her smile and was surprised by its sweetness. 'Does it matter? There's enough substance here to make it worth looking into. And it's worth looking into because it needs to be dealt with.'

'And how do we do that?'

A long pause. Then Stacey said, 'I'm not sure. But I think I'll know when we get there.'

28

He was going to have to try harder, that was becoming obvious. These women were like some sort of monster in a fantasy movie. Every time you cut off one head, two more appeared. Maybe he was more attuned to what was going on in the world around him. Living with Sarah, before she'd signed her own death warrant, he guessed he hadn't been paying so much attention to what was happening in the outside world. Or maybe it was the way that social media gave a platform to anybody, regardless of how screwed-up their message was.

One thing was certain. If Daisy Morton was anything to go by, they'd go to any lengths to twist things so they looked like the opposite of what he'd meant. How could anybody think Daisy Morton's death had been an accident? How do you accidentally turn on all the gas rings and stick your head and shoulders in the oven? How do you accidentally blow up a house with yourself inside it? He'd been enraged when he'd read that interview with her husband. 'Daisy must have banged her head when she was making sure the stove was working properly.' It beggared belief.

But most of the coverage had hinted that Daisy Morton's death had been intentional. It pointed out how vocal she'd been online and how much criticism, all of it legitimate in his eyes, she'd drawn to herself. Reading between the lines, the media view was the one he wanted the world to understand — that Daisy Morton had killed herself because of the pressure from people pointing out how wrong and stupid she was.

But he'd realised he needed to step up the pressure. To turn it into a wave that nobody could ignore. And so he'd moved a little sooner than he'd planned, because Jasmine Burton played right into his hands with her little holiday in Devon. All alone in her isolated cottage. It had been child's play to wait for her to come home at the end of the evening and knock her to the ground with a leather cosh he'd bought from a militaria website months before. This time, it didn't matter so much if there was damage to her body; the actions of the water would explain any bumps or bruises. She'd dropped like a stone and he'd had a couple of anxious moments, fearing he'd killed her too soon. That would have ruined his plan; he needed her to be breathing when he put her in the water. He needed her to drown.

He'd already collected the stones from further up the estuary, where he'd also left the template text. Virginia Woolf this time. Killed herself because she was an unfulfilled childless depressive who had no idea how to be a wife. Probably a lesbian too, so all the more appropriate.

Then he'd filled Jasmine Burton's pockets with stones and driven to a slipway on the estuary where he'd dumped her on an ebbing tide. Let them try to pretend that one was an accident. It served her right, spouting her crap about how women needed to be protected from men. Women needed to learn how to behave.

There was a beauty in what he was doing, he thought. An elegance. Nobody truly felt sorry for a suicide, in spite of what bleeding-heart commentators sometimes said in public so they could sound sensitive and caring. Mostly what people felt was contempt or anger. Contempt for people who were too weak to face up to their problems. Anger for the selfishness that didn't care about the pain inflicted on the ones left behind. So when he made their deserved deaths look like suicide, he was condemning them to a complete loss of respect. A loss of value. Nobody could take their opinions seriously when these women had opted for such a selfish, easy way out.

Slowly but surely, he was getting there. He just wanted to accelerate the process. He wanted to look out at a world where the women had learned their lesson and acted properly. That was all he wanted. A world where women like Sarah would never —

He slapped himself in the face. He needed to be stronger. He wasn't going to think about what Sarah had done. The pain of her betrayal remained so intense it was like a red-hot needle being pushed into his flesh. He wouldn't dwell on what she'd done. Instead he'd focus on how it had made him understand that it was time for someone to take these women on.

Take them on and win.

29

Good sense should have kept Paula's mouth shut until Carol raised the subject. But good sense had never prevailed where her former boss was concerned. As soon as she picked up the call, Paula said, 'Congratulations. Tony told me you got off yesterday.'

'That's not why I'm phoning.' The voice was frosty. Not a great start, then.

'No, of course, sorry, I . . . '

'How would you like to come and work with me again?'

A swirl of thoughts chased each other round Paula's head. *Yes! How? Where? Doing what? Something dodgy happened here . . .* 'I don't understand,' she said.

'It's not a trick question, Paula.' Carol's voice had softened. 'Would you like to come and work with me again?'

'Of course I would. But how? I mean, you resigned. You're not a cop any more.' Paula wished she could see Carol's face. Surely this couldn't be some sort of weird joke? Or was Carol setting up as a private eye?

'As of today, I am Detective Chief Inspector Carol Jordan again. Just to clarify, in case you thought I was crossing over to the dark side and going private.'

'What? You're coming back to BMP?' Paula heard her pitch rising to a squeak but she couldn't control it. Yesterday morning Carol had been facing disgrace. Now she'd somehow become flavour of somebody's month.

'No. It's a new initiative. John Brandon's fronting it up for the Home Office. We'd be a floating MIT covering six forces, only doing murders and serious sexual assaults. Maybe the odd armed robbery, but only if the local lads were pressed and we were at a loose-ish end. We'd be a small, tight team, with the locals doing the grunt work.'

Paula couldn't quite make sense of it. *Definitely something dodgy.* 'So I'd still technically be a cop?'

'You will hold the office of constable. You'll be considered to have continuous service and your pension rights won't be affected. You'll simply be reassigned to a different unit. A regional MIT, for want of a better name. No doubt some Whitehall mandarin is racking his brains trying to come up with a suitable acronym. ReMIT or something equally stupid. But we'd be like freelances, with our own budget. No more dealing with James Blake.'

'Or DCI Fielding,' Paula muttered. 'Are you serious, Carol? This isn't some kind of wind-up?'

'Never been more serious in my life. Yesterday morning, I thought my life was being flushed down the toilet. Now, I'm looking at the best prospect in years. What's not to like?'

Paula could hear the delight. And it was starting to rise in her too. Working for Carol again, doing serious, proper investigative work, using her interview skills on criminals who deserved the best filleting possible. Oh yes, that would be worth getting up in the morning for. 'Where would we be based?'

'Obviously there'll be a lot of travel. When we're working a case, we'll be there on the ground. But our home ground will be here in Bradfield. They're giving the top floor of Skenfrith Street a makeover as we speak.'

'Coffee machine?'

'On order.'

'In that case you'd better count me in. When do we start?'

'Officially, Monday. But if you want to show up tomorrow, that'd be good too. We won't have an office yet, but I'll text you to let you know where we're going to meet.'

'Have we got any cases yet?'

Carol laughed. 'Steady on. We've not even got a whiteboard yet.'

'So, we're going to sit around and drink coffee till we do?'

'Not exactly. I thought we might need a bit of practice to hone our skills.' There was a forced casualness in Carol's tone that prepared Paula for what came next. 'We could carry on taking a look at the cyber-bullying suicides. To get our hand in.'

'Oddly enough, I hoped you might say that. Are you busy this evening?'

* * *

Alvin Ambrose reeled in his line and stared gloomily at the untenanted hook. He'd been certain there had been something there. Well, obviously, there had been. Something that had taken the bait but not the hook. Something that was getting fatter at his expense. Angling was supposed to be calming. That's why his wife had bought him a basic set of gear for his last birthday. 'Go and sit on a canal bank and chill,' she'd said. What actually happened was that he sat on a canal bank and brooded. It wasn't the same thing. Not even remotely.

He shifted his considerable bulk on the tiny stool and, with a slight shudder, slid another maggot on the hook and cast the line. He didn't often encounter maggots at work; West Mercia wasn't exactly overloaded with murder scenes. But he'd come across them enough to have no love for them, in spite of their forensic usefulness. The heat and smell given off by maggot masses chomping their way through a corpse would turn the strongest of stomachs.

Ambrose sighed and looked down the bank. Two hundred yards away, another man sat hunched over a rod and line. He'd looked suspiciously at Ambrose as he'd walked past, offering no response to the sergeant's cheerful greeting. That was another thing. He was accustomed to being the only black man in the room a lot of the time — in the pub, in the CID, in the courtroom — although it was getting better with every passing year. But in all those other places, people acknowledged him. He'd never seen another black man fishing by a canal, and he'd never come across another angler who was willing to exchange more than the most basic of greetings. His wife tried to convince him that it was because angling was such a solitary pursuit. But she hadn't succeeded. So the pastime that was supposed to make him relax and feel calmer had turned him into a frustrated misfit.

His phone vibrated, breaking into his mood. If he was lucky, it might be work. Something interesting to get his teeth into. 'Chance would be a fine thing,' he grumbled to himself, standing up so he could wrestle his phone out of the pocket of jeans that were always tight on his muscular thighs. 'No caller ID,' the screen read. Almost definitely work, then. 'Ambrose,' he said, punching authority into his tone.

'Alvin? This is Carol Jordan. Remember me?'

As if he could forget. Carol Jordan, the woman who had plunged him into the most demanding investigations of his career. A woman who could eviscerate you with a look, but also fill you with pride and self-confidence when her smile reached her eyes. 'Ex-DCI Jordan,' he said. 'This is a surprise.'

'Almost right,' she said, a bubble of laughter under the words. 'It's not ex any more. I'm back in harness and I'm building a team, Alvin.'

His heart leapt but he told himself to hold back. She'd disappointed him once before, when she'd accepted a job that would have made her his boss then shocked everyone by walking away from the whole business of being a cop. He'd heard she'd had some kind of breakdown. *Once bitten, Alvin.* 'Back in harness?'

'I've been tempted back by the kind of offer you can't refuse. I'm going to be running a free-standing MIT that will cover six forces here in the North. We'll be the visiting firemen with back-up from the locals. It's a new initiative. We could be the future, Alvin. And I want you on my team.'

'I don't know,' he said. 'I'm used to how we do things down here.'

Carol chuckled. 'You were keen enough for me to come down there and shake things up a bit. Come on, Alvin, you know you're wasted in the depths of Worcestershire. Come and join me where the action is.'

'Who else is on the team?'

'Paula — DS McIntyre. You know her, best interviewer in the business. And Stacey Chen, the queen of digital forensics. Tony Hill, of course. I'm trying to persuade Kevin Matthews to come out of retirement to be my DI. And we'll have a couple of DCs. And maybe another sergeant to do the logistics.'

'Where will you be based?'

Carol listed the six force areas they'd be covering. 'But our home base will be Bradfield. It's going to take you away from the family to start with, I appreciate that. But if it works out, there's plenty of good places to bring up kids around here. What do you say, Alvin? What's it to be? Stick with the rut or reach for the stars?'

God, but she was persuasive. He could see why Tony Hill was trapped in her orbit like a captive moon. 'When is this thing getting off the ground?'

'We start Monday.'

'This Monday?'

'No time like the present. John Brandon, my old chief constable, is running the Home Office liaison. He'll arrange your transfer.'

'You don't hang around.'

'No. Ideally, I'd like you here in Bradfield tomorrow. We need to get our skills up to speed and I'm running a little exercise for us.'

'Tomorrow? That's . . . that's . . . '

'Eminently possible. You've got an afternoon to clear your desk and sort out your caseload. If you say yes, your DCI will get the message before you've found a box to empty your drawers into. I promise nobody will stand in your way.'

He had a strange feeling that was a promise she could keep. Carol Jordan had always had a handle on how the levers of power worked. He didn't understand how she cut through the red tape and bureaucracy but she seemed to have the knack. 'I need to talk to my wife.'

She sighed. 'I suppose you do. OK, you've got an hour. Then I need an answer.' The line went dead. He realised too late he didn't have her number.

But she clearly had his.

*   *   *

Carol took a deep breath. It was tiring, keeping up the image of having everything under control. She'd got past Paula and Alvin, but she wasn't sure whether she could pull off the same trick with Stacey. When you were dealing with someone who didn't expend much energy on human relationships, sometimes it was a struggle

226

to pull the wool over their eyes because they just couldn't see the wool for the truth. Carol forced herself into action and speed-dialled.

'Good morning,' Stacey greeted her. No name, no rank, no honorific. Bets thoroughly hedged, as always.

'How's things?' Carol asked.

'Pretty dull,' Stacey said.

'Not like it used to be.'

'No. Though it's been interesting to examine the cybertrolling.'

'How would you like to get back to the interesting stuff full-time?'

A pause. Carol could hear Stacey breathing. 'Has this got anything to do with your case being dismissed yesterday?'

Now it was Carol's turn to pause. She didn't know the answer to that question and frankly, she didn't want to know. But she had to find something to say that would keep Stacey on side. Admittedly, the digital specialist thought nothing of galloping headlong through data privacy legislation when it suited her, but Carol wasn't sure if her cavalier disregard would extend to what she feared might be classified as noble cause corruption. 'Only insofar as it means I'm eligible for a job that the Home Office wants done.' It was a twisty, wriggling sort of answer, but it covered the bases, she hoped.

'It must be quite a job, to tempt you back.'

And so she explained what Brandon was offering. Stacey listened in patient silence, then said, 'There's nothing to think about. Consider me on board.'

'I'm glad to hear it. We'd have had a huge hole to fill if you'd said no.'

Stacey gave a little girlish giggle. 'I know that. And Sam? He'll be joining us too?'

Carol felt the sticky silence expand between them. *Grasp nettle, bite bullet.* 'This is a very small team, Stacey. Everyone has to bring specialist skills to the table. I realise this is awkward for you, but Sam isn't the right fit for this team.' For an awful moment she wondered whether Stacey might withdraw.

'He's a good detective,' she said.

'I'm not disputing that. I'm sorry, Stacey. It's not up for negotiation.'

A deep sigh. 'I know. This is your team. And I'm glad to be part of it. I'm disappointed not to be working with Sam again, that's all. Is that why you're leaving him out? You don't want people working together who are in a relationship?'

'No, it's not that. I want this team to have a different shape from the old MIT.'

'Your call.'

'I'll let you know where we're meeting tomorrow.'

'I'm looking forward to it.'

★ ★ ★

That left Kevin. He'd celebrated his retirement by taking his wife on a month-long cruise. According to Paula, he'd never been so bored. He'd had an offer from a former DI to join his private investigation company in Manchester, but — again according to Paula — he wasn't keen to join a profession that people disliked even more than the police. He had planned ahead for his retirement in one respect, however — he'd acquired a half-share in an allotment tenanted by an elderly uncle whose arthritis meant he couldn't manage the plot on his own. The idea of Kevin rolling up his sleeves and digging over a vegetable patch was so entertaining, Carol decided she had to see it for herself.

The allotments were invisible from the road. They occupied an acre of land surrounded on four sides by houses that fronted on busy city streets in Harriestown, a formerly working-class area of Bradfield that had steadily become more gentrified in the wake of New Labour's arrival in Downing Street. Each street of terraced redbrick houses was bisected by an alley scarcely wide enough for a car, ending in a paved area big enough for two or three to park, so the allotment holders could load up their produce when the inevitable gluts came along. Carol knew better than to drive down; any strange car would immediately be a source of curiosity and comment. Instead, she parked on one of the streets and walked down an alley, following a narrow tarmacked path round the perimeter. In the middle of the day, the place was mostly deserted. A few figures were visible, doing indecipherable things to plants and sheds.

Carol spotted Kevin immediately. His copper curls were a flaming beacon, advertising his presence fifty yards away. She stopped in the lee of a tree and watched him. He was turning over the soil in a trench, muscles working hard over his wiry frame. His washed-out green T-shirt had a broad stripe of sweat down the back. He was attacking the job as if it was personal. He paused and swiped the back of his hand across his forehead, then bent to his task again. She moved closer and when she drew level, she called his name.

He looked up, startled, swinging round, spade at the ready. Still the instincts of a front-line copper, she was pleased to see. When he clocked who it was, his flushed face displayed an almost comedy expression of astonishment. 'What are you doing here?' he demanded. Surprised, not hostile.

'Looking for you,' she said. 'Are you going to let me in?' She gestured towards the padlocked gates.

He grinned. 'I think I could manage that.' He crossed to the gates and pulled a bunch of keys out of his dirt-stained cords. 'It's great to see you,' he said, leading the way back to the shed on his lot. 'Did Stella tell you where I was?'

'No, Paula.'

He gestured to a rickety bench outside the shed. 'Have a seat. I can't do hot drinks, but I've got a couple of beers inside?'

Carol shook her head. 'Not for me, thanks. But don't let me hold you back.'

He sat next to her. 'I usually wait till I'm done for the day.'

Carol gestured towards the vegetables. 'A bit of a surprise, all this. I imagined you with your head under the bonnet of some vintage sports car, not up to your elbows in fruit and veg.'

Kevin stretched his arms along the back of the bench. 'It kind of took me by surprise. I came down a couple of times to help out my Uncle Joe, and I surprised myself with how much I enjoyed it. It's hard work, but you've got something to show for it.' He shot her a sidelong look. 'I don't have to tell you that, from what I hear.'

'There's something in what you say,' Carol admitted. 'But for people like us, I think the shine wears off after a while. We miss what we used to do. Who we used to be.'

He straightened up and took a slightly squashed pack of cigarettes from his pocket, lighting up with the familiar metallic slide and click of his battered Zippo. 'Do we?' he said on an exhalation of smoke.

'I've nearly finished the barn. I'd started wondering what I might do next. And then I got an offer I couldn't refuse.'

Kevin shifted so he could see her better. 'What kind of offer? You're not talking cold cases, are you? Only, I had that slimeball Upcher on the phone a couple of weeks ago trying to get me on board for some cold case set-up.'

'Detective Chief Superintendent Upcher? They're letting him near some actual cases?'

Kevin smiled. 'I think it's a cosmetic exercise. It didn't feel like something with much traction. I told him I'd rather concentrate on building an asparagus bed.'

They shared a conspiratorial smile. 'But you might think about it if someone offered you a proper job?'

'Someone like you, you mean?'

She nodded.

He smoked in silence for a minute. 'I'm liking my life, Carol. I potter about down here, I'm rebuilding a vintage Frazer Nash with a couple of my pals, I go hill-walking on a Monday with the lads I used to play five-a-side with. I cook dinner three nights a week.'

Carol gave an exaggerated yawn. 'Rather you than me, Kev. I could keep that up for about a month, max. Then I'd start climbing the walls. But if you're happy — ' she threw her hands in the air — 'who am I to drag you away from it?' She could see the struggle going on in his head, curiosity fighting with contentment.

'Drag me away to what, exactly?' he asked.

And so she told him. But she knew that wouldn't be enough. There had to be something extra, something that would be a counterweight to what he'd regretted and resented about his career. It was something she was uniquely placed to offer, because she'd been the one who had been the agent of his disgrace in the first place, the one who'd uncovered his betrayal and refused to bury it. Once, Carol and Kevin had worked side by side as equals, two detective inspectors on the same team. Then he'd fallen for a woman who wasn't his wife. Worse, a woman who was a journalist, who wheedled his secrets out of him in exchange for excitement and lies.

He'd been lucky to escape with his job. What saved him was that their boss hated Carol even more than he hated what Kevin had done. He'd

232

been busted down to sergeant and he'd never managed to claw his way back up to his old rank. Not only that, but he'd had to watch Carol climb even higher. Along the way, he'd lost his best friend to a cornered child killer. Another man would have grown bitter and twisted under such a weight. Another man would have done everything in his power to make Carol's life harder. Instead, he'd swallowed his disgrace, absorbed his grief and turned into a loyal, dogged colleague. But she was banking on there being a knot of unfulfilled desire deep inside him.

So she leaned her elbows on her knees and gazed across the allotments. 'I need a DI, Kevin. Paula's not ready. But you? You know what's needed. You lost the chance to show what you could do. If you come back for me, I'll make you an inspector. You'll get the rank, the salary and the pension. And when you've had enough, this place will still be here. The Frazer what's-its-name will still be there. The hills'll still be there. Stella will let you back in the kitchen. I'm not asking you to give anything up. Only postpone it.'

He looked as if he might burst into tears. 'Why me? What's so special about me? Why couldn't you leave me in peace without waving temptation in my face?'

'Because I'm a selfish cow. Because this is a hard thing, Kev. And I need all the help I can get.' Her smile was a tired, sad thing.

He flicked his smouldering cigarette butt across the allotment and watched it arc over green shoots into a thicket of twisted yellowing stalks. His sigh came from a long way down. 'I've got a horrible feeling I'm going to regret this. But I'm afraid I'll regret it even more if I refuse you. I'll do it, Carol. But only for as long as you need me. Soon as it's secure and running like clockwork, I'm off. Is that a deal?'

She stuck out a hand and they shook on it. Then they clapped each other on the shoulder with their free hands. 'I'm very happy about this, Kev,' she said, getting to her feet and walking towards the gate. She turned back to face him and grinned. 'Better get digging. Did I mention we're starting tomorrow?'

30

Tony was surprised to see how unfazed Flash was by the clamour of the city. She trotted round the perimeter of the busy Minster Canal Basin a couple of yards ahead of Carol, pausing occasionally to check out an interesting smell, but always casting quick looks over her shoulder to check the whereabouts of her mistress. Tony sat on the roof of his narrowboat, feet dangling through the hatch, hands clasped round a cup of tea, watching Carol giving the dog a break from her confinement in the Land Rover. When he'd called to suggest meeting, she'd been the one to propose *Steeler* as the venue. He'd been taken aback; these days, she usually suggested neutral ground. Then she'd explained she needed to exercise the dog and the canal towpath was as good a place as any. That was how it was these days — a moment of elation quickly deflated.

By the time they returned, Paula had called to apologise that she couldn't make it; the news of her imminent departure had arrived and DCI Fielding was leaning on her to get all her paperwork in order so nothing would fall through the cracks of the handover. But as he explained to Carol, at this point he knew all Paula did, so he could bring her up to speed.

As they clattered down the steps to the galley and saloon below, the dog's claws scrabbling on the hard surfaces, Tony said, 'It's starting to look like we might have stumbled over something real.' He flattened himself against the stove to let Carol pass, then put the kettle back on the gas.

'Well, the cyber-bullying is obviously real,' she said, sliding on to the buttoned leather banquette that ran around the table. 'And so are the suicides.'

'But I think the connection might be real too.' He put a teabag in a mug for Carol. 'You remember I said there was something bugging me about Jasmine Burton? And I couldn't put my finger on it?'

'That's where all this started from.'

'Before I come back to that ... you know Paula was talking to Shakila Bain this morning? British Asian fashion designer who got trolled and harassed for saying the demonisation of young Asian men in the media was a recruiting sergeant for jihad?'

Carol nodded. 'She said she was going to use that as a smokescreen for getting the officers running the other cases to pass on their information.'

Tony poured boiling water into the mug and stirred it vigorously. 'What happened to Shakila was nasty and brutish, no getting away from that. But at least it was Hobbesian.'

Carol groaned. 'Stop showing off. What do you mean, Hobbesian?'

'Thomas Hobbes, the man who established many of the principles of European liberal thought. Human rights and that sort of thing. He described life without them as 'nasty, brutish and short'.'

'So, let me get this right. You're saying that what happened to Shakila didn't last very long?'

'Exactly. See? You're catching on. And that's quite interesting, because in many ways she's very similar to the dead women we're looking at. And what does that tell us?'

Carol rolled her eyes as he put her tea in front of her then gingerly sat down opposite, trying not to disturb Flash who was sprawled below the table. 'I don't know, Tony, what does it tell us?'

'If there is someone — or a group of someones, because when it comes to the net, you can't rule out a bunch of lowlifes egging each other on, upping the ante all the time — but let's say it is 'someone' for the sake of argument. So if he's deliberately pushing these women in one direction, his area of concern is quite precise. It's not simply gobby women in general. Because let's face it, there's no shortage of what internet trolls regard as gobby women who need to shut the fuck up. But what's interesting about our women is that they sounded off quite specifically about men behaving badly in relation to women. He wasn't interested in Shakila because he's not Islamophobic or racist. Well, he might be, but that doesn't push his buttons in the way that women having a go at men does.'

Carol sipped her tea. From the look of faint disgust on her face, he guessed what she actually wanted was a vodka and tonic. Late afternoon, the time of day when it was almost normal to need a drink. Almost but not quite. 'That's very interesting,' she said. 'I'm not sure where it takes us, but knowing you we'll end up somewhere we didn't expect to be. Hobbesian, for fuck's sake. So what's all this got to do with what was doing your head in about Jasmine Burton's suicide?'

'Well, nothing, yet. But something did occur to me. You know how it goes. Anyway, here's the thing: Kate Rawlins had a book of poetry in the car with her when she killed herself — *The Death Notebooks* by Anne Sexton. There were pages of a poetry book all over Daisy Morton's front garden — *Ariel* by Sylvia Plath. Both poets killed themselves, and in pretty much the same way as our victims. And then the light bulb went on in my head. Virginia Woolf.' He grinned triumphantly.

Carol looked blank.

'Remember the film, *The Hours*? The one where all the writers went mad and killed themselves?'

'Vaguely. Meryl Streep, and Nicole Kidman's fake nose.'

'You don't remember how it opens? Virginia Woolf walking into the river with her pockets full of stones. Pockets full of stones, Carol. Just like Jasmine. That was the echo I wasn't hearing.'

'But there's no book.'

Tony threw his hands up in frustration. 'We don't know that. The cops down in Devon think there's nothing suspicious about Jasmine Burton's death. They don't even know where she went into the water. For all I know, the entire east bank of the Exe is strewn with the pages of *Mrs Dalloway*.'

'I think they might have noticed that. But you do have a point.' He opened his mouth to speak, but she held up a finger to silence him while she thought. Then she looked at her watch. 'More than an hour,' she said, taking her phone out. She tapped the screen and put it to her ear. 'Bear with me,' she said to Tony.

He knew when it was answered because her face lit up in a smile. The warmth, he knew, would transmit down the line. 'So, what's it to be?' she said without any preamble. She bit her lip as she waited for the answer. He could hear the rumble of a voice, then her face lit up. 'That's great news. Now, I've got a job for you. Never mind coming to Bradfield tomorrow. I want you to go down to Exeter . . . ' A pause. 'Yes, Exeter. A woman called Jasmine Burton committed suicide last week. She walked into the River Exe with a pocketful of stones. She'd been trolled on the web. You can google her, and I'll get Paula to email you more info overnight. I need you to find out or figure out where she went into the river. What you're looking for — and I know it sounds bizarre — is a copy of a book by Virginia Woolf somewhere nearby . . . No, I've no idea which book. I don't know whether it matters. Just go and look, Alvin.' A pause, more rumbling. Then she chuckled. 'No, we're not hanging about. This might be a figment of our imagination. Or it might not be. There's only one way to find out. Talk to me tomorrow.' She ended the call and let the smile spread across her face.

'Alvin says yes?'

She nodded. 'Alvin says yes. This is starting to look like it might be a team.' She turned back to her phone and started composing a text. 'I need to get Paula to do him a brief.'

'Fielding won't like that.'

'Good. The day hasn't been wasted, then.' She glanced up. 'I will never forgive Fielding for the way she treated you.'

He shrugged. 'You sorted it out in the end.'

'It should never have needed sorting in the first place.'

Tony gave a little shrug. 'So, Chinese or Indian for our celebratory dinner?'

⋆ ⋆ ⋆

Stacey understood the importance of being prepared. The more information an interviewer of Paula's calibre had at her disposal, the more chance there was of persuading the suspect — or witness — to reveal all they knew. So she'd set herself the task of garnering as much data as she could on the five people who had repeatedly trolled Kate, Daisy and Jasmine. Where they worked. Where they lived. Who their friends were. Who they texted and what they said to them. It wasn't the most demanding of tasks, but it needed concentration and care.

She was entirely absorbed in what she was doing when Sam turned up with a Thai takeaway. She paused to accept a kiss, but let him get on with setting out crockery and cutlery. She was dimly aware of him moving around, then he cut through her focus, calling, 'Dinner's on the table, come and get it.'

Stacey blinked rapidly, saved what she'd captured and headed for the table. Sam had laid out bowls and chopsticks, spoons and forks alongside plastic containers with their lids flipped off. The mixture of aromas drove work from Stacey's mind, drawing her to the food like magnetic north, reminding her of how long it had been since she'd eaten.

They loaded up their bowls with jasmine rice and green curry. 'Ah, this is good,' Stacey said. 'You went to Mango Thai in Kenton Vale.'

'I did. Because you're worth it.' He picked up a morsel of chicken with his chopsticks and popped it in her mouth. 'What are you working on? You were completely absorbed when I came in.'

Stacey wished he hadn't asked. She knew he was going to be upset when he discovered he'd been left out of Carol Jordan's team and she'd hoped they could get through tonight without her having to break the news. 'Digging up full background for Paula.'

'Does Fielding know she's got you working for her?' DCI Fielding had once tried to recruit Stacey to her CID team, but she'd been thwarted by the DCI of the intel team who had been burying the analyst under a mountain of routine work.

'It's nothing to do with Fielding.' Stacey wished she was a better liar, but she knew there was no point trying to fool Sam. It was as if he had a secret lie detector tuned in to her frequency.

Sam frowned, a coconut prawn halfway to his mouth. 'What? Has Paula moved to another team? Has she escaped Fielding?'

'Kind of,' Stacey said.

241

Her reservation was a spur to his ever-ready appetite for information. 'Come on, Stacey, don't tease me. What's the story? Whose firm is Paula working on?'

'You're not going to believe this.' She knew she couldn't divert him, but maybe she could slow him down long enough to take the sting out of the hurt and disappointment he was going to feel.

He helped himself to some pad thai, not taking his eyes off her for more than a second or two. 'Sounds intriguing. It must be hot news, I've not heard a thing.'

'There's a new Home Office initiative about to be launched. A floating MIT, covering homicides across six forces in the North, including BMP. It's an incredibly small team. It'll be relying on local officers for a lot of the work on the ground.'

Sam perked up. 'And Paula's fallen for it? Sounds like a recipe for disaster to me. The local lads will take any credit going, and the floaters will catch the blame for whatever goes tits-up. I can't believe Paula would be so naïve.'

Stacey couldn't help a frisson of relief. Better he should put it down than feel put out. 'I've signed up for it too, actually.' She gave a self-deprecating smile.

Sam laid his chopsticks on the table. Now he was alert. 'Why would you do that? Why would you sign up for something so mad? You know it's mad, right?'

She had a mouthful of food but he waited, poised like a predator who sniffs something worth chasing. She washed the food down with the cold Singha beer and gave a smile that she hoped wasn't as nervous as she felt. 'Actually, I don't think it's mad.'

Now he leaned forward, ready to pounce. 'Why don't you think it's mad, Stacey?'

'I think it's something that could be effective. The smaller forces don't get enough complex homicides to develop the right skills, and the bigger forces could make better use of the detectives they've got on other serious crimes and on developing intelligence so they can prevent stuff happening.'

He cocked his head, as if listening to his brain analysing what it had heard. 'It could also go tits-up very quickly. I suppose a lot depends on who's running the show.' His voice was deceptively nonchalant.

Stacey took a deep breath. There was no avoiding it now. 'It's Carol Jordan,' she said.

Sam looked completely gobsmacked. For a moment, his mouth moved without any sound emerging. 'How?' he said at last. 'She was under arrest last weekend. Done for drink-driving. And now she's been spirited out of retirement to run some elite squad? How the hell did that happen?'

She stared into her bowl. It wasn't often that Stacey didn't know the answers, but this was one occasion when she was quite happy in her ignorance. 'The charges were dropped. The breathalyser was faulty.'

'You're kidding.'

'Apparently it happens sometimes. Three other people had the charges against them dropped too, it wasn't only Carol.'

Sam shook his head, incredulous. 'So amazingly, just when they need Carol Jordan, all the shit magically disappears? Who's running this show?'

'Carol's running the squad. But John Brandon is the Home Office liaison.'

He snorted. 'Of course it's John Brandon. Carol was always his blue-eyed girl. He'd move heaven and earth for her. Fuck. They got her off the hook. So of course she let them pull her out of retirement and hand her the poisoned chalice. That's got to be better than being pilloried as a drunk and a loser, right?'

'I don't think it's like that, Sam. We both know how good Carol is. She's the person you'd want running an operation like this, you can't deny that.'

He made a noise of exasperation. 'All the same. This stinks. To keep Carol Jordan squeaky clean, they've let three other drunks off the hook. All for the sake of giving Carol Jordan a shiny new job.'

'You've no right to say that, Sam. You don't have any evidence to suggest Brandon interfered with the course of justice.'

He shook his head. 'You can't honestly think that. You're far too smart. Well, good for you, Stacey. You get to walk away from all the crappy routine shit you've been doing lately. You get to go back to doing all the starry stuff that leaves everybody open-mouthed in admiration. Brilliant. Have you noticed something about all this, Stacey?'

She flinched at his tone but managed to keep her voice steady. 'What do you mean, Sam?'

He leaned forward, his face full of hurt. 'I didn't come in tonight full of exciting news. I didn't get the call to join the elite. I was there, right next to you, right at the heart of her last MIT. But did I get the summons?' He paused. 'Well? Did I?'

'I asked if she was going to include you.'

'And what did she say?'

Stacey felt a hard lump in her throat. She didn't want to cry, she was determined not to cry, but his hurt pride was so obvious. She hated to see him in pain and not be able to do anything about it. 'It's a small team and she wants specialists.'

He shook his head, refusing to accept what she said. 'You're a specialist, I see that. But Paula? She's just another plod.'

'She's the best interviewer I've ever seen.' Stacey didn't want to add to his hurt but equally, she didn't know how to back down from the truth. 'Carol didn't say you weren't good enough, only that you're not right for this job. It's not the same thing.' She put a comforting hand on his arm. 'Please, Sam.'

He looked as if he was about to burst into tears. She'd never seen him so naked. 'She never liked me,' he said bitterly. 'I worked my arse off in her MIT, but when it comes down to it, it's all about her not liking me.'

'Well, she's a pretty poor judge of character, then.' She got up and wrapped her arms around him from behind. 'Let's face it, anyone who prefers Tony Hill to you has got her hormones pretty scrambled. Don't let it get to you, Sam.

Besides, when it comes to promotion, MIT is a dead end. So few opportunities. You'll climb the ladder much faster in another firm.'

He reached up and gripped her hand tightly. 'Yeah,' he said. 'I'm not going to be defeated by Carol Jordan. Not while I've got you.'

31

Detective Sergeant Alvin Ambrose hadn't been in Devon since he'd been a kid. His parents had rented a tiny flat for a week in Torquay, two cramped bedrooms for them and their four kids. His dad was a bus driver, his mother a nurse, and they were determined that their kids should make their acquaintance with the sea and the sand, just as they'd done growing up in the Caribbean. They hadn't said anything, but when they got off the train in Torquay Alvin had read their disappointment in their eyes and the slump of their shoulders. The beaches of Devon had been stunning for a six-year-old from Smethwick, a place almost as far from the sea as it was possible to be in England. But for his parents, who had been dreaming of the white sands of Barbados, it was another letdown to add to all the others they'd experienced since they'd arrived in the fifties.

The kids hadn't cared. Alvin and his siblings fell in love with the beaches and the cool salt waters of the English Channel. They didn't even notice they were the only black family on the sands and that others tended to spread their towels as far from the Ambroses as was possible. But their parents noticed, and in spite of the kids whinging in the years that followed, they never went back to the English seaside.

He recalled that holiday as the motorway

crossed the border into Devon. There had been so much casual racism when he'd been growing up. There was the full-frontal stuff as well, but what had always irked him more was the thoughtless kind. The 'But where are you *really* from?' kind, as if he didn't have a Midlands accent. One of the things he'd liked about Carol Jordan's team right from the start was that they were such a mix — gay and straight, brown and yellow and ginger — and they genuinely seemed blind to difference when it came to working together. The only thing that mattered was solving cases and saving lives. That was one of the reasons he'd worked so hard at persuading his wife to let him make this leap in the dark. The commuting would be hard on both of them but, if it worked out, moving to Bradfield wouldn't be the worst thing that could happen to them and their kids.

Already, it was more interesting than most of the investigations he'd been following at West Mercia. The briefing Paula had sent him was puzzling in one sense; nobody had reported a crime, and yet that tight little knot of passionate investigators had sniffed it out and thrown at it all the resources they could muster. Alvin knew some hard-working coppers but he'd never come across any who went looking for work.

And the putative crime itself was fascinating. How did you make someone apparently strong and in control take her own life? What could tip a woman over the edge out of nowhere? He couldn't imagine anyone pushing his own wife into suicide. The only thing that might make her reach that pitch of despair would be the loss of her children. And even then, he thought she'd struggle on for the sake of the other people who loved her. So this really was a mystery.

Earlier on the drive, Alvin had spoken to the officer who'd been dealing with Jasmine Burton's death. Sergeant Paul Westmacott spoke with the distinctive West Country accent but Alvin knew better than to misread that as a mark of stupidity. Westmacott had sounded surprised at his interest, but Alvin had tried to shrug it off with a line about Jasmine's connection to another case they were working. The last thing he wanted was to put Westmacott on the defensive by suggesting there was something more complicated going on than the local lads had spotted. So he'd sounded a bit bored and offhand, only perking up at the prospect of scones with clotted cream.

Westmacott picked up on that and suggested they meet at a café outside the city, overlooking the estuary itself. Alvin called to say he was close, and they set a time. He was five minutes early and he filled the time with a call to Paula, asking if there was anything new he needed to know. 'I don't think so. Stacey's trying to track our victims' movements via their phones and Carol and I are off to do some face-to-face digging. God knows what Tony's doing. He's got Carol's dog, so he's probably walking some canal bank between here and wherever.'

There wasn't much to say to that, so Alvin didn't waste time saying it. He'd barely finished the call when the man he assumed to be his contact pulled up in a Ford Focus with the blue

249

and yellow Battenburg livery that was as subtle as a half-brick. The uniformed officer who emerged was, to put it politely, burly. With a stab vest stretched over his gut, he looked like a black gobstopper with legs. He crossed to meet Alvin with a gait that had to roll to accommodate his thick thighs. Alvin considered himself on the bulky side, but this guy must have a major struggle to pass his annual medicals. His head was round as a football, a fringe of short black hair curling from ear to ear, leaving the top of his head exposed and bare. It was hard to guess his age; the flesh padded out any wrinkles round the wintry blue eyes. There was nothing jolly about this fat man. 'You DS Ambrose, then?' he said, looking Alvin up and down.

'That's me. Alvin, call me Alvin.' He thought about extending his hand but he wasn't convinced Westmacott would appreciate the gesture.

'Right, then. Let's go and get some grub inside us,' Westmacott said, heading for the café, a charmless between-the-wars roadhouse pub that had been painted pink in a vain attempt to make it look like a country cottage. Inside was a distinct improvement. There were a couple of dozen tables, all with smart white tablecloths and an assortment of vintage china plates, cups and saucers. About half of the tables were occupied, the customers an odd mixture of older couples in walking gear and middle-aged women huddled over teapots and gossip. Westmacott led them to the furthest corner table and plonked himself down on a dainty wooden chair that creaked slightly.

Alvin perched gingerly on the chair opposite

and picked up the menu. 'Don't know why I'm even looking. I know what I want. A couple of scones with jam and cream and a big pot of strong tea.'

The shadow of a smile flickered on Westmacott's face. 'Proper copper choice, that is.'

A skinny blonde waitress with an overload of eye make-up pitched up alongside them. 'Hello, Paul, the usual for you?' she said, her accent straight from the Baltic.

He nodded. 'Twice over, Elena. My colleague here's having the same.'

She gave Alvin a brilliant smile. 'You'll love it, I promise. Are you Devon or Cornwall?'

'I'm not from round here. I'm from the Midlands.'

Westmacott chuckled. 'She doesn't mean where are you from. She means, do you put the jam on first or the cream? In Cornwall, they do it arse about face and put the jam on first, but up here, we cream up first then pile the jam on. Stands to reason, that way you get more cream.'

Who knew? Alvin smiled and Elena took off, weaving swiftly between the tables, making sure she didn't catch the eye of anyone she didn't want to hear from. 'This your regular watering hole, then?' Trying to build bridges on shaky foundations, but you had to try.

'I like to keep my ear to the ground.'

Alvin tried to erase that image from his mind and failed. If that was what diplomacy bought you, he was done with it. 'So, what can you tell me about Jasmine Burton?'

'Why are you so interested in her? I know you

251

said she had connections to another investigation you're working, but I don't see how you coming down here adds anything. This is an open-and-shut suicide.'

'You know what it's like when your boss gets a bee in her bonnet,' Alvin said, aiming for camaraderie.

'Huh. She probably thinks we've all got straw in our hair down here. Hell, you probably think that.'

'It's not like that. Nobody's saying you didn't cover all the bases.'

'Whatever. But I'm telling you straight. There's no question about it. She had the right water in her lungs, she had her pockets full of stones. OK, she was bashed about a bit, but you always get that with bodies that go in the water. The pathologist said her injuries were post-mortem.' He gave a casual shrug. 'Like I said, open and shut.'

Alvin smiled and nodded. 'I get that. It's a bit odd that she didn't leave a note or anything for her family, though.'

Westmacott screwed his upper lip into an expression of distaste. 'They don't always do that. I reckon I've seen a fair few in my time that've topped themselves, and about half of them don't bother with a note. I reckon they're only thinking about themselves at that point. They're not bothered about the poor sods left behind to clear up their mess.'

'You spoke to the friends she visited. How did she seem to them?'

There was a pause while Elena arrived with a

laden tray and distributed tea and scones, a dish of jam and a bowl of cream that would adequately have fed Alvin's entire family. And nobody in his family suffered from lack of appetite. He gazed at it and smiled contentedly. No witnesses to his greed except a man who was fatter than him. Result.

The two men tucked in. 'The friends?' Alvin prompted.

'They were genuinely shocked. They said she was a bit subdued but they reckoned that was because of what she'd been through with the harassment and the invasion of privacy. They didn't think she was suicidal. They said they'd never have let her leave if they'd thought there was any possibility of her doing away with herself. Nice couple, they were very upset. Kept saying they blamed themselves, which is just stupid, really. This Jasmine was obviously good at hiding how disturbed she was.' He rammed more loaded scone into his mouth and chewed vigorously.

'And nobody saw her after she left them? Nobody's come forward?'

Westmacott shook his head. 'Not a dicky bird. And with her being kind of notorious, if anybody had anything to say, they'd have come forward.'

'Was there anything at the scene?'

Westmacott gave him a sideways look. Alvin waited for less than the truth. 'We don't know exactly where she went in. There was nothing to be seen, according to the PC who took a look. There's a trail for cyclists and walkers down the east side of the estuary and we found her car parked in Exton near the trail. We reckon she must have gone in somewhere between Exton and Lympstone. It's easy enough to get down to the water. Given where and when she showed up, the local lads reckon the tide was probably running quite high when she went in. But it's rocky and it's either a proper wooden cycleway or a hard-packed path and there was nothing to see.'

And nobody was looking very hard because nobody was that bothered because it looked like an open-and-shut suicide. Which, let's face it, it most likely was. Nobody's saying she was pushed. Not at this stage. Alvin concentrated on his scone and said, 'And as you say, it was an open-and-shut suicide. Presumably you took a look at the cottage where she was staying?'

'I did that myself. Nothing out of the way at all. No diary, no letters, no nothing. Just a weekend case with a couple of changes of clothes, sponge bag, two or three magazines and her laptop. It was turned on, no password. I had a look at her recent email and there was nothing of interest. Mostly work stuff, one or two exchanges with friends. But nothing to say, 'By the way, I'm popping down Devon to top myself'. Like I said, we're not turnips down here. We didn't miss anything significant because there wasn't anything significant to miss.' This was delivered in a manner that invited no argument.

Alvin was mentally making notes. *Talk to the pathologist. Where is the laptop now? How did she know where to go? What was she wearing on her feet?* 'Has the laptop been returned to her family?'

Westmacott tightened his lips impatiently then said, 'Along with all the rest of her possessions, yes. No need to hang on to it.'

Alvin had stopped at the motorway services and bought a couple of maps. He pulled them out of his pocket and said, 'To satisfy my curiosity, can you show me where exactly Jasmine's car was found?'

Westmacott wiped his mouth with the back of his hand, leaving a shiny stripe across one cheek. 'You big-city boys know how to waste your time, don't you?' He grabbed the Ordnance Survey map and unfolded it, running down the line of the estuary with his finger. 'There.'

Alvin passed him a pen. 'Could you mark it for me?' He gave a conspiratorial smile. 'Then I can show my DCI I genuinely did need to buy it for work.'

Westmacott raised his eyebrows. 'Gotcha.' He turned his attention back to the map and circled a spot. 'That's where the car was.'

'I might take a run down there. Snap off a couple of pics to keep the boss happy. She loves to get all the detail nailed down.'

'You're not going to tell me what this is really all about, are you?'

Alvin tried to look innocent. 'Like I said, it's nothing more than a tangent on something else. The boss doesn't like loose ends.'

He harrumphed. 'Yeah, right.' He swigged the last of his tea, gathered the few remaining crumbs on the tip of his finger and licked them. 'The scones are on you,' he said, getting to his feet. 'Enjoy the rest of your waste of time.' He lumbered off without a backward glance. Alvin sighed and caught Elena's eye. At least the cream tea had been worth the trip.

32

The best way to follow someone was from in front. The first time he'd read that, he'd thought it made no sense. Then he'd read on and discovered what it meant. Discover a place where your target is going to be, then get there before them. Make yourself part of the furniture so they don't even notice you. Then you can watch them without having to insinuate yourself into the picture. Because you're already there. And if luck is on your side, you might even be able to find out where they're going next so you can tail them a little more loosely.

Waiting and watching had provided the discovery that Ursula Foreman spent Thursday afternoons doing her good deed for the week by helping out at the food bank. If it hadn't been so transparent it would have made him laugh. Did she honestly think she could make up for all the trouble she caused by giving up a few hours to patronise people who couldn't even feed their families? If it wasn't for women like her encouraging women to abandon their families for so-called careers, there would be enough jobs to go around. What was the point, after all? Ursula and her kind were the first to whinge about glass ceilings that blocked their path. There were no glass ceilings in a family. When you took care of the people you loved, the sky was the limit.

The food bank was in an abandoned shop in Brucehill, a bleak council estate that consisted of three tower blocks and a cluster of low-level maisonettes linked by galleries that provided a maze of escape routes for anyone chased by the local thugs or the police. According to one of the food bank volunteers he'd got chatting to, about a third of their clientele came from Micklefield, a warren of private housing arranged in closes, courts and groves just over the hill; nice, middle-class families who had hit the financial buffers and hadn't yet encountered the government's economic upturn.

The demand for handouts was growing, according to the volunteer. So they were very happy to have new faces like his coming along to lend a hand. Apparently it took a lot of organisation to give stuff away. He stayed in the background, opening boxes and sorting donations. He knew instinctively that wasn't where Ursula would be. No quiet unseen drudgery for her, oh no. She was up front, handing out whatever pitiful allotment the supplicants were being granted that day. The more he watched her, the more he thought she definitely should be next.

There hadn't been food banks when he'd been growing up. Even poor people had known how to feed their kids. Women knew how to make a little go a long way. They could cook. This lot thought cooking was putting a pizza in the oven or a ready meal in the microwave. That's what feminism had given the country. A generation of women who had no idea how to put a decent meal on the table. Before she'd started spending so much time at Greenham, his mother had always put a proper dinner in front of him every night. Even when money had been tight and the protein had come from lentils rather than meat, she'd managed. She'd have been ashamed to take handouts. That was something else that had changed; she talked about visitors to the camp bringing donations of food with them, as if it was a good thing that the peace women were so dependent. He wouldn't have minded betting that if there had been food banks back then, the Greenham women would have been first in the queue.

And Ursula and her kind would have been egging them on. She'd have been blogging about those marvellous women who tore families apart and left children standing at their bedroom windows crying for a mum who was never coming home.

Well, things were going to start changing soon. Ursula was just another brick in the wall. It wouldn't be — no, it *couldn't* be — long before somebody put the pieces together and started writing about this spate of suicides among women who'd seen the light, recognised the damage their proselytising was doing, understood how wrong they'd been.

He'd become a lot more sophisticated with experience. He'd seized the chance with Kate Rawlins because it was there. He'd let the opportunity control him, not the other way around. Now, he would leave nothing to luck. He'd chosen the model for the next one. Marina Tsvetaeva was a Russian poet. Among her brilliant life choices had been to put her daughter in a state orphanage during the Moscow famine rather than take care of her herself. The girl had died of starvation, which only went to show the kind of thing that happened when women abdicated their responsibilities. In the end, Tsvetaeva had understood the only way to atone for her life was with her death and she'd hanged herself in her own home.

He'd had a couple of candidates in mind. But increasingly, Ursula looked like the one who deserved to die next. Now all he had to do was make a connection with her. Enough so that she'd invite him in if he turned up on her doorstep when her husband was out. He'd slip the GHB in the cup of tea she'd be bound to make. In a short while, she'd be dopey and suggestible and easy to string up from the bannisters.

Meanwhile, he would be a well-behaved and biddable volunteer. He'd keep his head down until the right moment to make his path cross hers. And then he'd turn on the charm. She'd fall for it. They all did. Until it was too late.

These women thought they were so in control. But the truth was, they were so easy.

33

The cycle path was impressive, properly constructed with timber fencing and a remarkably even surface. Alvin had never seen anything quite like it on his own patch. It was almost tempting enough to make him take up cycling. But not quite. The thought of his muscular bulk on a bike was a bit like imagining a circus act. See the bald bear balancing on two wheels! He'd settle for his own two feet, leave the bikes for the kids.

He walked north along the cycle path, taking it all in. The tide was going out, leaving a jumbled slope of rocks, some emerging barnacled and weedy from the water. But these weren't the stones Jasmine Burton had filled her pockets with. They were too bulky; he'd have struggled to lift most of them with two hands. And somehow he couldn't picture her scrambling over a wooden fence to get to the water. Alvin thought the stones signalled that she wanted a peaceful death. He was no Tony Hill, but he was imaginative enough to consider that if you wanted to let go of life with serenity, you wouldn't start by scrambling over a fence when walking a bit further would offer much easier access. Even from here, he could see the path change to beaten earth bordered by thickets of yellow reeds.

He quickened his pace, convinced he was heading in the right direction both literally and metaphorically. As soon as the fence ended, Alvin moved close to the reeds, carefully scanning them to see whether there were any signs of them having been trampled down. It had been the best part of a week since Jasmine Burton had walked into these cold grey waters, but there might be flattened areas that hadn't recovered.

But there were no traces that he could see, and about half a mile on, a new fence began. Admittedly it wasn't solid, consisting instead of a couple of cross-members between each upright. Nevertheless, Alvin thought it was probably enough of a barrier to make a psychological difference. So he turned back, and this time he walked through the reeds to the muddy margin of the estuary, glad of the wellies he kept in the boot of his car as part of what he rather grandly called his Murder Bag. With this new assignment, he might finally be able to put it to proper use. The ground was firm enough, though every now and then it sucked at a boot heel. Peering at the surface, he doubted there would be any significant footprints now, especially since it had rained heavily at the beginning of the week. But he took his time, quartering the area, crossing back and forth, eyes attuned to any incongruity.

Of course there was litter. Haribo bags and Walkers crisp packets, wrappers from Mars bars and Toblerones, plastic Lucozade bottles and Diet Coke cans. They captured his attention then lost it as quickly. He was almost at the end of the reeds when he saw something odd trapped in the bare branches of a scrubby, dead-looking thorn bush. A splash of purple, the colour of the wax grapes in the old-fashioned fruit bowl on his mother's sideboard. Was it a book? Alvin approached cautiously, as if his prey was a bird that might be unnerved into flight.

If this had been a proper investigation, if they'd had any justification for claiming as homicide this 'rehearsal', as Paula had called it, he would have stood still and called the scenes of crime team. But it wasn't and they didn't and he couldn't. Instead, he took out his phone and started photographing the scene. Not that there was anything much to see. Regardless, he paused every couple of steps and took another shot.

And yes, it was a book. He could see that now. Purple cover with white writing. The weather had curled the cover and made it hard to decipher from a distance. There was nothing else that he could see. No footmarks, no handy bits of cloth snagged on the thorns. Alvin pulled on a pair of nitrile gloves and reached for the book.

A Room of One's Own, by Virginia Woolf. He dropped it in a paper evidence bag. Not poetry, like the others. But Paula had said Tony's prediction was that there would be something by Virginia Woolf, who had apparently walked into a river with her pockets full of stones. Which thought reminded him. Rocks. He took a few steps back then cut down to the river's edge again. The firm fluvial mud along the margin was studded with much smaller stones, milled smooth by the water. They were mostly the size and shape of avocados and mangoes, Alvin decided, knowing he was going to have to describe them later. He took more photos, setting his pen among them for scale. There was no sign that any had been removed, but it would be remarkable if there had been so long after the event, in an environment that was submerged or at least teased by the river twice a day.

There was nothing more he could think of doing there, so with a few final photos, Alvin made his way back to his car. It was a long way to have come for a cream tea and a rain-sodden paperback. But since he was here, he thought he might as well make the most of it. He dialled Paul Westmacott, who answered brusquely. 'It's Alvin here,' he said. 'A quick query. Who did the post-mortem on Jasmine Burton?'

'What? You think he might have missed something an' all?'

'No, I'm just crossing the t's. And I never said you'd missed anything.'

'You didn't have to. Anyway, you'll not find anything to complain about on the post-mortem. He's a top man. Professor John Chilton, up at the university. He did it himself, none of that passing it over to students.'

'And that's where I'll find him, is it? Up at the university?'

Westmacott chuckled. 'On a Friday afternoon? Not a hope in hell. He'll be on his boat, probably halfway to France by now. Proper sailor, the professor. It'll be Monday afternoon before we see hide nor hair of him back here.'

'You got a number for him?'

'I do, but it's more than my life's worth to hand it out to anybody who's going to mess with his weekend.'

'Oh for Christ's sake,' Alvin said, exasperated. 'I'm a fucking detective. You think I can't get this guy's number in five minutes flat? If you want to be an obstructive bastard, go right ahead. But you can bet your pension on one thing. When I do speak to Professor Chilton, I'll make sure to tell him I got his number from you.'

There was a moment of stunned silence. Then, in dull tones, Westmacott gave him the number before hanging up. What had been the point of that, Alvin wondered. All it had done was to raise his blood pressure and reinforce Westmacott's idea of him as a big-city tosser. Why did people have to be so territorial? He sighed and dialled the number Westmacott had given him. The voice that answered was brisk, posh and almost feminine in its pitch. Alvin explained who he was and what he was after.

'Ah yes, the drowning. My notes are in my office at the university, I'm afraid.'

Alvin's heart sank. Westmacott had apparently been right. 'When will you be able to access them?'

'Let me see . . . I have to pick my car up from being serviced . . . Can you be there in half an hour?'

Fuck you, Paul Westmacott. 'No problem at all,' he said. Chilton gave him succinct directions and that was that. As he drove back up to Exeter, he called Paula and told her what he'd found. 'I swear to God, I sometimes wonder whether Tony sacrifices goats on the high moor tops,' she said. 'How could he have known that?'

'His brain's wired differently to the rest of us. I'm going to talk to the pathologist. Not that I'm

265

expecting anything, but I want to cover the bases. What are you guys up to?'

'I'm waiting for Carol to finish up with the builders on the third floor, then we're going to talk to Daisy Morton's husband. Like you, we're covering the bases. Listen, I know you've got to drive all the way back, but do you fancy meeting me in Solihull later? It turns out Jasmine Burton was on my team, and Stacey's tracked down her girlfriend.'

'She's another one sacrificing goats on hillsides,' Alvin said darkly. 'I think I'll be done here in an hour or so, the M5 on a Friday will be hell but I could probably meet you about seven, if that'd suit?'

'OK. We'll sort out the details later. Have fun with your pathologist.'

Those were two words you didn't often find in the same sentence. 'Fun' and 'pathologist'. But Professor Chilton turned out to be surprisingly jolly. He was short and slender with a thick mop of wavy blond hair shot through with strands of silver that played completely into the mad professor image. He had the tanned leathery skin of a sailor, wrinkles creating white lines spidering out from his eyes. 'Come in, sit down, how delightful to meet you, you're not from round here, are you?' It all spilled out in one continuous flow, accompanied by a welcoming smile and an expansive gesture towards one of the visitor chairs that faced his desk. The office was Spartan, the desk bare. The only sign that this wasn't some temporary squat were the framed photographs of racing yachts that lined the walls. Wherever Professor

Chilton kept his library, it wasn't here.

'I'm based in Bradfield,' Alvin said, stumbling over the unfamiliar location. 'We're looking into a group of suicides of women who have been bullied online and we want to rule out any suspicious circumstances.'

The professor rubbed his hands together, as if he were washing them. 'Of course you do, why would you not? But you sound more like Birmingham than Bradfield, and your poor dead woman was from there, so I wondered, you know? Now, let me find my notes . . . ' He opened a drawer in his desk and produced a green folder. 'Here we are.' He opened it and frowned in concentration. He looked up. 'I can give you a copy if you want to take one away with you?'

Alvin nodded. 'But if you could run through the key points?'

Another cheery grin. 'Naturally. Healthy, well-nourished young woman. The cause of death was drowning. It was estuary water in her lungs, so we know she wasn't shoved under in the bath or swimming pool then dumped. We know she ate dinner with her friends — Thai chicken curry, green salad, apple crumble and custard — and we know they finished eating around nine o'clock. She had no alcohol in her system. I'd estimate the time of death, based on the stomach contents, at somewhere between 1 a.m. and 3 a.m.'

'What about drugs?'

'I won't have the toxicology report for at least a week yet.'

'Were there any injuries consistent with her being violently handled?'

Chilton gave him an inquisitorial look, bright eyes like a blackbird who'd caught a glimpse of a worm. 'Interesting question, but one that's very difficult to answer. The sea tends to give bodies a bit of a battering. Waves, rocks, soft tissue — it's no contest. If they've not been in the water very long, they can look as if they've taken a beating even though nobody's laid a finger on them. There were no marks on Jasmine Burton that were inconsistent with that conclusion. But equally, some of those contusions could have happened close to death. Even saying that, they could have been entirely innocent. It's a rocky shore there. If she took a tumble on her way to the water's edge, she'd probably have bruised herself. So my answer to you, Sergeant, is that there is no way of knowing.'

It was a long-winded way of saying 'no idea'. 'Makes sense. Thanks for clearing that up. Did she have shoes on when she was washed up?'

'One trainer. New Balance. The laces had worked their way into a tight knot, which is why it was still on her foot.'

Alvin made a mental note to check what Jasmine had been wearing earlier in the evening. It might be useful to know whether she'd gone back to her cottage in between leaving her friends and walking into the Exe. Or it might be completely irrelevant. 'What else was she wearing?'

Chilton flicked back to the beginning. 'What you'd expect. Relatively unscathed because she was only in the water for twenty-four hours or so before she washed ashore. Jeans, pants, sweater, long-sleeved top, bra. And over them all, a

268

padded coat, mid-thigh length. The pockets were filled with stones then zipped up. It wasn't a huge additional weight ... Here we are, 7.93 kilos. But it would be enough to affect her natural buoyancy. And of course she would have tired more quickly if she'd had second thoughts.' He closed the folder and sighed. 'People have this romantic notion that drowning is a peaceful way to go. Trust me, it bloody well isn't.' He tossed the folder across the desk to Alvin. 'There you go. I'll have my secretary make me another copy.' He stood up. 'It's been a pleasure, Sergeant, but other voices beckon me, as I imagine they do you.'

Alvin walked back to his car, brow furrowed in thought. From one perspective, nothing he had learned shed any light on the last hours of Jasmine Burton. But if you looked at it from the angle suggested by Tony Hill, quite a different picture began to emerge. Once was interesting; twice was a coincidence; three times was a pattern. And the rule of thumb was, three plus one is a serial killer.

34

There was something strangely comforting about the familiarity of it. Paula driving, Carol in the passenger seat, eyes on the road but her mind busy elsewhere. She was jacked up on a mixture of emotions — happiness at being back doing what she used to do best; anxiety that she'd lost her touch; and the low thrum of excitement that came from being on the trail of a killer. For even though a dispassionate observer might dismiss what they were doing as a crazy fantasy built on imaginary foundations, Carol knew there was something real and dangerous underpinning this investigation. She'd heard colleagues dismissing that kind of certainty as a hunch, or feminine intuition. But Tony had once explained to her that these convictions were based on a web of subtle and often subconscious indicators knotted together by the threads of experience. 'You might not be able to provide a logical explanation. That doesn't mean there isn't one,' he'd said. 'Trust yourself. We tend to jump to conclusions for good reasons.'

'Tell me what we know about Daisy Morton's background,' she said now as Paula threaded her way north through the city traffic.

'Bradfield born and raised. Respectable working class. Dad was a plumber, mum worked in the local newsagent. Daisy married young — she had two kids by the time she was twenty-two. They're grown up now, both at university. One in

Edinburgh, the other in Bristol.'

'That's hard on them, losing their mother while they're in the thick of doing their degrees. That'll fuck you up,' Carol said, remembering how vulnerable they'd all been in those days under their carapace of cool.

'I see it with Torin every day, that damage. I'm amazed by how well he's coped. I'd have gone right off the rails in his shoes. I hope Daisy's kids find the same resilience.'

'Hopefully they'll have people in their lives like you and Elinor. So, Daisy had her kids early? Then what?'

'When the children started school, she trained as a teacher. She'd been working part-time ever since she graduated. She taught four mornings a week at Harriestown Primary, the same school she went to when she was a kid. Her husband John is a full-time trade union official, and she became involved in local politics when she started teaching. She'd been a Labour councillor for just over six years. She was well-liked, although she wasn't scared of controversy.'

'A bit of a headline-grabber?' Carol thought she knew the type. Heart in the right place, but not averse to the limelight.

'Well, she was no stranger to the front page of the *Sentinel Times*,' Paula admitted. 'But nobody's had a bad word to say about her since she died.'

Carol harrumphed. 'They never do. Look at the way they treated Jimmy Savile. He was practically lying in state in Leeds Cathedral before the truth started to come out. Not that I'm suggesting Daisy Morton was anything like that. Just, you know, death puts people on a pedestal they never inhabited in life. You have to let the dust settle before you get near the truth. But tell me more about Daisy.'

'Stayed married to John. They lived in the house that blew up for fifteen years. Bought on a mortgage via John's employers that has five years to run. Nothing to indicate any problems in the marriage.'

'Except that he didn't know she was suicidal.'

'Exactly,' Paula said.

'Which means either they were a lot less close than he'd like us to think, or else she wasn't suicidal at all. So where is he staying now that his house is in ruins?'

'He's with Daisy's brother Phil and his family. Phil Adamson. He owns a local chain of butcher shops, he's done well for himself. Nice house up by the golf course, plenty of room for him and his wife and their two teenagers with a bit to spare for the grieving widower. Actually, from what Franny said, they're all grieving. They were a close family. Phil has a place in Spain, they all used to go over there together.'

Carol felt a momentary stab of pain. She understood loss; she'd had a brother, been close, shared space as adults. She knew that for John Morton and his family, the journey of grief was only beginning. If this had been suicide, he'd know the same burden of guilt she carried too, though for different reasons. 'Did Franny have anything to say about the threats against Daisy? Had she contacted the police?'

'No.' Paula turned into a broad tree-lined

avenue. Through the gaps between the substantial semi-detached houses, Carol caught glimpses of the unnaturally vivid green of the golf course. Living somewhere like this, you could almost forget you were part of a seething, diverse city, crime always a lurking presence. Up here, there was an illusion of calm prosperity. But behind those well-tended front gardens and smartly painted front doors, the truth was often just as nasty as you'd find in any inner-city alley. Paula slowed, checking the house numbers, then stopped outside a gabled mock-Tudor house fronted by a monoblock driveway. 'I said we'd be happy to come and talk to him at work, but Morton said he'd rather see us here.'

The glossy black front door was opened by a well-groomed woman in her forties. Her understated make-up blanded out any signs of mourning but her expression was serious. Carol gauged her wardrobe as Marks & Spencer rather than anything more extravagant; her black trousers and dark plum jumper suited her unremarkable figure and spoke of practical good sense. 'I'm Trish Adamson,' she said in response to their introduction. 'John's sister-in-law. Come on in, he's through in the conservatory. Would you like some coffee? Or tea?'

'That would be kind. Coffee, please,' Carol said.

'We're all still in a state of shock,' Trish said, leading the way towards the rear of the house. 'Every morning when I wake up I have to remind myself that Daisy's gone. She was so full of life, it's impossible . . . ' Her voice tailed off as she opened the door into a compact conservatory with a panoramic view of the golf course. A big man was hunched up in a wicker armchair, folded in on himself like a bird at rest. 'John, it's the police.'

Carol introduced them again as Trish withdrew. John Morton said nothing, simply acknowledging their presence with a tight little nod. Carol sat opposite him, taking in his long gaunt face, the dark hollows under his eyes. And the two-day stubble on his cheeks. His dark hair was shot with white, lank with the need of a wash. 'Thanks for agreeing to talk to us,' Carol said.

He moistened his top lip with the tip of his tongue. 'All I want is an answer.' His voice was dry and broken, as if his throat were damaged.

As they'd agreed, Paula took over. 'I appreciate that. And we're here to review the investigation, to see whether anything was missed at the time. I wonder whether Daisy said anything to you about something completely unexpected happening that day?'

He sighed. 'Not a thing. Look, you must hear this all the time from people after someone kills themselves. But Daisy wasn't the kind of person to commit suicide. She loved life. She loved her kids, she loved her job, she loved me.'

'She'd been at the eye of a storm for the last couple of weeks of her life,' Paula said.

He smiled with his mouth, but his eyes misted with tears. 'That didn't bring her down, believe me. She relished a fight. Daisy always said that was how you knew you were on the right track.

When the opposition came out fighting.' He looked up as Trish came in with a tray. 'Isn't that right, Trish? Daisy loved to take on her critics.'

Trish put the tray down and handed out mugs of instant coffee. 'That's right. She stood up for what she believed in and she didn't care who stood against her. She'd always been like that, even when she was a lass. She never took any nonsense from anybody.'

'But she'd had some particularly vile abuse on social media. I've seen some of what was directed at her and it was horrible. Didn't that upset her?'

John held his mug to his chest as if he needed the warmth. 'It shocked her a bit at first. But then it made her angry. That was how she was. She used the hostility to fuel her own spirit.'

'But something cut through that spirit,' Paula said. 'Do you have any idea what that might have been?'

'We've asked ourselves that every day since it happened,' Trish said. 'And we come back to the same answer. She never killed herself. It was some freak accident. The coroner agreed with us, he gave the open verdict, he knew it wasn't suicide.'

John stared into his mug. 'She would never have done something so selfish. All I can think is that she was maybe cleaning the oven and she was overcome with fumes. And the gas filled the house, and when somebody called her mobile, the spark set off the explosion. Nothing else makes sense.'

Stacey had accessed the forensic report into

the explosion, so Carol knew there had been no trace of oven cleaner at the scene. She also knew that Daisy had died from asphyxiation as a result of inhaling natural gas, and that wasn't something that happened by accident. 'Do you think she was perhaps not paying as much attention as she normally would because she was distracted by the abuse she was getting? Because it had gone beyond the online stuff, hadn't it? I imagine some of what was happening must have been quite frightening.'

'The brick through the window was,' John said. 'It made me scared for her, but Daisy was adamant that it was a coward's way. She said people who throw bricks are too weak to do anything face to face. And what happened proved it.'

'There is one other thing that puzzles me,' Paula said. 'When I was reading the reports, I saw there were book pages scattered all over the front garden.' Carol couldn't help admiring her sergeant's style. She somehow managed to combine acquiescence and compassion and still move the interview forward.

'She read a lot,' Trish said. 'Fighting for the library service, that was one of her big causes.'

'She'd have had a fight on her hands recently with that one,' Paula sympathised.

'She understood that books pave the way for working people to improve their condition in life,' John said. It sounded like a line he'd delivered more than once.

'So she was a fan of Sylvia Plath?'

Trish frowned. 'She never said. I assumed it

was a private thing, poetry. John?'

He looked dazed. 'I don't know. I don't remember her reading poetry. But she read all sorts that she didn't share with me. I'm a history man, me.'

'Why are you interested in a book of poems?' Trish asked.

Paula gave a self-deprecating smile. 'I'm a big Sylvia Plath fan myself, I was just curious, that's all.' And then the question to move the conversation away from the anomaly, so that wouldn't be the last thing they remembered talking about. 'This latest campaign of Daisy's — asking dads to step up to the plate? Was this the first time she'd addressed this issue in such a public way?'

Trish and John looked at each other, as if that would provide an answer. John shook his head. 'She'd mentioned it to me, in passing. But she'd never gone properly public with it before. Mostly she talked about local stuff. But the party were pushing her to consider standing for parliament and she wanted to show she could manage a bigger stage.'

'But she told me they liked that she'd stirred things up. That she was someone who could draw attention to issues,' Trish added. 'She was on her way up. That's what makes losing her so much worse. Especially in a such a tragic accident.'

John straightened up in his chair. 'Like Trish says, it has to be some kind of freak accident. Daisy would never have killed herself. And if somebody was going to do away with her, they'd have made it obvious, wouldn't they? Otherwise there would be no point.'

35

One question kept rattling round Tony Hill's head as he marched along the canal towpath, eyes on the ground, dog at his heels. What kind of serial killer wants their crimes to stay hidden? He'd investigated several, he'd interviewed others and read about dozens more. They generally didn't want to be caught, at least not at the start of their project. But they wanted their activities to be headline news. They wanted notoriety, respect and fear. They wanted to be acknowledged. But this killer — and Tony was convinced by now that there was a killer — seemed determined to stay below the radar.

In his experience, nothing enraged a killer more than someone else taking credit for his handiwork. A tiny part of them might be satisfied if blaming someone else meant they were left alone to go about the business that drove them so hard. But much bigger than that was the sense of grievance that someone else was reaping the glory — as they saw it — for their successes. But whoever was behind the deaths of these women appeared to be content with invisibility. An invisibility so absolute that in the eyes of the world, he didn't even exist.

Flash stopped to investigate a particularly intriguing smell and Tony paused too, finding a gap in his thoughts to feel surprised that he was actually paying attention to the dog. Normally when he was walking to think, he was so absorbed in his thoughts that nothing else penetrated. But the dog ticked some box in his brain that meant he was linked to it without making a conscious connection. He wondered whether the roots of his behaviour lay in his deep past, bound to the first person who had ever shown him love. Joan, the dinner lady who had taken on rescue dogs and later, the young Tony, a rescue boy. Joan, who had saved him from the otherwise inevitable consequences of a home without love, without affection, without compassion. He'd been a connoisseur of pain and loneliness till Joan had taken him under her wing on the pretext that she needed a hand with the dogs.

He'd always believed he didn't care much about the dogs. That it had all been about Joan and her brisk kindness. But perhaps he'd been wrong about that. He'd taken so readily, so unexpectedly to Flash. Maybe this mad-eyed collie had plugged into something so deep he'd never acknowledged it before. Not for the first time, Carol Jordan had opened something up for him.

Flash darted on ahead and he resumed his contemplation. So what reason could there be for a killer who wanted to hide his crimes, his identity, his very existence? The answer had to lie in the crimes themselves. This was a killer who was sending a message that was more important than the simple satisfaction of his ego. If he was in the limelight, the message would somehow be obscured. And that was the opposite of what he wanted.

The next step was to figure out what that message was. If Tony could tease that out, it might offer a path to the killer himself. It must have something to do with the women writers whose work formed part of the crime scenes. Inevitably, it would also be connected to power and control. And that linked in to the other key question that Tony needed to answer before he sat down again with Carol's new MIT. Was his target killing at one remove, by driving his victims to a place where the only way out was to take their own lives? Or was his a more active role? Was he actually hands-on, murdering them in a way that could pass for suicide?

When he knew the answer to that question he'd be a damn sight closer to finding the underlying explanation for whatever was going on here. Once they had that, they could pool their considerable skills to find a killer that nobody but them believed in.

★　★　★

Paula was pleased to discover that Alvin chose the same kind of place for a rendezvous as she would have. It was a proper pub, lacking loud music, supplied with craft beers and frequented by people old enough to be on their second major relationship. She treated herself to a half-pint of Hook Norton and found a quiet corner where she could update her notes on the interview with John Morton. Sylvia Plath was interesting. So was the fact that this was the first time Daisy's controversial views had taken flight

280

from the purely local to a wider audience. The other two victims had already had a higher profile; if someone was looking for victims, he would have come across them more readily than the old Daisy. But the new Daisy, the one in touch with her political ambitions, she was visible in a way she hadn't been before. It made Paula think they were looking for someone used to moving around the country, not someone bound to one place and uneasy in others.

She was pondering the implications of this when Alvin arrived. He stopped at the bar for a drink, raising his hand in the traditional interrogative gesture to Paula, who shook her head. He lowered his frame on to the stool opposite her and carefully centred his pint on a beer mat. 'Too much driving today,' he said, stifling a yawn.

'But you got a result,' Paula said. She'd still been with Carol when Alvin had called to pass on his news. 'Three's the charm.'

He took a delicate sip of his beer, savoured the taste, then took off a quarter of the glass in one easy swallow, smacking his lips with pleasure. 'I'm not entirely sure what the hell I'm doing here. Is this some kind of dry run? Are we going through the motions and playing with people just to get ourselves up to speed? Because if that's what's going on here, I'm not happy about it. We shouldn't be using real grief like a playpen.'

Paula scratched her eyebrow. 'I think it started as something Tony thought was a bit odd. He likes odd. But he usually keeps it to himself. Only, this time, he shared it with Carol, just when all this started to take shape. And once we looked at it a bit more closely, it began to feel like something that was happening for real.'

Her explanation seemed to appease Alvin. He drank some more beer and visibly relaxed. 'So tell me who we're going to see.'

'Jasmine Burton's girlfriend. Her name is Emma Cotterill and she's an architect. Works for the city council. According to Jasmine's secretary, they'd been together for around eighteen months. They didn't live together but they spent a lot of time together. If anybody knew what was going on inside Jasmine's head, it was Emma.'

Alvin sighed. 'Poor woman. It's bad enough the person you love kills themselves without having to dig it all up again for the likes of us.'

'Except that it might not have been as straightforward as that. And what we find out might make it feel a bit better.'

'I suppose.' He drained his pint. 'Come on then, let's get it over with.'

The house was a peculiar infill in a street of individually designed houses from between the wars. It looked like a miniature ocean liner, frontage like a prow, windows like portholes. Although it was clearly modern it had the feel of art deco about it. When Emma opened the door, Paula couldn't help thinking the architect had designed herself to match the house. Her hair was raven black and cut in a geometric bob. Her make-up resembled an advert from the twenties, and she wore a boat-necked striped sweater over the sort of bell-bottom trousers traditionally worn by stage sailors. 'You must be Sergeant

McIntyre,' she said, meeting Paula's eyes unflinchingly. Her accent was generically Southern, not a trace of Midlands creeping through.

'That's right. And this is DS Ambrose.'

Her perfectly shaped eyebrows rose. 'A brace of sergeants. I didn't realise you went around in pairs. Might I see your ID? We're always being warned on *Crimewatch* to take nothing on trust.' Her smile was as brittle as her words.

Channelling Dorothy Parker, just to match everything else, Paula thought as they followed Emma upstairs to a living room that had a glass wall overlooking the garden. The furniture here was thankfully contemporary, a long plum-coloured sofa and three pale grey armchairs clustered round a group of three tear-shaped low tables. It was a room that suited Emma but it wouldn't fit many other people, Paula thought. There would be no room for Torin's trainer-clad feet and nothing that matched Elinor's understated elegance.

Emma gestured at the chairs and sat down opposite them. No offer of tea or coffee or anything stronger. 'I'm curious,' she said. 'I wasn't Jasmine's next of kin so I heard what had happened on the radio news, like most people who knew her. You're the first police officers to come to my door, and you're not local.' She registered Paula's surprise. 'I checked. I'm not stupid. I know how devious journalists can be.'

'We're investigating incidences of extreme cyber-bullying,' Paula said.

'We're trying to identify persistent offenders so we can close them down,' Alvin added.

'And we thought that Jasmine might have talked to you about what she went through.' Paula produced her most sympathetic expression.

Emma smoothed her hair with one hand. 'Of course she talked to me. For the last couple of weeks of her life, that's more or less all she talked about. She was trying so hard to put a brave face on things, to stand up for herself in public, but privately she was unravelling.'

'That must have been hard for you,' Alvin said.

Emma sighed and turned her eyes wistfully to the darkness beyond the window. Paula wasn't entirely convinced. 'It was awful. To see someone so strong and self-assured coming apart before my very eyes. I did my best to help, but the attacks were relentless. I told her to stop going online, to let them shout themselves hoarse then move on, but she was drawn like a moth to a flame.'

'Did she consider reporting it to the police?'

Emma looked down at the floor. 'She thought that she wouldn't be taken seriously. It seems like the only cases where there are ever prosecutions against trolls is when property's involved, like in the riots.'

'That's not strictly true,' Alvin said. 'People have been prosecuted for threats of death and arson.'

'Not many,' Emma said tartly. 'Not enough to shut the evil little fuckers up.'

An awkward pause. Then Paula said, 'Did Jasmine have any strategy for dealing with it?'

'She was convinced it would blow over.

They're like magpies. Give them something more shiny to chase and they're off. She thought it was a matter of hanging on till life returned to normal. And actually, it was easing a little. Hardly noticeable, but a little bit less every day. That's what makes her death so hard to take.'

'What do you think happened?' Paula asked. A nice, open question to see how the land lay.

'She went off for a few days' peace and quiet. I made her promise not to do the social media thing, but she probably didn't stick to that, given how things turned out. I'm only guessing here, because I didn't speak to her that last day. I had a series of meetings and I knew she was having dinner with friends. I expected her to call me when she got back to the cottage. We facetimed most nights before we went to sleep. But I wasn't unduly concerned when she didn't make contact. I assumed she was having a good time and she'd got back late.' The mask slipped and Paula caught a moment of genuine pain.

'But she wasn't,' Paula said gently.

'No. She wasn't.'

'Did you think she was suicidal?' Alvin asked.

'Did I think she was suicidal? What kind of bitch do you think I am? Do you think for one moment that if I'd believed she was suicidal I'd have let her out of my sight?' Emma's anger subsided as quickly as it had flared. 'But you're right in a way. When I heard the news, I was shocked. But . . . I sort of wasn't surprised, if that makes sense? I thought she was more fragile than she was prepared to admit.' She sighed and clasped her hands tightly in her lap. 'But obviously I wasn't thinking it through. I should have understood how close to the edge she was. I let her down.'

'In my experience, you can't stop someone who's determined to take her own life,' Alvin said. 'It's not your fault, Emma. Do you think it's possible that the internet bullying pushed her that far?'

Emma nodded. 'I do now. I didn't think she was that desperate, but obviously I was wrong.'

'I'm sorry,' Paula said. 'But DS Ambrose is right. It's not your fault. There's one thing that's puzzling us, though. Jasmine didn't leave a note. Did she send you any messages? A text? An email? A letter, even?'

Emma shook her head. 'No. No word. And that hurts, believe me. I thought I meant more to her.'

'A lot of people don't leave notes,' Alvin said, his deep rumble conveying a weight of sympathy. 'I think they reach a point where they're numb. They're not seeing anything or anyone beyond the pain.'

'We do think Jasmine left something behind, though,' Paula said. 'Was she a fan of Virginia Woolf, by any chance?'

Emma looked bemused. 'Virginia Woolf?'

'She was a writer.'

Emma shook her head impatiently. 'I know who Virginia Woolf is, for heaven's sake. I don't think Jasmine ever mentioned her, though. We both read, but not that kind of thing. I read biographies mostly, but Jas was a big crime fiction fan. What on earth has Virginia Woolf got

286

to do with what happened to her?'

'They both chose the same method. Walking into the river weighed down with stones. And there was a copy of one of Woolf's books found on the shore where we think she probably went in,' Paula explained.

'A book? Which book?'

'It's called *A Room of One's Own*.'

Emma frowned. 'I've never heard of it, never mind read it. What's it about?' She gave a shaky little laugh. 'Obviously not cyber-bullying.'

'It's an essay. Not a novel. She's explaining why it's so hard for women to develop as writers. She says if you're going to be a writer you need a room of your own and five hundred pounds a year.'

Clearly baffled, Emma shook her head. 'All very commendable but nothing to do with Jasmine. I don't think she had any secret ambition to be a writer. She was doing a job that she loved, and doing it well. But those bastards undermined her so much she ran away from all of us.' She looked Paula in the eye. 'You people need to do your job. Track those shits down and prosecute them. Destroy their lives the way they destroyed Jasmine.'

36

It was almost like old times, walking through Bellwether Square on a Saturday morning first thing, before the shopping crowds had taken possession. Carol had crossed those worn York stone flags more times than she could count, heading down from the old MIT office through the warren of medieval alleys and courts that spread out behind the square. Her hairdresser, Wendy, had occupied a corner site opposite an old-fashioned cobbler and a designer handbag shop since she'd first opened her own salon twenty years before. Her appointment book was always full; you had to work your way up via one of the junior stylists before you had any chance of making it to Wendy's client list.

Carol had jumped the queue years before thanks to John Brandon's wife Maggie, who had been one of Wendy's first clients. Since then, she'd only ever gone elsewhere for a haircut when circumstances had forced her away from Bradfield. Even when she'd been based in East Yorkshire, she'd driven across the Pennines every five weeks to submit to Wendy's flying scissors. So today, to mark her return to service, Carol had made an appointment for a haircut.

She cut through the alleys with a faint feeling of trepidation. She hadn't been near Wendy in months. When her hair had become too annoying, she'd simply gone to the village salon where some anonymous junior had hacked it into something approximating a shape. Caring about how she looked felt like an impossible vanity in the wake of her brother's death. Wendy would be affronted at the end result.

Carol pushed open the door and Wendy peered over her glasses from behind the podium where the appointment book was guarded. 'Sorry, we don't see patients without an appointment,' she said, her tone caustic.

'Very funny,' Carol said. 'I know it's bad.'

'Bad? I've seen better-looking road traffic accidents. Who did that to you?'

'You don't want to know.' Carol shrugged off her coat and hung it on the rack by the door.

'I do, I want to put a contract out on them for bringing the profession into disrepute.' Wendy shook her head as she seated Carol. 'Carol, what were you thinking? Once, in an emergency, that I could understand. But this? This is wilful vandalism. You've got lovely hair, you should respect it.'

'And how have you been, Wendy?' Carol let herself relax into the chair as Wendy swivelled and lowered it so her head was over the washbasin.

'Busy,' she said, soaking Carol's hair and shampooing it briskly. 'Too bloody busy. I haven't been on holiday this year yet. And they say Lincoln freed the slaves.' Massage, rinse. Both women fell silent as Carol luxuriated in the pampering. Shampoo, massage, rinse. Condition, rinse.

When she was upright again, Carol tried to explain her absence. 'I've been renovating a barn,' she said. 'Out in the middle of nowhere.'

289

'What happened to coppering?' Wendy met her eyes momentarily, then went back to cutting and razoring.

'I thought I was done with it. But apparently it's not done with me.'

'Well, I'm glad to see you back.' They talked of nothing much as Wendy carried on. 'I think we're about done here,' she said at last, working some wax into the tips of Carol's hair and surveying the result in the mirror. 'Nothing short of a miracle.'

As she spoke, the door opened and a young woman with a terrifying shock of pink and ginger hair came bounding in clutching a newspaper and a carton of coffee. 'You'll never believe — ' Then she caught sight of Carol and blushed a deep unbecoming scarlet.

'You're late,' Wendy said.

'I thought we weren't opening till ten.'

'Hi, Tamsin,' Carol said.

'I opened early for Carol,' Wendy said. 'You remember Carol?'

Tamsin couldn't meet her eye. 'Hi, Carol.' She gave Wendy a beseeching look. Wendy paused. Carol couldn't quite see what was going on behind her, but it looked as if Tamsin was showing Wendy the paper.

'Ah,' Wendy said on a long exhalation. 'Carol, I'm guessing you haven't seen this morning's paper?'

'No, should I have?'

Wendy pursed her lips. 'I'd say so.' She plucked the paper from Tamsin's grasp and laid it with surprising gentleness on Carol's lap. The front page of the early edition of the *Sentinel Times* featured a large photograph of Carol, in mid-laugh, head tipped back, glass in hand. *Top Cop in Drink-Driving Mystery*, the headline screamed.

The room swam in front of her eyes. For a wild moment, she almost believed it was a tacky practical joke. But nobody leapt out to say, 'Surprise!' Wendy and Tamsin were both staring at her in the mirror in consternation. Carol forced herself to read on.

★ ★ ★

Mystery surrounds the dropping of a drink-driving charge against a retired top detective days before she was rehired to run a new crack squad.

Carol Jordan was a detective chief inspector with Bradfield Metropolitan Police until she retired recently.

Last Saturday night, she was stopped by police near her home on the West Yorkshire moors and breathalysed. According to a police source, she was 'well over the limit'. Later that night she was charged with drink-driving at Halifax police station.

She was due to appear before Halifax magistrates on Wednesday, but the Crown Prosecution Service told the bench the breathalyser had been faulty. Charges against Jordan and three other motorists were dropped as a result.

Our source said, 'This was a bolt out of the blue for us. We knew nothing about any faulty breathalyser till it came up in court. And none of our breathalysers has been taken out of service. Something very odd has gone on here.'

Two days after the collapse of the case against Jordan, she was revealed as the boss of a brand-new regional Major Incident Team in a Home Office initiative to cut costs and streamline homicide investigations.

A Home Office spokesman said, 'We have absolute confidence in DCI Jordan. There is nobody better qualified to run the new unit.' He refused to comment on what happened at Halifax Magistrates' Court.

Jack Lorimer, who was one of the other motorists who escaped prosecution thanks to the faulty breathalyser, said, 'I'm very glad that I was proved to be safe behind the wheel of my car. The police wouldn't listen when I said I couldn't possibly be over the limit, but I was right.'

DCI Jordan was not available for comment.

Carol folded the paper in half and handed it back to Wendy. 'Well, forewarned is forearmed,' she said, somehow managing to keep her voice steady. 'Thanks for letting me see that.'

'They make it sound like something dodgy went on,' Tamsin blurted out.

'That's what newspapers do,' Wendy said, tossing the paper into the bin. 'They take something perfectly straightforward and twist it till it looks like something completely different.' She brushed the loose hair from the protective overall Carol was wearing. 'Nobody that knows you could take this seriously.'

Carol stood up and slipped her arms free.

'Nice of you to say so, Wendy. But there's a lot of people out there don't know me from a hole in the ground.'

'Don't be daft. You're a local hero. The woman who masterminded the hunt for Jacko Vance. Not to mention all the other bad bastards.'

'That was yesterday's chip papers.'

Wendy put a hand on her arm. 'Never mind what the papers say. Fuck 'em. You're better than that, Carol. Now get out there with that bloody marvellous new haircut and put the world to rights.' She turned to Tamsin. 'And you, get the kettle on. We'll have our next client in ten minutes.'

Carol went to the podium to pay but Wendy shook her head. 'I'm not taking your money today. It's good to see you back.'

'I can't let you do that, Wendy.'

'There's a condition. You never, ever let that bloody savage loose on your hair again. It causes me actual physical pain to see lovely hair like yours butchered like that. Now bugger off and stop making the place look untidy.' She pushed Carol's hand with her wallet back into her bag. 'Don't brood. It'll be forgotten by Monday.'

But Carol couldn't help brooding. As she walked back to her car, she imagined people staring at her. The implications of the sensational article were obvious. Something corrupt had happened behind the scenes at Halifax Magistrates' Court. Which was nothing less than the truth. John Brandon had painted it as a good thing, a positive act; now it was exposed in all its ugliness. She was headline news for all the wrong reasons. Maybe Wendy was right. Maybe people had seen her as a hero.

They wouldn't now.

She'd be tarred with the label of bent cop. Drunk and bent. Exactly the sort of person you'd want investigating the murder of your child, your wife, your father. Every local nick they walked into, looking for support, they'd be faced with officers mutinous or contemptuous, laughing behind their hands at the drunk who'd had to be bailed out. The likes of Blake and Fielding and yes, John Franklin, would love every minute of her discomfiture and shame. John Franklin. Of course. She'd shamed him and his colleagues in the past and now he'd taken the chance to slap her down in return. Who else could supply anonymous quotes from inside the West Yorkshire force? She should never have asked them to call him. She'd invited the enemy into the tent and her new role must have seemed like the ultimate affront to him. Shopping her to the press was the perfect policeman's payback. Public humiliation coupled with permanent damage to her ability to do the job.

By the time she got back to her car, her hands were trembling and her mouth was dry. She wanted a drink more than she'd ever wanted anything in her life. She could taste the zing of a margarita on her lips, feel the popping bubbles of a vodka tonic all along her tongue, sense the cold slide of a Pinot Grigio down her throat. If she was going to be hung for a drunk, she might as well be a drunk. What was the point in trying to stay sober when everyone would have already made their judgement?

Carol jammed the key in the ignition and revved up the Land Rover. She could drive straight to the supermarket and load up with booze then head home. Nobody would know if she leaned on a little drink. She was meeting the team, but not till tomorrow morning. Plenty of time to have a few and sober up again before anyone was any the wiser. And she'd feel so much better with a drink inside her. She could take on the world with a quick hit to calm her down, settle her nerves, kill her fears of facing the world.

She smacked her fist against the steering wheel. 'Fuck! Fuck! Fuck!' It had to be Franklin. Who else would have done this to her? Who else would have betrayed her like this? Who else knew enough to put the pieces together? Not the local hack covering the mags. If it had been her, the story would have hit days ago. No, this had to be Franklin, the bastard. The only other candidate who came close was Blake, and she didn't think her former chief constable would take the risk of it blowing up in his face. He'd have other petty revenges up his sleeve, she didn't doubt that. But this didn't feel like him.

Jesus, how was she going to do this job if she had to watch her back every minute? But she couldn't retreat now. She'd given John Brandon her word. And besides, she had her team working on a series of deaths that nobody but them thought was suspicious. She couldn't walk away from that. Someone had to speak for the dead, as well as protect the living.

But yet, there was room inside that commitment for a drink. She had to swing by the canal basin to pick the dog up from Tony. But she'd hold it together. She'd tell him she had work to do, grab the dog and go. She'd be home inside an hour with a few bottles to tide her over till the humiliation subsided. It would be fine. She was in control again.

Carol put the Landie in gear and headed down the car park ramp. She threaded her way through the city centre streets and ten minutes later she was drawing up at the far end of the quayside from *Steeler*. She jumped out, not bothering to lock the door, and ran over the cobbles to Tony's mooring. She leapt aboard, pushing back the hatch and slamming the doors open.

He was at the saloon table, laptop open, hands startled frozen in mid-sentence. He looked at her in consternation. 'What the hell is it?'

All resolution gone, she crumpled on to the galley steps. 'I need a drink,' she wailed.

37

Paula was luxuriating in the rare treat of a lie-in. Elinor had gone to work, Torin was having a sleepover for his best mate's birthday and Carol had ordered her to take the day off. So she was enjoying the drift between sleeping and waking, dozing then surfacing, languid and loving it. Then she was prodded to the surface by the vibration of her phone. For a moment she thought it was a dream, but her hand was already stretching for the bedside table.

She registered the caller — Elinor — and took it without thinking further. 'Uh huh,' she groaned, not quite awake.

'Have you been online yet?' Elinor asked without preamble.

Paula swallowed and squirmed into a sitting position. 'No, why?'

'You need to look at the *Sentinel Times* front page. I'm assuming it'll be in the online edition. Otherwise you'll have to go and get a paper. I can't stop, I'm up to my eyes here, we'll talk later.' And she was gone.

Paula shook her head like a dog emerging from water. Had she just dreamed that? She yawned and stretched, then went downstairs to grab her tablet. While she waited for the kettle to boil, she rubbed the sleep from her eyes and opened up the Bradfield paper's website. And there it was, in all its glory: *Top Cop in*

Drink-Driving Mystery. 'Oh shit,' she muttered, reading on. In its usual attempt to prove it was as bold as the national red-tops, the paper sailed as close to the wind as possible without actually saying 'police corruption'. But you didn't need a magnifying glass to read between the lines. It was hard to see how it could be any worse.

Ignoring the kettle, Paula ran upstairs and called Stacey. 'Are you home?' she demanded.

'Yes, I'm home.'

'I'm coming round,' she said. 'We need to put our heads together.'

Stacey said something about Carol having told them to take a rest day. But Paula was already cutting her off and heading for the shower. Ten minutes later, she was running out the door, hair damp, rage fluttering in her chest. How dare they, the cheesy scumbags? Did they have no idea what Carol Jordan had done for this bloody city over the years? How many people were walking through their days without a care who might be six feet under if not for the job she'd done. Putting herself on the line for the ungrateful bastards. And if you were going to be completely selfish about it, how many bloody newspapers had been sold off the back of Carol and her team?

Once behind the wheel, she forced herself to calm down and drive attentively. The last thing they needed right now was another headline. By the time she rang Stacey's entry-phone, she had simmered down a little. But not much.

'Have you seen the paper?' The words were out before she was even across the threshold.

Startled, Stacey backed up a couple of steps. 'Only the *FT*,' she said. 'What's happened?'

Paula marched past and went straight to the work area. 'Which one of these can I use?'

'None, ideally,' Stacey said, slipping past her and into a chair. 'What am I looking at?'

'The home page of the bloody fucking *Sentinel Times*.' Paula drummed her fingers against her thigh. Even the speed of Stacey's solid state drives couldn't match her impatience.

'Oh,' Stacey said as she read the headline. She clicked on the story. 'Oh no.'

'That didn't happen by accident,' Paula said. 'And it didn't happen by routine either. If it had come from the local rag covering the court, it would have broken before now.'

'Mmm. It would have had to be reported the next day, there are rules about that sort of thing,' Stacey said slowly, letting her fingers move over the keyboard without actually pressing the keys. Paula had seen her do it often when she was considering what to do next.

'And besides,' Paula continued, 'she won't have been identified in court as ex-DCI Carol Jordan, she'll have been on the charge sheet with her name and address alone. That would've been meaningless to the hack who covers the mags for the *Halifax Courier*. If they'd noticed it at all, their story would have been 'faulty breathalyser put four drivers through hell of suspicion'.'

'Somebody leaked this, you're right.' Stacey stood up and gently pushed Paula back from the screens. 'Caffeine and sugar,' she said. 'I know you when you're insufficiently stimulated. Go out on the balcony and vape while I sort us out.'

Nonplussed, Paula did as she was told. Silicon Stacey was a changed woman. Love was slowly leaching the cool remoteness from her persona. Soon she'd be like the Cylons in *Battlestar Galactica*, indistinguishable from humans. Paula leaned on the rail of the small terrace and gazed unseeingly across the city. Who was so heavily invested in the failure of the new MIT that they would try to scupper it before it even began? 'Take a number,' she muttered, turning up her jacket collar against the thin breeze cutting across the rooftops.

Stacey called her inside and they sat round the kitchen table with a pot of green tea and a pile of buttered crumpets. 'Sam not around today?' Paula asked as she reached for a crumpet and some rhubarb and ginger jam.

'No, he's off with his mates,' Stacey said, busying herself with the teapot.

'So, I think we can assume that this was a deliberate leak from inside the tent. Somebody that wants to fuck us up before we even get out of the starting blocks.'

Stacey poured tea. 'That doesn't exactly narrow it down. Blake must be furious that she's back running his murder cases without actually being accountable directly to him. DCI Fielding hates her guts because Carol made her look even more stupid than she actually is. There's two without even thinking.'

'DCI Franklin can't be best pleased either. They've got history. She's made him and his team look like turnips a couple of times over the years. Then his officers make a righteous arrest — actually, four righteous arrests — and some hotshot at the Home Office decides they need Carol Jordan more than they need the law upholding on his patch. I'd be bloody furious if I was him.'

Stacey stared into her tea. 'He does have a point. I'm not entirely comfortable with how we got here.'

'It's a balance, isn't it? We know the good Carol Jordan has done in the past. We know the good she's capable of doing in the future. And this was such a small indiscretion.'

'This time,' Stacey said severely. 'She's been flying close to the edge for years, we both know that.'

'But it's pushed her into stopping drinking. So that's a strong positive to come out of it. I know if you take the high moral ground it's dodgy, but I think the benefit is much greater than the downside.'

'We'll have to wait and see. But those three — Blake, Fielding and Franklin — they're just the ones we know about off the top of our heads. There must be plenty of others. There's six forces involved in this project — I can't believe there aren't officers with an axe to grind there. Bosses pissed off at having the big cases taken from them. DCIs who think it should have been them.' She did a jerky shrug, as if she wasn't quite accustomed to so much animated conversation.

Paula stirred her tea and helped herself to a second crumpet. Exactly how she liked them.

Slightly crispy, running with butter. Thank God Elinor couldn't see her. 'We need to find out who's behind this in case they're not going to stop at one sabotage attempt. This is probably going nowhere fast, but there's real malice here. We need to stomp it into the ground, Stacey.'

'What do you suggest we do?'

Stacey nibbled at her crumpet, not meeting Paula's eyes. Nothing new there; she'd built a career on going deep inside herself when she needed to figure stuff out. 'Can you get inside the newspaper's system? There must be something in there. An email. A payment. A message. It's a big story, they wouldn't run it without a bit of to-ing and fro-ing.'

'There was no byline on the story,' Stacey said. 'I've noticed that sometimes these days on stories that pose potential problems for news organisations. It's as if they think they might come under attack and they're trying to make it as hard as possible for anybody to track things through the site.'

'I don't understand.'

'Say you're a newspaper and I crack your security and get inside your site. I don't want to be in there any longer than I absolutely have to be because you might have the kind of suspicious IT person who sets up tripwires against incursions like mine. So if I have the name of the person who wrote the story I'm trying to get to the back door of, I have a very direct starting point. I can go to the journalist's home on the server and, with luck, I can access all their notes and the evidence trail on the story. But if I don't have that starting point, I have to try to backtrack from the finished copy as it appears on the screen and try to get to that information the hard way. And that takes time. Time that I might not have if they're any good.'

Paula nodded. 'Right. I see what you mean.'

Stacey ran a hand through her hair, pushing it behind her ears. 'And now you're going to say, 'So can you do it, Stacey?' ' Her smile was ironic and without warmth. 'Can I do it for Carol?'

Paula felt wrong-footed. This wasn't the usual script. There was generally nothing Stacey liked more than a devilishly hard conundrum. Set her Mission Impossible and she was like a dog with two tails. 'So, can you do it, Stacey?' Paula raised her arms, bent at the elbows like a begging dog, and laid on her best pleading look.

Stacey smiled, apparently in spite of herself. 'I'll see what I can do. But I'm warning you, I've already got a mountain of work with the suicides. You wouldn't believe the amount of crap those women had dumped on them. Every time I step away from the screens I feel like I need a shower. It'll make a pleasant change to be dealing with journalists. The kind of sleazebags I'm used to.'

'That's good. Because we need to nail whoever is trying to sink this operation. It's not just Carol who's going to be holed below the waterline if we don't put a stop to it. We're all in the same boat now, Stacey. It's sink or swim for all of us.'

38

Sunday morning started gradually before the sun forced its way through the cloud layer and splashed the city with pink and gold. It was a light that flattered even a Northern Victorian metropolis like Bradfield, making the Minster Canal Basin almost picture-postcard pretty. Tony Hill stood on the roof of his narrowboat, hands thrust deep in the pockets of his padded jacket, eyes on the near horizon of renovated mills and brick kilns.

It had been a challenging passage of hours since Carol had pitched up in anguished desperation the day before. He was proud of her for not hiding her need, for not driving to the supermarket and loading up with booze, for not holing up in the barn and drinking the humiliation and anger into submission. Coming to him had been the brave thing to do. And it had cost her. Admitting any kind of failing had never been Carol's way. Failure had always been the spur to do better.

For Tony, her arrival had provoked a mixture of happiness and anguish. He was pleased to be the one she'd turned to when she couldn't carry the weight herself. But seeing her so unlike herself had been difficult. He was accustomed to the torment of others; he saw it every day in his clinical practice, and the empathy he felt for his patients was often the first step on the journey of healing and possible redemption. But it was easy to afford empathy when you weren't emotionally engaged with the person suffering. He didn't have that luxury with Carol.

But they'd made it. She'd showed him the story that had triggered her emotional storm, and he'd shared her rage and despair. They'd talked about what it meant to her and what it might mean to the opinions of others. They'd discussed and tested out various strategies for dealing with the fallout. He'd made innumerable cups of tea and coffee and had a takeaway delivered from their favourite curry house in Temple Fields. They'd walked right out of the city along the canal towpath and called a taxi to bring them back.

By ten, they were exhausted. Carol leaned her head in her hands and said, 'I should be going home.'

'What's the point? We're meeting the team here tomorrow, and you're knackered. It's daft to drive all the way home only to come back in the morning. Stay here, you know you're welcome.'

'What about the dog?'

'She's welcome too.'

'That's not what I mean. She's never spent the night away from the barn. And I don't have any food for her.'

Tony made great play of leaning down to check out Flash, who was stretched out under the table between their feet, fast asleep. 'Oh yes, because she obviously can't settle. I'll walk up to the all-night grocery store and buy a tin of dog food. It won't kill her to eat like the proletariat for once.'

Carol sighed. 'There's only one cabin. And it's your bedroom.'

'I've got a sleeping bag. You can stretch out here on the banquette, it's designed to be an extra berth.'

Carol looked at the banquette dubiously. 'I'm struggling with that.'

'The back cushions are on rails. They push up and back to cover the windows and give you extra width. Arthur designed half the gadgetry on this boat to his own spec. It does work. If you're dubious about it, I'll sleep here and you can have the cabin.'

And so it had been settled. Carol on the banquette, dog at her feet, Tony in his own cabin a few metres away. At first he'd thought he wouldn't be able to settle with her so close, and in his own space. But the emotional *sturm und drang* of the day had depleted more of his energies than he'd realised, and within minutes of turning out the light, he was drawn into deep sleep. When he finally woke after the best sleep he'd had in months, he lay wondering what had roused him, then realised it was the sliding of the roof hatch.

He emerged a few minutes later to discover the sleeping bag neatly rolled up, the banquette restored and the saloon empty. On the table lay a note scribbled on a paper bag. 'Gone for run with Flash. Back soon.'

Glad she hadn't woken mortified and driven to escape, he'd pulled on a jacket and climbed out on to the roof, drinking in the cool morning air, scanning the environs of the canal basin in the hope of catching a glimpse of Carol and Flash. The ruins of the minster looked spectacular in the low-angled light, but he had no interest in its beauty. The human scale had always been what interested him.

In between keeping watch, he checked his phone to see whether the *Sentinel Times* story had been picked up by other media. With a sinking heart, he saw it had found its way into the tabloids, though none of them had made a huge drama out of it. Probably worried about the potential for libel. He sighed, and turned back to his vigil. Eventually, his patience was rewarded. Two dark shapes on the distant towpath resolved themselves into detective and dog. They'd be back in time to have breakfast before the rest of the team pitched up. Tony wasn't quite sure how they were all going to fit into the narrowboat, but it was only a one-off. By tomorrow they'd have their new offices in Skenfrith Street up and running.

An hour later, they started to arrive. Paula was first, hugging a stiff-backed Tony as she greeted him on the quayside. 'Is she OK?'

'She's holding together. It was touch and go, though.'

'I'm fucking furious. Stacey's on the hunt for the mole. God help them when we find out who it is.'

'Yeah. There's coffee inside, Carol's here already.'

Kevin and Alvin drove into the car park one after the other. Judging by their body language, Kevin was bringing Alvin up to speed with the media shitstorm. Alvin's hands bunched into fists and he barrelled down the quayside looking like he wanted someone to hit. 'Do we know who did this?' he demanded.

'No, not yet. And we're not going to talk about it today,' Tony said firmly.

Stacey brought up the rear, laptop and tablet under her arm, face blank as a whiteboard when Tony asked her what progress she'd made. 'Not a lot,' she said, gesturing to him to lead the way below.

It was a tight fit, but they managed. The three women along the banquette, Tony in his leather swivel chair, Kevin and Alvin leaning against the galley countertops. Flash had retreated to the stern, sitting alert and fascinated at the life of the basin.

Carol kicked the session off. 'We started this inquiry as nothing more than an exercise. Tony's propensity for spotting clusters of connected events came up with some slightly unexpected suicides who had been the victims of vicious online bullying. We took a closer look and we found a very bizarre link. At each of the death scenes, there was a book. Or the remains of one. Two collections of poetry and one essay. The writers had all committed suicide themselves and in broadly the same way as the women we're looking at. And obviously there could be others that we haven't found yet. It's starting to look a lot like a pattern.'

'And if it's a pattern, they're not straight-forward suicides,' Tony said. It was as if there had been no interruption to the smooth flow of the MIT briefings. Everyone had slipped straight back into their old patterns.

Carol nodded. 'Thanks to the preliminary interviews we've done with people who were close to the victims, we can say with a degree of certainty that none of them was a fan of these particular writers. So there is some kind of significance in the presence of these texts at the crime scenes.'

'Unless there's been some secret collusion between the women — which makes no sense at all — leaving the books behind tells us there's somebody else involved, surely?' Paula cut straight to the heart of what they were all thinking.

'Exactly,' Tony said. 'The question is, precipitation or active participation?'

Alvin stirred, folding his arms across his chest. 'You're going to have to put that in words of one syllable for me.'

'You'll get the hang of his cryptic crossword announcements,' Kevin said. 'He likes to baffle us with science.'

Tony looked hurt. 'I don't mean to, I'm sorry. I don't always explain myself well.'

'You're so used to things being blindingly obvious to you that you forget we're a few beats behind you,' Carol said. 'Now tell us what you mean.'

Tony rubbed his hands over his head, screwing his face up in frustration with himself. 'I'm sorry. The question is whether the perpetrator is acting at a distance, pushing the women into a corner where they feel the only thing they can do is take their own lives, or whether he — or she — is taking an active role in their deaths.'

'You mean, actually murdering them?' Alvin asked.

'Well, technically, talking them into it would also be murder, I think. But yes, I mean actually taking an active part.'

'How would that work?' Paula chipped in.

'I'm not sure,' Tony admitted. 'Maybe using date-rape drugs to take control of their actions? You'd get away with something like GHB that wouldn't show up on a post-mortem tox screening because it breaks down so quickly. That would get round how Daisy Morton suffocated herself with natural gas, for example. Because if you were trying to do that to yourself, I suspect you'd pass out before you succeeded. And it was such a weird thing to do when there are so many other, easier, more straightforward ways to commit suicide.'

Alvin nodded slowly, unfolding his arms and leaning back against the countertop. 'And he could have walked Jasmine Burton into the water then walked straight back out again. It makes a kind of warped sense.'

'Given the available evidence, it makes more sense than the theory of pushing them into it from a distance,' Stacey said. 'I've been through most of the online attacks, and while there are a few that say things like 'I hope you get cancer and die', or 'women like you don't deserve to live', I didn't see anything that looked like a concerted campaign to undermine someone to the point of suicide.'

'What we seem to be saying is that if we accept there is a connection between these deaths, we should work on the presumption that the perpetrator was there at the end?' Carol said, summing up. The others nodded, grunted, mumbled assent. 'In that case, we need to go back and look at each of these cases. We have to use our new over-arching MIT status to ask all the investigative teams to revisit the cases and see if we can find any witnesses who saw a third party at what we're going to designate as crime scenes. So, did anyone see someone in wet clothes around the estuary area on the night Jasmine died? Was anyone spotted coming out of Kate Rawlins' house or garage at the crucial time? Did the neighbours see anyone hanging around Daisy Morton's house on the day of the explosion?'

'They're going to love us,' Kevin said. 'Surely we won't have jurisdiction to get the Met or Devon and Cornwall to help us out?'

'We'll ask politely, like we would have done when we were part of BMP. And if they drag their heels, I'll get Brandon to pull strings for us.'

Tony caught a fleeting look of dismay pass between Paula and Stacey. He imagined they were thinking John Brandon had already pulled enough strings for Carol. 'I'm sure it won't come to that,' he said repressively. 'You'll just have to ask very charmingly. There is another line of approach, of course.'

Carol made a gesture with her hand to indicate he should roll out his thinking. 'Come on then, don't keep us in suspense.'

He had to admit to himself that he enjoyed the eager anticipation on their faces as they looked to him for insight. 'He's not going to stop at this point. Not when he's beginning to get the hang of it and before he's made whatever point he's aiming for.' He frowned. 'And that's something I'm going to have to think about. What's this all about, ultimately? But in the meantime, we have to be aware he's trawling for other victims. If we can identify who they might be, we might be able to intervene. That way we save a life and we stop him. Two for the price of one.'

'That's easy to say,' Paula grumbled. 'But how do we do that when we don't know what he's trying to achieve?'

'We have to ask ourselves the question: why these particular women? What is it about them that meets his criteria?'

'So, what do we know about them?' Carol asked.

'They've all got a public profile,' Kevin said. 'They're not mega, but they have an audience already who support the kind of things they say.'

'They're all grown-ups too,' Paula added. 'They're not teenagers. In a way, they're not easy victims. They've presumably had to develop a bit of a thick skin to be doing what they're doing in the world.'

'So they're a bit of a challenge,' Carol said.

'But it's important to silence them.' Tony's fingers fidgeted, as if he longed for a whiteboard to scribble on. 'That's what this is about, isn't it? He's silencing women who have an audience to whom they say things that he finds unpalatable.'

312

'What they say? It's feminist.' Unusually within a brainstorming session, Stacey butted in. 'I've looked at their online history and it's not random rants. They're criticising the behaviour of men but they're doing it in explicitly feminist terms. So whoever is doing this, I'd say they have an issue with women who speak out for women.'

'Good point,' Tony said.

'I think it's a man,' Alvin said. 'I know there are plenty of women out there who don't support feminists being vocal about what they believe, but for a woman to be taking this kind of action, she'd have to be pretty far out there. And these murders have taken such careful planning and execution, if you were that disturbed you wouldn't be able to pull it off. Whereas, for a man, this way of thinking would be much easier to hold in your head as reasonable behaviour. Like you were doing the right thing, the manly thing.'

There was a moment's silence as they all digested what the new boy had said, then nods and smiles broke out. 'That makes sense,' Tony said.

'It does,' Carol said.

'Do we know anything about the writers whose books he's leaving behind? Like, why them in particular?' Kevin asked.

'I looked online,' Tony said. 'And I spoke to one of the English lecturers at the university. According to her, they're all writers who have been embraced by the feminist movement, even though they might not necessarily have self-identified as feminist.'

'That's helpful to know,' Carol said. 'But the big question remains: how do we use what we know to find his next victim? And how do we develop the evidence that will nail him?'

39

The heavy steel door clanged like a badly struck bell. Tony reached for the light switch and stepped inside his library. He closed the door, sealing himself into the shipping container with its maze of shelves and stacks of boxes waiting to be unpacked. He wanted to attempt a profile and he needed peace and quiet to think it through. Even after the team had departed to attend to their designated tasks ('Find who the trolls are attacking now, talk to the officers who investigated the suicides to see if there are witnesses, research women writers who killed themselves . . . ') *Steeler* wasn't a restful place to be on a Sunday. The canal boating community were very sociable; Sundays were an occasion for barbecues, parties and live music.

He could have gone to his office at Bradfield Moor, but when people knew he was in the building, they generally found reasons to come and pick his brains. Now he had an alternative. Some might say it resembled a prison cell more than a crucible of inspiration, but Tony liked the sense of isolation it gave him.

He opened his laptop and started a new file with his standard boilerplate introduction.

The following offender profile is for guidance only and shouldn't be regarded as an identikit portrait. The offender is unlikely to match the profile in every detail, though I would expect there to be a high degree of congruence between the characteristics outlined below and the reality. All of the statements in the profile express probabilities and possibilities, not hard facts.

A serial killer produces signals and indicators in the commission of his crimes. Everything he does is intended, consciously or not, as part of a pattern. Discovering the underlying pattern reveals the killer's logic. It may not appear logical to us, but to him it is crucial. Because his logic is so idiosyncratic, straightforward traps will not capture him. As he is unique, so must be the means of catching him, interviewing him and reconstructing his acts.

It was almost comforting to see those words on the screen. They anchored him to the discipline he'd been following for so many years. Now, he started making notes on screen that he could shape into a profile.

What are his goals? The silencing of outspoken women who criticise men, generally in overtly feminist terms.

What does that achieve? It sends a message to other women that feminism is a counsel of despair. It's the f-word, the forbidden fruit. He's telling them that pursuing such an agenda will lead to so much misery that suicide is the only answer.

Where are the roots of his hostility? Almost certainly in childhood or early adolescence. Men who are driven wild as adults by what they see as the damage done to them by individual instances of feminism tend to focus their anger very directly and personally in the form of domestic violence.

So what happened in his childhood to cause this warping of his outlook? A mother who disappeared from his life and a distorted version of the reason for her disappearance? Possibly a mother who became a lesbian and was forced out of the family circle? If so, this must have happened at a time when the courts still leaned towards giving custody to the father over a lesbian mother, so that would mean the killer was a small child before, say, the early 1990s. But the women he's killing are not all lesbian, so that may not be the reason. Whatever explanation he was given for his mother's departure from his life has provoked an extremely hostile reaction to feminism and women he perceives as feminist.

It's interesting that he doesn't see rape as a weapon in this context. His idea of exerting power and control is to erase these women, not simply to punish or humiliate them. He wants them gone for good.

Judging by the degree of self-control and planning we're seeing here, he's not young and/or impulsive. I'd estimate his age between 30 and 45.

Typically serial killers' behaviour links into the sexual homicide matrix, which generally has a clearly demarcated route that culminates in murder — poor school record, petty crime including acts of torture against animals, minor sexual offences and flashpoint acts of violence against weaker opponents. And so usually I recommend searching criminal records for traces of those who come into the frame as suspects; or checking out any persistent escalating offenders known to be on the patch.

But this perpetrator is different. There appears not to be an obviously sexual component to these murders. So I'm inclined to think he hasn't graduated to murder after a series of intensifying lesser offences. He's had the hurt that has provoked these crimes in his heart from the beginning and nothing less than this kind of annihilation would begin to quiet the nagging voice in his head. It won't have even occurred to him that torturing a cat or sexually assaulting a minor might be a satisfactory act. So he's not going to have the kind of criminal record that we'd recognise as indicative of serial homicide. Chances are he has no criminal record at all.

The leaving of literary texts at the crime scenes tells us something about his level of education and sophistication. He hasn't just googled 'famous suicides' and gone with that. He's specifically chosen women writers who would fit broadly in the category of feminist. That suggests to me that he probably has degree-level education and a professional status in his working life. His degree is not necessarily in English or American litera-ture, but it wouldn't be surprising if it was.

He has a high level of intelligence. To convinc-ingly fake a suicide is far from easy. To do it three times without generating suspicion is hard. It needs planning, patience and a cool head under pressure. Once he has identified and targeted his victims, he has clearly watched them and studied their lives without generating suspicion. So we know he's smart, patient and analytical in his approach. He's either self-employed or has a job that allows him a degree of freedom and mobility, given we're looking at victims in London, Birmingham and Bradfield. It's hard to see where he is vulnerable in the early stages of his crimes.

Except that he has to acquire his targets somehow. These are almost certainly women he doesn't know. Does he come across them by randomly trawling social media for somebody whose loudly expressed opinions piss him off? Does he go for women he's heard on the radio or seen in the papers? Does he pick them up from what's trending on Twitter? However he's doing it, I think he's doing it as a spectator. He may be joining in the general vilification, but if he is, it's only occasionally. He won't be a hardcore troll. He'll enjoy what others say and do but he won't get stuck in. He's too smart, too self-controlled for that. He knows how easy it is to be tracked down once you stick your head above the parapet.

This man is dangerous. He's going to keep on killing because he wants to create a climate of fear. I think his goal is to make women withdraw from public discourse, and that's not a realistic prospect. So there will continue to be plenty of prospective victims and he won't shy away from dispatching them. We need to catch him so we can stop him. And right this minute, I've got no idea how to do that.

Tony stared at his bleak conclusion and tried to think of a way to express it that offered some fragment of hope. But nothing was surfacing. 'You've lost your touch,' he told himself, closing the lid of his laptop and laying it on the side table. There were few things more frustrating than not being able to complete a piece of work because his imagination had let him down.

When all else failed there was one avenue he often found productive. Occupying his brain with something else seemed to liberate his subconscious mind. Left to its own devices, it would grind away like a hamster on a wheel until, more often than not, a solution would wriggle out into the daylight and make him smile with delight. Usually, his distraction of choice was some form of video game that required complete engagement of hands and mind. Creating a world or saving mankind, defeating a threat or building a railroad. They'd all played a part in making unpredictable leaps forward.

But he deliberately kept no games on his laptop, and there was nothing on his phone sufficiently immersive. The only distraction here was books. And there were no shortage of those. Reading wasn't the answer, though. It was the wrong kind of distraction, using the same part of his brain as the puzzle he was trying to resolve. What he could do was unpack and shelve some of the remaining boxes. Figuring out what needed to go where and how he could best arrange the collection was exactly the kind of challenge that would work.

He jumped to his feet, pulled off his jacket and made for the nearest box. Foucault's *History of Sexuality* was rapidly followed by Jon Ronson's

The *Psychopath Test* and Fiona Cameron's *Mapping Murder*. Oh yes, this would do perfectly. Tony started pulling out books and making decisions about where they should be placed. It was repetitive, slightly challenging and offered moments of distraction when something neglected for too long caught his attention.

More than an hour had passed. Three boxes had been emptied and he was contemplating a fourth when he stopped in his tracks. He slapped his forehead with the flat of his hand and rolled his eyes. 'Books!' he exclaimed. 'Bloody books, you numbskull.'

40

Stacey had set a series of routines in motion and was writing code to create more searches. This was the kind of thing that normally filled her with a Zen-like calm. Not today, though. Today she felt knocked out of kilter like an unbalanced wheel. The morning session with the team had been reassuring and interesting, reminding her of all the reasons why she'd been thrilled to be back on a team led by Carol Jordan. But then they'd dispersed, each with their own tasks, and she'd been left with nowhere to hide from the anxiety that had been fizzing away beneath the surface since the morning after she'd broken the news of the new MIT to Sam.

He'd been subdued all evening and later, when they'd gone to bed, she'd practically had to force him to snuggle with her. 'I know she doesn't trust me, but I deserve the chance to prove she's wrong about me,' he'd said. Like a child picking a scab, he couldn't seem to leave it alone. Stacey wished she could say something to make him feel better about himself. She knew he was a good cop; she wished she could make Carol Jordan see that.

She hadn't seen him since the morning after. He'd gone off, saying he was meeting up with some mates and they'd probably head over to Leeds to see some band. She'd texted him a couple of times and left a voicemail but he hadn't got back to her. She hadn't had much experience with men, but she did know that when their pride was hurt, they needed space and time to lick their wounds, so she was trying not to crowd him.

Stacey decided to go round to Sam's flat on her way home from the briefing. He didn't answer the intercom and she didn't have a key. When she'd given him a key to her place, he'd said, 'There's no point in me giving you a key to my flat. Why would we ever go there when we've got this place at our disposal?' She'd been charmed by his obvious appreciation of her home but now she wished she'd insisted. She didn't want to think of him sitting home alone, brooding about what he'd see as his failure. She wanted to comfort him, to reassure him that his career still had huge potential. But now there was nothing for it but to go home and get back to the endless routines that might take the squad closer to a callous killer.

Stacey understood the importance of her work but for once that underpinning wasn't enough to keep her focused. She checked her messages and emails every five minutes, irritated with herself for it. She felt out of place in her own skin and kept walking away from her array of screens to prowl round the flat, refill her water bottle or stare out moodily over the city roofs. Why wouldn't he let her help him? Wasn't that what lovers were supposed to do?

When her phone rang, she almost tripped over her feet in her haste to get back to her desk. Seeing Tony's name on the screen, she came close to not answering. But her sense of duty trumped her discontent and she fed the call through her speakers.

'Books,' he said without preamble. 'That's the way to find him.'

'What about books?' Stacey had worked with Tony for long enough not to dismiss him as a crazy man when he produced such gnomic utterances.

'I've been working up a profile and I couldn't come up with any useful suggestions that might help you guys track him down. It was frustrating because usually there's something I can offer that's like applied maths — it takes the theory and produces a practical application. And then it came to me. Books.'

'I'm not entirely clear what you're saying here, Tony.'

'He's been planning this for a while. He's not lurching from killing to killing. He's choosing the victims as they present themselves to him, but not the methods. He's got the books lined up. It's the only thing that makes sense. Otherwise how would he know there are enough to go around? Do you see? If he randomly started it, he couldn't know he'd find enough famous women writers who'd killed themselves to fuel a campaign. It's like the fatal flaw in *Se7en*, where the killer had obviously been planning the sequence more than a year ahead, but how could he have known he was going to end up with a cop whose sin was anger? He might have turned out to be despairing, or cowardly, or uncaring. That was bad planning. Our man is a planner too, and he looks to me like a good planner. I bet he has a nice little stack of books so he can mark each death and so the world will eventually notice there's a rash of these deaths that have a common feature. That women are killing themselves because they are ashamed of what they've said and they're copycatting each other by leaving books as suicide notes.'

Stacey felt a glimmer of comprehension. 'And you think he bought all the books at once?'

'Exactly,' Tony said triumphantly. 'I knew you'd get it. Now, I've done a bit of quick and dirty research here and you're not going to find all three of these books in your average high street bookshop. Your best bet would be an online retailer. And when it comes to books, we all know who the number one e-tailer is, right?'

'Valhalla.co.uk,' Stacey said. 'The evil empire.'

'Do you think they'd search their records and tell us if anybody in the last twelve months bought all three of those books?'

Stacey couldn't stop herself snorting in derision. 'Are you kidding? It'd be easier to get a Swiss bank to reveal who owns its numbered accounts.'

'That's what I thought,' Tony said. 'And everybody knows that, right? Everybody knows Valhalla are so paranoid about commercial confidentiality that they won't tell anybody anything about anything.'

'Exactly. So there's no point asking. Even if you got a warrant, it would somehow take months or even years to execute it.'

'Perfect.'

'What do you mean, perfect? I thought you wanted this information?'

'Of course I want it. But it wouldn't be there to be found if our perpetrator thought it would be retrievable.'

'Either I'm being very stupid or you're not making sense.'

'Sorry. This guy is smart, Stacey. He knows how to cover his traces. All I'm getting at is that the killer could safely order from Valhalla because he knows, as everybody knows, that it's an article of faith with Valhalla not to release any information. So he wasn't taking a risk by ordering all the books from Valhalla. He knew we'd never get our hands on that information legitimately. But what he couldn't know is that we have you.' Tony ended on an exultant note.

'So, let me be clear about this. You want me to make an illegal hack, break through the legendary security of Valhalla.co.uk and find out whether any single purchaser bought all three of the books associated with our victims?' She didn't even try to keep the incredulity from her voice.

'That's it. You've got it. You can do that, right?'

Stacey sighed. The trouble with being as good as she was was that everyone expected miracles as routine. Because none of them knew anything about what went on behind the front end of the systems they took for granted, they assumed that what she did was a level playing field of complexity. They thought it was as easy to hack a security-obsessed multinational corporation as it was to open a teenager's social media account.

'It's a big job, Tony,' she said. 'And I'm not sure I've got what it takes.'

'You're kidding, right? I never cease to be amazed at the back-door stuff you come up with. You've got a real feel for how systems work.'

'That's not what I mean. I'm talking physical kit. I'm not sure what I've got can do the job. I might have to build something and I'll certainly have to write some code. Or adapt some I've done before, depending on what I find in there. It might be easier and quicker to get somebody else to do it.' Stacey wasn't sure why she was making such an admission to Tony. Her standard operating procedure with her colleagues was to say nothing and get on with what they'd asked for. Maintaining her mystique as a hacker in a white hat. She never talked in any detail about how hard or how easy a particular task might be. She just presented results like a magician displaying high-level prestidigitation as if it was an everyday skill. If she was honest, she wanted them to think she was amazing. But her relationship with Sam had changed her in so many ways. Perhaps it was possible to admit to fallibility and still have people think she was amazing. If there was a safe place to do that, it was with Tony.

'Is that secure? Have you done that before?'

Stacey paused and took a deep breath. 'Yes. There are two people I trust implicitly. One of them I've asked for help before and he gave it, no questions asked. And all it cost us was a return favour, which is all paid off now. The other I've known since I first started writing programs. We've done stuff together for years, but nothing work-related. But — you know I have a private business, right?'

Tony laughed. 'Well, I figured out a long time ago that you either had some kind of business on the side or else you were siphoning money off from the Bank of England. You don't get a lifestyle like yours on a detective's salary.'

Stacey felt a momentary twinge of anxiety. 'Does Carol know?'

A moment's pause for thought. 'I'd say she chooses not to know. As long as it doesn't have any impact on what you do for the MIT, she's not going to pick a fight with you about what you get up to on your own time. What were you going to say about your own company?'

'Only that my friend has done quite a bit of work for me over the years and he's never let me down. A lot of what we do is commercially confidential. He could have destroyed my income stream pretty much any time in the last ten years and he's never given me any cause for concern. So if I do need help, there are people I can turn to.'

'And it has the added advantage of keeping your hands clean if it all comes on top,' Tony added, his tone wry.

'That doesn't hurt,' Stacey said. 'I don't want to go to jail. But neither do they. So the chances of it all going horribly wrong are vanishingly small. These are clever boys, Tony. They've been doing this a long time and they have a very clear-eyed understanding of what they can and can't do. So if I do have to outsource what you're asking me . . . ' She paused, considering. 'I think we'll come out of it in one piece. There's only one problem.'

'What's that?'

'If this is the key evidence that nails our guy, we're going to have to work backwards to find a different explanation for how we fixed on him. We can't go to court and rely on material that shouldn't be in our possession.'

Tony made himself sound positive. 'We've always found a way to protect you before. There's always something that emerges that we could reasonably have fixed on earlier in the game. I don't see why this should be any different.'

Except that they'd never been confronted by a killer quite like this one.

41

It was supposed to have been a bright shiny new start. But thanks to the weekend papers, Carol's eager anticipation had been replaced by a gnawing apprehension. She'd slept badly, knowing every time she woke up that if there had been a drink in the barn, she'd have swallowed it without a moment's hesitation. Though she'd hated him for it in the moment, she knew Tony had been right.

When she woke up for the seventh time a few minutes after six, she finally gave in and got up. She dressed in dog-walking clothes and took Flash up the hill at a steady jog. When they reached the top of the moor, Carol slowed to a brisk walk, gazing down the valley to the pale smudge in the distance that she knew was Bradfield. She tried to convince herself it would be all right. She'd overcome worse obstacles than a bunch of journalists, after all. It might be headlines today, but by next weekend, it would be history.

Except that every time she asked for support from one of her six client forces there would always be a question mark behind their eyes. Her integrity was tainted and it was nobody's fault but her own. She'd snatched at the chance to reclaim her life the easy way when she should have had the guts to accept that she'd forced herself into a corner. But it was too late to take back what she'd done. The damage was out there.

All she could do was face them down. Maybe one day, she'd manage to outrun this new past. Till then, all she could do was hold her head up.

By the time she arrived at Skenfrith Street, Carol had built her resolve brick by brick till it felt strong enough to withstand whatever the media could throw at her. John Brandon was waiting for her in the new MIT squad room, where a couple of electricians were putting the final run of sockets in place. 'Amazing job,' he greeted her. 'I didn't quite believe they'd get it done in time, but they've proved me wrong.'

'Thanks for making this happen, John,' Carol said, reaching a hand out to shake his. 'I'm sorry I made it harder for you than it should have been.'

He sighed. 'I won't pretend I don't wish it had been different. We'd have been fine if some shit hadn't leaked it to the press.' He tightened his lips.

'What line are we going to take? Because it's bound to come up.' She pushed her shaggy hair back from her forehead and let it fall.

'I thought about that over the weekend,' Brandon said. 'We're going to brazen it out.' He looked at his watch. 'Are you ready? I've got three chief constables and three deputies downstairs ready to nail a smile on their faces and say how bloody delighted they are that your MIT will be working with their dedicated detectives to bring serious crimes to a swift and satisfactory conclusion. Sound about right to you?'

Carol gave him a relieved smile and followed him down to the recently tarted-up media room at Skenfrith Street. To her relief, James Blake had passed the welcoming committee job on to his deputy, a former drugs squad chief whose face and uniformed figure seemed to consist entirely of straight lines and sharp angles. 'Good to see you back in harness, Carol,' he said in a clipped North Wales accent. 'Can't wait to watch your team in action.' She was almost convinced he meant it. She made her way along the rest of the top brass, all affable smiles and firm handshakes.

And then, suddenly, they were on the platform, staring down the barrel of a couple of dozen cameras. The room was crammed; there must have been sixty journalists and camera crew in a room designed for a maximum of forty. The buzz of their chatter stilled as soon as Brandon cleared his throat. He introduced himself and went along the platform before outlining the working of the new Regional Major Incident Team, ReMIT. Hearing the acronym, Carol couldn't prevent a quirk of satisfaction twitching the corner of her mouth. She'd been spot on.

Then Brandon turned to her. 'It gives me great pleasure to present Detective Chief Inspector Carol Jordan, the officer who has been chosen to command this elite specialist squad. DCI Jordan has had a long and distinguished career, much of it here in Bradfield, where she ran the Major Incident Team very successfully for a number of years. I'm not going to bore you with a catalogue of her triumphs because you've all got the internet at your fingertips. Suffice it to say I don't think there's another officer anywhere in the UK who can match her for experience and ability. When I was her chief constable, we called her the Closer because of her astonishing success rate.'

That was news to Carol. She suspected it was news to her team too. She wondered whether it had been the idea of one of the civil servants. It didn't sound like Brandon.

When she tuned back in, he was talking about the stellar quality of her team. The hacks were starting to become restive now, eager to get to something more juicy than an animated press release. Finally, Brandon wound up with the dreaded 'Any questions?'

Several started to speak at once. 'One at a time,' Brandon chided them. There were a few questions about the structure of the ReMIT, with individual senior officers being asked about the impact on their detective teams of the new elite squad. All very anodyne. Then Brandon pointed to the next questioner. 'Woman over there, blue top.'

The woman gave a frown to indicate her gravitas. 'DCI Jordan, there have been reports that you were arrested last weekend for drink-driving. Does that make you an appropriate person to run this elite MIT?'

Carol forced her mouth into a formal smile. *Come out fighting.* 'It's true that I was mistakenly arrested because of faulty equipment after a routine traffic stop. I don't see why being the victim of a broken breathalyser should have any impact on my ability to do my job.'

'Are you saying you hadn't been drinking?'

The reporter wasn't giving up yet.

'I'm saying that the case against me was dismissed. I left court without a stain on my character.'

'Are you denying that you've got a drink problem?'

Carol felt the tide of anger rising in her head. 'What is this? Character assassination or just another example of everyday sexism? If I was a bloke, this wouldn't even have caused a ripple. Because if you're a bloke who has a drink, you're one of the lads. But if you're a woman, you're breaking all the rules. You're given a hard time not for what you've done but because you refuse to fit the neat little woman box. The only problem I have with doing my job is people who know nothing thinking they know best.'

Brandon broke the stunned silence. 'I think we'll move on,' he said, pointing at a plump sweating man in the middle of the front row. 'You, sir?'

'Who discovered the breathalyser was faulty? And how was the discovery made?'

Carol maintained the smile. 'I have no idea. That's an operational question that's well outside my area of responsibility. You'd have to ask West Yorkshire Police that question.'

'Mr Brandon, is it true the Home Office intervened in this case?'

Brandon's bloodhound face creased in puzzlement. 'This was a local case resolved at a local level. Do you think Home Office officials have so little to do that they would concern themselves with something like this? Look, there's no story here, in spite of what some of you have insinuated.'

'The story's not going away though, is it?' The questioner was persistent. 'It's all very convenient for DCI Jordan.'

Brandon bristled. 'It's the opposite of convenient. All DCI Jordan wants to do is to get on with her job, but instead she's having to deal with cowardly innuendo and unfounded allegations. You lot are being used to blacken her name by jealous individuals who have been thwarted in their own empire-building.'

Carol's heart sank. She knew Brandon meant well, but in effect, he'd thrown more fuel on the flames. Again a cacophony of questions broke out. 'Can we focus on what actually matters here?' She cut through the noise with a voice like a blade. 'My team exists to save lives. Right now, there are killers we don't even know about yet. There are murderers in waiting out there. It's my job to stop them in their tracks. We've barely started yet and already we're on the heels of a killer nobody suspected existed till we started examining some recent cases. So can we kick the trivia into touch? I have more important things to worry about than rumour and gossip, and if you had any interest in doing your jobs you would have too.' A surge of adrenalin made her heart race and she pushed her chair back, unclipping her lapel mike.

Brandon caught the signal and got to his feet. 'And that'll be all for now, ladies and gentlemen. If you have any operational queries, please direct them to Pamela James in the press office.'

'Is it true you've got Tony Hill on the payroll?' The voice was familiar. Penny Burgess, the crime correspondent who had dogged Carol's footsteps for years, wasn't quite done.

'Ask him,' Carol said, turning away and leading the charge from the stage. Her relief at having got past the worst of the questioning was tinged with a niggle of worry. Why was Penny Burgess asking about Tony? She'd created more trouble for Carol and her team over the years than the rest of the press corps put together. When she showed an interest, it was never a good idea to ignore it. Before she could figure out what to do, Brandon was clapping her on the back.

'Brilliant job, Carol. You put them in their place.' His congratulations were echoed by the other officers on the platform, except for the Bradfield DCC.

He gave her an appraising look. 'You implied you're already working a case. Which one?'

'Early stages,' she said vaguely. 'We're not ready to take it outside the team yet.'

'Interesting. I thought today was your first official day in the job.'

She smiled sweetly. 'We don't hang about. Thanks for giving us your support. I look forward to a productive future relationship.' And she turned away, making a point of glancing at her watch. 'I'm sorry, I've got to go,' she said to Brandon. 'My team are waiting for me.'

Brandon nodded. 'Good luck.'

'Thanks. We'll need it, judging by that lot in there.'

'The eyes of the country are on you, no doubt about that,' he said. 'I know you won't let us down.'

42

Tony stared intently at the screen, trying to read the body language of the press conference participants on the CCTV feed from the media room to the ReMIT office. He was oblivious to the comments from the rest of the team, fixed on Carol as she shifted from apprehension to frustration at Brandon's line before finally arriving at confrontation. It was a beautiful shift; her whole body seemed to change in shape and size as she grew back into herself. You could see where game makers got their ideas about transformation.

And yet, he couldn't help a shiver of unease. The angry response that had come so naturally — and reasonably — from Carol was exactly the kind of statement that provoked the trolls. And hot on the heels of the trolls, the man who was killing women who didn't know their place. He shook off the idea. With so many vulnerable targets, this man wasn't going to come after a woman as strong as Carol.

The others were vocal in their irritation both at the press and at Brandon and the top brass. 'Don't even give them the satisfaction of a response,' Kevin growled. Then when Carol composed herself and issued her passionate mission statement, they howled in delight and punched the air. And then Paula made a celebratory coffee for everyone with their shiny new machine.

By the time Carol walked through the door,

they were in high spirits, ready to take on the next phase of their investigation, whatever that might be. They settled round the big table in the middle of the room and looked expectantly at Carol. 'So, now you know what we're up against,' she said. 'We're not getting a honeymoon period, and that's mostly down to me. I would apologise, except that I'm quite happy we're not being lulled into a false sense of security. I don't want to feel the love until we've actually earned it. So, Stacey, what have you got for us?'

Stacey tapped her tablet and studied the screen. 'I now have real-life IDs for all five of the men who repeatedly trolled Kate, Daisy and Jasmine. I know where they live and where they work.'

'So let's hit them,' Alvin said. 'Let's make those evil little shitbags wish they'd never been born.'

'Woo hoo, who's had too much caffeine?' Paula teased.

'He's not one of them,' Tony said. 'If he trolled the women at all, he'll only have done it once or twice and probably not gone down the death-threat route. It's too easy to be threatening online when you think you're anonymous. It's the kind of thing you do when you've had a few beers or a row with your girlfriend or a bollocking from your boss, especially if she's a woman. It used to take a fair bit of effort to deliver a proper death threat. To go to all the trouble of cutting the words out of a magazine and sticking them on paper then finding out where to deliver them to — that all required dedication. It wasn't a knee-jerk reaction.'

'But why does that rule out our killer? Just because anybody can do it doesn't mean he hasn't. If you see what I mean,' Paula said.

'Because he's careful. He's a planner. He thinks things through. And he's not stupid. He's going to know that once we understand what's going on, we'll be throwing all our resources at identifying the trolls. If he'd been an old-fashioned death-threat maker, he'd have used magazines from a bin. Something that had absolutely no connection to him. He'd have worn gloves every step of the way. He'd have bought paper and glue in different shops in different towns. He'd have travelled fifty miles in the opposite direction to post the letter. He's too smart to hurl abuse at a woman he's planning to kill. He'll be the one standing back on the sidelines and watching other people dig themselves a hole. He might even needle some of them to go in a bit harder. But the bottom line is that he'll have understood the importance of invisibility.' Tony gave a little shrug, spreading his hands. 'I'm sorry to sound so negative, especially since Stacey's done such an amazing job.'

'And it is amazing,' Carol said. 'I'm not going to ask how you got your hands on information that's supposed to be beyond our reach.'

'Better that you don't know,' Paula said.

'Quite. And I understand the point Tony's making, but right now, we don't have any other leads. So I think we should interview these losers. Shake them up a bit, and see whether, as Tony suggests, anybody urged them on.'

Tony caught Stacey's eye. She raised her

eyebrows and gave him a small nod. 'Actually,' Tony said, 'there might be something?'

Carol sat back in her chair with the air of someone whose expectations have been proved right. She smiled. 'Of course there might. What have you been cooking up behind my back?'

'The one thing we can track directly back to him is the books,' Tony said. 'They're what revealed the pattern. They show that what's driving him is more than simple misogyny. It's very specifically a strike against women who publicly stand up against traditional male attitudes and behaviour. He's using the writers as exemplars.' He made a quotation mark sign in the air with two curled fingers, ignoring Carol wincing. ' "When you think these bad thoughts, when you behave in ways that run contrary to what women are supposed to do, here's what your outcome should be. You should understand your life is insufferable now'. That's what he's saying and that's the key to everything that's happening here.'

Carol nodded impatiently. 'Yes, that all makes sense, but how do we make that work for us?'

'He's a planner, you said?' Paula spoke slowly. 'So he'll have worked this all out in advance, won't he?'

Tony pointed a finger at her. 'Give the girl a coconut. And that means, what . . . ?'

Paula's brows furrowed as she worked it out. 'He bought the books before he started the killing.' Her face cleared as she found a conclusion. 'He might have bought all the books from the same place at the same time.'

'Almost certainly,' Tony said. 'Because you

can't walk into the average bookshop and find them all sitting on the shelves. The Anne Sexton is out of print, for starters. When you do a search for all three titles together, there's only one retailer offering them all.'

'Don't tell me, let me guess,' Kevin said. 'Valhalla.co.uk.'

'I see why you chose this lot, Carol,' Tony said ironically. 'That's right, Kevin. Valhalla.'

Kevin groaned. 'Well, that's no use. They never hand over information. And — no disrespect, Stacey — even hackers can't get into their systems. They pride themselves on it.'

'There's a first time for everything,' Stacey said. 'No system is bulletproof.'

Carol looked at Tony then at Stacey. 'You're on this already, aren't you?'

'I spoke to Stacey yesterday when I had the idea,' Tony said. 'I reckoned you had enough on your mind getting through the press conference without having to contemplate more law-breaking.'

Carol covered her ears. 'Enough. I don't want to know. Just bring me the answers. And in the meantime, let's look at these abusive trolls. What's the geographical spread like, Stacey?'

'Two in London, one in Sunderland, one in Rochdale and one in Cheltenham.'

Carol thought for a moment. 'Paula, you've already made contact with an officer in the Met on this case, haven't you?'

'DS Lee Collins. He was managing the Kate Rawlins case.'

'What did you make of him?'

'He was helpful. Didn't get the hump at me

calling to basically ask him if he'd done his job properly. I thought he had half a brain too.'

'OK. I'll speak to his DI and brief him to interview our losers for us. Alvin — Cheltenham's not that far from your old patch, is it? How do you fancy taking off now and giving somebody a hard time on your way home?'

Alvin grinned. He'd left home that morning with no idea when he'd get home again. But it looked as if Carol was cutting him a break on his first formal day in harness. With any luck, he'd be home in time to put the kids to bed. That'd be a novelty. 'It would be my pleasure, guv.'

Carol chuckled. 'Correct response. Paula, Rochdale. And Kevin, short straw: Sunderland. I know you like a drive. Let's hit them at their workplaces if we can, put the pressure on to the max. And Stacey? Keep on doing what you're doing until you've got something to tell me.' She started gathering her things together.

'I already have something to tell you,' Stacey said, cutting across everyone's preparations for leaving.

'Let's hear it,' Carol said, stopping what she was doing and giving Stacey her full attention.

'We talked about the possibility of predicting who the next victim might be. I came up with a search algorithm based on the three women we already know about. It's not as sophisticated as I would like but I think it's a quick and dirty way of identifying possibles. I've got six definite maybes that tick my boxes.'

'Oh, Stacey,' Carol sighed. 'BMP were insane to have you doing routine data searches. You are a genius. Tony, any suggestions on how we approach this?'

'I'd suggest you go to Rochdale to monster the troll and Paula gets on the phone to these women,' he said, making no attempt to soften his proposal. 'You're good at being scary and Paula's better at drawing people out than anyone I know.'

Judging by her expression, that hadn't been what Carol expected. But she took it in her stride. 'I was thinking more about the angle of approach,' she said.

'Establish the facts — what they said that was so provocative, how long the trolling has been going on, what's been said, how many have been saying it. Then move on to the emotional stuff — how does it make them feel, what support do they have, do they want you to contact the local police on their behalf. And finish up with the practical suspicious things — have they noticed anyone hanging around? Following them? Any unexplained or inexplicable happenings lately?' He gave Paula an apologetic look. 'Only a suggestion. You'll have your own ideas.'

Paula scribbled in her notebook. 'Always happy to have input,' she muttered.

'OK. Back here tomorrow morning unless you hear otherwise. I'll be on the end of a phone as usual if you need me.' Carol got to her feet. 'Let's hit the bricks.'

'What about me?' Tony said plaintively.

'Keep on thinking, Tony,' Carol said. 'It's what you do best.' There was, he knew, a tiny buried barb there, but he was content to let it go.

On their way to the lift, Paula drew Kevin to one side. 'I need a word. Meet me in the canteen in five minutes.'

Kevin immediately looked anxious. In his experience, when Paula went off on one of her tangents, it always made for times that were interesting in the Chinese sense. She was a magnet for complications, and complications were what Kevin thought he'd finally left behind. He'd given up the quiet life for the time being but that didn't mean he was eager for full-on aggravation again.

He arrived in the canteen to find Paula in a quiet corner with a can of Diet Coke and a small stack of Kit Kats. 'The four main food groups,' she said as he sat down. 'Chocolate, chocolate, chocolate and Diet Coke. You want one?'

'Neither,' he said. 'Are you always like this when Elinor's not looking?'

Paula pulled a face. 'Pretty much. Not to mention that Torin hoovers up any stray biscuit, cake or chocolate in the house.'

'That's teenagers for you.' The weary voice of experience. 'So, what's the word?'

Paula looked wary, which worried him even more. 'Somebody leaked the story about Carol to the press.'

He flushed the dark blotchy red that sometimes afflicts redheads. Leaking was the sin that had cost him his inspector's rank all those years before. Was Paula actually suggesting he'd be stupid enough to commit the same transgression twice? 'I didn't even know the details,' he said quickly. 'Don't look at me, Paula.'

Her expression was aghast. 'God, no, Kevin, that truly was the last thing on my mind.' Her hand covered her mouth as if she wished she could swallow the words that had so upset him. 'No, that never even occurred to me.'

He studied her eyes for what felt like a long moment. 'OK. I'm a bit sensitive on the subject, even after all this time. So what are you getting at?'

'Like I said, somebody leaked. Stacey and I decided we needed to know who. It's always easier to deal with your enemies if you know who they are. And we need to know if this is someone inside or outside the tent.'

Kevin gave a grim smile. 'So Stacey went walkabout inside the *Sentinel Times* server.' It wasn't a question.

'And she couldn't find anything,' Paula said ruefully. 'Not a single electronic trace. No memo, no internal mail, no payment linked to the story. And no payment requisitioned in the name of anyone we recognise.'

'So why are we having this conversation?' He had a terrible feeling of impending doom. Someone had told him that was one of the warning signs of a heart attack. The way he was feeling now, a heart attack would be a better option than where he feared Paula was going with this.

'When elint lets you down, you have to go back to humint.' The sentence hung in the air between them. Paula's words were, Kevin knew, the opposite of what Stacey believed. Machines

345

have limits; human relationships are more flexible, more malleable. That was anathema to someone who had staked everything on the machines. But to the likes of him and Paula, it made perfect sense. And now he knew why they were there.

'Oh no,' he said. 'I can't go back there again.'

'I'm not asking you to do that. All we need is for you to ask the question.'

He shook his head. He tried to feel numb because he knew numb was safe. Numb was protected. 'She nearly destroyed my marriage. She nearly destroyed me.'

'I know. But someone's trying to destroy Carol and we owe it to her to try to put a spoke in their wheel. It's been years, Kevin. Surely it's ancient history for both of you now?'

He gave a bitter little bark of laughter. 'Have you ever had love like a virus? Something in your bloodstream that you can't medicate against? You think you're over it, you think you've recovered and then you see her and bang! It's like you're back at square one. Mad with it.'

'Oh yes,' Paula said softly. 'The demon lover. The one you can never outrun. The one who always has your number. Alison Young. I keep tabs on her even now, to make sure our paths don't cross because I'm scared I wouldn't be able to resist. How insane is that? I absolutely adore Elinor. I don't have a nanosecond of doubt about the love we have for each other. But I don't trust myself enough to be convinced I could walk past Alison Young. So yes, I do know exactly what you mean. I'm asking you to take

Alison Young out for a drink.'

Kevin closed his eyes and breathed slowly in and out. Then his eyes snapped open and he reached for a Kit Kat. He stripped off the wrapper and stuffed it in his mouth. It was gone in two bites. 'You want me . . . ' he spoke through a mouthful of chocolate wafer, 'to make contact . . . with Penny Burgess?'

Paula sighed. 'If she doesn't already know the source of that story, she could find out. And God knows she owes you.'

Kevin covered his face with his hands and rubbed, as if he was scrubbing himself clean. 'I almost wrecked my marriage. And my family. Stella and me, we've rebuilt our life together.'

'And that's your rock.'

'You think?'

Paula nodded, reaching out and taking hold of Kevin's trembling hand. 'I don't think, I know. I've watched you piece your life back together and I admire you for it. Kevin, I don't believe Penny Burgess should hold any fear for you now.'

He gave an unconvincing smile. 'You're only saying that because you want me to find out who shafted Carol.'

Paula shook her head. 'I won't deny that's important. Not just to me, but for all of us. But sitting here, seeing you like this, I can't help feeling that what's as important is for you to lay the ghost of Penny Burgess to rest. I mean that, Kev. You'll never be free in your head till you confront her and realise she has no power over you any more. If you won't do it for Carol, if you won't do it for all of us, do it for Stella.'

43

Ursula Foreman stared at her car in dismay. That the tyre was flat was bad enough. But it definitely looked as if someone had taken a knife to it. She'd grown almost blasé about the endless online vituperation, laughing it off in public and despising it in private. But if this was what it looked like, it represented an unnerving escalation. It was no big deal to rip into someone anonymously online. Slashing her car tyre was aggression of a different order. She looked around, as if half-expecting an attacker to be lurking in the shadows of the food bank car park.

But there was nowhere to hide and no one in sight. Just a handful of cars belonging mostly to volunteers; most of their clients couldn't afford to drive to the facility. Whoever had done this was long gone. There was no certainty that the attack had even been directed at her. There were some nutters around who were opposed to the food banks, suggesting that their very presence attracted people they considered to be human vermin — immigrants, the poor, the care-in-the-community cases with their mental health problems.

Ursula muttered under her breath and unlocked the car. The last thing she felt like doing was changing a tyre. All she wanted was to be home, eating whatever delicious meal Bill would have whipped up. He was off to London for a couple of nights in the morning, and he always made a point of cooking something special on the eve of such departures. It was as if he wanted to leave a reminder of himself in the aromas that would linger in the kitchen and the fridge.

As she popped the boot, another car drove into the car park and pulled up alongside her. Ursula glanced across and recognised the new volunteer she'd chatted to the week before. What was his name again? Mike? Matt? Martin? She pushed aside the pile of bags for life and raised the carpet of the boot. Matt, that was it.

Almost before she knew it, he was standing between the two cars, a look of concern on his face. 'Is something wrong, Ursula?'

'Somebody's slashed one of my tyres,' she said, leaning forward to unscrew the brace that held the spare in place.

'You're kidding. That's terrible.'

She paused and sighed. 'It's pretty upsetting, Matt. I'm used to being challenged for what I write, but it's never descended into a direct attack like this.'

He stepped forward. 'Let me help you with that. I'm pretty good with my hands.' He smiled, an open, disarming expression on his face.

She hesitated, but only for a moment. As a good feminist, she knew she should take responsibility for herself. But there were worse things than accepting help from someone, even if it was a man. After all, it wasn't as if she was playing the helpless little woman. She was perfectly capable of doing it herself but, if she was honest, she could live without the hard labour of changing a tyre and the concomitant mess. 'Thank you. I appreciate that.' She stepped to one side to give him access to the spare and the tools.

'I'll have this done in no time,' he said. 'I quite like getting my hands dirty. I don't get the chance much these days.'

He'd explained during their previous conversation that he was a systems analyst, working with small and medium-sized businesses to streamline their operations. It took him all over the country on an unpredictable schedule. She imagined he was good at his job. He seemed very precise and organised in the food bank. And he was pretty anonymous-looking, with his mid-brown hair cut neatly in no particular style, his regular features and his average build. There was nothing dramatic or threatening about him, nothing that would unnerve female clients or make men feel challenged.

Just like now. Without any fuss, he had the spare wheel out and the jack in place under the chassis. 'You're right, somebody has taken a blade to this,' he said, squatting down to study the tyre. 'That feels very personal.'

'It does,' Ursula said, unable to stop the shudder that ran through her. 'But maybe it's random. Somebody who hates the food bank.'

He shook his head. 'I don't think so. If they hated the food bank that much, they'd throw a brick through the window or put dog mess through the letter box.'

'That's a scary thought. I've had a lot of hate mail — I don't know if you remember me telling you I help to run an online magazine? Some people — let's be honest, some men — don't like the things I have to say. But this is the first time I've had a direct personal attack like this.'

He grunted as he strained the wheel brace against the nuts. 'That's not something you think about when you take up a controversial position. The people out there who are so offended they'll take up arms against you.'

'You're so right,' Ursula sighed. 'But I wouldn't have done anything differently. You've got to stand up for what you believe in. Otherwise, what's the point?'

The final nut gave way to his strength and he manhandled the wheel clear of its housing. 'I agree. The problems start when you have to deal with the fact that other people have a different set of beliefs. Sometimes ones that are incompatible with yours. And they would say they have as much evidence to back them up as you do.'

'That's a very good point. But surely the sensible thing to do is to talk it over? To agree to differ? Not fill people's inbox with abuse and slash their tyres?'

He jiggled the spare tyre, trying to align the bolts with the holes in the wheel. 'Some people are beyond rational argument, though. They won't shift their position even when you offer them compelling evidence that they're in the wrong.' The wheel clanked into place. 'Oof. Nearly done now. Are you heading off anywhere special?'

'No, I'm going home. My husband's off to London tomorrow on a business trip and he's cooking a special dinner.'

'Just the family?'

'Just the two of us. We don't have kids.'

'That's a shame.' He finger-tightened the nuts.

'No, we've no regrets. We decided there were enough children on the planet and we both have careers that we enjoy, and it would have been difficult to pursue them to the full if we'd had kids. And neither of us has ever felt particularly broody.' She shrugged. 'It works for us. What about you?'

He hunched over the wheel. 'Never met the right woman.'

Ursula, who still felt blessed by Bill after fourteen years together, had a momentary pang of sorrow for him. 'It's not too late,' she said. 'Lots of people find love later in life.'

He gave a dry chuckle. 'And lots don't. I think my standards are too high.' He wiggled the wheel nuts back on. 'Speaking of high standards. I could use a little advice from you.'

'Sure,' Ursula said, not sure what she was letting herself in for but aware that one favour deserved another.

'I've been doing this job for a long time now, and I think I've got a pretty individual approach to figuring out what companies can easily do to make their systems more effective. I thought there might be some money in a self-help book that would teach bosses how to work out their own streamlining.'

'You're probably right. After all, you can't be everywhere.'

'Exactly. Could I pop round sometime and have a chat with you about how I might approach it? From the practical side? I thought with your involvement in *TellIt!* you might have some useful tips.'

It was, she thought, not much of an ask. An hour at the kitchen table would easily repay his kindness. 'Yeah, sure,' she said. 'Any morning this week would be fine. I'll be at home working. I'm always glad of the chance of a coffee break.'

He smiled. 'You've no idea how much I appreciate that. I'll look forward to it.'

44

Every now and again, Stacey got to step out from behind her desk and play at being James Bond in a dress. The lengths she went to in protecting her sources and herself might have seemed paranoid to an observer. But Stacey knew exactly how many traces people scattered behind themselves every day, merely going about their routine business. Not leaving a trail in the era of electronic surveillance and cameras everywhere was impossibly difficult. But Stacey had schooled herself; she could have chosen 'hiding in plain sight' as a *Mastermind* specialist subject.

In her desk drawer she kept a stash of pay-as-you-go SIM cards, all bought with cash in a haphazard selection of shops all over the country. Whenever work took her to a different city, she would top up her stock. Now she selected a random SIM and slotted it into a phone that any teenager would have been embarrassed to possess, never mind to use. She sent a text that consisted of a string of numbers that were two digits higher than the actual number she was sending, which corresponded to a public phone on the central station concourse, ten minutes' walk from her flat.

When her text arrived, she knew her contact would leave his flat and scurry across the shopping centre to a bank of pay phones. Fifteen minutes after she'd sent the text, he would call the phone where she was waiting. It was, she thought, ironic that with all the advances in technology, the most secure way to communicate was by the practically prehistoric system of telephone landlines. But these calls couldn't be scanned or streamed through some government security system. They were pretty robust when it came to security, especially if you used pay phones rather than a home line that could, theoretically, be tapped.

Exactly a quarter of an hour later, the phone next to Stacey rang abruptly. She picked it up and said, 'Valhalla.'

There was a short pause. She could hear the man on the other end of the line breathing. 'DVLA,' he said.

'Done. Ten, K.' Transaction completed, she put the phone down. The arrangement was simple. In exchange for access codes for Valhalla's server, she would hand over access to the Driver and Vehicle Licensing Agency's database. Both would be time-limited, obviously. Any system worth having changed its access codes regularly. As in, daily or weekly. The handover would take place in row K of screen ten of the shopping mall's multi-screen cinema at the start of the next film being shown there. All beautifully random and, of course, invisible to CCTV because they'd be in the dark.

Stacey checked her regular phone. She had forty-seven minutes to kill before the next show-ing. She groaned. A romcom set in a Midwest college dorm. And she'd have to sit through enough of it not to look suspicious. The things she did for Carol Jordan.

She cut through the city centre to the shopping mall and slowly browsed her way through, doubling back on herself and lingering over displays of handbags and shoes. She was as certain as she could be that she had no pursuit on foot, so she made her way to the cinema, bought a ticket with cash and settled into a seat midway along the empty row K. There were less than a dozen patrons in the cinema; pensioners taking advantage of cheap matinee rates. Good for them, Stacey thought. Better here than sitting in a cold flat watching daytime soaps.

The lights dimmed and still she was alone. Adverts for cars and holiday destinations and fast-food chains; trailers for films she swore she'd never see; then finally the BBFC certificate revealing that *Cupcakes to Die For* had a 12A certificate. Halfway through the opening titles, a tall, lean figure folded itself into the seat next to her. He smelled of coconut and pineapple. What was it with hair product these days? Half the world smelled like a tropical fruit salad. 'Hey, Stace, how's it going,' a low bass voice rumbled in her ear.

'It's going, Harvey.'

He chuckled. 'It's later than we think, right?' He stuck a hand in his pocket and pulled out a taxi company receipt. In the light from the screen, Stacey could see a scribbled line of numbers, letters, slashes and dashes. 'This is good till midnight. Best I could do.'

She handed him a postcard of a Henry Moore sculpture from Leeds City Art Gallery. 'That'll see you through till Saturday midnight.'

'Ah. A bargain. I don't often get one of those from you. You must really want Valhalla.'

'You know the kind of work I do, Harvey. You can't put a price on saving people's lives.'

'It always warms the cockles of my heart, doing stuff for you. It's not often I get to feel virtuous as well as clever.' A low chuckle. 'You staying till the bitter end?'

Stacey sighed. 'One of us has to.'

'I tell you what, you bugger off and get back to saving people's lives. I've got five whole days to tease out what I'm after but you've only got till midnight before you turn into a pumpkin and your Jimmy Choos change into Uggs.'

Stacey couldn't hide her surprise. 'Thanks, Harvey.'

'Next time I'll make you watch a *Fast and Furious*. And then you'll be sorry.' He stood up to let her pass. 'Good luck with the life-saving thing.'

Five minutes later, Stacey was blinking in the daylight, heart racing at the prospect of forbidden fruit. She couldn't wait to get back to her flat. As she hurried through the mall, it struck her that she hadn't been this excited for days. A pang of guilt shot though her. What kind of worthless girlfriend was she, to be this excited when the man she loved was so clearly in a state of misery?

45

Carol had waited for the rest of the team to leave, calling Tony back as he was on his way out the door. 'What do you truly think?' she said, leaning against the table, her tired eyes belying the air of confidence she'd brought to the briefing.

'I think you're doing well, all things considered.'

She shook her head with weary humour. 'I wasn't talking about me. I meant the case. If there is a case. If we're not chasing shadows because we need to be doing something or we go mad.'

'For what it's worth, I think there is a case. But I also think we need to move fast because, before we know it, we're going to catch a live case from one of our suppliers. And then the heat will turn up underneath us. We need to crack this to show we've got what it takes to spot stuff happening under our noses. But also to remind us how good we are.'

Carol ran a hand through her hair. 'You're right.' She squeezed her eyes shut momentarily. 'Christ, but I could do with a drink. I have to keep holding tight to things to stop my hands shaking.' She looked him in the eye. 'I had no idea, really no idea how badly I was dealing with the drinking. I genuinely thought I was the one in charge.'

He laid a hand on her arm. 'It's never easy to be clear-eyed when it comes to ourselves. That's why I need my supervisor. Jacob isn't always right, like I'm not always right. But he always helps me to look at things from a different angle. That's all you needed, Carol. You're doing very well. Trust me on that.'

The door behind them opened and they both turned to face a tall, bony-faced young man with huge brown eyes, delicate eyebrows and ridiculously long lashes. He was wearing a dark blue suit that he might grow into one day if he ate enough canteen food. He smiled hesitantly. 'DCI Jordan? I'm DC Hussain. I was told that I'm being transferred to your unit?'

Carol looked him up and down. 'You know what we are?'

He nodded but looked uncertain. 'ReMIT. Like the old flying squad, only for homicide.'

'And incorruptible,' Tony said. 'Don't forget incorruptible.'

Hussain clearly didn't know whether this was banter or not. He looked pained. 'Yes, sir.'

'I'm not a 'sir'. I'm not even a cop. I'm Tony Hill. Dr Tony Hill. I'm a clinical psychologist.'

'Don't ask what he does around here,' Carol said. 'It doesn't make sense until you see it in action. I'm glad you've joined us. Sergeant McIntyre speaks very highly of you.'

'Thank you, ma'am.' His relief at being on safe ground evaporated when he caught her scowl.

'Don't call me ma'am. Guv, boss, chief, even DCI Jordan. But not ma'am. That makes me feel a hundred and four.'

'Yes, ma — guv.' He almost smiled.

'And what's your first name? We tend towards the informal here.'

'Karim, guv.'

'OK, Karim. You'll get a lot of responsibility on this squad. You'll have to learn fast and learn well. At this level, it's sink or swim.'

'That's fine by me, guv. I've got certificates for swimming.' He grinned, confident but not cocky.

'Well, let's throw you in at the deep end. You're with me. You can drive. We're off to Rochdale.'

'Hitting the high spots, then, guv?'

Carol rolled her eyes at Tony. 'God help me, another one that thinks they're funny. Come on, Karim, I'll brief you on the way.'

★ ★ ★

According to Stacey, Steve Fisher worked for an insurance company. One of the ones that rang up unsuspecting punters about to sit down to dinner to give them dire warnings about how much their premiums were going to rise if they didn't see the light and transfer immediately to them. The idea of doing that for a living depressed the hell out of Carol. It was easy to despise the cold callers, but she reckoned most of their employees were probably decent young people desperate to make a legal living, settling for shit jobs because there were no others. There would be some utter scumbags like Steve Fisher, but you got that everywhere. Even in the police.

She expressed this view to Karim as they

drove down the motorway towards Rochdale. 'You know all the trouble the uniforms get on a weekend? All the binge drinking and the fighting and the human wreckage filling up A&E?' he said.

'What about it?' Carol wondered how they'd got from cold calling to binge drinking.

'I reckon it's partly because most people my age are stuck in shit jobs like that. Every day's the same, your bosses hate you and they don't care if you know it, the job itself makes you feel like dog dirt on the sole of somebody's shoe. So come the weekend, all you want is to get totally blitzed and forget about how bloody awful your life is.'

'That's how you'd solve the problem, is it? Provide meaningful jobs for people?'

'Yeah, I reckon.'

'But back when I was a kid, there were plenty of shit jobs. Working down the pit or working in a factory — surely that was every bit as bad?'

Karim took the slip road that would take them to the industrial estate where Steve Fisher worked. 'The work was hard, yeah. And dangerous. But you were all in it together. They were mates. They were there for each other. And they had security. Jobs like that, they were for life if you wanted. My dad worked in a mill up in Blackburn when he first came over here and he says there was a real feeling that you could get on and make something of yourself. My generation? They don't feel like that. Most of the lads I know, they've got no optimism. I'm about the only one that feels like I've got a real chance at a good future. If I was working in a call centre, I'd go out and get hammered every chance I got.'

He had a point. Carol gave a wry smile. He was going to fit right in with the opinionated, gobby team that was his new home. 'Fair point.'

They turned into a wide road that ran between blocky brick buildings with small windows and zero personality. Their destination was conveniently plastered with hoardings that advertised the company name and its services. Karim paused by a space marked for the Finance Director and gave Carol a questioning look.

'Oh yes,' she said. 'Toes were made for treading on.'

They walked into a reception area so compact their presence made it feel overcrowded. Carol flashed her badge. 'I'm here to see one of your employees, Steve Fisher.'

The receptionist, a plump woman in her twenties with immaculate hair, nails and make-up, scarcely registered their presence. 'Do you have an appointment?' It was barely a question.

Carol delivered her most dangerous smile and spoke softly. It was a frightening combination. 'I don't need an appointment. I am the officer in charge of the Regional Major Incident Team and I'm here to see Steve Fisher. Now, if you don't have the authority to make that happen, I'd suggest you talk to someone who does.'

The receptionist managed a feeble eye roll as her last act of defiance. But she picked up the phone and pressed a button. 'I've got a cop here wants to talk to somebody called Steve Fisher

'. . . No, she didn't . . . OK.' She replaced the phone with a flourish. 'Mr Laskarowicz will be out in a minute.'

'And he is?' Karim asked.

'In charge.'

As she spoke, a door in the wall behind her opened and a burly man with a shaved head and sweat rings under his arms burst in. 'You're the police?' He sounded incredulous. 'What are you doing here?'

Here we go again. Carol introduced them and explained the reason for their visit.

'What do you want to talk to Steve about?'

Carol glanced at the receptionist. 'Can we do this somewhere a little less public?'

Laskarowicz muttered, 'Oh, for Chrissake,' under his breath and led them through into a dingy corridor. His office was the first door they came to. It was small but it was neat, the walls covered with photographs of him either shaking hands with other unattractive men or posing with a bunch of guys in football strips. It smelled of fried onions and the carpet was a mosaic of brown stains. There was nowhere for them to sit, so Karim leaned against the wall and Carol perched on the corner of the desk, enjoying the dismay on Laskarowicz's face. 'He's in the middle of a shift right now. This is very inconvenient. Why didn't you phone ahead and make an appointment to see him in his own time, not mine?'

'I need to interview Steve Fisher in connection with a series of threatening and abusive tweets that appear to come from his account.'

The manager looked genuinely shocked. 'Steve? Steve Fisher? He wouldn't say boo to a goose. He wouldn't threaten anybody.'

'If that's the case, I'm sure he'll be able to explain it all to us. Tell me, does he work a regular pattern of hours or is it shifts?'

'Why do you need to know that?' Carol waited him out, staring patiently and pointedly at him. He sighed histrionically. 'He's a dayshift co-ordinator so he works from six in the morning till two in the afternoon, Sunday to Thursday. Why?'

'In that case, it looks like he's sent quite a few abusive tweets while he was at work.'

'I find that hard to believe. This is just a bit of banter, right? Somebody with a sense of humour bypass has kicked off?'

Carol nodded to Karim, who took a sheaf of paper out of his pocket. ' "I want to see you burn, bitch." That's one bit of banter. 'It's about time you had some sense raped into you.' That's another.'

Laskarowicz had paled. There was a sheen of sweat on his top lip. 'He sent these from here?'

'That's one of the things we hope to find out from Mr Fisher. Perhaps we can use your office if you can find us a couple more chairs?'

He wiped his top lip and reached for the phone. 'We've got a conference room. It's more spacious.' He ran his finger down a list taped to the desktop then stabbed the phone buttons fiercely. 'Steve. It's Ray. I need to talk to you right now, in the conference room. Stop whatever you're doing and get down there now.'

He banged the phone down, breathing heavily through his nose. 'Jesus Christ. This is all I need.'

They followed him down the hall to a slightly bigger room furnished with a table and half a dozen plastic bucket chairs. Everything looked as if it had been rescued from a skip. Laskarowicz chewed the skin on the side of his thumbnail and bounced on the balls of his feet. A few minutes passed then the door opened to reveal a young man with a bad haircut and angry skin. 'You wanted me?' He sounded as if the pit of hell had opened at his feet. As he moved into the room, Karim discreetly occupied the space between him and the door.

'Not me,' Laskarowicz said, his voice grim. 'The police. You've got some answering to do, Steve.'

Fisher's eyes widened and he glanced behind him. His face revealed all; the momentary notion of flight, the realisation that the route was blocked, the terror of what was to come. 'I never did anything.'

Carol turned the tractor beam of her attention full on to him. 'Come and sit down, Steve. We need to talk. Thanks, Mr Laskarowicz, we'll speak to you on our way out.'

She waited till the manager made his reluctant way out of the room, never taking her eyes off the frightened young man whose Adam's apple was bobbing up and down as he kept frantically swallowing. Then she said, 'Steve Fisher, I want to interview you under caution in relation to the sending of abusive and threatening messages. You do not have to say anything. But it may harm your defence if you do not mention when questioned something which you later rely on in court. Anything you do say may be given in evidence. Do you understand?'

'What? Are you arresting me? Do I need a lawyer?' His voice rose to a squeak.

'At this point, I'm trying to establish the facts. If you want a lawyer, of course that's your right. We'll take you down to the police station and we can wait there till someone is available to act for you. Though I don't know whether you'd qualify for legal aid . . . '

'Or we can have a nice little friendly chat here,' Karim said, coming in from the side and pulling up a chair.

Fisher's narrow mouth pursed as he considered. 'OK, I'll talk to you.'

Carol took the sheaf of papers from Karim. She flicked through till she found the one she wanted. She placed it in front of Fisher. 'Are these your online identities? Twitter, Instagram? And the others?'

He swallowed hard. 'How did you get that? That's private.'

'Everything's private till you break the law,' Karim said harshly. 'Are they your handles?'

Fisher nodded. 'Yeah.' His shoulders slumped. He knew what was coming.

'Did you send these messages to Daisy Morton?' Carol laid two sheets of paper in front of him. ' "You're going to burn, bitch. You've dissed men once too often. We're going to fuck you up.' And what about this one? 'I hope your children die slowly from cancer, then you'll get what you deserve.' These are your handiwork?'

Fisher looked desperately from one to the other. 'Don't even think about trying some pathetic excuse about your mates nicking your phone,' Karim snarled. Carol was liking him more every time he opened his mouth.

Fisher cleared his throat and sat on his hands. 'Yeah. I wrote them.'

'How did you feel when Daisy Morton did burn? When her house blew up and she died and her family lost their home? Did that make you happy?'

He shook his head, giving her a pleading look. 'I never meant it for real, I was just . . . I don't know, showing off.'

'Acting the big man,' Karim sneered. 'So where were you the day Daisy Morton died?'

Fisher literally jumped in his seat. 'What?'

'You heard.'

'What's that got to do with me? She killed herself. I never had nothing to do with it.'

'You don't think piling all this crap on Daisy's head might have had something to do with her decision?'

Fisher pushed his chair back from the table, as if putting physical distance between him and his words would separate them. 'Sticks and stones, man. Just words, that's all, just words.'

Carol leaned forward. 'Where were you that day, Steve? Did you go round to Daisy's house to tell her to her face what you thought of her?'

'No,' he yelped. 'I never went near her. Look, I wasn't the only one who sent messages. There were loads of them. All I did was join in what everybody else was doing.'

'But she wasn't the only one you attacked like this.' Carol put more messages on the table. 'Kate Rawlins. 'You need to have some sense raped into you.' 'You're too ugly to rape. Not like your tasty daughter. We'll make her pay for your dirty mouth.' Kate killed herself as well. Where were you that day? Were you in London, persuading her to gas herself in her garage? And what about Jasmine Burton?' More paper on the table. 'What about this? 'Someone should stab you then fuck the hole.' What were you thinking, Steve? Where were you the night Jasmine walked into the River Exe and drowned herself?'

Now he was shaking, his whole body trembling, his teeth chattering like a man in the grip of a fever. 'I never. I never went near them. I never.'

'You abused them and now they're dead. It's a straight line, Steve.' Carol pushed the paper towards him and leaned back, arms folded across her chest, expression implacable.

He began to cry, fat tears spilling from his eyes and running down his cheeks. 'I never,' he gulped.

Carol exchanged a quick look with Karim. They both knew they weren't dealing with a killer. But their instincts didn't count as evidence. To discount Fisher, they needed evidence. 'Get a hold of yourself, Steve,' Carol said. 'We need you to prove to us you had nothing to do with these deaths. We need to see your time sheets. We need alibis from you for when these women died. And then maybe, just maybe, this will all go away.'

He gulped and gasped and looked piteously at her. 'You're not going to send me to jail?'

'That's not my decision. But know this, Steve. If you lie to me in one single tiny detail, you're going down. And when you come out, you'll be lucky to get a zero hours contract cleaning toilets. Now let's make a start, shall we?'

46

Driving to Sunderland and back gave Kevin plenty of time to consider how he was going to deal with Penny Burgess. There was the small matter of interviewing a potential suspect in between but it was obvious within a minute of meeting Robbie Percy that he probably thought Sylvia Plath was a topless model. He had a menial job on the production line in a car plant and had less sophistication than the machines he worked with. There was no way he had the brains or the personality to drive anyone to suicide unless it was to avoid the prospect of having to spend time with him. Kevin put the fear of God into him, humiliated him in front of his workmates and drove straight back to Bradfield, continuing to fret over where he could meet Penny.

He needed it to be a public place. The last thing he wanted was to risk being alone with her in private. Yes, it had been years since they'd been lovers. He'd only ever seen her since at crime scenes and press conferences where he was protected by his job and the presence of other people, but even so, he'd felt the old drag of attraction to her. She would always be trouble where he was concerned and he couldn't afford to take the risk of meeting her behind closed doors.

But it couldn't be the kind of public place

where they'd be seen by someone who recognised them. It would be ironic if a colleague spotted him and thought he'd returned to his old ways when he was trying to do the opposite of leaking. So that ruled out bars and coffee shops in the city centre.

Halfway down the A1 on his way home, the answer finally occurred to him. He pulled off at the next services and spent half an hour composing a text.

> Hi Penny. I'd like to buy you a coffee. No strings. Meet me in the café at Dobson's Garden World at 4pm? Kevin M.

She lived in a flat. There was no reason for her to be an habitué of the sprawling garden centre a mile from where she lived. Kevin was an occasional visitor now he'd taken up the allotment, but he and Stella went somewhere else when they were buying stuff for the garden, one that was nearer home. He'd never seen anyone he knew on his visits there, and the café was tucked away from the main concourse. What could be less redolent of adultery than a suburban garden centre?

Kevin arrived first. Nervous, he pottered around the tools section, settling on a new pair of secateurs and a different rose for his watering can. At five to four, he bought himself a Coke and chose a table apart from the handful of other customers. He wasn't worried that she hadn't replied to his text. She was the queen of wrong-footing people. Of course she wouldn't have given him the satisfaction of some anodyne reply.

He took a swig of his drink and instantly felt his stomach revolt. She'd always gone straight to his guts, he remembered that now. He could never eat or drink ahead of their rendezvous.

And then all at once there she was. She'd bypassed the counter and made straight for the table. 'Well. If it isn't Kevin Matthews,' she sighed. She scarcely looked a day older than when they'd first met. Her dark hair was the same cascade of mingled dark brown shades, her skin looked clear and soft, her lips slightly parted in that half-smile that was both knowing and inviting. There were a few more lines around her eyes, but they only made her look more interesting. As always, she wore clothes that were expensively simple, that emphasised all the right curves and disguised any that she wanted to hide. Her job might be provincial but Penny Burgess was anything but.

Kevin stumbled to his feet. 'Penny. Thanks for coming. You look great.' He hated himself for the words as soon as they were uttered. So much for playing it cool. 'Can I get you a coffee?'

She shuddered and sat down. 'God, no. It's one of those horrible machines. Press a button, out comes frothy milk substitute and a nasty, bitter brew. You know me, Kevin, I only settle for the best.' Her voice was not the one she used at press conferences. Then, she was forceful and strong, impossible to ignore. Here she was as impossible to ignore but for very different reasons. This voice was low and warm, intimate and subtle.

He sat too, thankful that she hadn't offered

her face for a kiss. His mouth felt dry and vast. 'I see your byline all the time. You've been doing some interesting work.'

She smiled. 'I have managed to extend the crime beat to cover all sorts of wickedness.' She leaned forward and put her hand over Kevin's. The shock was electric but he forced himself to look at the hand itself. Now he could see the signs of ageing that Penny had banished from her face. 'I missed you, my little ginger pig.'

'Yeah, well, sometimes we can't have what we want. Penny, this isn't me looking to revive things between us. I want to ask you a favour.'

She raised one eyebrow in a calculated move. 'And why would I want to do you a favour?'

Kevin drew his hand back. 'For old times' sake? Because I know that, in spite of what you want people to think, you're a decent human being? Because it never hurts to have a favour in the bank? All of the above?'

She gave a wry smile and shook her head. 'I'm amazed you'd even ask, after what happened to your career last time you got into bed with me, figuratively and literally.'

He forced himself to meet her eyes. 'Believe me, if there was any other way, I wouldn't be here. But we meant a lot to each other once. So I thought it was worth asking.'

'Ah, Kevin, you were always so serious. It was hard sometimes to have fun with you. It always had to mean so much . . . '

He shook his head. 'If that's how you want to play it, fine. But I know it meant something to you too.'

'Sweet.' Her expression was anything but.

'ReMIT. That's what I want to talk to you about.'

'Ah yes, the holy grail that brought you out of retirement and gave you your old status back.'

'It's a big deal, Penny, and it's on your patch. There's going to be a lot of great stories coming out of ReMIT, and because we're based in Bradfield, you'll be on the front line.'

'Well, duh, Kevin. I had worked that one out for myself. But surely you're not offering yourself up as a source?'

He shook his head with a rueful smile. 'I'm not that stupid, Penny. I don't want to throw away a second chance. And that's where I think we have something in common. We both have self-interest in making sure ReMIT works. Me because of the job. And you because of the stories.'

Penny crossed her elegant legs and sat back in her seat. 'You're interesting me now, Kevin. Where is this common interest going to take us?'

'You saw the story at the weekend? About Carol Jordan?'

She gave a scornful laugh. 'Oh yes. A mess of unsubstantiated innuendo and information that hadn't been knitted together properly. They should have taken more time with it and bottomed it properly. There was a good story lurking in there. Probably.'

'It nearly holed us below the waterline before we got started,' Kevin said. 'Obviously, we've got enemies. One in particular who took a chance on pulling together a half-arsed tale and leaking it.'

'And you want to know who that is.'

'Of course I do. And frankly, so should you. They're leaking to someone who isn't you, who doesn't know how to run a good story. But more than that, they're trying to bring down something that will keep you supplied with cracking good stories for years to come.'

Penny laughed. 'That's better, Kevin. I like it when you stop appealing to my good nature and go for my naked self-interest.' She gave him a long, considering look. 'Suppose I did find out what you want to know. You'd remember that down the line?'

'I won't leak, Penny. But when we have something we can release, you'll be the first on the list.' It was a promise he couldn't keep, but he didn't care. There would be no comeback. Because what he'd realised as the conversation had progressed was that although she made his heart race and his palms sweat, he wasn't helpless any more. He'd somehow grown up in the ways that mattered. Yes, he wanted her. But he knew he wasn't about to give in to that desire.

She sucked her lips in, then blew them out in a kissing motion. 'A business arrangement, then. All right, Kevin. I'll see what I can do.' She stood up. 'It's lovely to see you. Let's do this again.'

And she was gone as swiftly as she'd arrived. Kevin felt his body relax, his head swim. It was going to be all right. Really, it was going to be all right.

47

Paula had laid claim to one of the small interview rooms on the new ReMIT floor. It smelled of cut wood and fresh carpet, with a faint note of low emission paint underlying it. It felt slightly alien to her to be in police offices that didn't have the lingering tang of stale nicotine and male sweat. Décor was always low down on the budget totem pole; she reckoned the main Skenfrith Street incident room had last been decorated some time in the early nineties. And yet, there was something comforting about its familiar scruffiness. Here, there were no flyers and memos on the walls, their curling edges yellow with age, no squad rotas with their crossings-out and scribbled notes. Even the furniture was new, unscuffed and clean. The room had no history; it was a clean slate.

Time to change that. Paula opened a new A4 notebook and took out her phone. She woke her tablet from sleep and called up the briefing Stacey had prepared. The first woman on the list was Maxine Silvers, a successful businesswoman who had been appointed to a seat on the board of a Championship football club and dared to put her head over the parapet on the subject of homophobia in football. Stacey had provided a sample of some of the abuse she'd had on social media. Paula wondered whether the wives and girlfriends and mothers of these men had any idea of the vileness that spewed out on their computer screens. Somehow, she doubted it. No point in calling Maxine's number; she'd never answer a stranger, given the level of unpleasantness she'd had to deal with. Paula texted her instead, asking her to call via the BMP switchboard to reassure her.

She went through the same process with the next three women before Maxine Silvers rang on the landline. 'Thanks for getting back to me,' Paula said.

'No problem, I'm just glad somebody's doing something about these morons,' she said, a strong Welsh lilt to her voice.

'I understand you have reported the abuse to your local police?' That was, after all, how Stacey had found Maxine.

'Yes, and they were very sympathetic. But to be honest, I don't have any confidence that they knew what to do about it. It's one thing if you're a household name, then they get off their backsides because of the publicity, but if you're not an A-list celebrity, it's not such a high priority. The likes of me, we don't get the VIP treatment.'

'I'm sorry you feel like that. In this unit, we don't care what your status is, we want to do what we can to put a stop to this sort of harassment.' Not strictly true, but not a lie either. 'Can you tell me when you started to get these hate messages?'

'It was about three weeks ago . . . Let me check . . . Yes, the first one was three weeks tomorrow. Right after I had my little rant about

377

why men's football is so scared of acknowledging they have gay men in the game. The women are coming to terms with it, but the men seem to be running scared. That's pretty much what I said. And within minutes of it being reported, the trolls started. I can send you a copy of what I've been getting.'

'That would be helpful. Can I ask, what was your reaction?'

'Well, to be honest, I was shocked. Shocked and a bit shaken. I knew that kind of abuse was out there, but I really didn't think I'd said anything particularly new. There's a whole campaign against homophobia in football, for heaven's sake. The problem seems to be that, as a woman, I have no place in the conversation.'

'Did you take any action? Close down your Twitter account or your Facebook page or anything like that?'

Maxine laughed. 'God, no. My whole bloody life is online these days. No, once I was over the initial shock, I set about blocking the little bastards. You only get one pop at me, then you're gone, out of my life forever.'

'You weren't frightened by them?' Paula scribbled *Not scared off* on her pad.

She tutted. 'They weren't on my doorstep. The kind of people who resort to name-calling online, they're not the ones to worry about. They're stupid little boys shouting names in the playground. If I went round their houses and called them on it, they'd wet themselves.'

'And yet you reported it to the police?'

'It's against the law, isn't it? Threatening

people? It's nasty. I hoped that they'd get a fright like the fright they gave me. Some big bad policeman — or policewoman, I suppose — turning up on their doorstep and ruining their day like they'd tried to ruin mine. Didn't get me anywhere, though, did it?' Maxine sounded more disappointed than angry.

'The main thing is that you don't feel threatened.'

'Not threatened, love. Just pissed off. It puts other people off speaking out when they see the kind of crap that the likes of me get when we say what we think. And that's not a good thing, believe me.'

'Have you had any indication at all that any of the people making threats against you might put them into action?'

'Not a one. No bricks through the windows or scratches on my car.' She laughed, a throaty sound redolent of cigarettes. 'Well, except for the ones I put there.'

'No signs of anyone following you? No strangers hanging around at home or at work?'

'Not that I've noticed. Should I be looking?'

'There's no reason to think so, no. But I have to ask.'

'Fair enough. So what are you going to do about these morons?'

Good question. 'I wish I could tell you something concrete. We're trying to develop a joined-up strategy so we can deal with them. But I'll be honest. The problem we keep running into is the companies who run the social media sites hiding behind data protection legislation.'

Maxine grunted. 'Tell me about it. Well, good luck with that. If there's anything else I can help you with, call me. But I'm not losing any sleep over these bastards, let me tell you.'

Paula hung up and leaned back in her chair. She wasn't sure what the point of these interviews was. As far as she could tell, there was little in common between the responses of the three dead women. Kate Rawlins had been uncomfortable but dismissive, Jasmine Burton had been frightened and upset, and Daisy Morton had given them the metaphorical finger. Paula had a hunch that it wasn't their responses that counted. It was what they'd said. And on that basis, Maxine Silvers didn't fit.

She sighed. That didn't mean she shouldn't focus on the task she'd been given. For all she knew, her hunch was wide of the mark. There might yet be something lurking in the shadows. And as far as her colleagues were concerned, if there was anything to be got, she was the one to get it.

Three hours and five more interviews later, she was ready to concede defeat. Of the six possibles Stacey had identified, Paula reckoned only two fitted the pattern — Ursula Foreman, a Bradfield blogger and journalist, and a Norwich novelist called Zoe Brewster. They'd both expressed opinions that were similar to the dead women and they both had moderately high profiles.

The question was, what were they going to do about it? They didn't have any solid evidence to back up their theory and even if they did, and they had the resources to put surveillance on the women, it was doubtful whether they would know what they were looking for.

This case was like wrestling fog. Although she despised herself for it, Paula couldn't help longing for some twisted killer doing the kind of tangible things you could put your finger on and go, 'There. That's what he does. That's who he is. And here's how we find him.'

Had they lost their way? Had something gone horribly wrong? Had Carol been out of the game for too long? Had Tony and Carol finally gone off the rails and sent them all flying through the air on a wild goose chase? Paula put her head in her hands and groaned softly. Her head was spinning; she had no idea what to do next. Was this what it was like when the wheels came off?

48

Nothing was ever as straightforward as you thought it was going to be, Stacey chided herself. She ought to know by now. Armed with the access codes for Valhalla.co.uk, she'd let herself into the retail giant's site by the back door. On the basis that there would be traps for the unwary, she'd moved cautiously through the opening levels of security, doing the digital equivalent of peering round corners before she turned them. Eventually, after a few heart-stopping moments where screens froze on her or raced past at breakneck speed, she reached a place where she felt fairly confident she could move around with a degree of safety.

Her first attempt was a hopeful one, wondering whether she could enter all three titles in one search. Clearly it was possible but equally clearly it would take time for the system to spit out a result. Aware of the clock ticking, Stacey drummed her fingers along the edge of the keyboard, feeling the tension in her back and neck. After a few minutes, she actually got to her feet and did some shoulder stretches against the wall.

When she got back to her screen, she was faced with a moment of crushing disappointment. According to the search, not one single customer had bought all three titles together. Ever. She slumped in her seat. It had been a great idea of Tony's but it looked as if he'd been dancing in the dark once too often.

Because she was still in the system and she had some time left, she set up searches for all the possible pairings of the three titles. Almost immediately, the system spewed out 1,279 results for Woolf and Plath together. Stacey copied the list and printed it out, belt and braces as ever. Were they set texts, or something? Stacey had a vague memory of girls she'd been at school with fetishising Plath. What was it about suicide that was so appealing to adolescents? It had never crossed her mind, even at her lowest points. There was always the promise of better days over the horizon. New programs, new possibilities, new tricks to learn.

Given that result, it was all the more surprising that there were no results at all for the other pairings. Nobody who had bought *Ariel* and *A Room of One's Own* had bought *The Death Notebooks* with it, either at the same time or on a separate occasion. It looked as if the killer had gone elsewhere for a copy of the Anne Sexton. Unless of course he'd already owned it. That and the other titles too.

Stacey sighed. She hated to admit defeat but maybe this time the defeat had come at the hands of circumstance rather than her lack of competence. But she wasn't going to give in until she'd tried everything. She decided to do one last search, for the Anne Sexton on its own. And up it popped. Valhalla had sold eleven second-hand copies of the out-of-print title in the past year, which seemed amazing to Stacey. Eleven people who cared that much about a dead American poet she'd never heard of. She scrutinised the records, noticing that being second-hand seemed to put the book in a separate category to the new books. Could that be the answer?

Again, she copied the list then turned to one of her other screens, where she set up a comparison between the names on the Plath and Woolf list and those who'd bought the Sexton. Three names were highlighted by the computer. All women.

'Damn,' Stacey muttered. Because she couldn't help herself, she looked them up in Valhalla's customer database. One had an address at the English department in a Scottish university; the second apparently lived in France and the third had bought dozens of books of poetry, some of it by men. A further search revealed that the third was herself a published poet. Even if they hadn't agreed with Tony and Alvin that the killer they sought was a man, none of these seemed a viable suspect. It looked as if Tony's inspired suggestion had been a dead end.

Unless . . . perhaps there was a way of widening out the comparison? She'd asked only for exact matches. What if there were variations? Sometimes people set up new accounts when they changed their email address or the credit card they wanted their purchases billed to. She had some time left on the clock. Surely it was worth having another crack at it?

This time, she downloaded and printed the buyers of each of the three titles separately. Let her systems make the comparisons rather than

Valhalla's. There were pages of names now. It would be an almost impossible task for a human brain to sort them out. But for a programmer like Stacey, it was a minor challenge to set up a routine to weed out close variations.

She ran the comparison again, this time factoring in variations and using all three full lists. And this time, another match showed up. This time, one was definitely a man. Matthew Martin had bought both Woolf and Sexton. And MJ Martin had purchased Plath. How sweet it was when the machines delivered what no human could possibly manage.

Finding the personal accounts of both Martins was the work of moments. A few keystrokes, a few deft movements of fingers over trackpad and there it was. The credit card details were different. But the billing addresses were identical, and conveniently the same as the delivery address. The same instruction that if he wasn't home, his parcels could be left safely in the garden shed round the back. And a list of all the other purchases from both accounts.

He'd bought all sorts from Valhalla. Computer accessories. Pay-as-you-go phones. Vitamin supplements. Jeans. SIM cards. A hacksaw. MP3 downloads. And books. The three Stacey had gone looking for plus four others. Books of poetry by Marina Tsvetaeva, May Ayim and Alejandra Pizarnik. And a novel by Penelope Delta. Stacey had heard of none of them, but five minutes' googling revealed that all four were writers who had killed themselves. Hanging, jumping from a high building, poison and an overdose. It looked as if Matthew Martin was planning a major campaign.

For most people that would have been enough to take into the next morning's briefing. But Stacey considered that a mere baseline which she was obliged to rise above. With a name and an address she had the raw materials for a biography. First there was LinkUp, the site where people could post their beefed-up CVs and connect with everyone they'd ever wanted to impress. And there was Matthew Martin, civil engineer. A specialist in bridges. If you wanted to build a bridge or renovate or repair one, he was apparently your man. He'd worked on a wide range of projects overseas and in the UK. His most recent job seemed to have been in the Scottish highlands. Stacey followed the links for the project and discovered that the lead engineer on the project had been a woman. She captured the information and highlighted it. Not that she was particularly interested; but she knew it was the sort of thing Tony would latch on to.

His Facebook page wasn't very helpful. He had less than two dozen friends, almost all of them engineers. He owned up to no interests or relationships, even resisting listing his favourite albums, movies or TV shows. The last posting on the page was just over three months old and was a moody photograph of the Humber Bridge at dawn.

According to DVLA, he had a clean driving licence and owned a five-year-old 4WD Toyota Navarra pickup as well as a two-year-old Volkswagen Passat. Both were registered to the same address as his credit card.

Stacey wondered if she could get inside the ANPR system, the network of cameras that recorded in real time the number plates of the majority of vehicles on the road as they moved around the country. The last time she'd tried, she'd timed out before she got where she wanted to be. Since then she'd refined her security-busting software, tailoring it more precisely to the idiosyncrasies of the site, but she hadn't had a chance to try it out yet.

Tentatively she launched herself at the site. To her delight, she slipped inside as cleanly as if she had a set of master keys. If she could get what she needed, she wouldn't waste time trying to analyse it, just print it out and look at it offline. First she tried the Toyota pickup, typing in the registration. If he'd been moving his victims around, it would be a lot easier to get them in and out of the cab or the bed of the truck. She didn't know how much data was going to come up, so she set the search window for two days before Jasmine Burton had walked into the Exe. But nothing came up at all. Either she wasn't doing it right or he hadn't driven his Toyota anywhere the ANPR cameras were operating, which seemed unlikely, given they covered all the key trunk routes in the country these days. The other possibility was that he'd obscured part of his number plate with mud or reflective spray. Sometimes it was possible to hoodwink the cameras like that. And Tony had emphasised that they were dealing with a careful planner.

She tried again, this time using the registration

number of the Passat. And this time, up came a string of results. The car had dozens of hits over the past ten days. Stacey printed out the results, then stretched the time window back to the week before Kate Rawlins had died. The screen scrolled down and down and down as the results flowed in. He'd been all over the place, she thought as the paper spilled out of the printer. With all this information at their fingertips, they could go to the mobile phone companies and pinpoint the areas they wanted them to check for the phones and SIM cards they now knew Matthew Martin owned. There would be others too, no doubt. But they could make a start there. And for all her darkside skills, it was a search too far for Stacey to make. For now, she'd done all she could and she was willing to bet she had more to bring to the morning meeting than anyone else.

She stood up and did some stretches against the wall. It had been a long day and she didn't want to wake up stiff and sore. For the briefest of moments, she wondered where Sam was and what he was doing. Maybe she should text him one more time? Let him know she hadn't stopped thinking about him? But she pushed the thought away. She'd chased him enough. He knew how she felt. It was up to him to stop behaving like a child. If he didn't know her well enough by now to understand that she wasn't expecting him to grovel, he hadn't been paying attention. She'd let him sweat for another day or two, then she'd drop him a casual message suggesting dinner.

Then it would be up to him.

The decision nearly killed her. She wanted him back so badly. There was a physical ache in her chest; it felt as if her heart was actually bruised. And the effort of hanging on to the last shreds of her dignity was like clinging on to a high wire by her fingertips. Who was she kidding? If anyone was going to grovel, it would be her. She'd shame herself, no two ways about it.

The only red line was her job. This was the most excitement she'd had since the old MIT had been split up. She'd give up her dignity, her self-respect, her pride for Sam. But not her job.

49

Tony prodded the pan of chilli suspiciously with a wooden spoon. He could never remember the spice mix he'd used from one batch to the next. Sometimes the chilli heat was overwhelming, sometimes it was barely discernible. The cumin level was unpredictable and on occasions he forgot the oregano and coriander altogether. It gave a whole new meaning to pot luck. He tasted the mixture and yelped as he burned his tongue. 'Ow, that hurts!' Alerted by his tone, Flash wriggled out from under the table and cocked her head to one side, ears pricked. She checked him out, decided he was fine and headed back for her mistress's feet.

'Now you'll have no idea what it tastes like,' Carol sighed. 'I should have picked up a pizza.'

'You're over-excited because you're in the city and pizzas are a possibility. There's nothing wrong with my cooking. Well, nothing much.' Tony left the pot on the stove and sat down opposite her. 'You're going to have to come clean about what you're up to.'

Carol rolled her eyes. 'Since when have you been all about playing by the rules? Everything's fine. We're flying under the radar, everybody thinks we're quietly getting ourselves organised, ready to roll when the first big case rolls in.'

'And when's that going to be? It could be tomorrow morning. It could be happening right now. And then what are we going to do? We're already at full stretch and we've not even started on a proper caseload.' He rolled up his sleeves as he spoke. It was always the same when he started cooking on the boat. The temperature soon climbed out of the comfort zone.

'We'll cross that bridge when we come to it,' she said firmly. 'A few breaks from Stacey and we could have this wrapped up in no time at all.'

'You're going to have to set up an incident room if we don't.'

Carol laughed. 'What? You're missing writing on the whiteboards?'

'It's nothing to do with whiteboards, it's about having enough bodies to do all the routine actions that come out of what the team are doing. You know perfectly well that if you had a roomful of detectives bashing the phones we'd be further forward.'

Her jaw set in a familiar line of stubbornness. 'I don't know that, actually. This isn't a conventional case. There's so little to get hold of. No forensics, no loose ends to pull . . . '

'If you had a bigger team, you'd be taking apart those crime scenes. Looking at endless streams of CCTV, talking to potential witnesses, digging down into the victims' lives and their movements on the days they died.' He got up and stirred the chilli again. 'We wouldn't have to rely on Stacey's law-breaking abilities.'

'But I don't have the bodies and honestly, Tony, I don't have the justification. We're still woefully thin on evidence.'

He opened the oven and took out the pile of

tortillas he'd had warming through. He put them in a basket and dumped them on the table alongside a tub of sour cream and a bag of grated cheddar. 'I know. Believe me, there have been moments when I've wished I'd kept my mouth shut.'

'You don't mean that. You would never turn your back on a victim.'

He dished up the chilli into bowls. 'I know. But this is clutching at straws. I'm making a profile without anything solid.'

'Apart from years of experience and a unique degree of empathy,' Carol said softly, accepting the bowl. She dug her fork in and waved it around to cool down. Tasted it. 'Mmm, this is definitely one of your better efforts.' She stirred in cheese and sour cream. 'Thanks for feeding me.'

'It's more fun than eating alone.' He spooned chilli on to a tortilla and bit into it. 'Carol, we've got to cover our backs here. That story in the paper at the weekend proves what we already knew: we've got enemies out there waiting — no, longing — to bring us down. We don't want to give them a gift-wrapped opportunity to do that, to point to us and say, 'See, we told you they're a bunch of dangerous mavericks'. What are we going to do?'

'We're going to make the best of it. We're going to go in tomorrow morning and see what bones the dogs have brought us. And then, Tony, we are going to nail us a killer.'

He'd never got over her drive for justice. However bleak the prospect, it pushed her forward. He remembered a Scottish friend once defining his nation as 'the ones who run towards gunfire'. By that reckoning, Carol must have tartan in her veins. He hoped she also had a bulletproof vest.

50

You could tell by looking that this was a new squad, Carol thought. Familiar faces but with a new purpose. In spite of their years in the job, they all had an alertness and eagerness about them, a sense of being wound up ready to be let go. They looked well slept, showered and dressed in fresh clothes, a state she knew wouldn't last long once the hard cases started piling up. With the exception of Karim Hussain, she knew their strengths and weaknesses; she knew how to make the most of what they brought to the team. Tony was right that there were people on the outside who wanted to see them fail. But she thought there was enough talent here to keep them at bay.

Paula was last to leave the shiny new coffee machine. 'If this all goes to shit, we could set up as a coffee shop,' she said, plonking herself down at the table.

'Good to know we have an alternative,' Carol said. 'So who wants to kick off?'

Kevin started, reporting briefly on his trip to Sunderland. 'Complete write-off,' he concluded. It was the same story with minor variations from Alvin, and Carol asked Karim to run through their interview in Rochdale. Time the lad learned how to stand on his own two feet in the room. Everyone looked a little deflated, but Carol forced herself to sound upbeat as she turned to Paula.

'How did you get on?'

'The good news is that none of the women I spoke to sounded suicidal,' she said. 'But then, the ones who are already dead probably wouldn't have either, since they didn't actually commit suicide. However. When I talked to them in more detail about what they'd initially said that brought the shitstorm down around their ears, it seemed to me that only two of them fit the pattern in the terms that Tony was talking about. I mean in terms of the kind of things they've been vilified for saying. The three women we're looking at were expressing overtly feminist positions and directly attacking men for their behaviour. With some of the women I spoke to, like Shakila and Maxine, the nature of their attack was much less focused on those aspects. So they didn't interest our guy.'

She flicked open her notebook. 'On the other hand, Zoe Brewster is a novelist who lives in Norwich and had the temerity to suggest that computer games were misogynist and taught boys to despise women. Ursula Foreman is a blogger and journo and website designer who has written lately about everyday sexism in soaps and the damage it does to the self-image of young women and the attitudes of young men. They've both had the style and volume of trolling that our victims experienced. If he's sticking to the same sort of search criteria as, frankly, we are, they'd be the most likely current targets, I think. But what we can do about it — that's another matter. Since we don't know how he approaches his victims, I don't see how we can protect them.'

'We can't,' Tony said. 'Not even if we tell them they're at risk. Because, as you say, we don't have any clue how he's getting alongside them. And the questions I keep coming back to are: why this, why now, why here? And I've got no answers. Not a one.'

Glum faces all round. Except, Carol realised, for Stacey. Her face was unreadable as it often was but she definitely wasn't looking despondent. 'Stacey, have you got anything for us?'

She flipped open her laptop and looked round the table. There was an air of something suppressed about her that drew all their attention. 'His name is Matthew Martin.' She did something complicated on her trackpad and the interactive whiteboard on the wall behind her came to life. It showed a driving licence with a picture of a man with light brown hair and a full beard. 'He was born in 1975 in Bradfield. He's a civil engineer specialising in bridges and he lives here — ' a click of the fingers and the image changed to a small brick house standing alone at the edge of a stubble field — 'in Leicestershire. He's very close to the motorway network, so he can move around the country readily.'

'Bloody hell, Stacey,' Kevin exclaimed. 'Where did you get all this?'

'It was Tony's idea. Follow the books. So I did.'

'In a way we can admit to?' Carol asked.

Stacey gave her a long hard look. 'Not as such.'

'OK. We'll find a way round it. Leave that to me. That's very impressive, Stacey.'

396

Karim was staring at her as if he'd never seen a woman before, mouth open, eyes wide. 'How did you do that?' he stammered.

'Don't ask,' Paula said. 'Just accept it. You'll get used to it.'

Tony was smiling. 'That's beautiful, Stacey.'

She inclined her head graciously. 'I'm not finished.'

'Course you're not,' Paula said.

'He has two vehicles registered to him. A Toyota Navarra four-wheel-drive pickup truck with a double cab, and a VW Passat. The Passat is the one I've been able to connect to the dead women. Martin drove into London the day before Kate Rawlins died and he left the night she supposedly killed herself. I can put him on the A1 less than a kilometre from her house that afternoon.' A map appeared on the whiteboard, with the relative positions of the car and the house marked with red crosses.

It felt as if everyone was holding their breath, eyes on the whiteboard to see what was coming next. 'There's a similar pattern around Morton. He shows up four times in Bradfield in the two weeks before she died. Every time, he drove down the trunk road that runs within five hundred metres of Daisy's street. He shows up on the morning she died and goes in the opposite direction half an hour after the explosion.' A satellite image flashed up with a couple of roads outlined in red. 'I think there might be CCTV cameras here — there's a petrol station and a convenience store, they usually have cameras and they often pick up street traffic. But they're private, so I can't get into them remotely.'

'This is looking very strong,' Carol said. 'I'm amazed at what you've dug up, Stacey.'

'What about Jasmine Burton?' Alvin asked. 'Did you get anything there?'

Stacey nodded. 'Last and best.' An infographic appeared on the whiteboard. A series of red dots appeared, starting on the M69, moving to the M6, on to the M42 then the M5. 'Join up the dots and you get our man driving down to Exeter two days before Jasmine died.' A scatter of dots appeared on the A376 down the east side of the Exe estuary. Stacey hit a key and a scribble of to-ing and fro-ing appeared on the tail of the single line of the motorway journey. 'He was up and down that minor road five or six times. And the last time was the night Jasmine walked into the river.'

'Bloody hell,' Paula said. 'That's so impressive. I tell you, the way things are going, there's going to be no need for detectives out on the street, all the serious solving's going to be done by geeks like Stacey sitting in a cupboard with half a dozen screens analysing data.'

'Not quite,' Carol said. 'It's all circumstantial.'

'But it's more than suggestive,' Alvin said. 'Do we have phone details for this bastard?'

Stacey nodded. 'We have, but I can't access the tracking systems' records. But now we have an idea when he was in specific areas, they should be able to help us. I have details of his mobile plus a handful of pay-as-you-go phones and SIM cards that he was stupid enough to buy from Valhalla.'

Tony shook his head, an incredulous smile on his face. 'It's amazing, isn't it? This guy plans so carefully, yet he believes Valhalla when they claim they're invulnerable to hackers and resolute about protecting their customers' data from those pesky interfering lawyers.'

'Nobody's perfect,' Stacey said drily. 'Though of course he might have wised up and thought better of using the stuff he bought online. You can buy kit like that in any hole-in-the-wall newsagent's these days. I wouldn't pin too much hope on the phones.'

'Let's be grateful for what we've got already,' Carol said. 'I think it's time we picked up Matthew Martin. Before he can do any more damage. Kevin, Paula, Karim — let's take a little drive down to Leicestershire and see if we can lay hands on him.'

'No point,' Stacey said. 'Sorry, I hadn't quite finished. He's not in Leicestershire. He's here. In Bradfield.'

51

Matthew Martin was sitting in the passenger seat of his car. Another thing he'd learned about surveillance — spending a long time in the driver's seat of a car looked suspicious. On a residential street, neighbours grew wary. They might even call the police. But if you lounged in the passenger seat with a book or a newspaper in front of you, people assumed you were waiting for the driver to come back from some unspecified errand. It made sense so they didn't think twice about it.

Today was the day. The unsuspecting Ursula had told him she'd be at home this morning, and since her husband was going to London, once he left the house, he'd be gone all day. Martin sucked a mint; his mouth was dry but he didn't want to drink from his water bottle. The last thing he needed was a reminder from his bladder of how long he'd been watching and waiting.

He patted the pocket of his jacket, reassuring himself that the book of Marina Tsvetaeva's poems was there. Then he turned a page of the novel he was pretending to read while actually keeping his peripheral vision focused on the Foremans' front door.

Another five minutes drifted by. He slipped a hand into his trouser pocket, double-checking that he still had the wrap of GHB in his pocket. GHB, the magic powder that would place Ursula completely in his power. He wouldn't even have to carry her up the stairs. She'd cheerfully make her own way up if that's what he asked her to do. In an ideal world she should be prepared to do what she was told without the aid of pharmaceuticals, but he knew enough about Ursula to realise that was a vain hope. He imagined her husband was meek and henpecked behind the glossy black front door, in contrast to the self-confident and probing image he presented on the radio show where he interviewed people in the news.

And here he was, opening the front door, turning to say something over his shoulder. Bill Foreman, off to work, off to London, a pitiful jerk who couldn't persuade his wife to behave like a proper woman. Well, this would be the last time he went through this particular routine. Next time he came home it would be to a different world, a world where there was one less man-hating bitch trying to turn the tide against the proper order. Martin couldn't help a secret smile creeping across his face. As Bill Foreman walked towards him, he pretended to be engrossed in his book, not even glancing away from the page as the benighted husband walked past. He had no idea whether Foreman clocked him, and he didn't much care. Foreman wasn't going to do anything about some guy sitting in a car waiting for the driver to come back.

Martin stayed put for another half-hour. Then, a few minutes before ten, he pulled on his thin leather gloves, got out of the car and walked up to Ursula Foreman's front door. He pressed the doorbell and took a step backwards, not wanting to appear intimidating. Not yet.

The door opened and there stood Ursula, copper curls tumbling around her head, dressed in jogging pants and a scoop-necked T-shirt. 'Oh, hello,' she said, smiling at the sight of him. 'It's you.'

'I've come round for that chat we spoke about?' He gave her his most disingenuous smile. 'If it's a bad time . . . '

'No. No, of course not. Come in, come through, we'll have a nice cup of tea and you can tell me all about your idea.' She opened the door wide and stepped back to let him come inside. Just like that.

They were all so easy.

52

A moment's silence, then four voices speaking at once. 'When did he get here?' Carol demanded.

'Where is he?' from Kevin. 'He must be here for a reason.'

'Is he on the move?' Alvin asked.

'We need to get the phone company tracking his main phone,' Paula said decisively.

'Paula's right,' Carol said. 'Karim, get on to it.'

He looked momentarily stunned then moved away to the nearest vacant computer. 'I'm on it, guv,' he said.

Stacey looked from one to the other. 'He arrived last night. According to his credit card, he stayed in the motel behind Central Station. I've trawled his records and that's been his pattern. I presume he's been stalking them when he's visited before the actual killings. Every time he's stayed in a cheap chain motel. That seems to be where he stays when he's working too. He's not extravagant even though he earns enough to upgrade to something a bit classier.'

'Is there anything about this guy you don't know?' Alvin said.

Stacey looked across at Tony. 'Only everything that matters,' she said, sounding less than confident for the first time that morning. 'I don't know why he's doing this, I don't know what his plans are and I don't know how to stop him.'

Tony gave her a little nod of approbation.

'None of us knows these things and you're right to pick on them as the key points here. But here's what we do know, thanks to Paula's work yesterday. We know that there is one woman here in Bradfield who fits the pattern of the women he has killed already. Do we know if he's on the move already, Stacey?'

Her fingers were already flying over the keys, her eyes roaming the screen. The rest of her body was perfectly still; it was as if her hands were separate creatures, leashed to her without actually being part of her. 'Not according to what I can see,' she said slowly. 'That doesn't mean he isn't out and about, though. He could be sticking to side streets where the ANPR doesn't run. Or maybe part of his plate is obscured and it's not picking up.'

'OK,' Carol said decisively. 'Kevin, with me. We're going over to the motel. If he's there, we'll pick him up and bring him in. Stacey, stay with the screens and let us know if he shows up anywhere. Karim, hammer the phones.' She paused for a moment, frowning, distracted by the jolt of craving that shot through her.

'Ursula Foreman,' Paula prompted her.

'Yes, of course. Paula, you spoke to her yesterday, you're a familiar voice. Take Alvin with you. Talk to her, stay with her till we've got him locked down. Oh, and Karim? Soon as you can, get on to the local lads and get them to swing by his house, in case he's sitting at home playing *Minecraft* while his best mate is using his car in Bradfield. Nothing to spook him, just a fly-by, OK?'

'What about me?' Tony said plaintively.

Carol gave him a wild-eyed look, as if she'd almost forgotten he was there. 'You can either stay here with Stacey and Karim or come with Kevin and me,' she said, grabbing her coat as she spoke. 'Let's go, we're not taking any chances now. We've got nothing more than circumstantial evidence, so let's all keep our eyes peeled for anything at all that screams 'discrepancy' at us.' She took a couple of steps then turned back. 'Oh, and Stacey . . . ?'

'Yes?'

'Send that driving licence pic to all our phones, would you?'

A scramble of movement, half-finished sentences and a swoop towards the door and they were gone like birds scattering at the sound of a shotgun. Silence blanketed the room again, broken only by the sound of Stacey's fingers whispering over the keyboard. Karim cleared his throat. She looked up at him, face blank.

'I've never been tasked with anything like this before. Who should I speak to in Leicester?'

Stacey considered for a moment. She didn't want to betray her own inexperience in the field. 'I'd call the main number and ask for the duty inspector in the area that covers where he lives,' she said slowly. 'I think it's OK to ask uniform to handle this. It's not as if we want them to make an arrest. Just knock on the door and, if they get an answer, make up some cod story about a local burglary or something.'

He grinned, obviously relieved. 'Thanks. It's like being thrown in at the deep end here.'

God help him if he thinks this is the deep end. 'You'll learn,' she said, turning back to her screen. Now where the hell was Matthew Martin?

53

'Blues and twos,' Paula said, fastening her seatbelt. 'Till I tell you otherwise.' She gunned the engine and headed for the exit while Alvin fumbled with the controls for lights and siren on the unmarked CID car.

'You think it's that urgent?'

'Like Kevin said, he's here for a reason.' The lights flashed and the siren whooped as she pulled into the Skenfrith Street traffic. Six minutes later, she said, 'Turn them off now, I don't want to spook anyone.'

She slowed to a sedate pace and turned into the street of modest brick semis where the Foremans lived. The trim gardens and the well-tended trees were the only signs of life in mid-morning. Wherever the mothers and toddlers were, it wasn't here. Alvin called off the numbers as she drove. 'We're close and there's a space,' he said. Paula parked neatly and they fell into step on the pavement. As they turned in at the gate, the door opened and a man emerged from the house. Clean-shaven, closely trimmed receding hair going silver at the temples, clean jeans and checked shirt under a tweed sports jacket. Nothing to unsettle the cops; he matched the house. He looked startled to see them and paused, one hand on the handle, the door half-closed.

'Mr Foreman?' Alvin said.

'Yeah.' He looked concerned. But most people did, confronted by a big black man with a suit and a sidekick. Gangsters always knew Alvin was the law; the law-abiding were not always so certain. 'Sorry, I don't think we've met?'

'I'm Detective Sergeant Ambrose and this is Detective Sergeant McIntyre. Is your wife at home, sir?'

The man did a quick double-take. 'Ursula? No, she's down at the food bank in Brucehill, on Ramillies Road. She volunteers there. Is this about those bloody awful messages she's been getting on the internet?'

'I'd rather explain matters to your wife, if you don't mind,' Alvin said. 'Ramillies Road, you say?'

'Yes, that's right. Down by the shops.' The man pulled the door closed behind him. 'Now, if you'll excuse me, I'm running a bit late myself?' Alvin stepped to one side to let him pass.

'Sorry to bother you,' he said.

The man gave them a hasty smile over his shoulder as he turned into the street. 'No bother, officer.'

They walked back through the gate, almost bumping into an elderly woman making her slow way along the street, arthritic hands locked around the bars of a walking frame, coat a size too big for her shrunken frame. 'Sorry,' Paula said, taking hold of the woman's arm to steady her. Her forearm was like two sticks badly wrapped in a sack.

She peered up at them, her large glasses magnifying eyes as blue as hyacinths. 'Have you

408

all been visiting Ursula?' she said.

'We were hoping to see her, but her husband said she's not at home now.'

The old woman looked puzzled. 'That can't be right. Bill left for work at the usual time, over an hour ago. I saw him go.'

Alvin gave Paula a look that said *We haven't got time for this*. But her instincts told her something was off kilter. And she didn't need Carol telling them to look out for that very thing to know it was those moments that sometimes made all the difference. So she engaged with the old biddy. 'You must be mistaken, love. Mr Foreman only left a couple of minutes ago. Did you not see him come out of the house? He went off down the street ahead of us.'

The old woman shook her head, a stubborn pout to her lower lip. 'That wasn't Bill Foreman. I might be eighty-three, young lady, but I'm not gaga. I expect it was some friend of Ursula's from the magazine.'

'Did you recognise him, then?' Paula asked. 'Has he visited before?'

'If he has, I've not seen him. When he arrived this morning, that was the first time I'd ever clapped eyes on him.'

This time, the look they exchanged was one of alarm. 'You're sure? You're absolutely certain that wasn't Bill Foreman who left just now?'

The old woman nodded fiercely. 'Of course I'm sure. And anyway, Ursula's at home. She let that chap in and she's not gone anywhere since.'

Oh fuck. Paula swivelled on the balls of her feet but Alvin was already halfway up the path, charging at full tilt towards the door. Because if that hadn't been Bill Foreman then something was very, very wrong inside his house.

54

Kevin drove in a slow loop round the car park at the Sleeping Inn. 'His car's not here,' Carol said. 'Which doesn't mean that he isn't, of course.' She sighed. 'It's never bloody easy, is it? Let's park up and go inside and talk to the receptionist, who will have seen nothing and knows nothing.'

'You never know,' Kevin said. 'We might get lucky and get one of the Eastern European ones that never misses a trick.'

Tony lagged slightly behind, looking around at the car park and the bleak monolith with its uniformly square windows. 'You're not kind to yourself, are you?' He spoke under his breath. 'It's as if you don't dare let yourself get too comfortable. Because if you do, who knows what might happen? Like the song says, just when you least expect it you get just what you least expect. Much better to keep things low level, where you know what the parameters are.'

He caught up with the others as they reached the front desk. A dark-haired young man with prison pallor and dark hollowed eyes stared out at them, shifting his shoulders inside an ill-fitting uniform suit. 'Good morning, how may I help you?' he asked, his accent from somewhere east of the Danube.

Carol flashed her ID and leaned on the chest-high counter. 'You had a resident here last

411

night who is of interest to us. Matthew Martin was his name. Has he checked out yet?'

A flare of panic lit his eyes. 'I'm not allowed to release any information about residents.'

'We're the police, mate,' Kevin said. 'Whatever petty rules your boss imposes on you, we trump that. Now tell us what we want to know. Matthew Martin was the name.'

The receptionist flushed. 'I cannot do that. You need to speak to my manager.'

'So fetch him. Or her.' Kevin had always had a good line in bad cop, Tony reminded himself. It often came as a surprise, because he knew Kevin to be not only kind but soft in many crucial areas.

The receptionist backed away through the door into a back office. 'Fucking data protection. I bet that's what they come back with,' Carol said. 'They all hide behind it and none of them has any bloody idea what the act actually says.'

A couple of minutes passed, then a squat man with surprisingly wide hips emerged from the back room. His mousy hair was shaved close at the sides, an elaborate quiff resting on the top of his head like an éclair from a superior patisserie. 'You're the police, are you?' he said, his voice the epitome of Northern camp. 'Dimitri says you're asking about one of our guests? A Matthew Martin?'

'That's right,' Carol said. 'Is he here?'

The manager shook his head with irritating complacency. 'Oh no, you missed him.'

'When did he check out?'

'I've no idea,' he said airily. 'He used the

express checkout. When it was emptied at ten, his key and his checkout form were in there along with a dozen others. People don't have to check out in person any more, you know.' He spoke in the condescending tones of someone who thinks he's dealing with people so far below him that they have no understanding of how the better half lives. If it hadn't been so pitiful, his pomposity would have been laughable.

'Will his room have been cleaned by now?' Tony asked.

'I imagine so, we've got a very speedy turnaround here, you know. Let me check,' he said loftily. He moved to a computer terminal behind the counter and clumsily tinkered with the keyboard. 'Martin, Martin . . . Yes, room 302. According to this, the clean was done at quarter past nine. So he was obviously gone by then.' He heaved a weary sigh, his chins wobbling. 'Look, I'm not being obstructive here. He booked online. He checked in yesterday at 4.37 p.m. He charged nothing to his room. We have no idea what he did or where he went or how long he spent in his room.'

'You must have some idea,' Kevin said. 'Those electronic keys record when the punter uses them to enter the room.'

The manager smirked. 'Data protection, sir. Digital information. I'm not allowed to divulge that by law. Come back with a warrant and I'll happily tell you.'

'Told you,' Carol muttered. 'Come on, guys. This is a waste of time. He's not here and he's not coming back.' She turned away and led them back towards the car park. 'Our best hope is that he turns up at Ursula Foreman's house when Paula and Alvin are there.'

Right on cue, her phone rang. 'Alvin,' she said. 'Give me some good news.'

55

Alvin hit the door like a controlled explosion. The wood bulged and warped round the lock then splintered under the impact, swinging open as he staggered forward, struggling to stay upright.

Coming up behind him, Paula was momentarily confounded by the eye-level vision of two bare feet sticking out of two tubes of denim. Then her brain made the connections. A woman with a tumble of red curls was hanging by the neck from the balustrade on the first floor. Her face was purple, her tongue protruding, her eyes bulging. 'Oh Christ,' Paula groaned, running for the stairs.

Alvin righted himself, rubbing his left shoulder. He took in the implications of the scene at a glance. He looked around frantically, then spotted what he needed through the open kitchen doorway. He grabbed a solid wooden chair from the kitchen table and brought it back to the hall, placing it under Ursula's body. He noticed a book lying on the floor but didn't waste time on it. He climbed on the chair, bent his knees and curled his arms round her thighs. 'I'll take her weight,' he said, straightening his legs. 'Get that off her neck. You need to cut it, there might be DNA in the knot.'

'Fuck, yes.' Paula ran back down the stairs to the kitchen, fumbling her mobile out of her pocket and calling the emergency number as she went. She yanked open drawers, looking for a sharp knife, simultaneously talking on the phone. 'DS McIntyre, Regional MIT. I need ambulance and police backup,' she said. 'I've got an attempted hanging victim.' She was already running back up the stairs. 'Haxton Grove, number twenty-seven.' She dropped the phone and leaned over the bannister. With Alvin taking the strain, it wasn't hard to hack through the strong nylon cord that had bitten deep into Ursula's neck.

As the support disappeared, her body collapsed over Alvin's shoulder like a loosely stuffed sack. He grunted and staggered slightly on the chair but managed somehow to brace himself and keep his footing. Paula ran back down the stairs. 'Hang on, I'm coming,' she yelled.

Between the two of them, they clumsily lowered Ursula to the floor. Alvin carefully rolled her into the recovery position while Paula struggled with the ligature. The slip knot refused to slip back so she slid the knife blade between the cord and the back of Ursula's neck. It bit so deeply that Paula had actually to pull it free from the swollen flesh. She felt for a pulse, without much hope. Too bloody late. They'd been too bloody late.

56

The ambulance was pulling out of Haxton Grove, blue lights flashing and siren bleating, as Kevin swung round the corner. 'That's a good sign, isn't it?' Tony said. 'I mean, they don't hurry if you're dead.'

Neither cop graced his comment with a reply. Suddenly Kevin stamped on the brakes. 'That's his car,' he said, pointing at a Passat parked neatly with a perfect view of the Foreman house.

'Bingo,' Carol said. 'With any luck, it'll be a forensic goldmine.'

Kevin moved off and double-parked behind the two chequer-boarded squad cars; Carol was out of the car almost before he came to a standstill. One of the uniforms was threading crime scene tape through the shrubs that lined the wall at the bottom of the Foremans' garden. 'Never mind that for now,' Carol said. 'Get down the street and secure that VW Passat halfway down on the other side. Wait with it till the CSIs get here.'

Alvin was sitting on the wall, head hanging, hands clasped between his knees, looking wasted. He raised his head as they approached and gave a small, tight nod. 'Paula's gone with the ambulance. We got an ID from a neighbour. It's Ursula Foreman. It looks like she might make it. He made a rubbish job of hanging her. You do it properly, you break your neck. You do it badly, you strangle yourself slowly.'

'You did well,' Carol said.

'Not well enough. We let him walk right past us.' Alvin shook his head, his mouth tightening in an expression of disgust. 'He acted like he belonged here. Like he owned the place. We just assumed he was Bill Foreman.' He tutted at himself.

'That's all it takes,' Tony said. 'Behave as if you have every right to be somewhere and mostly you'll get away with it.'

Alvin sighed. 'He looks different from his driving licence picture. He's shaved off his beard and his hair's cut short. And it's greying now. He didn't look like we expected. Not like the driving licence pic at all. And we didn't spot his car because we came in from the other end of the street. I'm sorry.' He hung his head again.

'No point in beating yourself up,' Carol said. 'Get back to Skenfrith Street and organise an e-fit artist to work with you on a current likeness so we can get something out on the media and the internet as soon as possible.' She patted his shoulder. 'Look on the bright side. You and Paula have probably saved Ursula Foreman's life.'

'Even more important than that,' Tony said. 'You've almost certainly saved the lives of a bunch of other women as well. All those other books he bought — he had a list, but now it's blown.'

'That reminds me,' Alvin said, getting to his feet and wincing at the pain from his shoulder as he straightened up. 'There was a book on the floor under Ursula Foreman's feet. It was that Russian woman Stacey talked about.' He limped off to his car like a wounded bear as the minivan with the crime scene investigators rolled up.

'I'm going to talk to the CSIs,' Carol said. 'Cheer them up with the news that they've got a car as well as a crime scene to process.'

Tony sat on the wall and started to say something to Kevin but the detective's phone rang and distracted him. Seeing the source of the call, he twisted his mouth into a wry line then said, 'Sorry, Tony, got to take this.' He walked away, phone to his ear, eyes moving constantly to make sure nobody was close enough to overhear.

'Thanks for getting back to me,' he said.

'This is worth one in the bank,' Penny Burgess said. 'I had to be nice to someone I wouldn't piss on if he was on fire.'

Kevin felt a quickening in his chest. 'What did you find out?'

'The information came from a very reliable source.'

'Stop trying to tease me. Just tell me.' It was good to feel irritated with her.

'You're no fun any more, Kevin. That's nothing to be proud of.'

'Maybe not, but I'll live with it. The name, Penny. The name.'

'According to the assistant news editor who puts the credit payments through, we paid a woman called Susannah Dean.'

It meant nothing to Kevin. For a wild moment, he thought they might not have an enemy after all, only an opportunist somewhere in the admin unit at West Yorkshire. 'Never heard of her,' he said.

'That's because she's a beard. She's a dentist in Macclesfield.'

'So how does she know our secrets?' Kevin did a slow 360 degrees, making sure Tony was still sitting on the wall and Carol was still too busy with the CSIs to notice him.

'She has a brother.'

'Who is . . . who, exactly?'

'He's one of your own, Kevin. Sam Evans. From your old MIT team. Carol must have done something to really piss him off.'

The name was a jolt to Kevin's guts. Sam? He'd always liked Sam well enough when they'd worked together, even though they'd never been the kind of mates who went to the pub together. They didn't have much in common, that had been the main reason. 'Are you sure?' He didn't want to believe someone who'd sat at the next desk to him would do that to Carol. OK, he'd shamed himself all those years before by leaking stories to Penny Burgess. But he hadn't done it to discredit a colleague or even an enemy. He'd only passed on stuff that would have come out eventually at a press conference. The brass had accused him of jeopardising the investigation, but that was bollocks. It was a show trial, to draw attention away from the fact that they were going nowhere fast when it came to identifying a serial killer. What Sam had done was a different kind of betrayal. It was mean-spirited and deeply personal. It was the revenge of a petulant child who hasn't got his own way. Kevin licked his lips. 'Are you absolutely sure?'

'It's not the first time he's been a confidential source,' Penny said. 'That's why the payment system is already in place. I'm sorry, Kevin. I know it's not what you wanted to hear.'

Kevin stared down the street, not taking anything in. 'Thanks for finding out for me. And Penny — I don't like having debts hanging over me, so here's something in return. You know Ursula Foreman?'

'The blogger? Married to Bill Foreman from Bradfield Sound?'

'That's the one. She's been rushed into A&E at Bradfield Cross. You might want to check it out.'

'Has she had an accident?'

'I thought you were an investigative journalist?' He broke the connection as Carol called his name. He hurried over, trying to assimilate what he'd heard.

'We're going back to base,' Carol said. 'There's nothing we can do here. The CSIs are doing their thing, I've set up a door-to-door and I've got someone from Skenfrith Street picking up Bill Foreman and taking him to the hospital. Apparently he's still on air but they'll put somebody else on. We need to get an alert out on Matthew Martin ASAP, and I need to put together a briefing for John Brandon about the case. Now we actually have some hard evidence.'

57

Carol was trying to write a succinct summary of what they had on Matthew Martin and his activities, but Tony wasn't making it easy for her. He was pacing, as he always did when he was trying to order his thoughts. Up one side of her office, turn through ninety degrees and head for the next corner, then about turn and retrace his steps, repetitive as a Steve Reich tape loop. 'He knows we know,' he said. 'This has all been about creating a picture for the world. We're all supposed to think these women have been driven to suicide because the backlash against them has forced them to see the error of their ways. But when Paula and Alvin turned up at Ursula Foreman's house, he must have realised he'd been rumbled.' Pace, two, three four.

'Maybe not,' Carol said. 'Maybe he's waiting to see what we do next. After all, there are lots of reasons why the police could have been at the door. Alvin said he mentioned the online abuse. It's possible he thinks he's got away with it. That we think Ursula did in fact kill herself.' It felt good to be back in her traditional role of testing his theories to destruction.

Tony shook his head. 'He knows that he's blown. That we're on to him. You don't send two detective sergeants to investigate a bit of recreational cyber-bullying. So what's he going to do?'

'Make a run for it. They all do,' Carol said absently, tapping out another sentence.

He reached the corner and pivoted. 'No, he can't do that. Because there's too high a risk that he might be caught. Here's his problem, Carol. As things are right now, the suicide verdicts stand. We might argue till we're blue in the face that these were really murders, but without the evidence of his presence, we've got no proof. But if he's taken, the deck is stacked against him managing to keep his big project under wraps. Because once we start looking closely, we'll find his trail. And if we can prove the suicides are actually murders, then his whole project falls down. While the suicides stay on the record, there's a chance his plan will work and all you gobby women will shut up.'

'Fat chance,' Carol muttered.

Pace, six seven, eight. 'I keep coming back to why this, why now, why here? I don't know enough about him and that's infuriating when it comes to figuring this out. But there is one thing that makes sense.'

'What's that?' Still distracted.

'He's going to kill himself.'

Startled, she looked up from her screen. 'That makes no sense.'

'Exactly. Which paradoxically is the best possible reason for doing it. He can't afford to be taken alive or his whole plan is exposed in court and the idea that women behaving badly and talking about it like they're proud of it leads to them killing themselves is blown out of the water. The only chance he has to make his point now is to take himself right out of the picture.'

'But surely the truth will be splashed everywhere if he does? We can say what we like then, there's no legal comeback, no libel or slander implications. And if Ursula lives, she can tell the truth.'

Tony shrugged. 'But the internet will have an alternate reality. And the conspiracy theorists often shout loudest. No, he's smart. He'll understand how it's going to play out if he's taken.'

There was a knock and Stacey stuck her head round the door, almost knocking Tony off his stride. 'I've got a bit of background on Martin,' she said. 'I don't know if it's any use?'

'At this point, anything will help,' Tony said. 'Come on in and share it.'

'Whose office is this, again?' Carol grumbled.

'You know you want to hear this,' Tony said, gesturing to an uncertain Stacey that she should come in.

She sat in one of the visitor chairs and studied her tablet. 'He grew up here in Bradfield.'

Carol groaned. 'So he knows the ground. He knows how to disappear. Does he have family here? Parents?'

'I did some family records digging. He's an only child. His dad retired three years ago, sold his house in Harriestown and moved to an apartment in a seaside resort in Bulgaria. His mum died when he was eight. I found a report in the *Sentinel Times* archive. She was killed in a motorway crash on her way back from a trip to Greenham Common.'

'Yes!' Tony said emphatically, punching a fist

into the other palm. 'Of course. That's the underlying driver — Greenham Common. Those evil feminists took his mum away from him. She should have been at home, looking after him, not running off to Greenham with — what was it the *Daily Mail* called them? Woolly minds with woolly hats, or something. But she wasn't and she died. Everything he's doing now is about encouraging women to stay at home and save themselves. That's why this. And why here, too.' He paused in his enthusiastic monologue. 'But why now? I still don't know why now. What set him off? There's always a trigger, always a — '

Stacey cleared her throat. 'I don't know for sure, but I might have something there.'

'Let's have it, Stacey,' Carol said. 'You've done a brilliant job so far.'

'I did some digging around on social media sites. I figured since he's so savvy about that, he must have a presence. Anyway, I found a RigMarole page he deleted nearly a year ago and I followed the threads I picked up there. He had a girlfriend, Sarah Bell. They'd been together for a little over a year. I tracked a deleted message string between Sarah and one of her friends who was working in Australia. It turns out Sarah became pregnant when she was with Martin and decided to have a termination.'

'He wouldn't like that,' Tony said. 'He wouldn't like that one little bit.'

'There's more,' Stacey said patiently. Years of working with Tony had taught her the necessity of persistence. 'Seventeen days after the termination, Martin came home from a business trip to find Sarah dead in the bath. She'd washed sleeping pills down with vodka and slashed her wrists, according to the inquest. Martin gave evidence that she'd been racked with guilt over the termination. Friends posted online that they couldn't believe it — '

'They always do,' Tony said. 'It's a way of letting themselves off the hook. 'If I don't believe it, I couldn't have done anything to prevent it'.'

'One friend in particular said that Sarah wasn't depressed or guilty about the termination, she was relieved. This is the friend that went to the clinic with her. She messaged another of Sarah's friends on the evening of the termination to say Sarah was adamant that this wasn't the time for her to have a child, that she wanted to be more established in her career and she wasn't sure enough about the relationship to want kids yet. This was seventeen days before she allegedly killed herself.'

'She could have changed her mind,' Carol said. 'Funny things, hormones.'

'Or he could have killed her,' Tony said. 'Her killing his baby would be on a par with the feminists of Greenham killing his mother. Bad things happening because women deny their proper role in family structures. That's what set him off, it's obvious when you lay it out like Stacey did. He kills Sarah, making it look like suicide, and sees in her death the perfect template for doing this to other women. He sees himself as setting things right. Forcing women back to where they should be isn't limiting them or oppressing them in his eyes. It's about restoring the correct balance.'

'You're sure his father sold the family home?' Carol said.

'According to the Land Registry.'

'He didn't sell it to his son?'

Stacey shook her head, tapping her screen. 'He sold it to Harvinder Singh Khalsa.'

'Just wanted to be sure.'

'Have we got contact details for his father?' Tony asked.

'They're on the whiteboard.'

'Thanks, Stacey, that's all good stuff.' Carol thought for a moment then said, 'Is there any indication that he's in touch with any Bradfield school friends? He has to be holed up somewhere, that's a good place to start.'

'I'm on it.' Stacey headed out and Tony resumed pacing.

'Carol, I think he's going to kill himself,' he persisted. 'He can't complete his mission. The only thing he can do is try to make what he's done so far meaningful. And he can only be sure of that if he's beyond being held to account. Which means being dead.'

'I'm sorry, I don't get that,' Carol said, sighing with exasperation. 'He's expended all this imagination and energy in carrying out his fantasy. Why would he kill himself when he can disappear into the woodwork?'

Before Tony could answer, Carol's mobile rang. 'It's Paula,' she said, putting the phone on speaker. 'Hi, Paula, I'm here with Tony.'

He moved closer to hear Paula. 'The good news is Elinor's on duty and she says Ursula is going to make it. The bad news is that she's got some kind of drug in her system. Rohypnol or GHB or something similar, so the chances are she's not going to remember anything useful. Obviously they've taken bloods for toxicology tests, so that might be helpful.'

'Bloody date-rape drugs,' Carol said. 'But she's alive, which is a result. And at least we know for sure how he was getting them to comply. Is her husband there?'

'Yes. But he's in a state of shock. Knows nothing, saw nothing, all he cares about is that Ursula's going to be OK.'

'Fair enough.'

'The media are here already, by the way. Penny Burgess from the *Sentinel Times* and some teenager from Bradfield Sound.'

'Is the uniform who brought Bill Foreman still around?'

'Yes, he's hovering.'

'OK, leave him to guard Ursula. Get her into a side room on her own; Elinor should be able to sort that out for us. Nobody in or out except medical personnel with photo ID and her husband. And then I need you back here.'

'OK, chief.'

'You did a good job, you and Alvin. Getting her down. Saving her life.'

'Thanks. But we shouldn't have let him go.'

'Better to let him go than to let Ursula die,' Tony said. 'If you'd realised and given chase, it might have been too late by the time you got back to her.'

Not for the first time, Tony had hit on the

428

saving grace. 'Good point,' Carol said. 'See you back here.' She ended the call. 'I'm glad she's going to pull through.'

'Yeah,' Tony said, abstracted. He began pacing again. 'So if he's going to do it, I think he's going to stick to the programme. He's going to choose a death that reflects one of the women he'd already settled on. But he can't go back to his base to get drugs or poison. He's going to have to copy May Ayim and jump from the thirteenth floor.'

'I think you're reaching,' Carol said. 'I know you're very good at getting inside the heads of psychopaths, paranoiacs and general nutters, but this time it feels like you're making it up as you go along.'

Tony gave a half-smile. 'This whole case has been making it up as I go along. Sometimes you have to trust yourself.'

'I trust you. I'm not sure I believe you, though.'

He nodded. 'That's OK. I'll go away and think some more.' He waggled his fingers in a farewell and went back through to the squad room, where he studied the various details on the whiteboards then found a vacant computer. He spent a few minutes on the internet before he stood up and walked out into the sunshine. Time to do what he did best.

58

Kevin's head came up as soon as Paula walked in and he beckoned her over. As she approached, he called to Stacey. 'You got a minute, Stace?'

She looked up, blinking as if she was surfacing from a dream. 'Sorry?'

'A minute?'

She nodded and emerged from behind her bank of screens, stretching. Kevin tried not to look at the tautness of her blouse over her breasts. He'd spent years schooling himself out of sexist responses, but it was hard when women's bodies were so present, so attractive, so tempting.

Paula and Stacey gathered around the end of the table where he'd been working on tracking down old friends of Matthew Martin. 'I spoke to Penny earlier,' he said, casting an apprehensive look at Carol's open door.

'Any joy?' Paula said.

He scratched his ear. 'I wouldn't call it joy, but I have got an answer.'

'Who was it?' Stacey asked.

Kevin's voice dripped contempt. 'Our former colleague, DC Sam Evans.'

Stacey's face froze, her eyes unblinking, her lips parted. Paula drew her breath in sharply. 'Are you sure?'

'Penny's sure. And I've no reason to doubt her. She knows if she fucks me over, she won't get another answer from this squad ever again.'

While he was speaking, Stacey turned and walked back to her office, closing the door behind her. Paula stared after her. 'Oh shit,' she said.

'What's up with Stacey?' Kevin said. 'I mean, I know she thinks getting information from carbon-based life forms is beneath her, but at least I got what we needed to know.'

'She's been going out with him. Didn't you know?'

Kevin's face showed his shock. 'I had no idea. I didn't know Stacey did dating.'

'She doesn't, as a rule. That's why this is so devastating. This is going to break her heart.'

'Yeah, well, I'm sorry about that. Me, I'm going to break his legs.'

'No, Kevin. I think we should leave it be. If he's not with Stacey, he's not going to get anything to leak. We should make a point of letting him know we know, but that's all.'

Kevin grunted. 'As long as we let him know in front of other people,' he said. 'The people he works beside need to know he's a disloyal twat.'

'Agreed. We'll work something out as soon as we get Matthew Martin in custody, I promise. But no broken legs, no bloody noses.'

Kevin closed his eyes and gave a weary nod. 'OK, you win. Now roll your sleeves up and help me find somebody who keeps in touch with Matthew Martin.'

* * *

Tony stood in the foyer of the Skenfrith Street police station and took out his phone.

431

Sometimes when he was following a hunch, he didn't like witnesses. Nobody liked looking stupid when things didn't pay off. He keyed in a number, then waited. It was answered on the third ring. The voice on the other end was gruff and peremptory. 'Hello? Who is this?'

'Is that Mr Martin?'

'You called me, pal. You should know who you're calling.'

'My name is Tony Hill,' he said. 'I need to ask you a question that's going to sound a bit daft.'

'So why should I answer it? And who the hell are you, Tony Hill?'

'I'm the man who's trying to stop your Matthew doing something stupid. I haven't got time to explain, but I promise you, I mean him no harm.'

'I don't understand. You're talking nonsense,' Pete Martin said, his impatience obvious. 'What do you mean, 'something stupid'?'

'Just one question, please. Do either of these buildings have any family significance for Matthew — the Bradford Assurance Tower or the Exchange Hotel?'

'Are you some sort of nutter?'

'It's a harmless question. Please, Mr Martin.'

'Is this some kind of wind-up? I'm hanging up now.'

'No,' Tony yelped. 'I'm not a nutter and it's not a wind-up. It's vitally important. Honestly. How can it hurt you to answer that?'

There was a pause. 'We had our wedding reception at the Exchange. Are you satisfied now, you weirdo?' The line went dead, but Tony didn't care. He knew where he was going. His destination was across town, about ten minutes away. Walking would be quicker than persuading Carol to give him a police car and driver. Besides, if Matthew Martin was still alive, he might be spooked into jumping if he saw a liveried cop car racing up to the Bradfield Exchange Hotel.

Before he'd left the ReMIT squad room, Tony had googled 'tallest buildings Bradfield' and been grateful to Wikipedia for a list of buildings by height and by the number of floors. Even more usefully, the dates of their construction were also given. There were twenty-six buildings in the city with thirteen or more floors. Only two of them had been in existence when Matthew Martin had lived in the city. Tony operated in a field governed by probabilities; he thought it was most likely that Martin would find it symbolic to go for a building he remembered from his youth. And now his father had confirmed it had an emotional connection to a day when family life had been a beautiful promise.

The Exchange was the grandest hotel in the city. It had started life as the cotton exchange, where rich men gambled on the rise and fall of the commodity that had made the Lancashire mill owners rich for almost two hundred years. Above the soaring exchange floor were eight levels of offices. It was one of the tallest buildings of the age in the North of England. But by the time the First World War broke out, it had been overtaken by the Royal Exchange in Manchester, closing in the spring of 1915 after it was clear it wasn't going to be all over by Christmas. A shrewd businessman bought the decaying building for a song ten years later and took advantage of the cheap labour of the Depression to restore the exterior and fit out the interior as an opulent luxury hotel.

Tony had been inside twice. Once for a colleague's overblown wedding to a Cheshire stockbroker, and once for a conference organised by a rich Swiss pharmaceutical company. He'd found the interior intimidating and uncomfortable, but guessed that was the effect it was supposed to have on the likes of him. Today, he'd have to ignore its effect on him and concentrate on the man he was there to save. It scarcely crossed his mind that he might be wrong. He couldn't have explained why he was so certain. But he was.

As he drew nearer to the hotel, he slowed his pace and craned his neck to look up. He knew the tall windows that started at ground level were an optical illusion that actually ran the height of two interior floors. From Wikipedia, he'd learned that the hotel had fourteen floors. That meant Martin would be somewhere on the second level down. Among the pinnacles and decorative balusters it was hard to distinguish whether there was anyone there. Tony squinted and peered, but he couldn't see any movement.

He walked the length of the frontage and turned the corner. The Exchange occupied a whole block, so he'd be able to circle the entire building without any difficulty. He crossed the street for a better view but still he saw no one.

434

But when he rounded the next corner, Tony could see a figure outlined high above the street. He was outside the third window from the end, leaning on the stone parapet that came up to his waist. Tony barely paused, lowering his eyes to avoid Martin realising he was being observed. As soon as he reached the next corner, he stopped and took out his phone. When Carol answered, he said, 'I think I've found him. I need you and Paula here to arrest him when I talk him down. And probably to get me alongside him. Can you do that for me?'

'You're kidding.' Carol said, incredulous. Then, with resignation, 'No, you're not. Where are you?'

'Outside the Exchange Hotel. On the Midland Street side. I can see him on the thirteenth floor. Like I said.'

'We're on our way. We'll come round the front. See you there.'

Tony continued on his way back to the front of the hotel. He was itching to get to Matthew Martin but he knew that trying to make it on his own would only end in disaster. He'd freak out a chambermaid or terrify some innocent guest or get into a fight. Slowly, he was beginning to learn from experience to modify his impulses when it came to confronting the kind of people who didn't understand his therapeutic desires. He'd pushed his luck once with the call to Martin's father. Twice in a row would be too much to hope for.

He didn't have long to wait. Carol and Paula drew up outside the hotel less than seven minutes after he'd called. Carol didn't waste any time; she swept into the hotel with Paula and Tony scurrying in her wake. She flashed her ID and gave the receptionist the hard stare and in moments, they were in the office behind reception, talking to the duty manager, an elegant young man with a French accent. 'There's a man on the ledge outside the thirteenth floor,' Carol said.

The manager frowned. 'We do not have a thirteenth floor.'

It was a weird response, Tony thought. To be more concerned with the numbering of the floors than a potential suicide displayed a disturbing ordering of priorities. 'The floor below the top floor.'

'That is the fourteenth floor.'

'But it's actually the thirteenth floor,' Tony persisted. 'Only you don't have a floor called the thirteenth floor, right? Because people are superstitious?'

The manager pulled a face. 'If you say so. But yes, the floor above the twelfth is the fourteenth.'

'I'm glad we got that cleared up,' Carol said, failing to hide the sarcasm. 'Where exactly is he, Tony?'

'He's outside the third window from the corner of Midland Street.'

The manager's eyes strayed upwards, as if he was envisaging the layout above him. 'This is a bedroom,' he said. 'Fourteen forty-seven, I think.'

'What's the layout outside the windows?' Carol asked.

'There is a ledge and a parapet. The ledge

runs right along the floor. But you can't get out there from the bedrooms. The windows don't open far enough.'

'So how has he got out there?' Paula asked.

'He must have used the maintenance door. It's round the corner.'

Tony gave an exasperated sigh. 'Whatever he used, I need to get out there, and I need to get out there now, before he manages to wind himself up to the point where he can actually jump.' Seeing the manager's shocked face, he continued. 'What? You think he's up there for the view? He's going to kill himself unless I can stop him.'

The manager flushed. 'But that's terrible. You must stop him.' He pushed past them and headed out of the room, pausing to look over his shoulder. 'Come on, I'll take you there now.'

In the lift, the manager couldn't keep still, twitching and fidgeting like a sugared-up toddler. 'Why has he done this? Why has he come here? Does he have some grudge against us?'

'It's nothing personal against the hotel,' Tony said. 'It means something to him, that's all. Something from his family history.'

On the fourteenth floor, they hurried down the thickly carpeted hallway until they reached an anonymous door that was almost invisible against the dark walls. The manager held a plastic card against the electronic lock. It buzzed and released. He pushed it open a crack. 'I don't how he got through here. This should not be possible.'

'I'll take it from here,' Tony said.

The manager looked as if he was about to protest, but Paula put a firm hand on his arm.

'He knows what he's doing. You need to wait here.' Her voice was like the caress of a mother towards a fretful child. Tony nodded his thanks and slipped through the door.

59

The first thing that struck him was the wind. Barely a breeze at ground level, up on the thirteenth floor it was a gusty tug, ruffling his hair and chilling his ears. The traffic noise from below swirled round him in phases. Tony checked out his surroundings. The ledge was about two feet wide, a dirty kerb of gritty concrete; cheap material here where it couldn't be seen, unlike the ornate red sandstone and brick of the visible exterior. All around it ran a carved stone balustrade at waist height, its top about a foot wide. Deep enough to sit on comfortably, Tony calculated. He made his way gingerly to the corner, telling himself he was perfectly safe.

He moved round the corner, trying not to startle Martin. He needn't have worried. The other man didn't stir. He was sitting on the parapet, his legs dangling over space, his hands loosely gripping the edge of the sandstone. His features were drawn, his eyes screwed up as if it hurt to focus. 'Don't come any closer,' he said, his voice dark with tension.

'OK,' Tony said. 'I'm just going to come round the corner because I can't stand halfway round without it hurting. If that's all right?'

'Keep out of reach.'

'You've no worries on that score. If you're going down, I don't want to be dragged down with you. You're Matthew, right? Or do you prefer Matt? My name's Tony. Tony Hill. I'm not a police officer. I'm a psychologist.'

'You're wasting your time.' The tone matched the bluntness of the words.

'I don't think you've thought this through. Not properly.'

A quick sideways glance. 'You know nothing.'

Tony sighed. 'Actually, I know quite a lot. I know what happened to your mum. I expect that was devastating for you.'

'Leave my mum out of this.'

'I'd love to, Matthew, but you know I can't. She's the reason all of this happened.'

'You don't know what you're talking about.'

'I know that if she hadn't gone off to Greenham, none of this would have been necessary. If she hadn't listened to those women, she'd still be alive. Those women who don't understand what it means to be a wife and mother. That's the best thing a woman can ever be, isn't it?' He paused. Nothing. Time for a sideways shift from straight sympathy.

Tony leaned against the parapet, stuffing his hands in his pockets to keep them warm. 'I understand the point you've been trying to make. These women should shut up. They should stop trying to make men feel bad about wanting women to be proper wives and mothers. They should shut up, right?'

Martin turned his head. 'They can do what they want. But they've got no right to try and make other women think like them. If women want to be good mothers and take care of their families, nobody should tell them not to.

440

Nobody should try to turn them against men who want to take care of them.' It was a long speech in the circumstances and Tony was pleased to hear it.

'When your mum and dad came here for their wedding reception, all they wanted was to be a happy family.'

'Exactly. We were happy. She was happy. Till those women took her away from us.'

'It's what you wanted too, isn't it? To make a family with Sarah?'

Matthew flinched. 'I don't want to talk about Sarah.'

'But she spoiled all that.'

'Those so-called friends of hers, filling her head full of their shit, telling her it was too early to have a baby, telling her I wasn't good enough for her to make her life with. She should never have listened to them. But they overwhelmed her. They didn't give her space to think for herself.' He shifted his buttocks, edging slightly forward on the parapet.

'I can't imagine how I'd feel if someone I loved killed my child,' Tony said. Now it was time to start needling. To provoke a response. As long as they were talking, there was hope. 'I guess I'd be grief-stricken. And angry too. She didn't have the right to do that, did she?' The thrust met no parry. Martin said nothing; he carried on staring down at the street below. 'Any man would be driven to do something about it. The trouble is, Sarah was the tip of the iceberg. Everywhere you looked online, there were women pushing other Sarahs into doing the

441

same kind of thing.'

This time, Martin spoke. 'You have no idea,' he said, his voice grating in his throat.

'I do, you know. They're everywhere. I can see why you thought it would be a good idea to make it look like they'd come to their senses and killed themselves out of shame for what they'd become. It was a clever idea. And it worked. You got your suicide verdicts.'

He saw a tiny twitch at the corner of Martin's mouth. The smallest of smiles. The man was proud of what he'd done, even if he'd had to abort his mission before he was finished.

'You were a bit too clever, though. The books were good signposts, but once somebody like me realised it wasn't a one-off, it was obvious there was somebody controlling what was going on.'

Martin grunted again. 'They're easily led. They might have copied each other.'

'They might have, except that the cops didn't notice so the media didn't cover it so how would they have known about it? But still, you did get those verdicts when it counted. There's only one problem,' Tony continued. 'If you jump, the suicides won't stand.'

He shot a quick look at Tony. 'What do you mean? How can they not stand? The coroners gave their verdicts.'

'Verdicts can always be overturned. The woman cop who's running this show, Carol Jordan, she's a real bitch. She's furious with you, with the point you've been determined to make. She'll go to the ends of the earth to have those inquest verdicts changed. And with you dead, she's got carte blanche to say whatever she likes about you and what you did. She'll piss all over the point you've been making. She'll turn you into another internet troll, a mindless bully who hated women.'

This time, Martin turned his head to face Tony, who thought he could see the faintest look of consternation on the other man's face. 'She can't do that.'

Tony gave a regretful smile. 'Of course she can. With you gone, she's got all the power. And she's not afraid to use it. Like I said, she's a bitch. There's only one way you can get your point across.'

Martin gave a bitter laugh. 'I know what you're going to say. 'Don't jump, have your day in court.'' He rubbed a hand vigorously across his upper lip. Tony could see the tremble in his fingers. Sitting on the edge of his world was starting to get to him. It was all becoming too much. His head told him jumping was the only sensible thing to do, but deep down a powerful part of him was clinging to life.

'Pretty much, yeah,' Tony said. He was heading for the last throw of the dice, the appeal to vanity and the desire for posterity. The Achilles heel for so many killers. 'Because that's what makes sense. Otherwise, it's all been for nothing. You had something to say. You obviously think it was something worth dying for or you wouldn't be here right now. But if you give in and run away from the endgame, it's all been a waste of time. Because she'll turn it all into something it wasn't. Something sordid and twisted and meaningless. And you might as well not have bothered.' Martin turned away from him and Tony took advantage of that to inch closer. Now he was almost in touching distance.

He carried on pressing his point. 'You might as well have let Sarah and all those other women walk all over you, because Carol Jordan will walk all over you when you're dead. If that sounds like a good deal to you, fine. I'll walk away now and leave you to it. But if you do care about getting your message across loud and clear, unequivocally? Turn round and come back with me. Don't let the bitch win.'

He could see uncertainty in Martin's body language. There was a slump to the shoulders, a spasm in the fingers, a bowing of the head, as if a weight was pressing down on him. 'You promise I'll have the chance to say my piece, but that's bullshit. I'm not stupid enough to fall for that.'

Tony nodded. 'You go into the witness box and that's the one place you can say whatever you want and she can't stop you. Come on, Matthew, don't make it all for nothing. You're a bright guy. You know I'm talking sense.'

He straightened up, shoulders back, head up. Eyes front, chin up. He pushed down against the parapet with his hands. In that terrible moment, Tony knew he'd lost. But he wasn't ready to give up. He lunged forward and grabbed Martin's left arm just as he thrust off into space. Tony's body smacked into the parapet, the jarring shock powering through his body. But he didn't let go in spite of the joint forces of gravity and Martin's determination. Time seemed to spin like a sycamore seed falling to earth. He could smell Martin's sour sweat, feel his own heart pounding like a steam hammer in his chest.

And then Carol was there, strong arms reaching past his to lock around Matthew Martin's neck and shoulder. 'Oh no you fucking don't,' she snarled. 'You don't get out of here without paying.'

60

Much later, Carol and Tony sat on a bench near the all-night coffee stall at Central Station, a black-and-white collie at their feet, steaming cardboard cups in their hands. It was neutral territory they'd established a long time before. 'You did a good job up there,' Carol said.

'I felt sorry for him. He was always going to be damaged, given what happened to his mum. It was just a question of how the damage would manifest itself. If things had worked out differently with his girlfriend . . . '

'She'd still be alive,' Carol said, not an ounce of concession in her voice. 'I don't have your gift for compassion.'

They sat in companionable silence for a few minutes. Then Carol spoke. 'You don't think I'm a bitch, do you?'

'You were listening?'

She nodded. 'Paula and I were practically climbing over each other to get closest to the corner. You said it with such conviction,' she added, a little sadly.

'Of course I don't think you're a bitch. I was trying to save a man's life. I'd have said you were a people trafficker or a Tory if that had been what it took.'

Carol snorted with laughter. 'Don't do that when I've got a mouthful of coffee,' she protested. 'And it hurts my shoulder when I laugh.'

'You did well to hang on till the Fire Brigade got their ladder up. He was wriggling like a toddler.'

'Turns out being a builder did make me a better cop.'

More silence. The dog shifted, leaning her weight against Carol's shins. An infinitely long goods train grumbled its way across the bridge. 'I've been thinking . . . ' Carol said.

'Mm hmm?'

'The barn's nearly finished.'

'It is. You've done an amazing job. I didn't think you could do it, but I was wrong.'

She sighed. 'There's plenty of room, you know. I've plumbed in the second bathroom and the screens are coming this week to separate off the sleeping area.'

'So that means it's more or less completed?'

Carol ran a hand through her thick blonde hair. 'Unless I wanted to run bookshelves along one wall.'

'I don't want to sound rude, but I didn't think you had that many books.'

'No, but you have. And it would be so much more convenient than a shipping container.'

Tony frowned. There was no solid ground under his feet and he was certain that one misstep would be something he'd pay for forever. 'You're offering me a home for my books?'

Carol cleared her throat. 'More than the books, if you wanted. I kind of liked having you around. No strings, obviously. I wouldn't expect you to give up *Steeler*, you'd probably want to spend time there too.'

On the other side of the city, Sam Evans walked out of a nightclub, only slightly unsteady. He'd had a good night with a bunch of lads he sometimes played five-a-side football with. He'd been on the town every night since he'd walked away from Stacey, enjoying the life of a single man without a care in the world. But now it was time to knock all that on the head. To his surprise, he missed her.

Tomorrow, he'd text her. Suggest dinner somewhere smart. Somewhere that would show her he cared, in spite of her dissing him by not standing up for him with that bitch Jordan.

Sam yawned. There was a faint dampness in the air, as if rain was waiting to pounce on the unwary. He reckoned he'd avoid the risk by jumping in a cab. He was out of cash, but there was an ATM halfway down the next block.

He leaned into the blue light of the cashpoint and let the machine suck his card into its maw. He tapped in his PIN and waited. **PIN not recognised**, the screen said. Sam decided he must be more pissed than he thought. He keyed in the number again, and again it was declined. He shook his head as if to clear an internal fog and gave it one more try. **Your card has been confiscated on the orders of the issuing bank. Please visit your local branch to resolve the problem**.

'What the fuck?' It made no sense. Had he suffered a bout of amnesia and changed his PIN? Oh well, at least he had another card that would allow him to withdraw cash without it costing an arm and a leg. He inserted the card and this time, it accepted his PIN. The only trouble was that it wouldn't give him any money. He accessed his balance on screen and couldn't believe what he was seeing. His account balance stood at zero. Two days after payday. It was impossible. Somehow he'd been robbed. Robbed by his own bank.

He thought about using one of his credit cards to withdraw cash. It infuriated him to pay their charges, but on the other hand, he didn't want to walk home in the cold and probably the rain. But something was wrong with the credit cards too. They both claimed the card was at its limit and nothing more could be withdrawn. 'I don't fucking believe it,' he shouted at the machine. 'I'm a fucking police officer, by the way. I'm going to have you.'

Defeated by the technology, Sam decided he had no choice but to walk home. He turned up the collar of his jacket and hunched into it, taking the first steps of his new, electronically destroyed life.

* * *

DCI John Franklin hadn't been called out to the road traffic accident; he'd been on his way back to the station after a meal break when he'd seen the three cars twisted and shattered and obscenely amalgamated with the crash barrier where the road curved down the steep hill from the motorway into Halifax.

But he was the kind of copper who was always ready and willing to help out. So he pulled over and headed for the scene of the triple pile-up. 'What's the score?' he asked one of the traffic cops, a man he'd seen around in his own station many times.

'Carnage,' he said. 'Tearaway in the Vauxhall came round the bend on the wrong side of the road doing way over the limit. Went head on into the Mini and the two careered into the Ford Galaxy. Two dead in the Vauxhall, the Mini driver's off to casualty in a bad way. Two dead in the Galaxy. One died while the firemen were cutting her out.' He shook his head vehemently. 'I'm going to hear her screaming for a long time.'

Franklin looked across at the Vauxhall with its distinctive spoiler and flared wheel arches. He'd seen that not so long ago in the police compound. He walked over to the car, where the driver and passenger were still trapped in their seats. He recognised the driver at once and felt the heartburn of rage swell in his chest.

He couldn't recall the boy's name but the circumstances were burned into his memory. A week past Saturday. A clutch of drunk drivers righteously arrested then cut loose after a breathalyser was deemed to be unreliable.

The boy in the Vauxhall who had taken at least three other lives to oblivion with him had been one of those liberated by the overarching need for Carol Jordan to be clean. Franklin turned away in disgust. He looked forward with a kind of savage delight to making the phone call that would inform Jordan of the true price of her new squad. Whatever they achieved, they'd be doing it stained with the blood of innocent people. 'I fucking hope she's worth it,' he said to no one, knowing it was an impossible equivalence.

⋆   ⋆   ⋆

'You think it would be OK?' Tony asked.

Carol swallowed a mouthful of coffee. A gaggle of slightly drunk young men rolled up to the coffee stall, jostling and joshing as they ordered coffees and hot chocolates. Carol watched and Tony waited. Finally she said, 'You'd be doing me a favour. It's a lot easier to stay off the sauce when you're around. Plus it would be helpful with the dog.'

He tried not to show his delight. He failed. 'As long as your pal George doesn't come after me with a shotgun.' He looked into his coffee and smiled. A couple of weeks ago, he couldn't have imagined this outcome. It would have seemed impossible that he and Carol could move so far along the road of reconciliation. It was the next step on a journey that had started a long time ago, a journey waymarked in blood and hardship, a journey he wouldn't have missed for anything. 'Thanks for asking.'

His words were drowned out by the ringing of Carol's phone. Their eyes met; they shared a rueful smile. 'And so it begins again,' Tony said.

Acknowledgements

The great thing about inventing a police unit is that nobody can tell you you've got the procedure all wrong.

But of course there are plenty of other opportunities for that. And to help me avoid the pitfalls, I'm grateful to digital forensics guru Angus Marshall and to fire and explosives expert Naimh nic Daeid. I'm grateful to Simon Veit-Wilson for the novel use of a shipping container.

There is a whole squad of people out there who worked hard to put this book in your hands, among them Jane Gregory and her team; David Shelley, Lucy Malagoni, Thalia Proctor and everyone else at Little, Brown who supports me with such enthusiasm; Anne O'Brien, to whom I am eternally grateful that she gave up a promising career as a Jedi knight to be my copy-editor; and to my long suffering family who make everything possible.

Now turn the page for your free Val McDermid short story!

Guilt Trip

As neither of my parents was too bothered about religion, I managed to miss out on Catholic guilt. Then I found myself working with Shelley. A guilt trip on legs, our office manager. If she treats her two teenagers like she treats me, those kids are going to be in therapy for years. 'You play, you pay,' she said sweetly, pushing the new case file to me for the third time.

'Just because I play computer games doesn't mean I'm qualified to deal with the nerds who write them,' I protested. It was only a white lie; although my business partner Bill Mortensen deals with most of the work we do involving computers, I'm not exactly techno-illiterate. I pushed the file back towards Shelly. 'It's one for Bill.'

'Bill's too busy. You know that,' Shelley said. 'Anyway, it's not software as such. It's either piracy or industrial sabotage and that's your forte.' The file slid back to me.

'Sealsoft are Bill's clients.' Brannigan's last stand.

'All the more reason you should get to know them.'

I gave in and picked up the file. Shelley gave a tight little smile and turned back to her computer screen. One of these days I'm going to get the last word. Just wait till hell freezes over, that's all. Just wait.

On my way out of the door and down the stairs, I browsed the file. Sealsoft was a local Manchester games software house. They'd started off back in the dawn of computer gaming in the mid-eighties, writing programs for a whole range of hardware. Some of the machines they produced games for had never been intended as anything other than word processors, but Sealsoft had grabbed the challenge and come up with some fun stuff. The first platform game I'd ever played, on a word processor that now looked as antique as a Model-T Ford, had been a Sealsoft game.

They'd never grown to rival any of the big players in the field, but somehow Sealsoft had always hung in there, coming up every now and again with seemingly simple games that became classics. In the last year or two they'd managed to win the odd film tie-in licence, and their latest acquisition was the new Arnold Schwarzenegger and Bruce Willis boys 'n' toys epic. But now, two weeks before the game was launched, they had a problem. And when people have problems, Mortensen and Brannigan is where they turn if they've got sense and cash enough.

I had a ten o'clock appointment with Sealsoft's boss. Luckily I could get there on foot, since parking round by Sealsoft is a game for the terminally reckless. The company had started off on the top floor of a virtually derelict canalside warehouse that has since been gutted and turned into expansive and expensive studio flats where the marginally criminal rub shoulders with the marginally legitimate lads from the financial services industries. Sealsoft had moved into modern premises a couple of streets away from the canal, but the towpath was still the quickest way to get from my office in Oxford Road to their concrete pillbox in Castlefield.

Fintan O'Donohoe had milk-white skin and freckles so pale it looked like he'd last seen daylight somewhere in the nineteenth century. He looked about seventeen, which was slightly worrying as I knew he'd been with the company since it started up in 1983. Add that to the red-rimmed eyes and I felt like I'd stumbled into *Interview with the Vampire*. We settled into his chrome and black-leather office, each of us clutching our designer combinations of mineral water, herbs and juices.

'Call me Fin,' he said, with no trace of any accent other than pure Mancunian.

I resisted the invitation. It wasn't the hardest thing I'd done that day. 'I'm told you have a problem,' I said.

'That's not the word I'd use,' he sighed. 'A major disaster waiting to happen is what we've got. We've got a boss money-earner about to hit the streets and suddenly our whole operation's under threat.'

'From what?'

'It started about six weeks ago. There were just one or two at first, but we've had getting on for sixty in the last two days. It's a nightmare,' O'Donohoe told me earnestly, leaning forward and fiddling anxiously with a pencil.

'What exactly are we talking about here?' He might not have anything better to do than take a long tour round the houses, but I certainly did. Apart from anything else, there was a cappuccino at the Atlas café with my name on it.

'Copies of our games with the right packaging, the right manuals, the guarantee cards, everything, are being returned to us because the people who buy them are shoving the disks into their computers and finding they're completely blank. Nothing on them at all. Just bog-standard high-density pre-formatted unbranded three-and-a-half-inch disks.' He threw himself back in his chair, pouting like a five-year-old.

'Sounds like pirates,' I said. 'Bunch of schneid merchants copying your packaging and shoving any old shit in there.'

He shook his head. 'My first thought. But that's not how the pirates work. They bust your copy protection codes, make hundreds of copies of the program and stick it inside pretty crudely copied packaging. This is the opposite of that. There's no game, but the packaging is perfect. It's ours.' He opened a drawer in his desk and pulled out a box measuring about eight inches by ten and a couple of inches deep. The cover showed an orc and a human in mortal combat outlined in embossed silver foil. O'Donohoe opened the box and tipped out a game manual, a story book, four disks with labels reading 1–4 and guarantee card. 'Right down to the hologram seal on the guarantee, look,' he pointed out.

I leaned forward and picked up the card, turning it to check the hologram. He was right; if this was piracy, I'd never seen quality like it. And if they could produce packaging this good, I was damn sure they could have copied the game too. So why the combination of spot-on packaging and blank disks? 'Weird,' I said.

'You're not kidding.'

'Is this happening to any of your competitors?'

'Not that I've heard. And I would have heard, I think.'

Sounded as if one of Sealsoft's rivals was paying off an insider to screw O'Donohoe's operation into the deck. 'Where are the punters buying them? Market stalls?' I asked.

Head down, O'Donohoe said, 'Nope.' For the first time I noted the dark shadows under his eyes. 'They're mostly coming back to us via the retailers, though some are coming direct.'

'Which retailers? Independents or chains?' I was sitting forward in my seat now, intrigued. What had sounded like a boring piece of routine was getting more interesting by the minute. Call me shallow and superficial, but I like a bit of excitement in my day.

'Mostly smallish independents, but increasingly we're getting returns from the big chain stores now. We've been in touch with quite a few of the customers as well, and they're all saying that the games were shrink-wrapped when they bought them.'

I sat back, disappointed. The shrink-wrapping was the clincher.

'It's an inside job,' I said flatly. 'Industrial sabotage.'

'No way,' O'Donohoe said, two pale pink spots suddenly burning on his cheekbones.

'I'm sorry. I know it's the message no

employer wants to hear. But it's clearly an inside job.'

'It can't be,' he insisted bluntly. 'Look, I'm not a dummy. I've been in this game a while. I know the wrinkles. I know how piracy happens. And I guard against it. Our boxes are printed in one place, our booklets in another, our guarantee cards in a third. The disks get copied in-house onto disks that are overprinted with our logo and the name of the game, so you couldn't just slip in a few blanks like these,' he said contemptuously, throwing the disks across the desk.

'Where does it all come together?' I asked.

'We're a small company,' he answered obliquely. 'But that's not the only reason we pack by hand rather than on a production line. I know where we're vulnerable to sabotage, and I've covered the bases. The boxes and packed and sealed in shrink-wrap in a room behind the despatch room.'

'Then that's where your saboteur is.'

His lip curled. 'I don't think so. I've only got two workers in there. We've always had a policy of employing friends and family at Sealsoft. The packers are my mum and her sister, my Auntie Geraldine. They'd kill anybody that was trying to sabotage this business, take my word for it. When they're not working, the door's double locked. They wouldn't even let the parish priest in there, believe me.'

'So what exactly do you want me to do?' I asked.

'I don't want you questioning my staff,' he said irritably. 'Other than that, it's up to you. You're the detective. Find out who's putting the shaft in, then come back and tell me.'

When I left Sealsoft ten minutes later, all I had to go on was a list of customers and companies involved in returns of Sealsoft's games, and details of who'd sent back what. I was still pretty sure the villain was inside the walls rather than outside, but the client wasn't letting me any-where near his good Catholic mother and Auntie Geraldine. Can't say I blamed him.

I figured there wasn't a lot of point in starting with the chain stores. Even if something hooky was going on, they were the last people I could lean on to find out. With dole queues still well into seven figures, the staff there weren't going to tell me anything that might cost them their jobs. I sat in the Atlas over the coffee I'd promised myself and read through the names. At first glance, I didn't recognise any of the computer-game suppliers. We buy all our equipment and consumables by mail order, and the only shop we've ever used in dire emergencies was the one that used to occupy the ground floor of our building before it became a supermarket.

Time for some expert help. I pulled out my mobile and rang my tame darkside hacker, Gizmo. By day he works for Telecom as a systems man-ager. By night, he becomes the Scarlet Pimpernel of cyberspace. Or so he tells me. 'Giz? Kate.'

'Not a secure line,' he grumbled. 'You should know better.'

'Not a problem; this isn't top secret. Do you know anybody who works at any of these out-lets?' I started to read out the list, Gizmo grunting negatively after each name. About halfway through the list, he stopped me.

'Wait a minute. That last one, Epic PC?'

'You know someone there?'

'I don't but you do. It's wossname, the geezer that used to have that place under your office.'

'Deke? He want bust, didn't he?'

''S right. Bombed. Went into liquidation, opened up a new place in Prestwich Village a week later, didn't he? That's his shop. Epic PC. I remember because I thought it was such a crap name. That everything?'

'That'll do nicely, Giz.' I was speaking to empty air. I like a man who doesn't waste my time. I drained my cup, walked up the steps to Deansgate station and jumped on the next tram to Prestwich.

Epic PC was a small shop on the main drag. I recognised the special offer stickers. It looked like Deke Harper didn't have the kind of fresh ideas that would save Epic PC from its predecessor's fate. I pushed open the door and an electric buzzer vibrated in the stuffy air. Deke himself was seated behind a PC in the middle of a long room that was stuffed with hardware and software, his fingers clattering over the keys. He'd trained himself well in the art of looking busy; he let a whole five seconds pass between the buzzer sounding and his eyes leaving the screen in front of him. When he registered who his customer was, his eyebrows climbed in his narrow face. 'Hello,' he said uncertainly, pushing his chair back and getting to his feet. 'Stranger.'

'Believe me, Deke, it gets a lot stranger still,' I said drily.

'I didn't know you lived out this way,' he said nervously, hitting a key to clear his screen as I drew level with him.

'I don't,' I said. Sometimes it's just more fun to let them come to you.

'You were passing?'

'No.' I leaned against his desk. His eyes kept flickering between me and his uninformative screen.

'You needed something for the computer? Some disks?'

'Three in a row, Deke. You lose. My turn now. I'm here about those moody computer games you've been selling. Where are they coming from?'

A thin blue vein in his temple seemed to pop up from nowhere. 'I don't know what you're on about,' he said, too nonchalantly. 'What moody computer games?'

I rattled off half a dozen Sealsoft games. 'I sell them, sure,' he said defensively. 'But they're not hooky. Look, I got invoices for them,' he added, pushing past me and yanking a drawer open. He pulled out a loose-leaf file and flicked through fast enough to rip a couple of pages before he arrived at a clutch of invoices from Sealsoft.

I took the file from him and walked over to the shelves and counted. 'According to this, Deke, you bought six copies of Sheer Fire II when it was released last month.'

'That's right. And there's only five left now, right? I sold one.'

'Wrong. You sold at least three. That's how many of your customers have returned blank copies of Sheer Fire II to Sealsoft. Care to explain the discrepancy? Or do I have to call your local friendly Trading Standards Officer?' I asked sweetly. 'You can go down for this kind of thing these days, can't you?' I added conversationally.

Half an hour later I was sitting outside Epic PC behind the wheel of Deke's six-year-old Mercedes, waiting for a lad he knew only as Jazbo to turn up in response to a call on his mobile. Amazing what people will do with a little incentive. I spotted Jazbo right away from Deke's description. A shade under six feet, jeans, trainers and a Chicago Cubs bomber jacket. And Tony Blair complains about Manchester United's merchandising. At least they're local.

He got out of a battered boy racer's hatchback, clutching a carrier bag with box-shaped outlines pressing against it. I banged off a couple of snaps with the camera from my backpack. Jazbo was in and out of Epic PC inside five minutes. We headed back into town down Bury New Road, me sitting snugly on his tail with only one car between us. We skirted the city centre and headed east. Jazbo eventually parked up in one of the few remaining terraced streets in Gorton and let himself into one of the houses. I took a note of the address and drove Deke's Merc back to Prestwich before he started getting too twitchy about the idea of me with his wheels.

Next morning, I was back outside Jazbo's house just before seven. Early risers, villains, in my experience. According to the electoral roll, Gladys and Albert Conway lived there. I suspected the information on the list was well out of date. With names like that, they might have been Jazbo's grandparents, but a more likely scenario was that he'd taken over the house after the Conways had died or suffered the fate worse than death of an old people's home. The man himself emerged about five past the hour. There was less traffic around, but I managed to stay in contact with him into the city centre, where he parked in a loading bay behind Deansgate and let himself into the back of the shop.

I took a chance and left my wheels on a single yellow while I walked round the front of the row of shops and counted back to where Jazbo had let himself in. JJ's Butty Bar. Another piece of the jigsaw clicked into place.

Through the window, I caught the occasional glimpse of Jazbo, white-coated, moving between tall fridges and countertops. One or twice he emerged from the rear of the shop with trays of barm cakes neatly wrapped and labelled, depositing them in the chill cabinets round the shop. I figured he was good for a few hours yet and headed back to the office before the traffic wardens came out to play.

I was back just after two. I kept cruising round the block till someone finally left a spot that gave me a clear view of the exit from the alley behind the sandwich shop. Jazbo emerged in his hot hatch just after three, which was just as well because I was running out of change. I stayed close to him through the city centre, then let a bit of distance grow between us as he headed out past Salford Quays and into the industrial estate round Trafford Park. He pulled up outside a small unit with Gingerbread House painted in a rainbow of colours across the front wall. Jazbo disappeared inside.

About fifteen minutes later he emerged with a supermarket trolley filled to the top with computer-game boxes. I was baffled. I'd had my own theory about where the packaging was coming from, and it had just been blown out of the water. I let Jazbo drive off, then I marched into Gingerbread House. Ten minutes later I had all the answers.

Fintan O'Donohoe looked impressed as I laid out my dossier before him. Jazbo's address, photograph, phone number, car registration and place of work would be more than enough to hand him over to the police, gift-wrapped. 'So how's this guy getting hold of the gear?' he demanded.

'First thing I wondered about was the shrink-wrapping. That made me think it was someone in your despatch unit. But you were adamant it couldn't be either your mum or your auntie. Then when I found out he worked in a sandwich shop, I realised he must be using their wrap-and-seal gear to cover his boxes in. Which left the question of where the boxes were coming from. You ruled out an inside job, so I thought he might simply be raiding your dustbins for discarded gear. But I was wrong. You ever heard of a charity called Gingerbread House?'

O'Donohoe frowned. 'No. Should I have?'

'Your mum has,' I told him. 'And so, I suspect, has Jazbo's mum or girlfriend or sister. It's an educational charity run by nuns. They go round businesses and ask them for any surplus materials and they sell them off to schools and playgroups for next to nothing. They collect all sorts — material scraps, bits of bungee rope, offcuts of specialist paper, wallpaper catalogues, tinsel, sheets of plastic, scrap paper. Anything that could come in handy for school projects or for costumes for plays, whatever.'

Fintan O'Donohue groaned and put his hands over his face. 'Don't tell me . . . '

'They came round here a few months ago, and your mum explained that you don't manufacture here, so there's not much in the way of leftover stuff. But what there was were the boxes for games that had been sent back because they were faulty in some way. The disks were scrapped, and so were the boxes and manuals normally. But if the nuns could make any use of the boxes and their contents . . . Your mum or your Auntie Geraldine's been dropping stuff off once a fortnight ever since.'

He looked up at me, a ghost of an ironic smile on his lips. 'And I was so sure it couldn't be anything to do with my mum!'

'Don't they say charity begins at home?'

Other titles published by Ulverscroft:

THE SKELETON ROAD

Val McDermid

When a skeleton is discovered hidden at the top of a crumbling Gothic building in Edinburgh, Detective Chief Inspector Karen Pirie is faced with the unenviable task of identifying the bones. As Karen's investigation gathers momentum, she is drawn deeper into a world of intrigue and betrayal, spanning the dark days of the Balkan Wars. Karen's search for answers brings her to a small village in Croatia, a place scarred by fear, where people have endured unspeakable acts of violence. Meanwhile, someone is taking the law into their own hands in the name of justice and revenge — but when present resentment collides with secrets of the past, the truth is more shocking than anyone could have imagined . . .

NORTHANGER ABBEY

Val McDermid

Seventeen-year-old Catherine 'Cat' Morland has led a sheltered existence in rural Dorset, a life entirely bereft of the romance and excitement for which she yearns. So when Cat's wealthy neighbours ask her to accompany them to the Edinburgh Festival, she is sure adventure beckons. Edinburgh initially disappoints, but at a Highland dance class Cat meets Henry Tilney, a pale, dark-haired gentleman whose family home, Northanger Abbey, sounds perfectly thrilling. When Henry's father, the rigidly formal General Tilney, invites Cat to stay at Northanger Abbey with his family, Cat's imagination runs riot: an ancient abbey, crumbling turrets, secret chambers, ghosts . . . and Henry! What could be more deliciously romantic? But Cat gets far more than she bargained for in this isolated corner of the Scottish Borders . . .

CROSS AND BURN

Val McDermid

Someone is brutally killing women. Women who bear a striking resemblance to former DCI Carol Jordan. The connection is too strong to ignore, and soon psychological profiler Tony Hill finds himself dangerously close to the investigation, just as the killer is closing in on his next target. This is a killer like no other, hell-bent on inflicting the most severe and grotesque punishments on his prey. As the case becomes ever more complex and boundaries begin to blur, Tony and Carol must work together once more to try to save the victims — and themselves.

THE VANISHING POINT

Val McDermid

Stephanie Harker is travelling through the security gates at O'Hare airport, on her way to an idyllic holiday. Five-year-old Jimmy goes through the metal detector first. But then, stuck on the other side of security, she watches in panic and disbelief as a uniformed agent leads her boy away. The authorities, unaware of Jimmy's existence, become alerted by Stephanie's erratic behaviour. She finds herself brutally wrestled to the ground and restrained before she can finally inform them what has happened — and Jimmy is long gone . . . However, as Stephanie tells her story to the FBI, it's evident that this apparently normal family is not what it seems. What is Jimmy's background? Why would someone abduct him? And, with time running out, how can Stephanie get him back?